BLOOD LINES

A woman is lured to a remote spot in the Scottish Highlands and strangled almost to the point of death. As she begs for mercy, her tormentor begins to carve her face before burying her alive. In Edinburgh, unorthodox lawyer Brodie McLennan becomes tangled up in the case. Meanwhile in an asylum in Inverness, a deranged patient writes the name Brodie over and over in her own blood. Brodie is running scared from unknown forces, eager to see blood on her hands...

BLOOD LINES

BLOOD LINES

by

Grace Monroe

Magna Large Print Books
Long Preston, North Yorkshire,
BD23 4ND, England.

British Library Cataloguing in Publication Data.

Monroe, Grace
    Blood lines.

    A catalogue record of this book is
    available from the British Library

    ISBN   978-0-7505-3312-6

First published in Great Britain by HarperCollins Publishers 2008

Copyright © Grace Monroe 2008

Cover illustration by arrangement with Arcangel Images

Grace Monroe asserts the moral right to be identified as the author of this work

Published in Large Print 2010 by arrangement with HarperCollins Publishers

Magna Large Print is an imprint of Library Magna Books Ltd.

Printed and bound in Great Britain by
T.J. (International) Ltd., Cornwall, PL28 8RW

Acknowledgements

From Maria:

Lots of love to Jenny Brown at Jenny Brown Associates who is the most amazing agent; your kindness and support has been invaluable.
To the girls at Avon, you are the best team. Special thanks to Maxine Hitchcock and Keshini Naidoo, whose insight into the manuscript was awe-inspiring. It has been many years since I have been a lawyer and I am grateful for the support given to me by my friends in the legal profession, especially John Mayer, who keeps me on track.

From Linda:

Lots of thanks as always to the hordes of lovely ladies behind all of this – particularly Keshini Naidoo (who gets first shout this time for having had to trawl *so* many edits and for the sheer imagination of her contributions to our Men on Friday afternoon discussions); Maxine Hitchcock (for always sounding like a little ray of sunshine in the midst of nasty discussions about murderous modes and deadlines); Sammia Rafique (for possessing a full deck of technological abilities and email friendliness – things I aspire to possessing myself one day); Sara Foster (for fantastic copy editing and allowing me to keep in all the dodgy Scottish slang and sweariness); and, again, again, again, Jenny Brown of Jenny Brown Associates for top-notch agenting stuff and words of wisdom on everything in the world ever.

Thank you all – see you in six months, Linda xx

Gordon, Caitlin, Patrick, Brogan and Keanu
you are my raison d'être. Maria

Still appreciating you really, Dr Cairney.
Linda xx

Prologue

Ruthven Barracks
August 2005

The Jacobite ruin stands high in the evening mist. Ruthven Barracks, set on a mound in the Scottish Highlands, echoes with ghosts and lovers' tales. The settlement which had existed there for over a thousand years is long gone, but the rumours of betrayal and obsession are as fresh as if whispered yesterday. Alisdair Mor mac an Righ once made his home here, but few round these parts referred to him by that name then and nor do they do so now. One of the blackest bastards ever to walk through Scotland's history, the son of King Robert II lived in barbarous times – times which he, the Wolf of Badenoch, made darker and more murderous every day he lived.

Now the earth which the Wolf walked is hard from the constant tramp of tourist feet. The day-buses and walking tours have long gone as the low evening clouds scurry past the moon. It is almost midnight, but it is as bright as day underneath the startling Scottish night sky. The lovers walk up the steep gravel path from the roadside and, hand-in-hand, enter the stony ruins. They sit down amongst the ancient stones, their heavy voices echoing with lust – and revenge.

A hip flask is taken from the backpack of its owner. It is handed to the other, who fingers it anxiously, thinking of past indiscretions.

'Take the whisky and seal the deal,' come the words as the dark fluid is thrown down a throat parched from the wanting. The breath of the lovers is sweet in the night air. They search for words, for an appropriate toast to what they feel for each other. Both seem content to drink in the surroundings and the presence of the other alongside the liquid from the pure waters of the nearby distillery.

This is a betrothal. A consummation. The reverberations of words exchanged and vows underscored will last beyond this night.

The Earl of Badenoch had ruled these lands in a cruel way – always taking more than he was entitled to, yet never satisfying himself. He knew the meaning of betrayal; he knew the cost of love. When he deserted his wife for his mistress, the Church ruled against him – and entire towns paid the cost. The Wolf sought revenge in an orgy of ransacking, burning and murder, eventually offering superficial repentance in order to win his way back into society.

But he, more than most, knew that what lies on the surface matters nothing compared to what lurks beneath.

Legend interrupts fact with the Earl's story at this point and says that his final visit to Ruthven was for an infamous chess battle to the death – with the Devil. As the Devil called 'checkmate', a terrible storm of thunder, hail and lightning surrounded the place. In the silence of the morning, all of the Wolf's men were found blackened and dead outside the castle walls, with their master discovered lifeless in the banqueting hall, unmarked but with the nails from his boots ripped out. The Devil had won yet again – as the Wolf had always known he would.

'Don't you want me?' comes the voice from the seated woman, who raises the hip flask to her lips once more as soon as she has whimpered the words.

'Don't you want me?' she asks again, her craving for love more overwhelming than the feeling of fear which batters these walls. The betrothal is not going as planned. Where are the dual commitments? Where are the exchanged vows of lifelong adoration? As the woman reaches out to touch the face of her beloved, she also raises the pewter flask above her head as a sign of dedication. Her voice echoes around the ancient stones, joining the many pledges made there over the centuries.

'Join me,' she says, but her words do not invite, they beg.

'May the hinges of our friendship never rust, nor the wings of our love lose a feather,' she continues, trying to ignore the silence of her beloved. '*Slainte.*'

The whisky warms her heart as she takes another sip. Warms her heart more than the presence of the one she loves. As it trickles down her throat, the taste awakes demons. It dribbles down her chin as she tries to wipe it away with the back of her hand. Her co-ordination is all wrong – has her old friend affected her so quickly? She drinks more, but the dribbles increase, and the woman looks to her love for help.

The words that reach her do not comfort.

'You greedy bitch. I should have known. That whisky was the one thing I needed to rely on – and the one thing I couldn't control. You didn't disappoint me, did you? You just had to drink it, you just had to take what you wanted, just like you always do.'

The woman beseeches her lover with her eyes. Why is there such cruelty in the words? Why is there such hatred in the face of the one she worships?

'My legs aren't working properly. Help me.'

Even to her own ears, the words sound slurred as she falls heavily to the ground. The woman's tights rip on the rough stony hillside of the barrack floor, but her darling moves towards her, bringing hope. Her arms are pulled together above her head and held there as she is dragged still further. There is no help, there is no hope. The soldiers' latrines await her as she is hauled round a corner.

'This is for you,' whispers her darling into her ear. The woman fleetingly thinks of love, of surprises prepared by the keeper of her spirit. As she is thrown into the hard-packed six-foot trench, lovingly dug just for her, her hopes are dashed and her heart knows that it has been betrayed. Silently she screams, incapable of making a sound.

'If I'd known you were so fond of the taste of sodium pentathol, I'd have tried it years ago,' come the words, but the woman is too busy watching what is happening to pay attention to the one-sided conversation. Her lover has picked up the spade resting on the rough stone wall and starts to dig afresh.

'Normally it's injected – but I find needles really ... unpleasant...'

The pile of earth is considerable now. It has also managed to change the channel into something else. With the presence of the woman within, it is no longer a trench.

It is a grave.

Such alchemy.

The legs and the arms of the woman are useless. They are drugged into stillness, numbed into inefficiency but it is the loss of love which immobilises her totally. The voice she once adored now drones on as the owner of it continues to dig.

'Truth serum. That's what most people know it as. Isn't that funny? Isn't that ironic? I couldn't be less interested in your truths, my darling. I've had to put up with them for long enough. I think it's much more worthy of reflection that this stuff is also used in executions.'

The face of the woman manages to contort with fear – no mean feat given the amount of paralysing drug she has willingly swallowed.

'You betrayed me. You put your truths before everything. Before me. Before our love. Do you know what that does to someone? To me?'

She cannot answer, she cannot plead for her life or use her words to escape the fate she knows is awaiting her. Flecks of spittle foam around the mouth of the one she loved to kiss. She longs to wipe them away, to show a caring touch even with the knowledge that her lover has become her executioner. Pins and needles start in her fingers as the feeling spreads throughout her entire body. The winding sheet starts at her feet as her beloved ineptly wraps her in a shroud. This will be her bridal dress, this will be the culmination of their love.

'My love, my love – why did you make me do this?' asks the undertaker of her heart.

A tear escapes the woman's eye as she is wrapped tenderly in her beloved's arms who, struggling with the dead weight, lays her roughly in the grave. Still the woman cannot speak. The tears run down her face unchecked – her hands are close enough to scratch her nose but they are bound and crossed on her chest where there is no strength to break free.

The shovel of earth hits her heavily, knocking the wind and the life out of her body. Painstakingly, the grave is filled, each load crushing her body and stealing her soul.

There is hope.

Her head and neck are uncovered. She tells herself that this is no more worrying than a game children will play at the beach when they bury each other in the sand.

At any moment, her love will release her, they will embrace and their betrothal will continue.

As the knife pierces her cheek, the sensation returns to her body as pain slices through – as does the awareness that this is no childish game, this is no lovers' diversion. The metallic smell of blood joins the stench of terror. The woman's face is warm and wet as her beloved rubs dirt into the open wounds over and over again.

Finally, strength returns to her fingers – as the first dirt lands on her face.

She tries to claw her way out.

She breaks her fingernails to the quick.

She feels the blood run down.

She cannot see for the suffocating darkness.

She cannot breathe for the earth in her nostrils.

She cannot scream for the muck in her mouth.

What starts in pleasure always ends in pain.

As the final words of the treasured one scrape against the ancient stones, the Wolf of Badenoch enjoys what he sees, savours what he hears.

'Who will love you now?' asks the beloved one as the knife cuts, the blood pours, and the Wolf howls with delight.

Chapter One

My knickers felt cold and squidgy when I pushed them into my jacket pocket. I tried not to notice. the embarrassingly large bulge that they created. If I didn't look at it, it wasn't there. I liked that view of the world. At least for now. I was obviously quite good at only recognising what I wanted to recognise, given that whatever I had expected when I left the office last night hadn't involved squelchy undies and drunken sex.

Especially with him.

I'd felt so moral going in on a Saturday – it's usually the quietest time to work, much better than Sundays when people sometimes panic and decide to get a head start on the week. Even Lavender sometimes isn't there to give me directions on how I should spend my time. But yesterday, a combination of dull reports and accounts followed by too much rotten wine in a nameless Rose Street pub had brought about a distinct lack of continuation of my moral superiority.

Where the hell was my left shoe? I was at the stage where staying and looking would have probably been more embarrassing than leaving in my bare feet and answering lecherous questions from a taxi driver.

'Are you looking for this?' a voice called from the bedroom.

Shit.

No escape.

I'd have to go back and retrieve it now or have him think I was too lovestruck to face him rather than too hung over to think about it. If only I had just gone home after the office. If only I hadn't bumped into him making his way back from a Saturday shift. If only I hadn't said hello and noticed how bloody gorgeous he was. I hobbled my way along the hallway like Long John Silver on a bad day – although, for all his worries, I'm sure he didn't have to deal with not taking his mascara off and being covered in stubble rash the morning after.

With one shoe off and the other dangling from his hand, I lurched towards him. Towards it. Towards my shoe. Towards Mr Jack Deans, Esquire.

I was very upset. Very, very upset. Unlike me, the bastard looked good. Even in the morning light after a very heavy session I could see why I'd finally been unable to resist. Before last night, I'd only ever seen him in his work clothes – crumpled suit, clichéd raincoat. Now, covered only by an impressively white bath towel, he looked damn fine. Just back from the South of France – research, I'm sure, not a piss-up – he was dark, handsome, and absolutely chock-full of himself. A very useful bout of food poisoning had knocked a stone off him and there wasn't a moob in sight.

'I bet you're just thinking what a lucky girl you are,' he crooned as he launched himself off the bed and walked towards me, twirling the shoe on one finger.

'No, no ... I was "just thinking" that fat looks better when it's brown.'

'Liar,' he whispered into my ear, giving it a surreptitious lick for good luck.

I was back to our familiar double-act of winding each other up much quicker than he was. I took the end of my jacket and wiped the inside of my ear dry. My gesture of dismissal was wasted because Deans was already in the kitchen – with my shoe.

What had once looked a very attractive half of an LK Bennett leopard-print combo was now just pissing me off. It was a shoe, not the bloody Holy Grail, yet he was dragging it from room to room as if I was in thrall to the wonder of a well-turned heel at the cost of my pride.

The offending article was on top of the kitchen table.

'Don't you know that's bad luck?' I said, forcing my foot into the shoe. It scraped on my skin, hurting my little toe. Actually, come to think of it, they'd always nipped – I should have left the buggers whilst I had the chance.

'Let me guess, Brodie – that's one thing you don't need more of.' He wriggled his pelvis at me in a way that would have put a geriatric Chippendale to shame. 'Aw, I don't know – looks like your luck might have turned. Do you want sugar in your coffee?'

'You know I don't take sugar.'

'With a face like yours this morning, you look as if you could do with a little sweetness.'

'You weren't complaining about my face last night.'

Damn. I was the first one to obviously refer to the sex thing.

'Last night I thought *I* was the sugar you were needing, darling.'

'You must have been drunker than I thought then. But definitely nowhere near as comatose as me – obviously.'

'Frankly, Brodie, I was a bit hurt that you were going to sneak out without saying goodbye. I felt used. A piece of meat. Just a plaything for you.'

For the first time that morning I actually looked into his eyes – only to see his smile lighting them.

'I'm in no mood for jokes, Jack. I'm pissed off, I'm late, and my shoes hurt.'

'I can see that. Well, I can see the pissed-off bit anyway. Christ knows what you'll be like when you get a look at your face – it's dragging along the ground.'

I tried to ignore him, took my coffee and wandered round his tiny kitchen. I did what I could to avoid facing the fact that he was almost naked.

'What are you up to today?' he asked.

I hesitated to answer in case he was going to ask me out.

'Don't worry – you're safe. I'm just going to bide my time and catch you when you're lonely – again.'

'Was I that pathetic?'

I didn't have to turn to know that Deans was nodding his head.

'Actually, I do have plans. I'm supposed to be seeing my grandad and my moth– and Kailash – they tell me they're worried about me, so I need to go and calm them down.'

'They're not the only ones bothered,' he commented.

I looked at him sharply. Insulting me, glorying in finally getting me into bed, I could take – but care and concern?

'Not me.' He looked as aghast as I felt. 'It's the hairy-arsed sheep-shagger you hang around with who's all het up.'

'Glasgow Joe?'

'Aye, the one and only.'

'Jack – you're the only one I know who could consider Glasgow the heart of sheep-shagging land. It fits in so well with your impeccable journalistic credentials. Never let facts get in the way of a good insult.'

My heart started racing at the thought of how Joe would react if he knew what we'd done.

'Whatever you want to call him, he's the one who's concerned.' I sighed. One problem after another. Right now, there was one particular issue that I had to bring up with Jack.

'Jack? Do me a favour? Don't mention last night to Joe.'

'Don't worry, I won't – under usual circumstances it would be the talk of the steamie, but…'

'But you're rather attached to your bollocks?'

'No, it's not that – actually, Brodie, you won't understand this, but I like Joe and I wouldn't want to hurt *him*.'

'Don't give me that crap – if you really felt like that you wouldn't have dragged me back here last night,' I countered.

'As I recall, Miss McLennan, it was you doing the dragging.' He paused for effect.

Jack moved towards me at the kitchen table – I expected him to kiss me or try to do the dragging to bed this time. I don't really know whether I felt relieved or disappointed when he only reached down for his battered briefcase which he threw on the table.

'Like I said, Kailash and old man MacGregor. aren't the only ones who are concerned,' he said, handing me some sheets of paper. 'Take a look at this.'

'You sad git, Jack. I didn't know you were into tracing family trees. It's the new train-spotting for blokes your age, isn't it?'

'No – blokes "my age" have got other things to do with their time.' He managed to say this whilst looking lecherously at me – I was touched: I looked a right state but he was still so desperate he wasn't kicking me out.

'It's your family I'm digging at, Brodie, not mine. Now stop being so vain and put your specs on to look at it properly. Don't worry about me seeing you less than perfect – I've seen it all now, even…'

'I'm putting them on,' I said loudly, cutting him off mid-sentence.

I looked at what was in front of me.

My line.

My blood.

The blood that I didn't even know I had running through my veins until just about this time last year. At the bottom of the page, I saw my own name and that of my parents. If you could really call them that – a paedophile and a whore. A match made in heaven. My blood parents.

Alastair MacGregor————Kailash Coutts
|
Brodie McLennan
(bastard)

The line ended with me.

Even on the sheet of paper I looked lonely.

'Cheers, Jack, I'm moved. It makes me feel all warm inside. How nice of you to remind me what I came from.'

I threw the papers down on the table.

'Don't get bloody touchy with me, Brodie. Those bits of paper simply state facts. You always knew your dad wasn't around, you always knew you were a bastard – you just have to understand that now you are a high-class bastard.'

He poked his fingers at names above my own.

'All high-court judges. All above the law. They're protected, Brodie. To a man.'

25

'My father wasn't safe, though, was he?'

I still felt odd calling the man who had raped Kailash by that title. And poor dead Mary McLennan, cold in the ground with only me to remember that she was the woman I considered my *real* mother. She'd taken me on with more love than most people receive in a lifetime. Running through it all in my head made me think I was reading the TV listings guide for a particularly tempting episode of *The Jerry Springer Show*. There wasn't much to laugh at when it was my own life, though. Jack's words dragged me away from my reflections.

'Alastair MacGregor *was* protected, Brodie. He was protected by the law – not the law that you and I live by, but the law that has protected men like him and their interests for centuries. That's why Kailash had to kill him. He had gotten away with it for decades. All those girls, all those boys, with no families to worry about them, being taken out of the care homes and sent to be abused by good, upstanding legal men like your father? Fucking protected to the hilt, the lot of them. I'd rather there were a thousand Kailashes than one of him. She may not be the usual type of mother, but she knows right from wrong – and she fights for what's hers.'

I imagined my mother in her work guise as Scotland's most notorious dominatrix, running her girls across the country, and doing it all with beauty and style. I wasn't much closer to under-standing her than I had been a year ago when I represented her – not knowing then that our connection was so much more than lawyer and client – but I did realise that she loved me – in her own way.

'You're not your father, Brodie. Just like he wasn't his. All the stuff you learned last year might make your head spin, but it's true – it's your truth, the truth of who you are. It's not every day your mother asks you to defend her for killing your father. But there are decent people in your blood, Brodie – your grandfather is a good man. Like Kailash, he loves you and knows that his only son was an evil bastard. What more evidence do you need? He saved Kailash, he stands by her now – and they both want one thing: they want you to be careful.

'Yes, you have enemies. You've made a lot in the last year – but they'll back off if you decide to toe the line. You have to listen to the old man, Brodie.'

'Has Grandad been speaking to you?' I said accusingly.

'Maybe…'

'Family trees, now cosy chats with my grandad? I'll just nip out and get you some slippers and a pipe. The years are taking their toll.'

'I'm not daft, Brodie – even if I wasn't … *keen* on you,' he raised his eyebrows at me as he found the right word, 'I'm a journo, I'd have to be stupid to ignore everything in my line of work. Look at this…'

Jack pulled his laptop across from the table at the side of him and fired it up. My heart sank as I saw that the *Journal of the Law Society* was in his favourites list. He clicked on the icon and opened up an article I recognised only too well. The words in the piece were engraved on my mind,

27

because – rightly or wrongly – I had felt they all applied to me. Complaints about falling standards were pretty predictable from the old guard who moaned every century or so when they were nudged out of their complacency by the recognition that there were others out there who wanted to drag law into this millennium. But this article was far more strident than usual. The author had chosen to remain anonymous, which was very rare in itself. They must be pretty well in with those at the top of the tree if they were being allowed to hide. Whoever was behind it – and I had my suspicions of who it might be – was on their high horse about the fact that they believed solicitors were looking on what they did as a business, not a profession. They rattled off a few sound bites about whether they were lawyers or ambulance chasers, which had got a few snippets of coverage from the papers. However, the most interesting – or irritating – point for me, was the remark about 'rumbles' from last month's meeting of the Edinburgh Bar Association, where, allegedly, there had been talk about how one firm in particular was going to be reported to the Law Society for blatant touting.

'Come on, Brodie, you know all about this – you're one of the lawyers they're particularly worked up about. You're too successful – they prefer mediocrity to brilliance.'

I stared at him long enough for him to feel uncomfortable.

'And gorgeousness too – obviously, gorgeousness too.'

'Yeah, that's it, Jack. They're terrified of my

28

brain *and* my thighs. In the real world, I think you'll find it's all down to what it's always been about with lawyers – money and power.'

'Fair enough,' he said, 'but ask yourself this – just how many clients can one firm represent without there being a conflict of interests?'

'No idea, Jack, but I guess I'll find out pretty soon.'

'Alex Cattanach is keeping an eye on you. You don't want head-honcho accountants on your tail at the best of times – you certainly don't when they are telling everyone in town that they have enough to take you down. I'm usually all for smart-arses, Brodie, but you can't keep annoying the Bar Association or they'll take you out. They might be wankers ... but they're not stupid wankers. You can't watch your back the whole time.'

'You watch it for me then, Jack.' I threw back at him and wiggled my arse right out his door, vowing never to return.

Not even I believed it.

Chapter Two

'I don't know how you've managed it, but you've achieved in months what no man has done for the past two hundred years – you've united the Bar. Unfortunately, it's against you.'

Lord MacGregor, my newly found grandad, was sputtering his words out. I was still coming to

29

terms with things. Until recently, I had thought of another woman as mother, another man as father – albeit an absent one – and didn't think I had a grandad to call my own. It was a lot to take in – on top of that came the spectacle of the man who was universally recognised as one of the greatest legal minds to ever come out of Scotland lying half-naked on a table in front of me. Behind him, the masseur gave a deep-tissue massage to help loosen the old man's blue-veined limbs, which were becoming knotted with arthritis. I didn't want to imagine the conversations Malcolm, my mother's gay personal dresser/ masseur friend, could be having with the pillar of the legal community when I wasn't there. What could they possibly have in common? Apart from a genuine admiration of Kailash Coutts, I couldn't come up with anything.

I shook myself out of my reverie.

'Have you finished yet?'

'You'll know exactly when I've finished with you, young lady.'

This was something else I was having to get used to. To him, I wasn't kicking thirty now, nor did I have a career of my own – I was just the wee lassie who needed to be kept in line.

It irked and delighted me at the same time. His face was turning puce, whether from temper or the pain of the massage, I couldn't tell.

'Grandad, I was speaking to Malcolm.' It still felt weird that, a year ago, I had virtually no family to speak of, and now, here I was calling one of the most important and influential men in Scotland 'grandad'.

'Five minutes, Brodie. I told Lord MacGregor that if he cancelled this appointment, I couldn't fit him in for another ten days. I'm very busy with colonics these days, you know.'

'If you'd arrived when you were supposed to, Brodie,' started my grandad again, 'I'd have met you with my breeks on. But that's the state of Edinburgh today – I can't get help with my arthritis for the citizens of Edinburgh wanting the shit washed out of them. More money than sense. In my day we went to the toilet ourselves.'

Malcolm rolled his eyes dramatically. As usual, he was immaculately turned out in purple and green tartan trews. His black patent dress brogues twinkled beneath the massage table as he pushed and pummelled my grandad. The scent of warm lavender oil filled the air. Pig farmers have been known to use that essential oil to stop sows eating their young – but it wasn't working on my grandad and his savaging continued.

'Kailash? Kailash? Where are you, girl?'

Lord MacGregor looked like an old tortoise without a shell as he craned his neck upwards to shout for my birth mother.

Malcolm pushed his client's head down onto the table. Lord or not, Malcolm would allow no one to be harsh with Kailash.

'She's making some tea. It's no good getting yourself all hot and bothered – you only make your blood pressure go sky-high.'

Malcolm was from Inverness via San Francisco. His curious lilt soothed the belligerent old man in front of him; either that or it was the vision of loveliness that kicked open the door carrying a

31

butler's tray of steaming cups.

Kailash floated in, dressed in soft white linen. Her black hair rippled around her shoulders. It was obviously freshly washed, whereas mine felt itchy and I fought the urge to scratch the crown of my head until her back was turned. To make things worse, the smell of Malcolm's unguents and potions were bringing on my hangover again. Seriously dehydrated, I almost snatched the mug of steaming tea from Kailash's beautifully French-manicured hands. Rats were chewing at the base of my skull and I gingerly reached out to find a seat.

'Are you still on that diet?' Kailash queried.

'I didn't know I was on one,' I answered.

'I could have sworn last time we spoke you mentioned something.'

I knew what she was doing. Her underhand tactics weren't going to work on me, but maybe I could lay off the booze for a couple of days. Or months. In truth, I was quite impressed that she had managed to cotton on so quickly to that mother's way of hiding insults behind innocent comments. I bit my bottom lip.

'Show it to her, Kailash,' interrupted my grandad. 'I don't think she's seen it.'

Kailash reached down to a chair and picked up today's paper. They had all paused their various activities to look at me. I sensed that it was going to be news best taken standing so I feigned dis-interest and moved over to stare out of the window.

Kailash's voice was slow and warm. I tried to listen with half an ear, sure that that the words she spoke were not going to be good. I stared out of the windows in Ramsay Gardens and watched the people scurrying below in Princes Street. I loved my grandad's flat. There wasn't a garden but the place snuggled in deep beside Edinburgh Castle. Built before planning regulation, it was a delightful hodge-podge of styles. There had been dwellings on this site for centuries and, as I looked at my grandad lying there, I wouldn't have been surprised to hear that he had been amongst the first residents.

I turned my attention back to the pedestrians below. I wished that I was one of them. Even the road-sweeper's job looked alluring right now. Kailash's words brought me back to the moment.

Cash laundering link to missing law chief

Scottish solicitors suspected of money laundering are to be interviewed by detectives investigating the disappearance of the chief accountant of the Law Society of Scotland.

Former Scottish rugby internationalist, Alex Cattanach, has not been seen for ten days. Cattanach is known to have launched what colleagues describe as a 'fatwa' against corruption in the legal profession.

Police are probing a theory that Cattanach was the victim of a revenge attack ordered by a lawyer whose criminality was about to be exposed.

Cattanach, characterised as 'a tough customer' by more than one top lawyer, is understood to have spearheaded a recent crackdown on all forms of misconduct relating to finance, including money laundering.

At present, sixteen Scottish solicitors face charges. A Lothian and Borders Police source said, 'We will be questioning people we suspect have been involved in money laundering, given that Cattanach's team would normally investigate them. There are some guys – especially some guys in criminal practice – who give us a lot of concern because of the people they associate with.' One police officer who wished to remain anonymous added, 'These solicitors are not whiter than white themselves. They know some pretty disreputable characters. Characters who are proud to let it be known that they can make problems – or people – disappear.'

Police will, also this week begin sifting through all Law Society files that were being dealt with by Cattanach and the team of twelve accountants. They will be looking for anyone who had a grudge against Cattanach or who may have feared being investigated. The police source added: 'It'll be a pretty long list.'

Silence.

I didn't turn round. I continued staring down, ignoring my racing heart as much as I could.

Lord MacGregor, now dressed in a robe, tapped me on my shoulder whilst Malcolm and Kailash scurried in the background pretending not, to listen.

'Now, lass, I'm not suggesting that you're one of the lawyers that's going to be investigated.'

By his glinting eyes, I guessed that something must have shown in my face. The wily old fox was used to reading witnesses.

'Tell me things haven't got that bad?'

He moved on to shaking my shoulders roughly. I shrugged him off.

'Brodie – the Edinburgh Bar is gunning for you. You are building a practice that is enviable – but you've no protection. The clients that you are representing are coming to you from somewhere. Someone else's pocket is empty since you've got so popular.'

I continued to look as disinterested as I could muster. 'Other lawyers.' Kailash butted in. 'You're taking money from their purses and they're getting worried and angry.'

'If they can't keep their clients happy, that's their problem.'

I sounded more bullish than I felt.

I thought of all the complaints from the Law Society that I had received. Their headed note-paper was usually green – every letter I had was in red. Warning letters. Even Lavender was worried.

'Don't take that tone with me – I know better,' said my mother. 'The Bar might be full of absolute tossers, but they're razor-sharp when it comes to protecting their purses, and I, for one, wouldn't cross swords with them lightly.'

'Well then, it's lucky someone in this family has guts,' I responded.

Kailash and Grandad looked at me. I was a bit worried; the seriousness of my situation had stopped them laughing out loud at me even though they should have. I was behaving like an impudent young pup – no wonder they were treating me like a child. I was Grandad's last blood relative, so I really couldn't doubt that my best interests were of paramount importance to him.

And yet I tried.

My grandad tried again to make me see sense.

'Brodie – I know about the letters of complaint. I've tried to buy you time. I've been told that if you mend your ways, pull back on your empire building a bit, and stop annoying everyone in the entire field, then they will be put on the backburner until we can find a different path for you.'

I was furious. How dare they lecture me like this?

'Might I remind you both that my life was going well until you two became involved in it again. "The rising star of the Scottish Bar" – that was me. And then you...' I pointed at Kailash, 'decided to settle your differences with my senior partner by involving him in a sex scandal and splashed it all over the papers. So what happens then? *My* firm gets plunged into debt because of the defamation charge going against us and unless *my* firm pays off its overdraft then *I'll* be bankrupt and unable to practise on my own? Thanks to, you, Mummy dearest, I'm looking at a future of being someone else's cash cow, so don't start telling me what to do when the best thing is probably that you keep well out of things.'

Kailash didn't look fazed in the slightest. I suppose a lot worse had been said to her.

'Brodie,' she went on, as if I hadn't spoken, 'you play the cards you're dealt. If you could win carrying on the way you are – making enemies left, right and centre – I'd say go ahead. But you simply can't win.'

'You don't trust me?' I asked her. 'You don't trust me to do things properly?'

'Too bad,' she cut back. 'Your life is at stake now – and that's far more important.'

'You're using a lot of gambling terminology Kailash,' I commented, trying to move the conversation on. 'Are the rumours correct?'

'Yes, they are. For once. I've taken over the Danube Street casino.'

She mentioned it as if she'd bought a new handbag. And that was the rub. I knew that all I would have to do would be to ask either of them for money to buy my way out of the firm. Lothian and St Clair would see the back of me and I would be, technically, free. I knew that Kailash and my grandad would give me as much as I needed without a second thought, but my damned pride insisted that I had to do it my own way. If I did rely on the money of others, who would I choose anyway? Which fortune was more acceptable to me? The one made recently by one woman's ingenuity and willingness to do anything to survive, or the other based on old, aristocratic money handed down through the ages? I told myself it wasn't a choice I was ready to make.

'Enough of these diversionary tactics. Kailash – can't you see what she's doing?' Lord MacGregor was shouting.

He was a great lawyer in his time, my grandad, but the judge in him took over now. There was only one person in charge in his drawing room and it was clear that it wasn't going to be me.

'Brodie – the only route open to you is to take

37

a position as a sheriff. Put in a few years in the lower courts and then get a seat in the College of Justice. Join the family firm and become a judge. It would make me very proud to see you wear the red robes.'

'Easy as that, is it?' I asked. 'Just say what you want and it all comes together? Even for your annoying bastard granddaughter?'

He looked slightly flustered. Unusually.

'Well, the only reason I can even suggest this is that the powers-that-be are looking for more women to become judges. Political correctness or some other such bloody nonsense. It can work in your favour, my dear.'

'Follow in my father's footsteps?'

'If it will save you from being ruined, then yes, do whatever you have to continue.' Kailash joined in the shouting match.

'Some people would bite their arm off for the chance we are offering you.' Grandad's voice was raised.

We. I didn't want to know about Kailash's involvement. Thinking about what favours she was pulling in on my behalf made my blood run cold. No one likes to think about their mother having sex, much less for money or other favours. It was enough to keep me in therapy for years.

My grandad's next words made that thought disappear.

'Bridget Nicholson is wining and dining as we speak. That girl is desperate to be elevated to the bench.'

'Girl? She was born middle-aged, and she's certainly looked it ever since I've known her.

38

She's probably excited by the huge pension.'

'Whatever her reasons are, Brodie, could you really imagine yourself scraping and bowing before *Lady* Nicholson?'

And there he had it – my hot button.

I didn't want it, but I was bloody sure I didn't want Bridget Nicholson to have it either.

Chapter Three

'Have you been sleeping there all night?'

It's surprising how sharp and hard a ball of rolled-up paper is when it hits you in the face. I had been sleeping, head down on my glass-topped desk, and I could feel the drool running freely from the side of my mouth.

'Was I snoring?'

'Like a pig in clover – and the resemblance doesn't stop there. Did you go home last night or have you been working in the office all night?' Lavender looked sniffily around my office, which was littered with files.

'When I finished at St Leonard's with the custodies, it was hardly worth going home. I was busy at the weekend and I hadn't had time to prepare the trial files properly.' The mere mention of the word 'weekend' made my mouth go dry – Lavender Ironside wasn't just the best secretary in the firm, she also knew me inside out and I was terrified she'd make me spill the beans about Jack.

'If you employed an assistant they could do some of the preparation,' she pointed out.

'You know we can't afford it,' I replied.

Lavender snorted. 'I know the money that comes in for criminal fees – you're paying more than your fair share into the partners' pissing pot. Why don't you ask the others to cut down on their expenses and get the overdraft down?'

'If I had the energy I'd laugh, Lav.' The very thought of the rest of them walking to work or taking clients to McDonald's was risible. 'I need some caffeine – would you?'

I knew that I must still be looking pathetic when Lavender switched the coffee machine on without a murmur. I wouldn't get away without a few comments, though.

'For all your money, Brodie, I wouldn't have your life.'

'Is that some sick joke, Lav? You of all people know I'm skint.'

She considered her options. 'Well, even for your body I wouldn't have your life – well, I might consider it.' Lavender self-consciously smoothed her hands over her rounded rump before continuing. Like a hound dog she turned on a six-pence – for all her flaws, I loved her to bits, and knew that it was reciprocated. She presented me with a steaming cup of strong black coffee before delivering the killer punch.

'You've been shagging this weekend – haven't you?' Her bright blue eyes were hungry for details.

'Come on, Brodie, share – don't spare my blushes.'

'Your interest in other people's sex lives is, frankly, obscene.' I tried to sound superior, but we'd had too many of these conversations in the past to take the moral high ground.

'Oooh, you're not denying it then?'

'I didn't admit anything– I was merely commenting on your unhealthy obsession with second-hand sex.'

'Do I know him?'

She pressed her face into mine, and for some bizarre reason sniffed as if she believed she would get his scent.

'What the hell do you think you are doing, Lavender?'

'Trying to get inside your aura.'

'My what?' Lavender came up with the oddest things sometimes. I'd known her ever since I was a student doing part-time work at the firm and she was a secretary there – over the years we had become friends much more than workmates, and I trusted her more than I trusted myself at times – but she was still strange on occasion.

'You know that I've been going to the College of Parapsychology to increase my psychic ability,' she said, as if she'd just signed up for woodworking. 'Well, this weekend I went to an introductory course on psychometry.'

Keeping up with Lavender's fads was quite beyond me. I adopted my usual tactics – I put my feet up on the desk and switched off.

'I found I was good at reading people's auras – probably because it works at an emotional level.'

If Lavender was trying to imply she was good at sensing other people's feelings she was either

41

lying to herself or ignoring mine. Knowing her, she would simply be disregarding my desire for privacy.

'This man – the one you won't tell me about – he's very drawn to you, you'd be surprised at the depth of his feelings.' Her head moved from side to side like a snake as she read me.

'Was it Joe? Did you sleep with Joe?'

I ignored her, but she continued undeterred.

'Brodie, did you know that feelings get trapped inside material items? So…'

There was a long pause whilst she stood up, before she pounced like a cat.

'All I have to do is figure out what you were wearing when you were with him. And, unlike most women, you only seem to have one pair of shoes.'

She snatched my shoe off my foot. She held it aloft and ran round the office, avoiding the piles of files and law books that were scattered on the floor. Those shoes could tell a tale or two, she was right there.

'I'm not in the mood, Lavender.'

'You were in the bloody mood on Friday night,' she snapped back. 'And Jack Deans is a piss-head.'

I was impressed and it must have showed on my face.

'And you need to stop drinking so much. I saw you go off with him. You were like a bitch in heat, dragging him out the door, too busy to notice anybody watching you.'

'So much for your aura-reading, Lavender; you're just a nosy cow, aren't you?'

42

The shoe hit me on the arm. There was no time for explanations or apologies as the agency lawyers started to appear and Lavender went to pour the coffee.

This was where recent events started to hit home. The Edinburgh Bar's latest meeting had concluded I was to be shunned – sent to Coventry. This decision went beyond social niceties; it was an unwritten rule that members of the Bar watched each other's backs. No one can be in two places at once, but often the court diary decreed that I was in two or three courts at 10 a.m. I might have a deferred sentence in Court Four, a plea in mitigation in Court Two, and a trial in Court One. I would turn up at Courts Four and Two; ask the clerk in Court Two to hold back my plea in mitigation until the end of the roll – in Court Four I would expect another lawyer to cover the call-over for me – gratis. At 10 a.m. on the morning of a trial that is assigned to a court, the sheriff has the case called. This involves the clerk shouting out the name of the accused person to make sure that he has turned up. If they fail to appear, a warrant is taken for their arrest; it's purely administrative and anyone who wears a gown can do it. The practice was that if a fellow lawyer was in another court, then I would stand up for them. But as the Bar had taken the huff with me, it meant I had to get cover for every single case I had in court – even if I was only there for five minutes. They kept trying to trip me up, hoping that if I didn't have cover I'd be found in contempt of court – thus losing my practising certificate and my livelihood.

I needed to use agency solicitors because I couldn't afford to hire full-time assistants. I hired the agents on a daily basis. They got a higher rate of pay than full-time assistants would, but I only paid them to do the things that I couldn't do myself. I had been working ridiculous hours lately, but even I recognised that I couldn't be in two courts at once.

As a rule, firms were reluctant to use agency solicitors because they were loose cannons. Most lawyers didn't choose to be agents, they went down that route because some setback had forced them out of private practice.

I preferred to think of my agents as outsiders. I needed my agents to take shit from the Edinburgh Bar and they were tough enough to do it – trainees were not. Typically, Robert Girvan appeared first. Sober and freshly dressed, he was the odd man out. Handsome, intelligent, personable – he made my flesh creep. He was my dark doppelganger. If everything went tits over arse, then I would be like Robert Girvan. I kept him around as a cautionary tale to myself; whenever I felt like slacking off, his face would flash before mine and I would keep going.

'Brodie.' He nodded in my direction as he took his suit jacket off to stop it crushing, laying it carefully on my desk. Censure flicked through his eyes as he surveyed my mess.

'Are you checking out my backside?' he asked Lavender as she handed him the coffee.

'Absolutely, Robert – and you've been working out. Good boy.'

'Buns of steel, that's me – I've got to be careful

how I sit.'

Silently I agreed with him, but for different reasons – beneath his joking, my overriding impression of Girvan was that he was anally retentive.

I could already hear the shuffling and coughing in the corridor that meant one thing. Lavender stood at the ready with a double espresso in one hand and a couple of paracetamol in the other.

Eddie Gibb was about to arrive.

His entrance didn't disappoint. His sandy hair was messier than mine, and his suit jacket hung off his shoulders as if he had shrunk in the night. Eddie, like all of us, carried his court gown over his arm. The main difference being that Eddie's was a nasty shade of green. I surmised that it was some strange yeast growth from all the beer that had been spilled upon it as it lay discarded in some spit-and-sawdust pub that would still sell him drink.

Of course, that wasn't the image Lavender saw. Her eyes lit up as she looked upon his craggy wee face. Why did I employ this waster? Not just because of Lavender. Eddie Gibb sober was quite simply the greatest court lawyer I have ever seen. He never looked at a file during a trial, saying that it confused him. Eddie questioned and probed police witnesses until they cried. Right-wing judges were putty in his hand and, at that moment just before any case collapsed, Eddie always believed he was at his best.

There was someone missing.

'Where's David? Did you instruct him, Lavender?' I asked. I was beginning to get anxious. It

45

was past 8 a.m. and we hadn't started the court meeting yet. We had trials set down for courts outside Edinburgh and they needed to be handed out and discussed so that the agent could arrive on time.

'I phoned him last night to confirm he would be here, but there was no answer. It seems Edinburgh has turned into Sodom and Gomorrah – everyone's having sex except me.'

Lavender looked at Eddie wistfully. I ignored her and so did he.

'Well, to be fair, every weekend's pretty much like that for David,' commented Eddie before Lavender could rugby tackle him to the ground with her demands.

'Maybe this weekend was different,' added Robert Girvan. 'He told me he's met a soul mate at the Fire Island club and he wants to spend some time basking in young love's delusion. I hope he's got the sense to lock up his valuables.'

This was a recurring pattern with David. He'd married young in an effort to convince his mother he wasn't gay, and as soon as she was lukewarm in her grave, he was off with the scoutmaster. Like all his relationships, it didn't last long. David couldn't decide whether he was a slut or a hopeless romantic. It didn't bloody matter – I was one body down.

'Don't worry – I've taken care of it.' Lavender bristled with efficiency. 'I've instructed Laura McGuigan.'

Everyone groaned.

Laura McGuigan was an absolute bitch. The only female agent used by the firm, she tended to work as a criminal assistant for her boyfriend, Neville Boardman. This was a man whose only personality trait was his dandruff. Under normal circumstances, Neville's chronic eczema would elicit sympathy, but as chairman of the Edinburgh Bar Association, he was one of my main adversaries. I wasn't the only one to detest him, though, and the fact that Laura had now defected away from him made me want to believe that she might be open to leading the swing against Neville and the Bar Association.

Maybe I needed someone like that around, someone two-faced, more than I was willing to admit.

On cue, Laura walked in. We shuffled a little uneasily in case she had heard us, but she would be so grateful for the work after leaving her meal ticket, both professionally and personally, that she wouldn't say anything anyway. Her silver shiny suit looked as if she had raided a Next January sale twenty years ago. I had to hand it to her – she had tried with her remaining wisps of hair, which were carefully plastered down with Vaseline by the looks of it.

As Lavender handed out the court files, Laura smiled at me and I felt incredibly uneasy.

'We still have a problem,' Lavender said.

'*We* do?'

1 looked around and saw the appropriate files in the correct hands. I checked my photocopy of the court diary again. 'It's not in there. I haven't entered it.'

It's a sackable offence not to enter a date in the court diary. Lavender knew this to be the case –

not because she had ever been careless enough to do it, but because she had heard me rant on about it ad nauseam.

She waited a few seconds before announcing, 'I didn't put it in there because I don't think you should do it. Tanya Hayder's been lifted. She was taken into Leith police station this morning. She won't get legal aid, she's no money, we have no one to appear for her, and she's going away for a long time, so it's not an investment, Brodie. You can't represent her – it's not just your arse you're trying to keep out of the fire – I need this firm to survive too. I don't have a rich grandad to support me.' I knew why Lav was doing this, why she was twisting the knife; but we both knew it wouldn't work. Tanya Hayder and I went way back. Irrespective of whether it had been put in the diary or not, I would be there for her regardless of the cost, and we all knew it.

Chapter Four

My Fat Boy roared past Edinburgh Sheriff Court, and I took my time making sure that all the punters saw us – my Harley Davidson motorbike was my greatest marketing tool.

Slowly, I did a U-turn past the pompous statue of William Chambers before coming to a regal stop directly outside the gates to the Sheriff Court. There was a parking place for solo motorcycles further up the street, but I always parked

Awesome where he could be seen.

Riding my bike was my greatest source of joy, a pretty sad indictment on my life. Awesome was eight years old, and I can't pretend that the one lady owner was careful. Oil dripped onto the road where I parked, but I wouldn't part with the Fat Boy for anything. The bike had been a twenty-first birthday gift from the one man who truly loved me. Unfortunately, I had an easier relationship with the bike than I had with my benefactor, Glasgow Joe.

The upside of riding a motorbike was that you could get through Edinburgh's congested streets and find a parking space in relative safety from the parking wardens. The downside was that I had to arrive early to change out of my leathers.

As I dismounted, I remembered another draw-back. Helmet hair.

It was 9.30 a.m. and the usual suspects were beginning to gather at the court entrance. Polyester suits were in abundance, and teenage girls with pussy pelmet skirts clung to the arms of aged Lotharios.

My eyes drank in the scene, looking for my clients. At least I didn't have to make them up any more. When I had first started building my practice, I noticed that the successful lawyers carried lots of files. They then made a great show of standing in the atrium of the court before the call-over of cases where they shouted out their clients' names. The more successful you were, the more names you hollered.

In the beginning I had one slim file. It was embarrassing. To keep myself amused I took old, fat files out of storage, stood next to the busiest lawyers and barked out fictitious names. The number of clients I called for, naturally, was always greater than my rivals.

Mary McLennan, the woman I would always think of as my mother, used to tell me, 'Be nice to those you meet on the way up, as you never know who you might need on the way down.' Feeling alone today, as usual, I wished that I had listened to her.

'Brodie!'

Panic ran through my veins. I wasn't expecting him to be at court today. Had I missed a date?

Moses Tierney sauntered out of the shadows. The leader of the Dark Angels – and my most important client – looked his customary picture of sartorial elegance. His peroxide hair was spiked and gelled with military precision, and kohl enhanced his grey, wolf-like eyes, making his skin seem even whiter.

The Dark Angels were rarely seen in daylight. Rather dramatically, they prided themselves upon being creatures of the darkness – which is difficult in Scotland during the summer months. Recently I suspected that Moses was trying to model himself on the London gangsters of the Fifties. Moses had made it known that he was now a legitimate businessman, flashing his money about and being a bit more careful about who he was dealing with – which would have been bad news for me if it had been the truth. In fact, his few legitimate ventures required the services of commercial lawyers so I was able to refer him to my partners.

'What the fuck are you up to, Brodie?'

Moses grabbed me by the collar of my leather jacket, and pulled me into the corner, away from the gathering crowds.

'What do mean?' I genuinely had no idea why he was so upset.

'Look at that radge there.' Moses pointed into the opposite corner where a Dark Angel stood looking shame-faced. I would have placed him in his late twenties, so he was quite old to be a member of Moses' gang.

'Who is it?'

'See? That's my point, Brodie. You should know who he is.'

I had a good memory for faces and I definitely hadn't met this one.

'See, Brodie, when you let yourself down, you let me down. Know what I mean?'

Frankly, I didn't know what he meant, and it must have shown on my face.

'Do I have to spell it out for you? That gadge works for me – and the arsehole got himself lifted by the polis.'

I saw Moses' point now. I knew that I had never met this gang member, but it was customary that if a Dark Angel was arrested by the police, then they asked for me to represent them. I had never seen him before so he must have another lawyer representing him today. One of us was slipping, and there was no way even I could suggest it was Moses.

'Who is he?' I asked again.

'That arsehole calls himself "The Alchemist". Fucker.'

'What's he into, Dungeons and Dragons? You

51

the Dragon Master now, Moses?'

'Don't push it – this is serious. The Alchemist's my chemist. Smart boy – not smart enough, though. He's got a degree from Aberdeen University, he makes the legal drugs that I sell through my Internet business.'

'What's he up for? Possession? Intent to supply?'

'Naw, nothing like that. Big arsehole just got himself done for breaking and entering.'

The surprise must have shown on my face as Moses proffered an unasked-for explanation.

'That twat…' he threw his head in the direction of the Alchemist, 'went to a private school, but he's got this romantic notion of being a criminal. Butch fucking Cassidy and the fucking Sundance Kid don't have a look-in with him. Of course, he's been fitted up on the present charge – so he's pleading not guilty,' Moses hastily added.

No Dark Angel was ever found guilty of an offence – it was more a question of what they knew rather than who they knew. Moses might be slinging mud at me today, but we both knew he was slipping if the Crown Office had decided to prosecute.

'Bring him across,' I said.

I was pissed off. I was busy enough today without having to deal with a public-school tosser who had been given enough privileges in life to know better. I had to get him to sign a mandate saying that I was now representing him and then I'd have the aggro of handing the piece of paper over to the now-redundant lawyer in person. This would all be done in full view of the Edinburgh lawyers, compounding their belief that I was lining my own pockets at the cost of theirs.

Could this day get worse?

My mobile vibrated softly in my pocket. Five missed calls. Four from Glasgow Joe and one from Jack.

'Welcome to hell,' I muttered under my breath.

'Sorry? I didn't catch what you said?'

The Alchemist had a soft, cultured voice, and the spaced-out look that comes from permanent brain damage. Brain damage caused by handling too many hallucinogenic drugs with a hole in your rubber gloves.

'Sign this.'

I shoved the mandate under his nose. I could take the details later. Right now I had to find the lawyer who was supposed to be representing him and get the document to them.

'Who was supposed to be representing you?' I asked.

'Bridget Nicholson.'

Shit. With the way my day was going I should have guessed it would be her.

As always, when I entered the agents' room I was struck by how bland it was. Not to mention the fact that there was absolutely no privacy.

Bridget Nicholson brushed her peroxide-blonde hair. She caught me looking distastefully at the hairs that were landing on her black court gown and falling on the floor.

She deliberately swung her skanky mane at me and I jerked backwards. Her lips were bright red, which made her teeth look yellow. I tried to remember those makeover television shows. I'm sure they would advise her to use a lipstick with more blue in it.

I couldn't deny some men found her attractive, but then again, there's no accounting for taste. At thirty-nine, Nicholson looked years older than Kailash – I didn't want to imagine what she'd been doing to make herself look so haggard. I put my scuffed bike helmet down on the carpet, beside her well-polished stilettos.

As I straightened myself up, I became uncomfortably aware of the hush that had settled on the agents' room. No one was making any pretence of not listening. Reaching into my trouser pocket, I pulled out the crumpled mandate and handed it to her. She looked at it as if it were a steaming pile of shit.

The hordes clustered round, waiting for a scene. They looked like a gang in pristine black gowns – all except Eddie Gibb in his funny-coloured green gown. Still, at least he had a gown on. I was the outsider and felt that they were all willing Bridget to rip me apart.

'How much did you pay him?' Nicholson asked.

'Pardon?'

'You heard me, Brodie. How much are you paying your clients?'

I ignored her and pointed to the appropriately signed mandate.

'Come on, Brodie,' she went on. 'You must be making some kind of profit out of this – so what incentives are you giving these young men? Maybe it's not financial? You handing out blow jobs like your mother?'

I wanted to hit her, but Eddie Gibb showed previously hidden speed, and his surprisingly steady hand held mine as he spoke to Nicholson.

'Brodie has a legitimate mandate – failure to furnish her with the papers will result in a complaint to the Law Society.'

I was surprised by the gravitas in Eddie's voice.

'Speaking of the Law Society – have you been interviewed yet about Cattanach's disappearance, Miss McLennan?' Nicholson shouted loudly so that her public could hear every word. 'Don't look so surprised; everyone here knows you're being investigated – that's why we're not bothered by these.'

She threw the mandate back in my face. Eddie pulled me close and whispered in my ear.

'Stay calm – you know that she and Cattanach were an item.'

I followed his advice because I knew it was the right thing to do and I couldn't think of a smart retort. I took the file from Nicholson and ripped out the complaint – the piece of paper that stated what the Alchemist had been charged with – then handed the file back to her. As I walked out of the agents' room to change for court, I heard her shout.

'Cat got your tongue, Brodie? Or are you just upset that you can't shag your way out of this one?'

Chapter Five

'You look as if someone is squeezing your balls, Brodie!'

Robert Girvan shouted at me as we scurried between courts like black rats trying to find their way round a maze.

The weight of the files was hurting my arm. I was struggling just to be in the right place at the right time, without even considering how good my performance was. This morning's work was purely administrative, a chimpanzee could have done it, in fact there was one ugly bastard at the Bar doing a grand impression of an orang-utan.

I missed the easy camaraderie of my early years, when all the old letches were falling over themselves to help me. Either I had lost my charms or I was even more unpopular than I wanted to know. I didn't know which was worse. No one had stood up for me earlier except Eddie, and I wasn't daft enough to think that was for any other reason than the fact that I paid him.

I had finished my morning's work except for the Alchemist's intermediate diet – meaning I would have to tell the court whether or not we were ready to go to trial – and a probation hearing for Tanya Hayder. I'd won the battle of wills with Lavender – stubbornness usually does win the game, and it was always a foregone conclusion given the history between Tanya and myself. Both cases were in different courts at different ends of the building. Eddie, Robert and Laura were in trials that were about to start. I had intended to cover one of the trials, but the Alchemist situation was one which definitely required *'delectus personae'*, not just because he was an important client, but because the courtroom would be filled with spectators hoping to see another fight. Tanya Hayder would have to go on the backburner and I prayed that everything would run smoothly.

The glass and marble halls of the new Edinburgh Sheriff Court are sharp and clean, easily wiped-down surfaces to erase the mistakes of humanity that appear there on a daily basis – the lawyers, not the clients. There is obviously a large police presence at the Sheriff Court, but the court cops are a different breed. Whether by accident or design, the powers-that-be have reassigned the best negotiators to work there; they are so skilled they should be in the diplomatic corps sorting out the Middle East.

The Alchemist lounged against the glass balcony outside Court Seven. Moses wasn't there. Instead, the Alchemist's entourage consisted of two sixteen-year-old schoolgirls, who were definitely not Dark Angels. This was very unusual because the gang were a clannish bunch – once you were in the inner circle, which this boy obviously was, you didn't taint yourself with outsiders.

I don't know why I called him a boy – probably more due to thinking he must have made some daft choices to end up here rather than his looks. As I studied him more closely I would have placed him in his early thirties: tall, about six foot three, and 1 guessed he'd weigh about nine and a half stone soaking wet. His Adam's apple was the largest I'd ever seen and it bobbed about nervously in his scrawny neck. I sensed that he was nervous because he was having difficulty swallowing. One of the first signs of fear is a dry mouth.

He had all the trademarks of a Dark Angel but there was something different about him, more than just his age. The peroxide-white hair was gelled to perfection, but it was sparse and I just wasn't used to seeing a balding Angel. It didn't fit. The Dark Angels were beautiful, in their own unorthodox way.

His skin was pale, except for an angry shaving rash around his chin and a cold sore dominating his thin blue lips – I knew that Malcolm would give an alternative reason for this, nothing as boring as a virus but the consequences of 'angry words not spoken.' Maybe Malcolm was right in this case. The Alchemist looked the type of coward to keep all his rage inside.

'Georgia, Alice, this is my lawyer Brodie MacGregor.'

'McLennan. It's Brodie McLennan.'

Had he done that on purpose? And what was the deal between posh girls and criminals? Judging by their customised uniforms, these girls went to St Charles', Edinburgh's most exclusive girls' school. They were beautiful in the way only the daughters of the very rich can be, as an ageing pop casanova once said. Their skin was creamy and blemish-free, their confidence was overwhelming – so why were they hanging around this loser?

The Alchemist was clearly much more interested in them than me, and I sensed my time for getting information out of him was fading. I needed the details and I needed them fast.

'What's your name?' I asked.

'The Alchemist,' he replied instantly, turning round and grinning at his harem.

'Well, unless you want to do six months for perverting the course of justice or contempt of court, you'll stop being a smart-arse and tell me your given name ... now.'

He stared at me to check I was serious. I didn't blink.

'Bernard Carpenter.'

I'd call myself 'The Alchemist' with a name like that too, but the girls' adoration wasn't dented.

'It says here,' I wiggled the complaint under his nose, 'that on the fifteenth of May, you were caught breaking into a house in Morningside Road. I spoke to the Procurator Fiscal earlier because today is an intermediate diet. I have to say that I have all the prosecution statements and any defence witnesses are ready. Now, the Fiscal told me that you've been caught with your dick flapping in the wind. The Crown have productions – namely the jewellery that was taken from the house, and they say that it was found in your possession.'

'No way – that lying bastard DI Bancho is just out to get me. There is no way that was on me when I was taken to the police station. As a matter of fact, I threw that jewellery away.'

I sighed.

'Thanks, Bernard – you don't even have the

courtesy or common sense to keep your mouth shut. Now that you've told me you did it, I can't argue in court that you didn't.'

I was really getting angry with this idiot. He must be a pretty spectacular chemist for Moses to put up with his amateurish attitude. I had a duty as an officer of the court that if a client told me they were guilty then I couldn't argue that they were innocent. Sweet Jesus, most of the prisoners in Scottish jails were still protesting their innocence.

Georgia – or was it Alice? – lifted his heavy leather coat and put her arm around his waist. At least she had the sense to know that we were in deep shit.

'I'm going ahead with this trial – they can't prove it,' he protested weakly.

'I'm telling you that they can prove this – they have the jewellery, and the DI who says he found it on you.'

'Bancho is lying, I've said that already – and it's up to you to prove it. Moses says you're the dog's bollocks – well, he doesn't want me sent down, it's bad for his business, so you'd better do it if you want to stay in his good books.'

Bridget Nicholson sauntered up to us. 'More trouble, Brodie? Morning, Bernard – you should have stayed with a lawyer who knows how to look after her clients.'

How much had she overheard?

'It's never too late, Bernard,' she called as she walked off. I think he might have gone with her if she hadn't kept calling him Bernard.

I followed her into court, all the way thinking

60

that there was no way I could see myself bowing to her if she became Lady Nicholson. But I would have to, unless I took my grandad's advice and applied myself. I couldn't see it happening – me? Lady Brodie McLennan? I was too young, but if Grandad said it could happen, then maybe I just had to believe, even if it filled me with dread. The very idea of sitting on my arse all day listening to cases would be one of the worst parts. There was no challenge in that for me. Maybe when I was a coffin dodger like the rest of them it would be a grand way of life. But not now.

Court Seven was packed. Lawyers lined both sides of the court walls as they waited their turn. I put my name in to the sheriff clerk, but there was no way they could really call my case any quicker. Sometimes they would do me a favour and call my clients first, but that depended on me having the time to get in there before Court started and, speak to them nicely. The set-to I'd had with Bridget Nicholson had delayed me, and all morning I'd been trying to catch up with myself.

The queue moved slowly as the judge was a temporary sheriff. His day job was as a property lawyer and he'd never been in a courtroom in his life, so he was taking his time to make sure there were no mistakes. There was a shortage of judges when they had to resort to using clowns like this. Maybe I did have a chance of being Lady Mc-Lennan – or should I take my father's name and follow in his footsteps?

'Bernard Carpenter!'

The last case was called. I stepped forward and took my place in the well of the court. The Alchemist sloped into the dock.

'Are you Bernard Carpenter?' The clerk's voice was dry and hoarse; it had been a long court roll.

'M'Lord, my name is Brodie McLennan. I appear on behalf of the accused.'

'Are you from the same firm as Ms Nicholson, because it says that she represented the accused on the last occasion?' The judge wasn't just a pedant, he was also a hermit if he hadn't heard who I was in the last year. His prissy half-moon rimmed glasses fell to the end of his nose as he peered at me suspiciously. I shouldn't have been surprised – that's exactly what happens when the criminal Bar encounter their fellow professionals. Like oil and water, they just don't mix.

'I have a mandate to act for Mr Carpenter now,' I answered.

'Well, this young man can't think just because he changes his mind that he can hold up the judicial machinery. Are you ready to go to trial? Because I'll tell you now, I'm in no mood to grant an extension just to satisfy this young man's whims.'

It had been my intention to ask for an adjournment, but I knew I was on a hiding to nothing, and so I said what I knew I would regret.

'The defence is ready and prepared for trial.'

I had one official paper and a scribbled statement from my client. If I was Eddie Gibb I would have been ready to go to trial and win, but no sober lawyer would proceed on that basis. I noted the trial date down, two weeks from today. It would be hard work, especially as the Alchemist was insisting that I prove that DI Bancho had fitted him up. Now I'd had time to think of Bancho rather than push his name out of my mind, I had to admit that we went way back. He was a colleague of an old flatmate, Richard Sturgeon, and a crowd of us used to go out on Friday nights. However, there was no love lost between Bancho and me now, in spite of a couple of drunken snogs in the police club in Gorgie.

As it was, the last case called before lunch meant I had to stand and wait until the court was cleared; which really meant until the judge had left the bench. It was like watching a kettle boil. Eventually, I could go. As I left, Andy, the court macer, approached me.

'Sorry to bother you, Brodie.'

Andy was a nice guy, and I could tell by his face that he hated to be the bearer of bad news.

'Don't worry, Andy, I won't shoot the messenger.'

'You might – you put your name in to represent Tanya Hayder? Her case was called and you didn't appear. I did everything I could because I saw you were having difficulties this morning. The sheriff clerk kept it back right to the end – it only called five minutes ago. You were just too late.'

'Story of my life, Andy. So what's to happen now?'

'It's Sheriff Harrison and he wants to see you at two o'clock in chambers. He's pretty mad – he was playing golf at Muirfield and he's had to cancel because of this.' Andy patted me on the back and we left the court together as I moved towards my next run-in.

'Bernard! I want a word with you – in private.' I was past being polite. 'You heard what went on in there.' I inclined my head towards the court, not giving him the chance to wriggle out of my question.

'I ...' he started to stammer.

I cut him off.

'This trouble is of your own making. If you want to go to trial on that defence in two weeks make sure you have five grand in my hand before close of business on Friday.'

I turned and left without waiting for a reply. I was stopped in my tracks by a voice I knew only too well.

'Charging Kailash's prices now?'

Glasgow Joe was back.

Chapter Six

Joe never had approved of me lying on tombstones.

'Aren't you scared of the dead?'

'It's not the dead you should be afraid of, Joe – it's the living.'

Greyfriars Kirkyard was the nearest green space to the court, and my favourite lunch spot. Mary Queen of Scots had opened its gates to the townspeople of Edinburgh when it was still a rural site. Glasgow Joe and I had left court to get some peace and quiet – and, despite the tourists and snogging teenagers, we almost managed it. I was at my usual dining spot, Alexander Scroggie's flat tomb. With raised legs, it looked rather like a small mossy table, situated in the best site in the graveyard, under a large oak tree. I liked to lie on it and watch the clouds go by whilst I ate my sandwiches. I didn't mind that it was hard and cold. The only drawback was that crumbs fell down my neck, and I knew that at four o'clock I'd still be finding them inside my bra.

'Are you in trouble, Brodie?'

'Of course. Didn't you used to tell me that trouble was my middle name?' I said to evade his real question.

'You were seven. I thought you'd grow out of it.'

Joe and I had been at junior school together. The girl whose mother had aspirations for her never fitted into the tough Leith environment – but when the hulking ginger ogre that was Joe, even as a kid, descended from the West, I knew I had a friend. The fact that he was still around owed as much to his doggedness as my lure. He'd saved me more than once, and I hoped he'd always be there to do so. If he found out about Jack Deans, though, it could be the end of what we had established over years.

I watched a cloud that looked like a dragon pass in the otherwise clear blue sky.

'You had a lucky escape then, Joe.'

'Is that what you think? Is that what you think happened to us? I escaped you?'

I didn't like the way this conversation was heading – how much did he know? I tried to make the peace – we had fallen onto the edges of an argument far too quickly today, and I didn't want him, of all people, to be upset or angry with me.

'What difference does it make, Joe? Our past is far away, and all we've got to worry us is whether you've eaten all the chocolate brownies.' Maybe I could distract him – if only Awesome was parked on one of the graves; that would get his attention. He loved that bike as much as I did. In fact, I sometimes marvelled that he'd ever been able to hand it over for my twenty-first, given how much he still treated it as his own possession.

'Here, Joe – do you think the ghost of Burke's watching me?' As I lolled on the grave, I could almost imagine the days when the famous resurrectionist used to sit nearby watching the burials, so he could come out after dark and dig up the bodies.

'Don't act tough and intelligent, Brodie, I know you're just soppy about that daft wee dog,' threw back Joe.

'What? A scruffy wee Skye terrier holding me here? Not even a very bright one at that – he didn't even recognise his master was kicking up the daisies for years.'

Joe stood beside the gravestone, his kilt swinging as he swayed back and forward, chewing a hot meatball baguette. His legs were muscular and well-formed, black hand-knitted kilt socks lay in puddles at the top of his polished Caterpillar boots. For a biker, Glasgow Joe was fastidious and it showed in the whiteness of his cotton shirt. The cuffs had been carelessly rolled up to his elbows, showing his thick muscular forearms. Unusually for a redhead his skin was golden brown. The epitome of a Highland warrior, he stood six foot four in his size-thirteen stockinged soles. Even though he was off limits for me, I could still appreciate the fact that he was gorgeous as fuck.

A group of Italians on a walking tour of the graveyard had spotted Joe. It wasn't hard. Like flies to a corpse they swarmed over to him. The girls stood shyly at his side, elbowed out of the way by their buxom mamas who placed their arms around him, and found enough English to ask him what he was wearing beneath his kilt. Joe managed to find a smile for the photographer. He always did. He should be getting a fee from the Scottish Tourist Board given the number of times he found himself in the memories of visitors. They all shouted *arrivederci* and he shrugged off their thanks. Alone again, he turned to me.

'Will you sit up, Brodie? Don't you know it scares the shit out of me seeing you lying there like that? And it brings back some crap memories of the last time we were in a graveyard together.'

I ignored his last comment – did he mean when we considered grave-robbing or when my blood father's widow tried to kill me amongst the memory of a thousand dead Highlanders? No, I wouldn't go back to Jerry Springer territory again. My back was beginning to hurt anyway. 'I would have moved sooner but I didn't want to interrupt your fan club.'

He stared at me for longer than he needed to. 'Have you ever considered that men welcome a bit of appreciation?'

'They get far too much bloody attention as it is,

Joe. And if you just let yourself go a bit, the world wouldn't stop spinning. You're vain, that's all it is.'

He looked at his watch. 'You're a rotten liar, Brodie McLennan. If I'm not worth your time, how come you've been here so long?'

I checked my own watch and couldn't believe how much of the afternoon I'd wasted talking nonsense with him. God, I'd miss him if we did fall out over this Jack Deans business. I picked my jacket up and ran, with Joe following me. It was easier to deal with Bridget Nicholson and Sheriff Harrison. The problems with Joe put a big tick in the box in favour of being a judge.

'Joe,' I wheezed as I ran past the statue of Greyfriars Bobby, 'you're forgetting I like cats, not dogs. I'm going to be an old lady with cats.' My voice was almost lost in my rush.

'Do you think I came up the Clyde in a banana boat?' he replied. 'You're like that wee dog, loyal to a fault even when it gets you into trouble. Why else would you be representing Tanya Hayder? Everyone else gave up on her long ago.'

As I ran down George IV Bridge, I knew it was true. And I also wondered why, if he knew all about my life, he hadn't stuck his nose into what I'd done with Jack?

Chapter Seven

Even I didn't believe that Tanya Hayder had changed her life around like she always promised she would. From time to time I checked on the website for the escort agency she was linked with, just to make sure she was still alive. Tanya's official photograph on the *Flowers of Scotland* site still showed her in the first flush of youth. Before sex and drugs had taken their toll, she was the most alluring girl I had ever seen, apart from Kailash. Now, she looked at least double her age and with damn few years left. I often thought the trading standards officers could do her under the Trade Descriptions Act if they saw her advertising pitch.

'Are you all right, honey?'

That's why I liked Tanya: she was the one behind bars but she was worried about my mental health.

'You're looking a bit peaky, Brodie. You under any stress?'

I rolled my eyes upwards and she understood.

'You can't let those bastards grind you down – you're better than that,' she continued to try and calm me. 'We go back a long way, Brodie. Don't bail out on me now because of some stroppy bastarding men getting to you.'

I never needed to tell Tanya anything because she always assumed it was 'bastarding men' who were behind anything and everything. Occupational hazard, I suppose. But she was right – we did go back a long way. Tanya was my first client, I'd had little else to do and so I lavished more care and attention on her than a firstborn. Tanya had been a heroin addict since the age of thirteen, chasing the dragon to escape memories of childhood abuse, which were unfortunately not suppressed. She was a real dripping roast in the early years – her constant appearances in court made her a good source of income for me – but I always supposed (or hoped) that she would escape her destiny. During one interview in Cornton Vale Women's Prison, she had handed me a white gemstone. I didn't want to dwell on how she'd managed to smuggle it in.

'It's faith,' she had told me. 'The stone represents faith.'

I'd taken it from her all those years ago and still had it in my purse. Foolishly, I believed that as long as it was safe, we both had a chance.

'We don't have long, Tanya, you know the form.'

'Enough that I know you're in bigger shit than me. Where were you when they called my name out?'

'A victim of my own success, Tanya.'

'Get me out of here, Brodie – I can't do another stretch. Please, Brodie, I promise you this time I'll straighten myself out, just get me into rehab.'

'Tanya, I told you last time that I got you the deal of the century – probation with your record? And what did you do with that great chance? You shagged a police officer – how many times have I told you not to have any drugs on you when you're on the game?'

Drugs were an illness with her; she was more to be pitied than punished. I knew that with Tanya I overstepped the mark, but someone had to care. The Fiscal claimed to understand when she was a Crown witness at the age of twelve, but where was the therapy or stable home when she needed it? Now, her background reports sounded like tired old tosh trotted out by lawyers and social workers, although it didn't make it any less true.

'I did not. I always double-check with the hotels to make sure they're not the vice squad. This gadge had a suite so I thought I was safe – vice are too tight to take a suite. Anyway, when I got there it was a police officer, they had ordered a few working girls to entertain some business colleagues so I thought it was okay. I've got some scruples, I didn't go with the pig, I went with the pal. Nice black guy. I could tell he was using because his top lip was covered in sweat. He paid me in smack – it was good stuff and I was hoping he would ask for me again but I never got the chance. That pig booked me for drugs. I tried to tell them I got them from their pal but they wouldn't believe me. Said his pal was a fisherman from Pakistan, but that was a lie 'cause I used to work the boats in Peterhead and all the men there have rough hands and he didn't. Really rough hands. They get them from mending the nets.'

'It doesn't matter.' I cut her off as quickly as I could. There was always a story with Tanya. 'You were caught with drugs. There is not going to be a trial. You'll be sentenced for your original offence today and for the breach of probation.

It's not your first offence so they don't need social enquiry reports – you're off to prison this afternoon, Tanya, for a long time.'

As I said them, I thought my last words were unnecessarily hard. They were true, of course, but there was no need to kick her when she was down. Apparently, Tanya thought so too.

'Who were you with, when you should have been representing me?' she asked angrily.

'You wouldn't know him.'

'You'd be surprised who I know. Must be somebody important to make you abandon me.' She liked to twist the knife. Most addicts are experts at emotional blackmail.

'I bet it was one of those Dark Angels – you seem to be Moses Tierney's personal tart these days.'

I ignored her insults, but she went on.

'Get me probation and I'll give you information that will help your client. I don't need to know who he is just now to know that I've got a link to practically everybody in this city – and information on most of them.'

'There's no way I can get you probation today, Tanya, but I will try.'

I ignored the line she was throwing me about the Alchemist. I would have put up a good spraff for her anyway, regardless of the personal cost.

Chapter Eight

'Are you still hanging around here? You're like a bad smell in a toilet.'

'Has anyone ever told you – you don't do yourself any favours, Brodie?'

I was still really annoyed with Bridget Nicholson and I suspected that the only reason she was still here was to witness my humiliation when I asked for probation for Tanya. She swept past me into Sheriff Harrison's court.

As a rule, after lunch, the Sheriff Court is almost deserted as the swathe of human detritus has completed its tasks in the morning and only a few ongoing trials remain. A courthouse is a horrible place to be. It shows you the very worst that humanity has to offer. Greed. Malice. Violence. Debauchery. Old lawyers' tales tell of a young man in the seventeenth century about to sit his Bar exams who had a vision that he was at the mouth of hell. It sounds pretty likely to me that he got to live his vision when he became a lawyer.

'Sheriff Harrison will see you in chambers now,' said Andy, the macer, interrupting my thoughts.

Whenever I get anxious my bowels turn to water, and this, annoyingly, was one of those times. There was no way I could keep his Lordship waiting, so I breathed deeply and clenched my stomach muscles as the sweat formed on my brow. This was one situation where my nerves always made an appearance – too much was beyond my control.

The doorway to the sheriff's inner sanctum looked innocuous enough: an expensive, plain light-oak door. Gingerly I knocked on it, trying to wet my lips with my parched tongue.

'Enter.'

Sheriff Harrison wore his twilled silk gown but his wig lay on a pile of law reports. If this was his attempt at informality, he was failing. In spite of my best efforts – head up, shoulders back – he must have known I was afraid.

'I suppose you've heard? I've missed my tee-off time at Muirfield.'

'I'm very sorry to have inconvenienced you.'

'Well, of course you are – your slip-up has led to you standing before me now, and even I recognise that's not a nice experience.'

'Yes, M'lord.'

At this point there was no limit to the grovelling I thought I would have to do, or indeed, that I was prepared to do.

'Actually, I'm quite intrigued to meet you, Miss McLennan. Your father was my devil master and we were in the same stable before he was elevated to the bench. Of course your actual existence was news to me – I don't know how your father managed to keep it secret for so long.'

I bit my tongue and said nothing. I was uncomfortable talking to anyone about my father – hardly surprising given not only the recent discovery of the fact but also what I had found out about his predilections.

'I suppose everyone has told you that your resemblance to him is remarkable?'

I was shocked. Most people did not even mention my father, and within my circle of friends and family no one would upset me with the knowledge that I *looked* like him. I had to stand there and take it, so I smiled blandly and nodded. At least he was viewing my absence as the oversight of a lawyer with the proper blood in her veins and not as contempt of court.

'I've spoken to your grandfather, of course – marvellous man – and he has assured me that he's taking you under his wing, putting you back on the straight and narrow and so forth. You will be showing some spark of intelligence if you listen to him.'

I nodded dutifully, all the while thinking he looked like Owl out of Winnie the Pooh, filled with his own importance. I was so lost in this imagery that he had to repeat his question twice. Me – part of the establishment? It was surreal to even consider it fleetingly.

'So what is it you want for your client?'

'I respectfully submit...'

'Yes, yes, of course you do. Just tell me exactly what is your desired outcome.'

'Well, I'd like her probation to be continued and for her to be placed in a rehabilitation, unit.'

'My, my, Christmas has come early to Edinburgh. I suppose the taxpayers will be funding this little jaunt of hers?'

What could I say? We both knew it was a pointless, expensive exercise, but that little white stone made me think maybe this time Tanya could do it. I knew that this would have to be dealt with in open court so I nodded and was about to leave when he extended his hand towards me. His fingers gripped my wrist, and, grasping my right hand, he interlaced his thumb with mine. I was thrown off guard, unsure what to do, so I fumbled, pressing his knuckles. He stared through me and smiled. I left the chambers unsure of what, if anything, had occurred. It then struck me that the whole interview between us had taken place without the presence of the sheriff clerk. There were, unusually, absolutely no witnesses to what had transpired.

The courtroom was remarkably empty. The sheriff clerk sat in the well of the court and the macer had gone to bring the sheriff onto the bench. Tanya sat in the dock, looking more optimistic than she had any right to. Of course, Bridget Nicholson sat centre stage, having bagged her ringside seat early to watch my downfall.

The owl came onto the bench, and nodded to the public benches. Without ceremony, the sheriff clerk called Tanya Hayder.

Tanya's record was horrendous. No one would admit to being her if they were not, but formal identification was necessary.

I joined in the play.

'My name is Brodie McLennan. I represent Tanya Hayder.'

The sheriff clerk handed the papers up to the judge, who began to speak immediately.

'I took the opportunity this morning to read over this case thoroughly. Given the details of the last social enquiry report on Miss Hayder, I have decided to take the unusual step of deferring sentence in this matter until the end of the probationary period. In addition, I want the recommendations that were not followed in the last report carried out, namely a place must be found for Miss Hayder at Castle Fearns rehabilitation centre.'

He handed the papers back to the sheriff clerk.

'You're a gentleman, sir, a gentleman.'

I turned to quieten Tanya before she got done for contempt of court or a bad rendition of some Dickensian dialogue. She wouldn't shut up, though, turning her pleasure to me.

'That was some result, Brodie. What did you have to do to pull that rabbit out of the hat?'

Sheriff Harrison heard every word from his position on the bench. I blushed and tried to push Tanya into the arms of the police, so that I could get out of there. Bridget Nicholson's face looked as if I had slapped it, before worry clouded her eyes. I'm sure she was picturing her seat on the bench being pulled from under her. She skulked out of Courtroom Three whilst I sat quietly in the aftermath. Sheriff Harrison had left the bench and the clerk busied himself tidying away the papers. The Fiscal wanted to talk. But all I could think, as I looked at his face, was that I missed Frank Pearson. Frank had been a great ally in the Fiscal's office but it wasn't for selfish reasons that I missed him. He had asked for a transfer to Inverness because he couldn't hold his head up after spurious photographs of him during auto-erotic asphyxiation were circulated round the Bar common room. A Fiscal can only find so many latex thongs in his files before he realises his credibility has gone.

The corridors were quiet. I checked my phone for messages. Ten texts from Lavender, every one of them telling me she had been right about something or other. I deleted the ones from Joe, as I had seen him since he had sent them, and cautiously opened the one from Jack.

meet u in the drs after court

What harm could it do?

The Doctors was a famous pub near the court and even nearer to the old hospital, hence the name. I pushed the door open. Jack was standing at the bar getting a round in; his wallet was open and he waved his hand expansively towards a motley crew of journalists who occupied an alcove.

'Stranger!' he said as he caught sight of me. 'You were the last person I expected to see here.'

'Cut the dramatics, Jack, you invited me.'

'I know, but I didn't think you would come. Hang on a minute – you want something, don't you?'

He stopped and allowed his eyes to rake over me.

'Enjoying the view?'

'Brodie, we both know that I do, and I'm not going to hide it.'

'Except when Joe's there?'

'Well, that's a given. What do you want to drink?'

I hesitated; Kailash's voice ringing in my ears.

'Diet Coke.'

78

'Are you sure?'

'I'm driving.'

I banged my battered black bike helmet down onto the bar.

'Fair enough. I'll be back in a minute – they turn nasty if you're slow with their drink,' he said, tipping his head towards his fellow waiting hacks.

I watched him walk away. He'd been working out and definitely was a different man to this time last year.

'You were checking me out,' he stated on his return.

'I was not. I was wondering who was with you.'

'You were checking out my arse. I could feel your eyes, Brodie. My bum felt quite hot with your lust.'

I knew he was joking, but I still felt mortified.

'In your dreams.'

'Yep. What do you want my wise counsel on?'

I reached out and took his right hand, grasping his wrist with my fingers, intertwining our thumbs. He stepped back as if I had bitten him. I couldn't tell if it was the frisson of excitement that ran down both our bodies, or if it was the significance of the gesture. More worryingly, I didn't know which one I wanted it to be.

'Mahabone,' said Jack.

'I wouldn't have come to see you if I had a clue what that meant.'

'Okay, it's part of a Masonic ritual. It's the Master Mason's word. It developed in Scotland in the mid-sixteenth century and involves the shake of the Master Mason. It's also known as the "lion's paw"; whoever shook your hand like that is pretty high up. He was extending the hand of continuing brotherly love – a bit different to the sort I'd like to extend to you. Did this guy do you a favour?'

I nodded.

'I thought so. A big one?'

I nodded again.

'Well, I hope it was worth it, because it might be called in.'

'How many judges are in the Masons, Jack?'

'Who knows how many judges, police officers, tax inspectors or anything are in the Masons? They try to keep their secrets.'

I had a nasty taste in my mouth. Sure I'd got a great result for Tanya, but at what cost? I was disgusted with myself, using my blood line to oil the wheels of justice, even if I had bought myself some time.

'Jack! Jack! You haven't finished your story!'

Some blonde floozy in the corner was jumping up and down trying to get his attention.

'Your bimbo's wanting you, Jack – and by the glazed look in her eyes, you've invested quite a bit in her.'

'Are you going?'

He stroked my arm, urging me to stay.

'How did you guess?'

'You're a big girl now, Brodie. You'll wake up one day and no one will be there.'

'I can always join the Masons,' I shouted at his back.

He turned for a moment and looked at me.

'I thought you already had.'

Chapter Nine

I walked in and realised that I'd kill for a cup of tea.

It hit me hard that I had no one to make it for me.

I slammed the front door shut in disappointment. The noise ricocheted off the old walls, and drew my attention to the damp patch on the ceiling. I meant to get a man in to see to that. I'm sure Tanya would say that I needed a man for a lot of things, as long as I didn't put my trust in them.

Black tea didn't hit the spot I wanted it to. Cup in hand, wandering through the hallway to the drawing room, I was uncomfortably aware of the dust lying on the thick Georgian skirting boards. Even the smell of the house was unlived-in. I wondered for a moment if I needed a housemate. The company would be welcome and the money would help keep this old pile of stones habitable. I just didn't need one anything like the last. Fishy had more than put me off flatmates for a while.

The doorbell rang.

I placed my empty mug down amongst the other dirty dishes on the coffee table. The bell continued to ring. Whoever wanted to see me was impatient. Was it Joe or Jack? Either would be welcome. But the face I saw when I opened the door wasn't one I'd hoped for.

'Are you Brodie McLennan?'

'Christ, Duncan, you know I am – what game are you playing today?'

'Brodie McLennan – I am arresting you under Section Fourteen of the Criminal Procedure Act.'

'Is this a joke, Duncan? What are you talking about? On what grounds could you possibly arrest me?'

I tried not to raise my voice because I didn't want the neighbours to hear. This wasn't the kind of area where the polis came calling.

He ignored me and went through the routine.

'You are not obliged to say anything. If you do say anything, it may be taken down and used against you in a court of law.'

'Can't you at least come in and say your piece?' I fought the tears.

'Get your shoes, Brodie.' He'd given up looking at me when he spoke.

'Duncan – can't you be reasonable?'

'I'll come in – while you get your shoes.'

Detective Inspector Duncan Bancho stood silent and stony-faced whilst I put my bike boots back on.

'It's a few years since I've been here, Brodie, but this place has gone downhill,' he said. I got ready and walked down the stairs with Bancho. I sat like an automaton in the back of the police car, mercifully unaware during the journey to St Leonard's.

Sergeant Munro was on the front desk. Did that man ever go home? He was restrained and businesslike as he took my details. I even saw a spark of pity in his eyes. Then I knew I was in trouble. I couldn't afford to lie down and let DI Bancho kick me.

'Are you going to tell me what this is about?' I asked, as I sat down on a hard plastic chair in the interview room.

Duncan nodded curtly at his colleague. 'Detective Constable Margaret Malone will be assisting me today,' Bancho informed the tape machine.

DC Malone smiled across at me. She looked as if she must have put weight on recently; either that or she had shrunk her shirt in the wash, because the buttons were straining fit to burst. Her wispy blonde hair was in a bun at the nape of her neck, and she looked more like an air hostess for a budget airline than WPC Plod.

'Call me Peggy,' she said as she reached over and shook my hand.

Peggy responded to Bancho's unspoken put-down.

'What? It's not as if she's your average criminal. She's entitled to be treated with a bit of civility.'

Duncan's eyes flickered with anger, but interestingly he said nothing. Peggy, on the other hand, lifted her chin and looked up into his eyes. It was obvious that she had just put him back in his place and I couldn't help but smile.

Peggy Malone bent over the table, her tight black skirt clinging to her. Duncan Bancho stared at her, entranced, probably hypnotised by the hip–waist ratio of the creature in front of him who was fiddling with his recording device. I gratefully watched this domestic tableau, because it meant that he was ignoring me.

Bancho walked up and down, towering over me. He left for five minutes but it seemed like an eternity.

'Would you like a cup of tea?' Peggy broke the silence and smiled at me.

'She's getting nothing at the moment,' said Bancho, walking back in.

'Are you two playing good cop, bad cop with me?' I asked.

Peggy smiled again.

'Do you want us to inform anyone that you are here?' Her voice was quite posh, obviously well-educated – probably from a good girls' school. What had made her join the police?

Normally, this was the stage when I got a call from my clients.

'No. No one.'

I was too ashamed.

'Well, everyone probably knows already – you know what the jungle drums are like when they get a piece of news as tasty as this one.'

Duncan spoke this time, glad to stick the boot in. Peggy looked as if he had personally slapped her. Either she was really excellent in her role as the good cop or she was in the wrong profession.

'If they're talking about me they're leaving some other poor sod alone.' I feigned a bravado I wasn't feeling; even I could hear the crack in my voice.

Bancho sat down opposite me. After explaining who was present and the date and time, he threw a newspaper at me, an updated version of the story that Kailash had read out.

'So? Cattanach is missing. What's that got to do with me?'

'Jesus, Brodie – I thought you were supposed to be bright? Cattanach was investigating you in particular – in fact everyone at the Law Society is saying that you were the piles in Cattanach's arse.'

'Cattanach had it in for me because of Bridget Nicholson – everyone knows she hates me.'

Peggy watched me intently; maybe they were a good team after all.

'Cattanach's a professional – you're kidding yourself if you expect anyone to believe that you were being investigated for no other reason than Cattanach's girlfriend doesn't like you.'

It did sound petty and unlikely, even to my ears.

'Where were you on the fourth of August?'

Strangely enough, I knew the answer to that question.

A smug smile broke out on my face.

'I was at the MacPherson Clan gathering in Newtonmore, with my grandad and another three thousand people.'

'Your grandfather? What was a MacGregor doing at the MacPherson show?'

'He's friendly with the clan chief.'

'Oh, as he would be – well, don't expect me to be influenced by your high-ranking relatives. He's no better than you.'

Obviously, Duncan Bancho was angry at my cast-iron alibi. I stared him out and leaned back in my chair. He would have to release me soon, unless he was simply being a bastard.

'Switch that damned thing off and go and get us some tea,' Bancho shouted at Peggy, who clearly responded to him when he was masterful.

The door clicked behind her. Duncan and I were left facing each other. The ghost of my ex-flatmate, Fishy, hung between us. Duncan was wearing well. Expensive haircut, the right amount of product in his light brown hair, and a carefully sculpted beard that screamed too desperately 'I'm an individual'.

'Still biting your fingers, I see.'

The skin around my nails was broken and raw. Mechanically, I pulled them back and hid them under the table. I was annoyed at giving him the upper hand. We were at war – psyching one another out.

'You've got a dick and a brain, Duncan, but only enough blood to run one at a time. What do your superiors say about you and Miss Money-penny?'

'It's none of their fucking business and it's certainly none of yours. You never change.'

'You're right, I haven't changed – when did your beard go grey?'

'Piss off. Its a goatee.'

'Bit sensitive about your facial hair there, Duncan.'

He leaned over the cheap table and spoke into my face. Little flecks of spit landed on my cheeks.

'Don't think I'm impressed by your family connections – the MacGregors were cattle thieves and blackmailers. You come from criminals and nothing's changed, no matter how you dress it up.'

My first thought wasn't to wonder how he knew about all that, but of how much he knew about my father? Had Fishy said anything about him, or about me? I was on the back foot; sometimes I should just learn to shut up. After all, it's what I told my clients.

'I think you should look at the clan motto it says, "My race is royal".'

'It can say anything it bloody wants, Brodie. Doesn't mean it's true.'

'You know me, Duncan. Do you really think I could be capable of disposing of Cattanach, or anybody else for that matter?'

'You did a really good job of stitching up Fishy and he was your friend – what would you do to someone who was threatening your career, your livelihood, your dreams? Your work is all you've got, Brodie. Now tell me, if you were in my position, wouldn't *you* wonder?'

I couldn't explain to him about Fishy in case I gave too much away. Another thing I had to thank Kailash and my father for. There was no way he could or would know the full story – how embarrassing for them that the boys in blue hadn't noticed a psychotic paedophile serial killer in the canteen. They weren't the only ones though – I'd shared a flat with him during the whole episode and had still thought he was innocent. Really, me and the cops were on the same side when it came to Fishy – he'd stitched us all up – but they'd never admit it.

'Are you going to release me now?'

'No.'

'You know you have nothing on me – unless

87

you're saying that Lord MacGregor, the ex-Lord President, was my accomplice in murder.'

'Who said anything about murder?' Bancho asked.

'Come off it, no one thinks Cattanach has simply had a hissy fit and walked off in a huff.'

'I'm not releasing you, Brodie – you're in for the full six hours. And then who knows?'

'Are you threatening to stitch me up?'

'Well, you believe that little bastard – what does he call himself?'

'The Alchemist.'

I finished his sentence for him, even though I remembered it was something he'd always hated.

'Yeah – you believe him. I'm bent, aren't I?'

'I don't believe him...'

He didn't give me a chance to finish.

'You don't believe him? Then why are you persecuting me and spreading it round the Sheriff Court that I fitted him up? That I planted evidence on him?'

A fine film of sweat beaded his top lip, and for some reason I thought of Tanya Hayder. An overwhelming hunch told me not to irritate him. I had painted myself into a corner and I had to find a way out. Bridget Nicholson had obviously overheard my conversation with the Alchemist and had wasted no time in causing further trouble for me.

'I don't believe him, but that's not my job. My job is to investigate his defence. He's entitled to a defence.'

Wheedle and cajole, those were my instructions to myself.

'Do you sleep well at nights?'

'Very well.'

I lied. It just slipped out; I had meant to agree with him. Anything to get home and wash the smell of desperation that clung to these walls from my hair. He shook his head and circled me.

'When you were a little girl did you dream of representing scumbags like Bernard Carpenter?'

I didn't reply.

'You lawyers are all the same – authorised pickpockets.'

'It's my job,' I shouted after him as he closed the door, leaving me alone with his insults, which naturally I replayed. I objected to being called a legalised thief. I worked within the system. It was how things operated. In the last two years of practising law I had come to think of it in a straightforward way. The law was a bulky, decrepit engine that dragged in individuals, ruined their lives and wasted their money. I was just an engineer. I was a specialist at going into the engine, repairing things and taking out what I needed in return.

I had fallen out of love with the law. The law-faculty philosophy about the merits of the adversarial method, of the weighing scales of justice, seemed like shit to me now. There were too many hopeless cases, too many miscarriages of justice, too many vested interests. Something had changed for me. I used to believe in the law more than anything; I'd lost a part of myself when that changed. My quest for truth had recently been abandoned. The law was not about justice. It was about arbitration, amending and stage management. I didn't deal in guilt or blamelessness, because everyone had done something wrong. This fact was of no consequence, because every trial I took on was laid on shifting sand. A case built by worn-out and poorly paid drudges. The police didn't have the time or staff. They made mistakes. And then they papered over those mistakes with lies. My trade was to strip the paper and find the cracks. To insert a crowbar into those cracks and open them. To make them so wide that the case fell apart, or my clients slipped through.

Much of humanity thinks of my type as the devil incarnate. But they are wide of the mark, I am a slippery seraph. I am the true dark angel, necessary to both sides. I think of myself as an engineer, but I am more important than that. I am the oil and I allow the cogs to keep turning. I help keep the engine running.

But, more importantly, I hate to lose.

The Alchemist's case would change things.

For me.

For Bernard Carpenter.

And certainly for Duncan Bancho.

After all, I had nearly six clear hours to focus on his downfall.

Chapter Ten

I got through the six hours – of course I did, I had no choice – but I wasn't left unscarred.

As usual, I'd started off a difficult morning with a run. However, instead of calming me, I felt awful. I didn't know what was worse, the nausea or the fear. One threatened to choke me, whilst the other chilled me to my marrow.

I stood at the river's edge. The water was an accusing finger curling towards me, searching for me. I felt as if it wanted to touch me, to mark me. My world was collapsing.

'I did this! I did this to myself!' a voice screamed in my head.

Those six hours when I was supposed to be plotting Duncan Bancho's ruin? Well, it didn't happen. All I saw was my own defeat staring me in the face. There was no help or escape. DI Bancho had made it quite clear that his mission in life was to see me behind bars for the murder of Alex Cattanach. Trouble was, my actions for the past God knew how many months made it look as if I had a pretty good motive. My grandad was right, Kailash was right, even Bridget Nicholson was right to a point – I was obsessed with making as much money as possible – but I did it to feel safe. As long as I was joint and severally liable for the debts of Lothian and St Clair WS, then I was weak. One of the downsides of becoming a partner was that I was responsible for any outstanding debts if the firm went down, so I was making sure that there was enough money floating around to stop that happening – the only way I knew to lessen the feeling of fear was to bring in as much work as possible, make myself a cash cow that they would never be tempted to slaughter.

I'd thought that the other firms I was taking from, pissing off along the way, didn't matter. I couldn't waste time or sympathy on whether some overindulged lawyer was a few grand down a week. But I did have to care about what effect all of this hostility could have on me and my security.

I could see why Duncan might think I was an obvious suspect. We hadn't had the sort of relationship where he knew me inside out – thank God – so he could very well believe I would be pushed over the edge by all that had happened to me in the last couple of years. He might also think that I believed I was now protected by my blood line. These were all possibles. Cattanach had been missing for too long. Foul play was the obvious conclusion, given the investigations that had been going on. And, on paper, I looked like a pretty good candidate for the perpetrator.

I tried to comfort myself that at least I wasn't a complete fool. Even I knew that the offer of a judicial position would be withdrawn now. When Duncan Bancho had arrested me, he had snatched my best hope, even if I hadn't seemed too keen on it when it was offered to me. There is nothing like something being taken away from you to make it seem attractive.

'At least your plooks have disappeared.'

A familiar voice shouted at me through the trees. A woman jogger looked affronted, as if the remark had been aimed at her.

I didn't bother to turn around. 'Is that supposed to make me feel better? I don't have spots any more?'

'Yeah – when the shit hits the fan, you have to be grateful for small mercies.' Glasgow Joe's voice came in short bursts as he climbed down the steep embankment.

'Keep your *Reader's Digest* homilies to yourself, Joe. Have you been looking for me for long?'

'I went to St Leonard's once I heard the gossip, then that wanker Bancho sent someone out to move me along. I wanted to be there – when you were released – but I must have got my timing wrong.'

'What do you mean you got your timing wrong? You thought I'd be out quickly, didn't you? Well, so did I, Joe, so did I. When he kept me in for the full six hours, did you think that meant I was guilty? Do you think I did it? Do you think that's why Duncan Bancho kept me in for the full six hours?'

'Calm down, Brodie – of course I don't think you did it. I mean, nothing's even been proven to have happened. Maybe Cattanach was bent and ran off with money from the investigations? I don't know what the fuck's going on, but I do know that Bancho wanted to see you sweat, to make you cry – you didn't cry, did you, Brodie?'

'Of course I didn't.'

'I did – the first time I was arrested. I bawled

93

my eyes out begging the constable to get my mammy.'

'You were eleven, Joe.'

'True, but there were bigger boys than me greetin' for their maw.'

'Do you know his sidekick, DC Malone? She was nice to me.' I believed I would be eternally grateful for that woman's common decency.

'Do you mean Peggy?'

'You do know her then?'

'Everybody knows Peggy Malone – and I do mean everyone.'

'Well, she looks a pretty settled item with Duncan Bancho.'

'That'll never happen.'

'Well, I'm telling you it has.'

'Peggy Malone would never settle with a man – she's too into women for that.'

'Don't tell me she fancies me.' I felt faintly uncomfortable – had all that bum wiggling been for me.'

'No – she'll be shagging Duncan Bancho all right, I'm just saying he won't be the only one.'

I didn't want to ask Joe how he knew so much about Peggy Malone; after all, he had never claimed to be celibate.

I turned to face him, throwing myself against his chest and listening to the Water of Leith run past me over the stones. His leather jacket was soft against my face. I pressed in so hard I could hear his heartbeat. I had my excuse ready. I was only protecting myself from the midges if Joe asked why I was getting all cuddly and soppy. He didn't.

I suddenly thought of something. 'How did you know where to find me?'

'I knew you thought you needed a miracle – and when divine intervention is your only hope, you come to St Bernard's Well.'

'It's never worked before,' I whined.

'It has – I told you; your spots have gone.'

We came to the well when I was thirteen to wash my face in the healing waters, because Joe told me pilgrims had been coming to this site since the thirteenth century.

'Nothing happened, Joe, I was still acne-ridden and, at thirteen, spots are social suicide.'

'And where's your acne now, Brodie?'

'It disappeared when I was sixteen.'

'See? I told you it would work. Some miracles take longer than others. Your spots disappeared and your chest arrived – that seemed pretty miraculous to me.'

Was it my imagination or was his heart beating faster? Reluctantly, I pushed myself away from the safety of his arms. That was a bad habit of mine, rejecting protection. It was sod's law that the midges really started to swarm around my head and munch on me.

'I see they still like you then,' Joe commented.

'Parasites always do.'

I waved my hands around my face like a lunatic and, as a result, the little bastards promptly bit them. I climbed up the riverbank to the glorious pseudo-Roman temple that occupied the site of St Bernard's sacred spring. Maybe, like the holy man, I had been restored by the waters, because I certainly sprinted up that bank. Waiting for Joe to join me, I leaned against one of the ten Doric pillars that supported the temple roof, and I stared at Hygieia, the goddess of health.

'What's happened to you now?' shouted Joe. 'Any chance you've perked up there? What's wrong, Brodie?'

'Everything, Joe; everything in my life is shite.'

'Not everything – you can see and you can hear. Helen Keller couldn't do any of those things and she danced on Broadway.'

'At least she didn't have to listen to people criticising her all the time. Did you ever think of that, Joe? I am just so tired of snide remarks.'

'Well, do something about it, then. When did you become so pathetic?'

It was a question I had been asking myself since Duncan Bancho had arrested me. Somehow it seemed so much more insulting when asked by someone else.

'You have choices,' stated Joe.

'What? What choices do I have? Private practice is becoming impossible, thanks to the Edinburgh Bar complaining about me to the Law Society. The complaints about me haven't stopped – that's all the mail I get from them these days. One way or another, it'll ruin me.

'The one thing keeping me going recently was the thought that I could escape private practice and become a sheriff. Now, thanks to Bancho, that can't happen. Before becoming a judge I have to sign an affidavit that there are no court actions outstanding against me. I can't do that. Even if Bancho fails in hauling my arse into the High Court on some trumped-up murder charge,

96

he has promised he'll still do me with wasting police time.'

'You don't need to be a lawyer, Brodie. There are other ways to earn a living.' Joe's whisper entered my ear, curled all the way down the inside of my neck, into my chest, where it stopped my heart.

And, for the first time in years, I realised I wanted to do this job. I'd been kidding myself. I loved fighting with the Crown Office. I relished my small victories of holding on to someone's liberty. Punters who had been given every opportunity in life and squandered them annoyed me. I was only too aware that I could have gone either way. Each time I looked into a client's face and heard about their tragic background, I thought, there but for the grace of God go I... Luckily for me, I'd had Mary McLennan. It was the thought of her – the woman I still considered to be my real mother, even if she hadn't carried me in her belly and brought me into the world – that kept me going through all of this.

The clock on the church tower in St Stephen's Street interrupted my thoughts as it chimed eleven bells. The sky was bright and clear. Summer in Edinburgh was a gorgeous time. The birds made noises as they flew overhead. They circled slowly before roosting in the trees that lined the walkway by the Water of Leith. I should have expected it. But even as I felt the wet blob land on my head I didn't want to acknowledge what had happened.

'That's lucky, you're destined for greatness,' said Joe, smiling as he took his clean white hankie to my hair. 'You've got to read the signs, Brodie. Before I spoke to you this morning, I thought you had two choices: take your grandad's advice and become a sheriff or be hounded out of the profession.'

'Has he been speaking to you as well?'

Joe nodded.

The old man was nothing if not thorough.

'Kailash wants me to get out as well. I suppose I should listen to her – after all, she is my mother.'

'Your mother is dead, Brodie. I will never consider that woman to be your mother.'

I wished he hadn't said that because, although I denied it to Joe, when the cell door slammed shut on me I *was* crying for my mammy, and it wasn't Kailash Coutts. Joe saying what he had just made me feel her loss even more, because he had adored her too. Mary McLennan fought for me and she would have taken on Duncan Bancho too. But, as Joe had brought home to me, she was dead.

His hatred of Kailash struck me as odd, and I wondered if there had ever been anything between the two of them. I knew Joe wasn't a monk, and she was very attractive. Even so, I shuddered at the thought.

'Anyway, I've changed my mind. You still have the two choices – jump or wait until you're shoved. But, you're a fighter, Brodie – you can think of something else, and I'll stand by you when you decide to do that.'

I considered what Joe had said – jump or be pushed.

Or fight.

'Maybe I do have another option,' I said to him, as I got up and he followed me.

'What if I decide to fight him?'

'Who?'

'Duncan Bancho.'

'It would make a damn sight more sense for you to take on Lord MacGregor than to fight Lothian and Borders Police, Brodie.'

'Well, it makes no sense at all for me to fight my Grandad, he's on my side.'

Joe looked more worried than angry. 'So am I, and I'm telling you – leave the police alone. Run away, Brodie, because it's the only way to win this fight.'

'He's a corrupt police officer,' I replied.

'Says who?'

'The Alchemist.'

Even in my temper I knew I was on shaky ground.

'Give me a break – the Alchemist, or whatever poncey name he calls himself by tomorrow, would sell you for a bag of smack. There's no honour amongst thieves, Brodie, you know that. Just because Duncan Bancho decided to give you a taste of your own medicine doesn't mean he's a bent copper. How would you like it if he was going round spreading rumours about you?'

'Joe! He is! He's saying I murdered Cattanach – or at best that I'm money laundering!' I spluttered. Bancho didn't seem the innocent victim in all of this.

'Face it, Brodie. Bancho's not bent, he's just human. You can't pin all your problems on him.

Word will get out, everyone will know that you were hauled in by mid-morning. Edinburgh is a village. I should know – I get told everything you get up to.' He had turned his back to me but I still heard him whisper the last words. 'Even when I wish that I didn't.'

I wasn't going to let on that I heard that, as I had the uncomfortable feeling he could only be referring to Jack Deans.

'I know that Duncan Bancho is bent.'

'Don't give me that crap – just wanting someone to be crooked to fall in with your plans doesn't work.'

'I know, Joe, I just know. And I'm going to prove it.'

'Are you going to tell me it's women's intuition, Brodie?'

Joe was shouting now – people on the streets up ahead were beginning to look back at us.

'Tell me, just tell me this – if your intuition is so bloody good, how come you're in this fucking mess?' He was pulling at his hair, his face was red with frustration, and beads of sweat formed above his eyebrows.

'You're a stubborn cow, Brodie, always have been.'

'And you'd know, wouldn't you, Joe? Just like you know everything, always know what's fucking right for me?'

Glasgow Joe stopped, pulling me back by the elbow as he did so. His face went back to a colour closer to normal, and he looked me straight in the eye.

'I knew you as a girl, Brodie McLennan, and I

100

know you as a woman. Nothing's changed. The fact that you were once my wife doesn't make a blind bit of fucking difference.'

Chapter Eleven

I couldn't bear to go into my own flat but I knew I had to.

I'd run as quickly as I could from Stockbridge, no mean achievement, but I had the hounds of hell at my feet given what Joe had dredged up. There were certain things we never spoke of, places neither of us wanted to go – that he had crossed the line terrified me, and reminded me of how much I depended on him. If we went down that path again, the one that he had broken every rule by mentioning, it could finish us forever.

I lingered for a long time at the front door. Long enough to become embarrassingly aware of the signs of neglect. The black gloss paint was starting to peel and the ornate brass door-knocker was tarnished. I ran my finger around the outsized lion's head. It was an original Georgian feature. As I stared at it I expected it to speak to me, warn me to mend my ways.

The twitching of my neighbour's curtains was all the encouragement I needed. I had entertained them enough for one day. I followed the smell of hot coffee and cigarette smoke into the drawing room. It was in darkness, the curtains still drawn from when I'd got up that morning after my night in the cells, lit by a single red tip. As my eyes adjusted, they followed the cigarette to the lips of Kailash.

Rather than open the curtains, I switched the main chandelier light on, hoping it would hurt her eyes or, at least, make her feel less at home.

'How did you get in?' I snapped at her.

'Is that any way to speak to your mother?' she shot back.

In the harsh light Kailash appeared shattered and, for the first time, I noticed the fine lines around her eyes. She was vulnerable. The disadvantage I had in being an only child was that I knew I had put that look in her eyes. Motherhood was a lot easier for Kailash to get into than it was for her to get out of. I could have kicked myself for even letting that thought into my mind, remembering too late that my mother had been repeatedly raped by a paedophile before giving birth to me and signing her own expected death sentence. I couldn't deal with the guilt I felt – so I did what I always do when I am uncomfortable about facing emotions. I attack – the best form of defence.

'You didn't answer my question – how did you get in here?'

The tone of my voice cut into her. I thought I had never seen her so exposed.

'Don't be so bloody naïve, Brodie – your inexperience is hurting us all.'

Kailash stood up and stubbed out her cigarette. She had only taken a couple of draws on it and the long stem broke in half before she crushed it beneath her fingers. Leaning against the mantelpiece, she took a deep breath to steady herself.

Her tone changed slightly, becoming about a millionth of a degree warmer. 'Brodie – when did you last change the locks on your front door? You don't have a burglar alarm. How many people have had access to your keys since you moved in here? Do you know the lock on that front door was so loose I could have put my shoulder to it and it would have caved in?'

'What is this? Twenty questions? I know we've missed a few Christmases together, Kailash, but...'

'You think you're invincible,' she cut in. 'Well, I've got news for you – you're not. A life can be bought in this city for less than four grand.'

I didn't want to ask how she knew.

'How much do you think it would cost to get your hands on a set of keys for any flat? Within six degrees you know anyone in this world. It's a whole lot less in Edinburgh. Everybody knows your business – especially if you're not careful. And you, Brodie, you're not careful one little bit.'

Kailash left me to think about what she had just said, and I was reluctantly forced to follow her out of the drawing room. Her scent lingered in the air; an expensive handmade perfume whose basis seemed to be attar of roses. Like Coco Chanel before her, my birth mother believed that without perfume a woman was not complete. The odour of bike oil was not, in her opinion, an adequate substitute.

A strange nasal sound was emanating from my kitchen. Undulating notes carried along the long hallway – I strained to make out the words. Jesus

103

Christ, who was murdering Dolly Parton beside my kettle? I had gone right off the woman since finding an odd CD of her in Frank Pearson's flat last year. What I eventually discovered inside back then was a damn sight more unnerving than an inflated blonde pygmy wearing cowboy boots. Mind you, Dolly herself couldn't have looked more kitsch than the current singer of her song.

'Tell me who did that to you, Malcolm, and we'll set Glasgow Joe on him,' I laughed.

'Very funny, Brodie – it's lovely to see you too.' He self-consciously touched the cast over his nose that had appeared since I last saw him. Ever since he had taken up with a younger man, Malcolm had taken every opportunity to 'freshen' himself up. Derek was a dancer getting to the end of his performing career. I personally thought he viewed Malcolm as a meal ticket, but he was happy, so who was I to throw a bucket of cold water on his romance with vile Derek?

'Derek's down in Blackpool finishing out the summer season, so I thought why not? As you get older your nose doesn't stop growing I don't think – every time I looked in the mirror I saw bloody Pinocchio staring back at me. So enough was enough – after all, a girl's got to take care of herself. Speaking of which, this place is a bloody disgrace. If you can't clean it yourself, Brodie, get a woman in.'

Malcolm turned his attention to my bin and started furiously scrubbing the tomato sauce off the lid. Tutting all the whilst under his breath, satisfied that he could see his face in the stainless steel, he peeled off his novelty rubber gloves.

104

'Aren't they divine?' he asked me as he saw me staring. 'An early birthday present from Derek.'

He lovingly placed the deep pink gloves with black marabou trim around the wrist and a fake diamond ring onto the countertop. Switching on the kettle he trilled, 'Anyone for tea?' Malcolm in love was a sight to behold. Then again, weren't we all?

I nodded at his offer of a cuppa. At last, someone to make me a cup. In that instance I envied the relationship between Kailash and Malcolm – not even vile Derek could stop Malcolm's love for her.

The kitchen was sparkling. Thankfully Malcolm had brought his own cleaning products, presumably when he had decided to come with Kailash to the tip I called home, and hadn't had to rely on the unopened tub of ancient scourer that lurked beneath the dishcloths. He'd done a great job – and the unexpected bonus was that it was easier to talk to Kailash's reflection in the window than the real thing.

Her black hair hung like a waterfall to her shoulders and a pale cream jersey dress sheathed her body, showing exactly why she had made so much money in her chosen profession. I stared at her face, hoping to find some resemblance in the tilt of her ears or the shape of her mouth, but all I could focus on was Sheriff Harrison's words that I resembled my father.

'Why are you here?' I asked, hoping she would simply say she wanted to see me, to check that I was all right.

'Moses asked me to bring the money for the

Alchemist's trial.' She reached into her chilli-red Gucci handbag and threw five thousand pounds in well-used, grubby notes onto the table. Malcolm pushed aside the money and placed two china cups and saucers there.

I looked at them wistfully. 'I'd forgotten I had them.'

'They're beautiful,' replied Malcolm. 'They were buried at the back of the press.'

I fingered the cup lovingly.

'They belonged to my mother; she only used them on special occasions. They were far too good for us, so she kept them for visitors.'

I could never understand that aspect of Mary McLennan. The woman had raised me and worked herself to death for me. I used to tell her she would be the best-dressed corpse in the cemetery because at last she would be wearing the clothes she kept for best. Out of the corner of my eye I saw Malcolm reach across and touch Kailash's forearm.

She pointed to the money on the table.

'Aren't you going to count it?' she snapped.

'For Christ's sake, Kailash, if I can't trust you, who can I trust?' Malcolm made a grand cup of tea and I slurped it greedily, uncomfortably aware that I hadn't eaten since breakfast.

'No one, Brodie. You can trust no one. But that…' she pointed to the cash again, 'you haven't even given me a receipt for it – and that's not trust, it's laziness. No wonder Cattanach was investigating you.'

I gulped down the last of the tea before tackling her.

'Since you know everything, you tell me why Cattanach is so keen to bust me. I know I've done nothing wrong. In fact, I think Cattanach has been put up to it by Bridget Nicholson.'

'Alex Cattanach was honourable – get it into your head that Cattanach's principles could not be bought and sold. So what if Alex made a mistake? It was a mistake based on something tangible.'

'Like what?'

Kailash paused before she began speaking again. 'Tymar Productions. What does that mean to you?'

'Nothing, I've never heard of it.'

Kailash stared at me.

'Really. I've no idea.'

I was telling the truth, but I also had a knot in my stomach which suggested that it was memory lagging behind rather than being completely ignorant. Something was niggling, I just didn't know what.

'Well, if you read the papers you'd know that Cattanach was looking for details of that company to link you to money laundering. You know as well as I do that Cattanach believed a partner in a law firm isn't tempted by client funds when the bank balance is healthy, but if it's over-extended at the bank and it's difficult for lawyers to meet the standard of living they have become used to...'

'Like Lothian and St Clair?'

'Exactly – like Lothian and St Clair. Remember, Alex Cattanach had seen your books. The rest of the fools in the Edinburgh Bar think you're making a fortune.'

'So Cattanach thinks I fit the profile for a crooked lawyer?'

'Let's not fool ourselves, Brodie. You do. Your connection with me doesn't help – and by the way you are the only person still talking about Cattanach in the present tense. The murder investigation is hotting up. It's on *Crimewatch UK* this week, and the police won't want to be shown slacking after that.'

Kailash began to clear the money off the table and back into her bag. I stifled a protest.

'You need help, Brodie. You didn't give me a receipt, you didn't even think of it. How would you have explained five thousand in cash to the Law Society? You haven't followed a single one of their accounting rules.'

I desperately needed another cup of tea. The cup Malcolm had given me, though pretty, was just too damned small, as I was used to huge mugs that satisfied my caffeine requirement. I reached out for it anyway but Malcolm was fiddling with it. He had it turned upside down and was twisting it round three times in an anti-clockwise direction. Picking it up, he held it to the light and peered into it. I got up and stood behind his shoulder. All I saw was a jumble of tea leaves.

'There are six powerful men in your life – like snakes all messed up and writhing to get out on top,' he intoned.

'Sorry to disappoint you, Malcolm, but there are two and, as far as I'm concerned, that's two too many.'

'Your cup definitely shows six, Brodie. They're not all your friends. You need to beware –

especially of the friends acting in your best interest but making mistakes. That could cost you dear.'

'Have you been encouraging Lavender?' I asked.

'I have indeed. She told me you were a sceptic, which is nothing I didn't already know. Stop trying to change The subject and listen. God knows, by the look of this cup you need all the help you can get. Your danger doesn't truly come from the men in your life, but the women. I see two who are troublesome to you.'

I looked over to my mother. 'Does that include Kailash?'

'I don't know details, Brodie – I just see that there are two women who are problematic.'

If Kailash was hurt, she concealed it well. I resolved to learn that lesson from her.

'Enough of tea leaves,' she declared. 'Take this.'

It was a cheque for five thousand pounds drawn on a company bank account for The Rijks Property Company. My surprise at the name must have shown in my face. The poker countenance obviously required a bit of work.

Kailash took a deep breath as she looked at me. Her gaze then turned away to Malcolm, who immediately came forward to hold her hand as she spoke.

'After you were born, Brodie, I escaped to Amsterdam. Your grandfather had taken me to Newcastle originally, but he was the father of the bastard who had raped me for years – how could I trust him? I stole away and hitchhiked on a lorry doing the ferry crossing. I had to pay – I didn't have any money, but I knew the currency men

109

traded in. I didn't know then that your grand-father was watching me from a safe distance – but safety wasn't exactly what I found myself in. Thirteen and living by my wits? It wasn't easy.'

That was some understatement. I knew that Kailash had been whoring herself out since then – the only difference now being that she was in charge. When Malcolm first met her she was one of the many skinny wee things he was employed to patch up and send out onto the streets again. When Kailash left, Malcolm did too.

It made my troubles seem petty.

Kailash looked uncomfortable with her con-fession, or maybe I was, and we didn't make eye contact. Anyway, it was less painful to look at her feet. She wore Jimmy Choos, as always. Maybe her love of luxury wasn't so indulgent after all. As usual, her foot tapped a restless rhythm, as if it would be dangerous to stay in the one spot too long. She cleared her throat and brought me out of my daydream.

'There wasn't a lot of beauty in my life then, and I found a nicer class of client basked in the company of Rembrandt. For turning my life around, I will always be grateful to the Rijks-museum.'

'Hence the name?'

Kailash didn't add anything. I felt even guiltier that she had wanted to share her story with me, but I didn't feel ready to deal with the burden of her pain. The atmosphere lay heavily between us.

Malcolm made mutterings of disappointment as he collected their coats and held the front door open for her. If he'd expected an emotional reunion with me calling her 'Mummy' he would have to leave dissatisfied.

Kailash turned to face me just before she left.

'Why won't you do it, Brodie? Why won't you ask for my help?'

I gave her a look that Mary McLennan used to describe as silent insolence. I didn't see her hand move but I felt it when it slapped my cheek. Tears of frustration ran down her face.

'There is no need for any of this,' she hissed. 'You know I would give you the money to pay off Roddie Buchanan's debts, to get you out of anything.'

Malcolm ushered her out before I could reply. I leaned against the door. I knew she was right, but I could never buy my way out of trouble on her money. Not because I didn't feel anything for her or was too stubborn, but because the money she had was earned by her pain.

The answering machine flickered, alerting me to messages from the men in my life. Wriggling snakes trying to charm me to do their bidding?

All I could think of was Kailash's eyes, because I knew I was the one who killed the light in them.

Chapter Twelve

'Wipe that face off now. Nobody is anybody until they've been arrested, Brodie. Look on it as an education for the job.'

If I had been expecting tea and sympathy from

Lavender, I was sadly mistaken. I'd stayed in the flat on my own all night after the rotten afternoon I'd had with Kailash and Malcolm. I hadn't returned any calls – not to Joe, not to Jack, not to Kailash, and not to Lavender herself. They were probably all pissed off with me, but only Lavender had the chance to show it to me now.

'The problem with you, Lavender, is that you never know when enough is enough.'

She wouldn't stop. 'Just think of all the famous jail-birds: James Brown, Jerry Lee Lewis, Johnny Cash…'

'I don't think Johnny Cash ever actually spent any time behind bars, he just sang there a lot. And…'

'Well, there's…' She ignored me. Like I said, the problem with Lavender was she never knew when to stop.

'Hitler?' I finished her sentence for her.

'Well, if you're going to be stupid about this…'

Then I saw in her eyes the look I really didn't want to see. Lavender was fighting hard to stop herself from hugging me. We both knew that if she did she wouldn't be able to hold back the tears that were giving her eyes such a romantic dewy look. Eddie should come in now and sweep her off her feet.

The clock showed that it was shortly before 8 a.m., so there wasn't really much chance of him turning up. Lavender had collected the post from Rutland Square at 7.30 a.m. It was all ready for me to open. Rutland Square is an internal postal service that means lawyers and ancillary bodies don't have to rely upon the vagaries of the Royal

Mail. It is very handy, especially at Christmas time; it's a bit like scout post with attitude.

The opening of the mail isn't a menial task in a legal office. It's normally carried out by partners because it's supposed to indicate that you have your finger on the pulse of the firm. In theory this means that if you have a rogue employee, be they a secretary or a lawyer, you should find out about it. Theory is all very well, but what if that rascal is you?

'Another red letter, Brodie. What do you intend to do about it? I have files of complaint letters from the Law Society of Scotland, all red tabbed.'

Lavender was looking over my shoulder, to make sure I didn't dodge any necessary action.

'And in your file of complaint letters are there any from clients?'

'No, you know there aren't, but...'

'But nothing. All the letters are from lawyers complaining that I'm touting, taking their clients. As I told the President of the Society – punters have the freedom to choose the best legal representation they can have.'

'Which happens to be you? Always?'

'Of course. Our team is the best.'

'And how did all of that go down with the President of the Law Society?'

'Like a lead balloon. Which is why we keep getting these ridiculous red letters.'

'Do you mean to tell me, Brodie, that red isn't their corporate colour?'

I shook my head in disbelief. Had we never had a letter from the Law Society about normal stuff?

It didn't matter. Lavender had a point. I had to come clean.

'Lavender, I haven't exactly replied to those letters, and if I don't read them then they can strike me off. It's just...' I didn't have to finish my pathetic almost-apology. Lavender was off like a rabbit from a trap.

'I'll have a set of draft replies on your desk by the end of business today. That,' she pointed at the file, 'is a bigger and more immediate threat to us than Duncan Bancho.'

It was unorthodox, but Lavender knew as much about all of this as I did. Who was I kidding? In a lot of cases she knew more about the running of the office than me. The letters were all complaints from members of the Bar claiming I had exerted undue influence on their punters. In a way I should have been flattered. Some days it was just nice to think I had any influence at all.

By the time Lavender came back with the coffee I was ready to look at the diary.

'When I heard you were lifted yesterday, I got extra cover in, Brodie. I wasn't sure if you would ... well, you know.'

'You didn't know if you'd need someone to represent me?'

'Well, even if I had, I can tell you they wouldn't be queuing up. The bright side is that you can stay in the office today and get things organised.'

The desk jumped as she laid the court files down on it. On top of the pile was a photocopy of the day's work She had even marked the name of the lawyer against the court case.

'Lavender, you make me feel redundant.'

'Is that your way of saying thank you?'

'I see Eddie's instructed...'

Lavender was easily distracted where Eddie was concerned. A slow, satisfied smile stole across her face as I turned round to see why.

Eddie Gibb had broken all records. This was the earliest I had ever seen him in the office and surely the only time he had been the first one into the court meeting.

He even looked clean.

Lavender got up and straightened his tie, an unnecessarily intimate action.

'Eddie was the one to phone me and tell me the rumour on Monday night. Which, I might add, I didn't believe because I was sure that if any such calamity had occurred you would have phoned me,' she said pointedly.

'Yeah, well...'

'It was running riot round the bars. I was in the Tilted Wig when Bridget Nicholson came in. She had that sly look on her face and she couldn't wait to tell me and everyone else who could hear her – and that was everyone in the bar. She was so loud. Really loud. I didn't know she could be so...'

'Loud. Yes, I've got the picture, thanks very much, Eddie.' I stopped him mid-flow as Robert Girvan and Laura McGuigan traipsed in.

'I'm surprised to see you here,' said Girvan.

'I pay you large sums of money every month, Robert. Lavender makes out the cheques and I sign. You could at least give me the courtesy of silence if you can't manage support.'

'You've got it all wrong, Brodie, because you're

115

too damn touchy as usual. All I meant was, of course I knew that Duncan Bancho would release you. It's just that it must have been a hellish experience and I would have expected you to take more than one day off.'

Lavender thrust a cup of coffee into his hand and answered for me.

'For your information, Robert, Brodie will never let the bastards grind her down.'

She sounded a lot more certain than I felt. I handed out the files in a daze, distributing the work evenly between them. They were great courtroom brawlers, they needed no pointers from me. Usually I made a pretence at directing them just to let them know who was boss. But they were mavericks and I knew that they would go their own way once they stepped inside the arena.

'Robert?' Lavender's voice cut across the room. 'Are you free next Wednesday to do that jury trial in Wishaw?'

'No, sorry, Lav. All next week I'm in a complicated fraud case in Linlithgow for Bridget Nicholson.'

Two days ago, Robert Girvan would not have taken work from Bridget Nicholson because he knew that he more or less worked permanently for me. It indicated to me that he was covering all bases. He expected me to go down, if not for this, then for something.

'Rat,' Lavender hissed after him, as they all began to file out with their cases.

A strange silence fell upon me after they had left. It had been at least three years since I had still been in the office at nine o'clock Even on holiday I couldn't relax between the hours of 9.30 a.m. and 11 a.m. because I was conditioned to act like a headless chicken running from court to court.

'You can't go in there,' I heard Lavender shout from the reception area outside my office. It wasn't like her to raise her voice, and it was enough to make me move. I jumped over my desk in case she was in trouble. Clients with drink and drug problems aren't ever easy.

'I've got a warrant.'

'Show it to me now, before you take another step.'

I recognised Duncan Bancho's voice. He must have timed this to make sure he didn't have me to deal with. I was gratified to realise that he now knew Lavender was no pushover. He'd have had an easier time with me.

I opened the door. Lavender was barring his way with one hand, whilst slowly reading the warrant she was holding in the other. As soon as Bancho saw me, he shouted:

'Serious Crime Squad, we've a warrant here to uplift your client files.'

That wasn't for my benefit. He was shouting loudly so that the commercial-department clients would hear. In the space of about five seconds, over his shoulder, I saw one portly businessman go up to the receptionist and walk out. It was a sight Bancho didn't miss; his eyes narrowed as he sneered at me and pushed his way into my office.

'Tell your minions to get me the list of files on this warrant. You can stall if you want but we both know this warrant is kosher.'

I nodded to Lavender to co-operate. Top of his list was Tymar Productions. Good luck to him if he could find it because I sure as hell had no idea where it was, although the name 'Tymar Productions' was starting to ring a bell. Lots of bells. Alarm bells. It had just dawned on me that it was the name of the company my senior partner, Roddie Buchanan, had been setting up in Switzerland the weekend my father was murdered.

I stared out of my office window. It still sounded strange to say *my* office. I had demanded it from Roddie after Kailash's trial last year. I knew he had cursed me and probably still cursed me every day, but even he must have thought it would have taken me longer to fall this far.

'Brodie!' Lavender shouted through to me from her adjoining office. 'It's the *Evening News* on the phone – they're running a story on Alex Cattanach and they're going to mention you. Do you want to speak to them?'

'Christ, no. Tell them "no comment".'

I could hear Lavender getting rid of them before she nervously crept into my room.

'If they were going to run the story anyway, why did they want you to comment?' she asked.

'If I spoke to them, they could pretend to me they were doing a balanced piece and then they would stitch me up with my consent,' I answered.

'I'm sure I shouldn't show you this.' Lavender's hands were behind her back, concealing something from me.

'How much worse could things get?'

I knew that was a stupid thing to say, but it got me what I wanted and she threw a cheap lilac

118

envelope down onto my desk.

'It doesn't look much.'

The envelope was unopened. I really would have to praise Lav for controlling her nosiness. The writing on the outside of the envelope was semi-literate and flowery, like an eight-year-old girl's. I opened it quickly – no letter-bomber would act like this, I was sure.

Hiya Brodie!

I told you if you got me into rehab then I would help you!

Woman of my word!

Only kidding I would of helped you any way cos you and me go back a long way and I know you've always been there for me.

About that tosser the Alchemist?

I remember now. I had been lifted by the Leith police and I was pretty pissed off cos it was 1 of my busiest nights of the year – better than Xmas. I was raging. It was in May at the start of the Church of Scotland Asembly and thats always a busy time. Those ministers are randy bastards – thats why I remember. I look forward to it all year cos its such easy pickings. But some gadge accused me of stealing his wallet after we'd you know ... you'd think he would have been embarased but the sneak wee bastard called the cops.

I get taken in to St Leonards as per usual. And thats where I saw him. Bernard? What a stupid name that is, no surprise that he calls hisself by a nickname. Anyhow he was screeming at the top of his voice get my lawyer get me Brodie McLennan get me Brodie.

Then I heard DI Bancho sayin you were crap and that he would be better off with a real lawyer like

Nicholson. Bridget Nicholson.

Too be fair Bernard just ignored him and he started shouting that he didn't need a lawyer cos they had nothing on him. I heard him emptying his pockets and shouting he had to be relesed cos they had nothing on him. Nothing at all.

They put him in the cell next to me. I spoke to him cos I bort gear from him before and he was so scared he was wetting his knickers.

The thing is he told me that he had done the job <u>BUT</u> he'd thrown the jewelery over a hedge before the cops nabbed him. When they lifted him he was clean.

I know that that's the same story I always give you but I believed him for 1 reason. When DI Bancho had taken him into a room I heard a phone call to the desk sergeant. It was from a man phoneing the cops to hand in a necklace and bracelet that he had found in a garden.

Now I put 1 and 1 together and how come that jewelery has suddenly ended up as evidence?

If you can answer that Brodie then I think – in spite of the rehab – you owe me one.

Your Friend
Tanya
(Hayder)

'What's the smackhead saying now?'

Lavender was itching to know as she looked over my shoulder.

'She says I owe her a favour.'

'Again? Do you?'

'We'd better hope so.'

And with that, I began to pray as best as a non-believer scumbag lawyer could.

Chapter Thirteen

'Two pounds fifty to terrify, yourself? You have lost the bloody plot, Brodie. There are plenty would do it for free for you.'

Lavender handed over five pounds to the attendant, but she wasn't finished with me yet.

'I don't mind you frightening yourself but I've got more than enough going on without having to actually witness you having a freaky fit.'

'It's aversion therapy. If I force myself to confront my fear of heights then I will feel very brave. I need someone to come with me and you're cheaper than a psychiatrist.' I didn't say that I also needed something to take my mind off Tanya's letter before I decided what to do about it.

The Carrara marble statue of Sir Walter Scott and his beloved dog Maida looked as if they were mocking me. I didn't blame them. This wasn't exactly a life or death situation, but I still wondered how I could summon the courage to climb the 287 steps of the two-hundred-foot monument.

'I've paid the money so you are climbing to the top.' Lavender stood to the side to allow a group of enthusiastic Japanese tourists to pass. She grabbed me roughly by the arm and marshalled me into the stairway.

'Don't even start about your claustrophobia. What I don't understand is how you can drive that bike at breakneck speed and yet be frightened of a little thing like this.'

By step fifty-five I was already sweating, from fear as well as exertion. Lavender was behind me, poking and prodding me up those steps. At seventy-five I stopped and faced her.

'Why do I get the feeling you are enjoying this?'

'Because I am – now turn around and get moving, look out at the scenery. There's no lesson to be learned unless you face your fear.'

I felt myself being pulled to the edge magnetically. Down below, office workers enjoyed an alfresco snack in Princes Street gardens. Little did they know they were in real danger of experiencing my own mid-morning nibbles, as nausea started to overwhelm me. I pulled at the neck of my blouse, trying to cool myself down.

'Get moving.' Lavender nudged me. I rushed to the first floor and the museum, faking interest in the superb stained glass windows.

'What does that mean?'

I followed Lavender's pointing finger.

'What am I – a tour guide?'

'No. You are, or at the very least were, a nerd, and I bet you know exactly what that means.'

She was right. 'This is the third window and it shows the coat of arms of Scotland – the Lion Rampant.'

'But what does the motto mean? *Nemo me impune lacessit?*'

'No one provokes me with impunity.'

'Sounds like a good mantra to take into your appointment with Lord MacGregor, Brodie.'

Her words spurred me on to a charge up the

steps. If I couldn't face looking over a perfectly safe two-hundred-foot precipice, what chance did I have looking into Grandad's face and explaining myself? I shouted historical details at Lavender as I raced upwards. It kept me distracted.

'The Scott Monument was built after his death because the people of Scotland wanted to commemorate him. No public funding was used in the original build.'

'Don't worry, Brodie, if you kick the bucket I'll put a fiver in for your memorial.'

We stared out over the Waverley Valley. It was nothing to Lavender but I felt triumphant. I waved at the people down below and ventured to put my arm around her shoulder.

'Keep your fiver – if I'm out on my arse, Roddie will make sure that you're not far behind. Race you down.' I pushed my way down the stairwell, in two minds about the direction I was going, for every step took me closer to my meeting with Grandad.

Lavender walked me to Awesome, parked at the bike spaces near the Waverley train station. She'd refused to ride with me from the office, preferring to walk, but she had a soft spot for the Fat Boy, knowing how much that bike meant to me. Gingerly she pointed her shoe at a small drip of oil.

'You need to get that leak fixed – do you want me to phone Joe and get him to arrange it?'

'I'll speak to him myself.'

Lavender's eyes lit up.

'Oh, I thought that you were avoiding him.'

'You think too much for your own good

123

sometimes, Lav.'

I yanked my bike helmet on – she knew that now I couldn't hear her – and threw my leg over Awesome. I jumped down on the kick-start and the engine roared into life.

I sped off down Waverley Bridge, narrowly avoiding dozy packs of tourists who were more interested in wolfing down their McDonald's than taking care of their lives. I turned left at the roundabout down past the Edinburgh Dungeons, where the queue was massive. The ragged skeleton in the cage seemed to wave at me as I drove past. I was taking the long way round to my destination – I could have walked from the office or from the monument, but I needed an excuse to get on the bike.

With the thinking time I'd created for myself, I wondered how bad my punishment could be and felt quite cheered as I pulled into Parliament Square, the Fat Boy announcing my arrival with a roar. I circled the statue of King Charles the Second astride his horse and then parked. I could almost hear the sniffs of disapproval but I felt bullish.

'Miss MacGregor!'

The man's voice rang out round Parliament Hall as I made my way inside. Parliament House is no longer the residence of the Scottish Parliament, although it did sit there until the Union of 1707, when those members bribed to do so signed away Scottish independence. They had some scruples, and the treaty of Union was not signed in this hallowed hall but in a pub cellar in the High Street. Not much has changed, and most advocates still do an inordinate amount of business in the pubs up and down the Royal Mile. Why had Lord MacGregor insisted on meeting me here?

'Miss MacGregor!'

The voice was insistent. He, along with everyone else associated with this place, knew I was still calling myself McLennan. Footsteps came steadily nearer at a speed belying his age.

'Miss MacGregor!'

Childish, I know, but I was refusing to turn and answer to that name, pretending to be consumed by the intricate details in the vast black mantelpiece. The grate was empty in deference to the time of year, but, in spite of the fact that it was summer, it was a Scottish summer, and consequently chilly at times.

He finally caught up with me.

Prather tapped me on the shoulder, continuing the icy mood. He was a law unto himself, and within this Parliament House he was used to being obeyed. Prather's status was difficult to define. The closest that I could come to it was to say that he was rather like Jeeves – a lackey who's infinitely smarter than his employers and with little done to conceal the fact. Nothing happened in Parliament House, home of the Scottish High Courts and Faculty of Advocates, without Prather's consent or knowledge.

He ran a tight ship by virtue of an excellently trained staff of underlings, the average age being seventy-five. He was, as usual, immaculately dressed in livery with silver buttons, his white hair slicked down. Intelligence shone out of his small brown eyes as he cocked his head to the side before he began speaking to me.

'Miss MacGregor – your grandfather has asked me to direct you to the lower corridor where he is waiting for you.'

It reinforced my grandad's clout in the Scottish court that Prather deigned to deliver this message in person.

I walked along the corridor, my biker boots sounding heavy on the worn flagstones. Idly I looked at the boxes of counsel papers. When an advocate is called to the Bar, they are given a box and instructions from solicitors are placed in it. The box starts outside Court Nine, then, as advocates die, your box moves up. It's a slow process.

'You, took your time.'

'Good to see you too, Grandad.'

'If I didn't know better, Brodie, I'd say you were avoiding me.'

'Now, why on earth would I do that? Anyway, I saw you on Sunday.'

'I'm not stupid, Brodie. I know that since then – well, shall we say, a few things have happened to you. Come here, I want you to see something.'

My grandad stood in front of a large blackened oil-painting. He placed his hand in the small of my back and pulled me into him. I felt tiny beside him for he was surprisingly tall for his age. Reluctantly, I acknowledged that was because his posture was so good. Mary McLennan had shouted at me for almost half my life to put my shoulders back and stop slumping, especially when I morphed in to a sullen, dull-eyed teenager. Which was exactly what I felt like now.

126

Lord MacGregor's gnarled arthritic finger pointed at the picture. I shook my head in ignorance.

'Am I supposed to recognise this?'

'*The Hale Fifteen.*'

Shrugging my shoulders sullenly, I indicated without whining that he had lost me.

'*The Hale Fifteen* is, as you can see, an ancient picture – it represents the beginning of the Scottish legal system. The history of the position of the judge was that *he* was to take the place of the King in the administration of justice. But Stewart Kings believed they were appointed by God – naturally, James IV thought that one man alone could not take his place so he decreed that all fifteen would have to sit together.'

'I must be slow, but I don't see what this has to do with me or my life.'

'Look at the painting closely – see the anomaly.'

His finger poked at the ancient depiction. I looked over my shoulder to see if anyone was going to pull him up for vandalism.

'Fifteen men in judicial robes,' I said. 'Fourteen of them wearing the Templar Cross.'

'So, you are awake? The fifteenth man is dressed in black, and not the traditional red and white. He is a judge – the bastard son of the Lord Advocate.'

I felt him swell with pride – he did not share my aversion to secret societies. Thankfully he did not tackle me on that subject.

'And I am the bastard child of the Lord President,' I helped him out.

Pointing at the painting again, my grandad

restarted the story. 'The black bastard was his own man, and he forged his own path. There's nothing to stop you eventually following him.'

'Eventually?'

I knew what he meant but for some masochistic reason I needed him to say it.

'I can't help you get a seat on the bench just now, Brodie – even a position as a temporary sheriff is out of the question.'

'I know that. You don't have to take it badly, Grandad. I'm not sure I want to be a judge at the moment.'

'I'm not entirely senile, Brodie. Your feelings on this matter have been adequately communicated to me. That wasn't the news I was trying to break to you.'

A pain gripped my gut like a knife being twisted. It was prophetic.

'Prather contacted me last night. He didn't want you to suffer unduly when the news was announced.'

I felt stupid and weak. Prather's unasked-for kindness was about to be my undoing, I thought. I fought back the tears even before I heard the news.

'As we speak, my dear, Bridget Nicholson is being offered a position as a Senator of the College of Justice. Of course, it will take some time before the position is officially announced, but, there is no question about it – you will be bowing before Lady Nicholson.'

Words failed me.

I turned to run.

He grabbed my shoulder. It hurt. He pulled me

up in front of his face and hissed.

'If you ignore everything else I say, Brodie, obey this – make a friend of your enemy.'

Pulling myself free, I ran. My heart told me he was right but my stomach felt sick at the thought of sucking up to Lady Nicholson, even if there was nothing I could do to stop it.

Chapter Fourteen

I am one of the ninety-five per cent of dieters who sabotage themselves by comfort eating.

And right now, I didn't give a damn. My only worry was how fast I could stuff the hot and salty chips into my mouth.

'That's unnatural. You shouldn't be able to get a whole bag of them in at one time, Brodie.'

I smacked the hand trying to grab a piece of my white pudding.

'There's no need to turn nasty.' Moses Tierney, leader of the Dark Angels, shook his hand dramatically.

'What are you listening to?'

He didn't wait for an answer, rather he pulled one of my earphones out and shared them with me. Moses was caterwauling along as he listened in.

'Johnny Cash has never sounded so bad, Moses. Who told you that you could sing?'

'Everyone. Everyone does. They all say I'm the dog's bollocks.' He looked genuinely surprised.

'Makes sense. Who in their right mind would tell you what you didn't want to hear?'

'Too true, Brodie, my girl – I mean, who really needs some whinging bastards around who keep disagreeing with you; present company excepted. I pay you too well to just get lip service.'

Moses and I have a disturbingly close relationship. He has watched over my safety for more years than even I know. Our lives are linked, whether I want it or not, through Kailash. He was another survivor of the sadistic paedophile ring headed up by my father and the experience shaped him into a unique character. Moses was the undisputed leader of band of renegade teenagers for years, and he took pride in the fact that they were like Teflon, non-stick.

'Shift your arse up.'

My Harley was on its stand and I was leaning against it outside the Rag Doll pub. Moses placed, his rather more slender hips against the seat. It was intimate but not uncomfortable or remotely sexual.

'He's watching us,' he commented.

'Who?'

'Don't give me that. You know. Glasgow Joe is in his office pretending to do his accounts but he can't take his eyes off that surveillance camera.'

'How do you know?'

'You should know better than to ask me questions like that, Brodie – on this occasion I'll answer it. I always approach the Rag Doll via the backyard, not being a big fan of CCTV in general. I only came round the front 'cause I wondered what he was watching so intently. I should have known.

Nothing grabs Joe's attention like you. Poor bastard.'

'Don't be impudent, young man.'

Moses mockingly moved to defend himself from an imaginary blow.

'Seriously, the guy is hard. Wouldn't like to be the one that gets between you and him.'

'If *you're* saying he's tough, he must be.'

'Joe's nothing like me, Brodie. That man is your original freedom fighter. He's got ethics.' Moses spat the word out as if it was dirty – it was all front; he had his boundaries just like Joe.

'Stop being so dramatic, Moses.'

Moses was the original drama queen, which made him difficult to handle at times – still, given his past I thought he deserved a bit of leeway.

'You can say what you want, Brodie, but you can't argue with facts. He was recruited for the IRA through a boys' football club. He was in Gaddafi's training camps. You know better than me that he ran to America to escape prosecution.'

'You're right, I do know all this. Are you writing his CV?'

Moses tapped Awesome with his walking cane.

'He went underground in LA and joined the Blue Angels – they don't wear the Hells Angels' colours – they're their own men.'

'You don't know everything, Moses.'

'I know. He won't tell me some stuff…'

Moses' wolf eyes stared at me eagerly, prodding me for information, but there was no way I was telling him the truth. Unfortunately, Moses is not sensitive to other people's feelings. What he'd said was all true but Moses had no idea how catastrophic all of Joe's choices had felt in my world.

'You were out there for a bit, weren't you?' He kept digging. Maybe if I gave him a few snippets, he'd shut up.

'I went out to join Joe in Las Vegas at the end of my fifth year at school. I had all the qualifications for university but I had made up my mind I wasn't going to be a student.'

'Your ma must have been pleased.'

There was no use denying it, Mary McLennan was furious. Of course, she blamed Joe, but when I left Turnhouse Airport I wasn't even sure I could find him. For ten days I searched Las Vegas, asking every scruffy, dangerous-looking biker I could find.

'I didn't know where he was – I had cards printed up with my photo and name on it and gave them to everyone I met in case they saw him and could pass one on.'

'Were you scared?'

'I was seventeen, Moses. I thought I was invincible. When Joe eventually got in touch, we spent our first night fighting.'

'That must have been bad.'

'I smashed God knows how many beer bottles at him for being ungrateful. I'd travelled round the world for him and all he could do was criticise me for putting myself in danger.'

'You might no longer be seventeen, Brodie, but age hasn't knocked any sense of self-preservation into you.'

I gave him a sharp kick on the ankles.

'Why'd you leave Joe in Vegas?'

'My mother was dying.'

'Mary?'

I wanted to slap him – of course Mary. I knew that he adored Kailash, but it offended me to think that Mary would get usurped for her. I kept quiet – and also didn't say that whilst I was at home grieving, Joe had gotten a quickie divorce from the State of Nevada.

I screwed up my chip paper and walked over to the bin.

'I think we've kept him waiting long enough,' I said. But as the doors of the Rag Doll swung open, I began to regret my words.

Joe was kissing someone.

Not a friendly 'great to see you' kiss, but a full-blown passion-igniter.

'Is that his new fancy piece?' Moses asked, adding, without waiting for me to reply: 'I've never seen him with anyone before – I mean I didn't think he was gay or anything, but ... funny, I always thought you two would end up together.'

'Brodie!'

Joe shouted at me across the bar when he came up for air. He didn't look embarrassed. Well, why should he? But then why did I? He tapped his woman on the butt and she scurried out the door.

'What do you want to drink?'

Joe shouted our orders to his barman and led us to a table. Nothing had changed since my last visit – still the same torn red leatherette benches and Formica table – so why did it feel so different?

'How's business, Moses?'

'Not too hot, Joe, not too hot. I'm getting hit

133

from all directions. I was hoping you might be able to help me out actually.'

'Sorry, Moses, but these guns aren't for hire.' Joe flexed his biceps, more for himself than me or Moses.

'I'm not looking for that, Joe – the only muscle I'm interested in is the one between your ears. No, this is a whole other business. Here,' he said, as if he had just thought of it, 'like that lassie – very nice by the way.'

Joe handed us our drinks. Moses, as usual, stuck to Irn-Bru. Mine was a neat Glenmorangie. The little display I had been treated to when I first entered the pub had made up my mind to take a taxi home.

'*Slainte*.'

Our glasses clinked in friendship and union. For better or worse, our lives were linked together.

'What's up?' Joe asked, looking at me. Moses butted in.

'You know I'm trying to go legit, big man?'

Joe coughed politely and, to his credit, said nothing. Moses didn't even have the courtesy to blush.

'Well, someone is cutting in on my supply lines. When I go to my dealers, they're not there, so they are getting their gear elsewhere, and the worst of it is they're not afraid. Even that idiot the Alchemist ignored my instruction and got Bridget Nicholson as a lawyer instead of Brodie.'

I kept silent. I was in no mood to do the Alchemist any favours by sticking up for him and repeating what Tanya had written about him asking for me.

'Do you want another one?' Joe had noticed that my glass was empty and rather disapprovingly ordered a refill.

The music in the background started up and the lunchtime dancer leaped onto the makeshift stage. She wasn't the worst that I had seen Joe employ, but, like most of the girls who freelanced here, it was most definitely her last-chance saloon. Not that this deterred her small band of ardent admirers, who whooped with delight. I think because she wasn't that bonny even the toothless old men thought they had a chance.

'Brodie – what's troubling you?'

Where would I begin? On safe ground, I thought.

'It's Duncan Bancho – he's determined to stitch me up with Alex Cattanach's murder.'

'Well, the word on the street is you're equally determined to stitch him up for planting evidence on the Alchemist.' Joe did not look amused.

Moses interrupted. 'Tell me you're kidding, Brodie? Go after Bancho if you like, although I don't think you should, but even I don't believe that the Alchemist is innocent.' Moses poked me on the shoulder, forcing me to look at him.

'I'm not defending myself.'

'Do you have any idea what it means to attack the police so directly? It's madness.' Moses was staring into my eyes, trying to detect signs of psychosis.

'I didn't start it – I'm only trying to find a way to finish it.'

But already the doubt was creeping in. Had Bancho thrown the first punch or had I?

'Well, Brodie, if you're successful Duncan Bancho will, lose his career and get at least five years in Saughton,' said Joe cynically.

'Don't give her a hard time, Joe – he's bent all right. If you want proof, I contact him through a chat room for singles looking for a date. There's a password, which I'm not saying in front of Brodie in case she misuses it. Anyway, I arrange with him a time to send an instant message, which is completely untraceable, and he tips me the wink about the things that are going on in his patch. He's useful and I don't want him busted. Contrary to what it says on the news, bent coppers are not ten a penny, they're hard to come by these days.'

'What information do you buy?' I asked, feeling totally vindicated.

'Shops or warehouses that have dodgy alarms mainly – then I know we'll have a clear run at a job.' Moses continued, 'Obviously for a gold standard service like that I pay him – well, I deposit his money in the Swiss bank near George Street; it's a numbered account so there's no name. If you're hoping to trip him up then you'd better be good because he always watches his back, covers all the angles.'

'I'm having difficulty with a bank account too,' I added. 'It's no secret that Alex Cattanach thought I was dodgy after the Law Society had examined the books. Our margins were just too small and our overdraft too big. Cattanach's convinced I was laundering money and putting it into an account named Tymar Productions.'

I never heard Joe's reply. Our attention was

taken by a stramash at the front door. A group of drunken Dark Angels barged in, led by the Alchemist. It was the first time I had seen any of them with colour in their faces; some of them looked rosy with drink, others looked green.

'You're no' doing us any favours, Moses,' shouted one skinny bilious male Angel. Moses did not react, even when the boy started pointing a finger at him. The others looked shaken, as though they would like to disassociate themselves from him, but if they did he would have fallen flat on his face.

'Shut up, Bruce.' The Alchemist was trying to shush him, but the boy still had a point to make.

'Your days of controlling us are over, Moses. Your loyalty seems to belong to her, not us,' he said, twitching his head over to me. 'The Alchemist had a good lawyer and you made him change and take her. She's nothing to us, Moses, she's not an Angel.'

'Can't argue with that,' Joe whispered in my ear.

'You can't control nothing any more, Moses. We're out of here – come on, boys.'

They turned drunkenly on their heels and left the pub. Moses hadn't uttered a word throughout. He watched the closed door. After five minutes he stood up, saying 'I'll catch you guys later' as he walked out. How could he be so calm? I needed to take lessons from him, I thought.

Joe and I sat there in silence after Moses had left. He was always a hard act to follow. 'What's going on there, Brodie?' Joe finally asked. 'Moses

137

getting none-too-subtle threats from his own guys? Not like him to sit back and let that go on.'

I nodded in agreement, before the silence settled on us again. We both realised it at the same time – Moses wouldn't accept it.

Joe knocked a stool over as we ran through the crowded pub. We reached the door just in time to see Moses underneath the lamplight across the road.

He had made no sound and the Angels hadn't heard him.

We watched as he placed one arm around Bruce's neck.

Bruce fell to his knees, forced to stare into Moses' face.

Moses whipped a stiletto knife out of his boot.

With skill and accuracy he cut out his victim's eyes.

It was like watching a butcher slice a pig.

Blinded, Bruce fell to the pavement. Blood poured from the sockets of his eyes. He searched around for his companions but they had all fled with Moses over the cemetery wall.

'We've got to help him, Joe,' I whispered, terrified.

'He's beyond help, darlin'. He won't die, but no surgeon in the world can help him now.'

'What's going to happen to him?'

'Moses will take care of him. Blind Bruce is now valuable to Moses – he's a cautionary tale.'

'You can't leave him.'

'I didn't say I would leave him. I'll see him right but you have to get out of here – find Cattanach.'

Joe placed the helmet on my head; at least it

muffled the sound of Bruce's cries.

'He's getting no help till you've gone,' he told me as I lingered on Awesome.

I must be a Good Samaritan at heart, because I was like a bat out of hell as I drove up Coburg Street.

Chapter Fifteen

'A friend in need is a pain in the arse. Go away, Brodie,' Lavender shouted from behind the door.

'Just open up, Lavender.'

I followed her into the hallway when she finally consented to let me in. Barry White was crooning in the background and the smell of coq au vin made my mouth water. My nose led me straight to the kitchen stove. Lifting the lid off the pot, I asked, 'Whose favourite dish is this?'

'Well, even if it's yours, you're not staying.'

I picked up a wooden spoon, stirred it and naturally had a taste. 'It needs a little more seasoning.' I cracked the sea salt and pepper corns into it, and tasted again.

'That's not bad, Lavender.'

'Don't kill me with your praise, Brodie. We're not all aiming for Michelin stars.'

'What, or who, have you set your sights on with this little lot?'

Unusually, Lavender wasn't forthcoming, but I was determined to get an answer. I made my way to the kitchen window, which overlooked Hibernian football stadium. Lavender's flat was a fanatic's dream; for any member of the normal population it would be a nightmare. I had often wondered what had possessed her to buy it, then each time remembered that Eddie was a fan.

'Tell me, who's the mystery guy?'

Still she didn't say a word, busying herself with setting the table. For two. When she placed the candles on the table I knew she was serious. I looked out over the football ground again. I was missing something. Barry White was still warbling on repeat.

'You've got something in common with the Walrus of Love, Brodie.'

'Is this going to be some smart-arsed reference to me having put on weight?'

'As if. That would be the kettle calling the pot black. No, Barry was a fellow jailbird, he got done for stealing Cadillac tyres and...'

'Can't you let me try to forget about it, Lav? That's why I came up here. I thought we could just chat and talk about shoes or whatever else you find interesting.'

'Do you know what Barry's last words were?'

'Obviously, not being a fully paid-up member of his fan club, no, I don't.'

'"Leave me alone – I'm fine." You could learn from his mistake.'

'Thanks for those words of wisdom, Lav. What do you want me to say? That I'm terrified? I don't know where to turn? Everywhere I do turn it's just getting worse?'

'Okay, you can have a cup of tea,' she buckled.

'That's a relief. I thought I was going to have to

cry before you put the kettle on – are you worried that I'm going to interfere with your heavy date?'

'You aren't being given that option – if he's early you're shinning down the drainpipe.'

I wandered over to her bookcase. It was filled with chick lit and some frankly embarrassing self-help titles.

'Do you really think you should have these books on view?'

'What's wrong with them?' asked Lavender huffily.

'Any man is going to run a mile if he sees *How to Get Your Guy in 10 Days* or *Stay Close by Sharing Hobbies* on the shelves.'

'And I should take advice from you on men? Oh, just put them in the bedroom, Brodie; or, on second thoughts – stuff them into that cupboard over there.'

I opened her overflowing cupboard and put the books in. I had some difficulty in closing it.

'Have you ever taken any of their advice?' I asked her.

'Of course, that's why I have such a vibrant love life.'

I was drawn to the window again. Could her unrequited love of Eddie be so strong that she'd bought this flat just to get him interested? Was this how Lavender 'kept him close by sharing hobbies'? I didn't want to draw Lavender out on this subject, I didn't want her to think I was mocking her, but maybe she was taking those books too seriously.

'Right, Brodie. I'm obviously not getting rid of you as quickly as I would like – so, what can I do to help you?' She handed me a large mug of tea and an outsize Galaxy bar.

'This is a good start.'

'What's happened?'

I told her about Moses. She wasn't his greatest fan at the best of times. She'd met too many like him during her time in London, so what she said surprised me.

'Don't be too hard on him.'

'Don't be too hard on him? Didn't you hear what I said? I watched him cut a man's eyes out.'

'I know – but were any of the Angels drugged up?'

'Probably– they were too drunk for me to really tell.'

'Exactly. Moses doesn't drink or take drugs – he wouldn't even take a cup of coffee that had caffeine in it. What's the one condition he lays down for joining the Dark Angels?'

'They have to have a letter from a GP that they are not on any form of prescription drugs.'

'He doesn't believe in taking methadone – he says it has to be cold turkey, they must be clean. I heard he refused a guy until he'd finished his antibiotics for the clap.'

'So, what's your point?' I asked her.

'My point is, Moses and I don't always see eye to eye,' I ignored her unfortunate turn of phrase, 'but he guards and takes care of those kids better than anyone else could. The guy he blinded?'

'Bruce.'

'Well, I'll bet Bruce and the Alchemist are challenging his authority – even to the point of giving the younger ones drugs.'

'So, Freud, you're saying that because his mother died of a heroin overdose, he acts like that in their best interests?' I asked.

'I prefer Jung, and, yes, Moses would protect those kids from drugs with his life.'

'So really – blinding Bruce wouldn't even make his heart skip a beat? He'd see it as part of a bigger matter that he was dealing with perfectly?'

'I'll tell you something else,' went on Lavender, 'I bet next month's pay packet that he takes Bruce back into the fold.'

'That's what Joe said,' I admitted.

'What else did he say?'

'He said we had to find Alex Cattanach. I desperately want to get my hands on the witness Tanya Hayder overheard.'

'Do you really think he exists?'

'Call me naïve – but I think it will be easier to find that witness than Alex Cattanach.'

'Don't bet on it, not if Joe's on the case. Anyway, I'll put an advert in the *Evening News* personal column thanking the person for handing in the jewellery – I think we'd better offer a reward.'

'But what are we going to do about Cattanach?' I dipped a piece of chocolate in the hot tea and waited for inspiration to hit me. Lavender sat at the computer composing the ad.

'I think we should involve Jack Deans,' she stated.

'What? Lavender, I thought you said he's a dickhead?'

'Well, he is compared to Joe, but he's also a great investigative journalist. We can use him.'

'What if we didn't include Jack and we just put in Cattanach's physical characteristics and searched the web for leads?'

'You're absolutely right, Brodie – we could do that or we could go to the wishing well in the museum and see what turns up. I'm emailing Jack now.'

The doorbell rang. She was still busy.

'Do you want me to go?' I offered.

'I wanted you to go twenty minutes ago but you didn't take the hint.'

Before she answered the door she turned Barry off and rushed to the mirror.

'I don't have my full slap on today – I thought he might prefer it if I was more casual.' Lavender looked at me for reassurance.

'You look lovely. George Clooney is a very lucky man.'

'George Clooney?'

'Well, who else would be worth all this trouble?'

'Smart-arse.'

'Seriously, Lavender. This is all for Eddie, isn't it? When I first got here I thought you'd found someone else. Someone who would appreciate the nice meal and the effort. You've gone to all this trouble for a drunken wee waster who just wants a free view of the match. What do you see in him?'

'He's gentle and he's loyal...' she began.

I cut her off mid-sentence. 'Are you looking for a man or a Labrador?'

'He's funny and he's a genius at what he does,' she went on.

'True. He's especially brilliant and funny in

144

that window just before he passes out.'

'He likes a drink but he's not an alcoholic.'

'He's an alcoholic.'

'He doesn't think he is and neither do I. But just supposing you're right, lots of addicts are functioning human beings. Mozart was a poly drug user, Beethoven's liver had been ravaged by drink.'

How could you argue against logic like that?

'You're a big girl now, Lavender, and if he stops you quoting bloody lists at me, I wish you all the best.'

'Brodie, you're my best friend – can't we agree that I always tell you you're thin and you tell me Eddie is the man for me?'

The doorbell and knocker hadn't stopped since we started our discussion.

'Prince Charming is champing at the bit,' I told her.

Alcoholic fumes announced his entrance; so did his rather loud rendition of 'Mack the Knife'. The carrier-bags of booze clinked as he put them into one hand to give me a kiss.

'How are you doing, Brodie? You've had a hard time these last few days, doll.'

I felt tears prick my eyes because Mary McLennan had called everyone 'doll'. I managed to stutter that I was fine, when he gripped me in a bear hug. Eddie is not small but he's definitely not tall. As a teenager he must have been stunning, but he was one of those men who hadn't grown into his looks – rather, they had dissipated around him.

As usual, his suit looked as if he had shrunk

overnight. Long, dark brown hair, streaked with grey, brushed his collar, which was worn and had seen better days. He had led an interesting life – his father had died when he was eleven and his stepfather was a member of the Rosicrucians, an occult society. The only effect it seemed to have on him was that he threw himself into football to escape the memories of his dad. He was good too, until a devastating knee injury ended his career and banished him to the terraces.

'Where have you been, Eddie?'

I was making polite conversation whilst Lavender finished up at the computer. Not that it was necessary. He made himself at home, opening the wine and pouring two glasses. I looked at him askance. Eddie obviously thought I was outstaying my welcome too.

'Sorry doll, I thought you were driving.'

He handed Lavender a glass and switched Barry back on. He was certainly at home here – this wasn't a first visit by any means.

'Where've you been, Eddie?' I asked again.

'The Cabbage and Ribs in Albert Street,' he told me. Most nights the Hibs pub is packed with fans reliving the glory days.

'Actually, something interesting happened. DI Bancho came in looking for Moses. Apparently he's knifed another Dark Angel. I thought it was unlikely but they're looking for witnesses – I told him he had no fucking chance. Who would grass on Moses Tierney? Then your name came up – if I didn't know better I'd say Bancho fancies you. He brings you into every conversation. Either that or he thinks you're a criminal mastermind.'

I ignored him but drink did not stay his tongue.

'You're in for another busy night, Brodie. Bancho is looking for you and, unfortunately, he knows where to find you. Moses always co-operates with the police so he'll hand himself in rather than go into hiding.'

Strangely, that was true. Moses did always hand himself in to the police because he thought he was invincible. However, after the death of my father, the ace card Moses had carried was buried with him.

The only one who didn't seem to realise that yet was Moses.

Chapter Sixteen

'Has Bancho been in touch yet, Moses?' I asked.

'No need to. He knows that I always hand myself in,' replied Moses.

'About that...' I had to broach the subject sometime. 'I was thinking you don't have a get-out-of-jail-free card any more, not now that my father is dead.'

'I know that, Brodie – anyway, that's not the reason. I always co-operate with the police because of the one time I didn't. I was fourteen. There was an outstanding warrant for being in possession of an offensive weapon. The police had a crackdown. A whole weekend of dawn raids. I thought I was ready for them – when the knock came I jumped naked into a divan bed. I'd carved

147

a hole in the fabric so I could hide. They tippled me and had great fun kicking at the mattress pretending to look for me.'

'Happy memories, Moses.'

We were hiding where all Leithers hide, in the Citadel in Dock Street. It was built in 1650 to house Cromwell's troops, but all that remains is a tunnel.

We'd had to jump a fence to get in once I'd found him after leaving Lav's flat. Now we were both in hiding from the police.

'It smells of piss in here, Brodie.'

'Thanks for drawing my attention to it. Look, it's going to be a long night, Moses – we might as well focus on pleasant things.'

'It still smells of piss, though.'

The sound of a foghorn broke our silence; the haar had come in over the Firth of Forth, and the mist gave us a false sense of security. The hum came again, reminding me that the whole of the Edinburgh Bar was waiting for me to go down. I looked at my watch – now I had less than twenty-three hours to go until...

'Do you want a Pringle?'

'It's a pretty pathetic last meal, Moses.'

'They're paprika ones.'

'That makes all the difference.'

'Life's too short to be sitting in a stinky tunnel, Brodie.'

'Well, why are you still here?'

'I don't want to leave you on your own – you're not used to this life.'

'I never dreamed I would have to be.'

'We could always be like Bonnie and Clyde.'

'They died, Moses.'

My bum was numb. I got up to walk around and rub it for a bit. Just as the feeling came back, my mobile rang.

'Brodie! I've found Alex Cattanach,' said Jack Deans, breathless and excited.

'What's going on?' asked Moses. 'Put your phone on loudspeaker so I can hear.'

I did as I was asked and Jack's voice continued breathlessly, 'I've found Alex Cattanach in Inverness! I think I should collect you and we can go up there together.'

'When? When can we go? And, how? How did you manage?'

He paused for a moment. 'I'm free after four tomorrow.'

'No chance, Deans. I need to go now. I need to get out of Edinburgh tonight.'

'Inverness is only three hours away. We'll go tomorrow – make it a bit earlier, but there's nothing we can do until morning.'

'Trust her. She has to leave tonight, Jack.'

'Is that Moses? What are you doing with Moses?'

'I don't have time to explain, Deans. Come down to the docks now. The Citadel.'

'This is getting worse, Brodie.'

'Just get your arse down here, right away.'

I hung up. Moses straightened his long leather coat. Remarkably, his make-up was still intact. His kohl stuck to him as if he were a Hollywood icon. He raised two fingers to his temple and saluted me. Saying nothing, he disappeared into the fog, and all I had left of him was the tapping of his cane.

He had made his decision. Moses had gone to meet Duncan Bancho. Rightly or wrongly, all three of us knew that any assault charge Duncan brought against him wouldn't stick. Nonetheless, Duncan's efforts would delay him and buy me some time.

It was not the first time that Bancho and I had crossed swords over Moses. The last time I had won and it cost Bancho a promotion. Bancho thought then that he had busted Moses' car-theft ring. It was alleged that the Dark Angels stole cars in and around the central belt of Scotland. They were said to have taken the cars back to a yard that Moses owned. DI Bancho had a tip-off that a fresh load of cars had arrived. He turned up with a warrant and Moses wasn't there. Bancho took the cars. His first problem was that it was late on a Friday and there were no police trucks available to uplift the vehicles, so he used his initiative. Bad mistake. Bancho instructed a local garage to pick them up and put them in their yard.

At five they locked the gates with chains and went home.

Moses' story was *he didn't steal cars,* so when he was walking home and saw his cars in a strange yard, the first thing he did was call the garage owners to find out what the score was. They weren't available because it was the weekend.

The next thing he did was cut the chains and take *his* cars back.

When Bancho went to collect the evidence on Monday morning, it wasn't there. He couldn't charge Moses with theft because he had no evidence. He did have CCTV footage so he charged Moses with breaking and entering. The second charge was an attempt to pervert the course of justice; the third charge was breach of the peace.

On the morning of the trial, I pointed out to the Fiscal that her case had more holes than Emmental cheese. She was young, a more experienced Fiscal might have run it. Okay, I bullied her when I pointed out that in Scotland you can't be guilty of breaking and entering unless you intend to steal. How can you steal your own property? If there's no theft, there's no court case, so how can you pervert the course of justice?

Then I said my client would plead to a breach of the peace.

In the plea in mitigation, I said he was very sorry for having sworn at the police officers but he was justifiably upset at being accused of a crime he did not commit. Moses got a fifty-quid fine instead of the seven-year jail sentence Duncan Bancho thought he would.

Bancho had been mad at me ever since. That didn't mean I was ready to roll over and let him win.

Alex Cattanach was alive, and that was the best news I had heard in ages ... even if I did have Jack Deans to thank for it.

Chapter Seventeen

'How much for a blow job, darlin'?'

A 1967 white 3.8 S-type Jaguar sedan pulled up at the kerb. I ran out from the close where I had been taking cover.

'Nice to see you too, Jack. Drive.'

Jack Deans leaned over and kissed my cheek. My body betrayed me, as it often did, and I turned to face him. I had heard that fear heightened sexual response. Could I use that as my excuse?

'Tell me about Cattanach. How come you managed what the police couldn't?'

'I'm proud to be one of the best muckrakers around.'

'Muckraker?'

'To get answers, you've got to stir shit. "Investigative journalist" just makes it all sound so antiseptic. You know I'm not that type.'

He stroked my face at the traffic lights and I kicked myself for not telling him to piss off. The streetlights twinkled in the fog, and Edinburgh took on a mysterious feel. I saw myself as a raunchy Nancy Drew, off to solve a puzzle.

There was little traffic and the journey across the Forth Road Bridge was smooth. Jack fondled my thigh – or was it a reassuring pat?

'You've had a hard time the last few days.'

'My life would be easier if you put both hands on the steering wheel and then told me what shit you had to stir to track down Alex Cattanach.'

The haar disappeared as soon as we left the east coast and started moving inland. Jack, on the other hand, was immovable on the subject of his contacts.

'Are you expecting me to put out, Jack, before you tell me what I want to know?'

'What age are you? Fifteen?'

'Well, why don't you tell, me, then?'

'You don't have any rights here. I have to protect my sources. I'm able to find out facts that the police can't because I use sources that they don't. Did you know the Salvation Army reunites ten people every day with their families? They're a damn sight more reliable – and pleasant – than the cops. Everyone on the run shits themselves if they see a copper – but a nice Salvation Army wifey is a different matter.'

'So the Salvation Army found Cattanach?'

'I didn't say that. My job is to seek out and expose scandal. My sources have to trust me. You can trust me too.'

'Are you going to do a story on this?'

'It's what I do, Brodie.'

'So, how come wherever Alex is didn't work out that the headliner on "Crimewatch" was within their midst?'

'We're talking the North of Scotland, Brodie. The Highlands barely even recognize television, never mind watch it.'

'Oh, come on, that's a crock of shit, Jack – they're not exactly stuck in the Stone Ages. Do you want the Scottish Tourist Board putting you on a hitlist as well?'

'Seriously, Brodie,' he said. 'It's another world up there. They get a different local regional news programme to Edinburgh – and Edinburgh was where Cattanach went missing, so it's seen as a local angle. Just the same with the papers – it was huge in the Edinburgh *Evening News* because they'd already been following all the Law Society stuff and running interviews, but anywhere else? No story.'

'And that's where you come in with your sleuthing skills and dodgy contacts?' I asked.

'Well, it's certainly where I come in with my willingness to get bored titless phoning every hostel and guest house and possible resting place for Cattanach's weary head.'

'So where was it? Hostel? Guest house?'

'Hospital actually. Usually one of the first stops, but not always the best as it depends on whether you get Nurse Ratchett answering the phone or not. I'd put it off as I'd had a bad experience doing a story a while back where a guy walked out of his house one morning and never came back. All searches turned up blank, then eventually someone told me he had been seen at Inverness Royal. I set up camp to see if it was him – it was, but it turns out he wasn't an amnesiac patient, it was a straightforward running off with his fancy piece who worked on the switchboard rather than an international spy scandal or anything. Abuse I suffered made me a bit wary of Inverness's finest medical frontliners though...'

'And Cattanach? Tell me about Cattanach?'

I was trying to concentrate on Cattanach because I didn't want to think about Jack. Being close to him after last Saturday night was odd. It hadn't felt like this in the pub – probably because we hadn't had the chance to do anything there. Now? We could do what we liked. If we liked. And I wasn't sure whether I liked or not. If I was honest with myself, I would admit that I was thinking about Glasgow Joe. When he sent me the divorce papers, I couldn't breathe without it hurting. It took me years to live again, and then just when I could live without him, he showed up.

So why did I feel like this about Jack? Why did I feel that I wanted him? He put his hand on my leg again; we both pretended it was for reassurance. I closed my eyes and feigned sleep. It was easier than having to work out how to respond.

When we passed Perth, I felt the energy outside change. We were moving into the Highlands. Jack nudged me awake.

'I'm starving, Brodie. Let's stop at the chippie in Dunkeld.' I didn't want to admit that I'd already eaten at a chip shop that night, so I was forced to wolf down a fish supper by the cathedral. I must have consumed fifteen thousand calories today. I regretted not giving Moses that chip.

'Did you see the sign for Birnam Wood?' Jack asked.

'From *Macbeth?*' I replied.

'Yes, from *Macbeth.*'

'I don't want to think of tragedies and ghosts and people falling from grace at the moment – thank you. And I certainly don't want to think of men named Banquo.'

'Suit yourself.'

'I hate it when you're tight-lipped, Jack.'

'I don't like it when you play hard to get.'

'If I dropped my knickers you'd tell me what you know?'

'Don't flatter yourself – but if you'd like to put it to the test, I'd be willing to participate.'

'It's ten o'clock – can we see Cattanach tonight?'

'No – we'll have to wait until the morning. Do you want to get a room?'

'Jack – you bastard.'

'We can get two rooms, since I find it difficult to resist temptation. Anyway, you were the one who insisted on coming up tonight.'

'We'll sleep in the car,' I decided.

I think, just to spite me, Jack chose a lay-by in Drumochter, the highest and most exposed mountain pass in Scotland. I closed my eyes in terror as the car shook from the force of the juggernauts speeding past on the A9.

'It's beautiful, Brodie. Just look at that sky.'

We were surrounded by Munros and, although it was late summer, there was still snow in the gullies. Outside it was so light it was impossible to sleep. I regretted not checking in to a hotel. With all the worry of the last few days I had slept very poorly indeed – a post-coital snooze might have been just the thing.

Jack was suffering from no such problems. His snoring actually didn't bother me as it meant that I knew he was asleep, so I was free to check him out. A sneaky voice in my head suggested that I might need to have erotic memories if I ended up in prison, so I gave myself permission to dream. I must have dropped off, because after what felt like no time I woke myself from drooling onto my jacket and heard Jack laughing at me as he drove.

'Whatever was going on inside your head, it sounded great. I wish I'd been there,' he said.

I felt myself flushing – I didn't like to tell him that he was.

'Where are we?' I asked, to change the subject.

'We're in the grounds of Craig Dunain,' he answered. 'It's a hospital in Inverness. Apparently Alex Cattanach has had a nervous breakdown; my source said they think it was caused by overwork. No one worked out who they were dealing with – a combination of the aforementioned media daftness up here alongside, and the fact that our Law Society accountant is in a bit of a state. It took a fair few bungs to a fair few people to track this one down, I can tell you. You've been asleep for ages, Brodie – so have I, but at least I remembered what we were here for. You looked like you were in a bloody fairy story lying there sound asleep.'

'I'm going to ignore all of that apart from you saying overwork brought Alex Cattanach here. I'm not going to argue with that – Cattanach was a workaholic, especially when it came to nailing my arse. A nervous breakdown sounds a lot better when you compare it to murder, too. What else did your "source" say?'

'She – obviously it was a "she" darlin' – suggested that we look here. There wasn't any point in me looking anywhere other than hospitals and loony bins. I knew you hadn't killed anyone – I think I'd be first on your list for that – so I took a different tack to the cops. They were looking for a body; I wasn't. Brodie, this is a bloody strange

157

business; but that's been where your luck lies. Because it's so bloody weird, the receptionist I spoke to remembered her pal here telling her about it, and Bob's your uncle.'

'Was nobody else looking?' I asked.

'Nope – they don't even get *Crimewatch* up here. It's all *North Tonight* and sheep-shagging programmes as far as I can tell.'

Jack said that the medical staff insisted that Cattanach had complete rest, and, as a result, were really picky about visitors. Especially at this time of the morning, I guessed.

We parked and made our way into the hospital, via the fire doors. It was deathly silent, but, in my experience, that could hide anything.

Chapter Eighteen

Silence meant little to Alex Cattanach. Whether it was a friend or an enemy didn't matter. Whether it helped or hindered was irrelevant. Since the attempted murder at Ruthven Barracks, it was just more background noise. The noise of nothing.

There was little of note in the surroundings of Room 404.

A small window, out of which could be seen a few trees and pathetic-looking bushes.

A print on the wall of some flowers, which attempted to bring colour, but failed in its banality, the cheap clip-frame doing nothing to enhance the pitiful lack of artistry.

A shaky metal bed with a thin duvet and a hard cotton cover.

A locker that held nothing. In fact, the locker wasn't even expected to hold anything as it had no padlock, no means to secure it. It swung open and shut sometimes as hospital staff went about their duties. The metal clanged against itself, the ragged edges of the side never quite fitting into the frame.

A chair, which was facing not the window but the wall.

And curtains.

Some curtains.

All of the curtains in this place were the same. How many rooms? At least 404, and each glimpse that Alex had of any other room confirmed that someone, somewhere, had made all of the curtains in the same fabric and in the same manner.

They were hung in the manner of the 1980s.

Thick fake-pine curtain poles with fake-pine finials at each end. Each curtain had rings which slid onto the pole, and at each end the rings were aided by tiny little silver screws.

Alex liked the curtains – and the metal locker, and the unimaginative flower print.

The little silver screws were useful as they could gouge a line across wrists, across arms, in a slow but effective way. Alex had found that, if this action was repeated many, many times (and what else was there to do?), then blood would flow. It wouldn't gush, but it would flow.

The metal locker was another matter. If Alex crouched down, then the ragged side – lethal, one of the nurses had warned – could be moved up and down any appendage or body part. Again, arms and wrists were easy, but any port in a storm – as long as some blood could be squeezed out, what did it matter where it came from?

The face.

The face could be dragged along the metal edge too, although that was trickier, to be honest.

The flower print had been glued into the clip-frame and the front piece of glass had been attached securely to the backing plywood.

It didn't matter.

The corner could be smashed and the broken edge of glass used for whatever purpose necessary.

And there was indeed a necessary purpose.

The tiny screws.

The locker edge.

The broken glass-frame corner.

Added together, they were enough.

Alex utilised all of the materials available.

Wrists were cut, arms were gouged, the face was slit.

Alex was pleased. There was work to be done. As the blood flowed, as the skin gave up its secrets, Alex sat and knew that it was time.

Armed with as much material as could be gained under such restrictive circumstances, the word was written on the wall.

The deal was, indeed, sealed.

Chapter Nineteen

'Are you sure this is necessary?' I asked as Jack had handed me a white coat that he'd stolen from a doctor's locker.

'It's best that we don't attract attention to ourselves. It's hard enough for a stranger to pass unnoticed in the Highlands. At least if we wear the uniform they'll think we are legitimate Sassenachs.'

We stopped outside Room 404, where Jack had been told Cattanach stayed. It was six in the morning, so the night shift were having a break before waking the patients. We didn't encounter a soul.

'Will we go in?' I nervously whispered to Jack.

I was wary about bursting in on Cattanach, even though I was pretty angry at how much trouble this disappearing act had caused for me. Jack didn't wait; he walked in without knocking. I peered over his shoulder. It was difficult; I had to stand on my tiptoes.

The stench of human excrement and blood was overwhelming.

'Don't look, Brodie! Just get the fuck out of here,' Jack shouted as be tackled me backwards. I fell against the wall but it was too late.

I had seen her.

Alex Cattanach was unrecognisable from the woman we both knew.

The former female rugby internationalist was a shadow of her former self. When I had last met Alex she had been full of muscles and strength. A big-boned woman. As I looked at her the only phrase that came to mind was that 'there were no big-boned people in Auschwitz'.

Jack broke the silence.

'Jesus, what happened to her face?'

'Shit, Jack, she's been mutilated. There's a pattern to the cuts on her face. What sick bastard could have done that to her mouth?'

Alex Cattanach's mouth had been cut from her lips to her ears.

A sickening smile.

Cattanach moved, but not in recognition. Her blank eyes were motionless as she swayed. Her swaying drew our attention to the wall.

'What the fuck has she written there?' Jack asked.

There was no need

We could both read the two-foot-high word written in blood and shit.

BRODIE

'Do you mind explaining what you are doing here?'

The voice was soft and cultured; they speak the best Queen's English in Inverness. The doctor looked like a tired teenager. He had come in whilst Jack and I were staring at the wall, staring at what Alex Cattanach had written there.

'Sorry Doctor...?'

'MacPherson. Doctor MacPherson,' he replied

162

cautiously. 'Are you family, may I ask? It's only close relatives who are allowed to visit Miss Cattanach at the moment.'

The bags under his eyes indicated that it had been a long, hard night. Dr MacPherson reminded me of a bloodhound, with lanky brown hair falling like jowls around his face. I hoped that his resemblance to a bloodhound stopped with his looks.

'Not exactly.'

In my impatience I interrupted Jack's attempts to silence me with looks.

'Doctor MacPherson.' I noticed on his nametag that his Christian name was Callum.

'May I call you Callum?'

'No, you may not. I am Doctor MacPherson and I think even you can see that this woman is very ill and she is *my* patient.' I had taken it as a given that he would consent to a chatty approach because of his age. I assumed he would like informality, but now he was pulling rank. 'Now tell me why you are in her room, at this ungodly hour, without permission?' he continued.

'Doctor MacPherson, I understand that you have a very responsible job and I apologise for the fact that we didn't inform you of our intention to visit ... Alex.'

This caught the doctor's attention. 'Alex? You know her? You know her name?'

Jack saw his opening and a chance to trade his information for some coming the other way. Whilst Jack tried to repair any damage he thought I'd done, Alex was paying no attention to us whatsoever. Nor did she show any sign of recognising us. She was swaying back and forth, picking at the scabs on her face with fingernails that were broken to the quick. I felt sick to my stomach as I recalled how much it hurt just to break one fingernail. Her hands looked swollen and infected; mercifully, I couldn't imagine what she had done to herself to make this happen.

'Doctor,' continued Jack, 'your patient is called Alex Cattanach and she's a rather high profile missing person in Edinburgh. Can you tell me what's going on here? I've seen a number of colleagues who have suffered a nervous breakdown from pressure of work, but none of them have ever self-harmed to such an extent.'

'Is that what you think this is?' asked the doctor. He gently took Alex's hand and pulled her towards us. She was impervious to our existence. MacPherson ran his finger down her cheek, like a merchant touching an exquisite vase and pointing out the intricacies of its colour and pattern. I noticed the raw, jagged edges of the swirling patterns on her cheeks, the fresh black stitches holding her face together.

'No – she wasn't mad enough to do this to herself. It was this which facilitated the madness. Now, you know who I am and you know Miss Cattanach. I am the only one in the dark and I don't like it. Please answer the question I first put to you. Who are you? And what is your business here?'

I was so mesmerised by the mess of Cattanach's face, lost in her pain, that I didn't hear the door open behind me.

Not until I heard Duncan Bancho's voice did I

realise he was there.

'Thank you for keeping them here until we arrived, Doctor. I think I can answer your questions, although I understand all too well why you want to keep your identity a secret,' he added, looking at me.

I could have protested that I wasn't concealing my name but no one would have believed me.

'I've been watching you, Brodie. I knew you couldn't resist it. I knew you'd want to see it through, you wouldn't leave a job half-finished. Looks like I got a bonus – you and Alex Cattanach in one swoop. Got you Brodie McLennan!'

As Duncan shouted out my name, Cattanach went berserk.

'Brodie, Brodie, Brodie...' On and on like a stuck record. Before anyone could stop her, she grabbed me, her brown eyes staring at me like a raven's, cocking her head back and forth. Ravens are alleged to carry the souls of the dead; it looked to me like Cattanach was stranded.

'Brodie.'

She whispered my name this time, stroking my hair with her shattered hands. 'Brodie? Is that you? Or the ghost of Brodie?'

It was an odd thing to say, but this was an odd situation all round.

'Alex, I am Brodie. I came to see how you are.'

It was a lie, but what else could I say? If I could have given the poor soul some comfort, it would have been a relief to me. I motioned with my hands for everyone else to stay back. It seemed to bring her some ease to touch me, to feel I was real. I put my hands out in the air in mock crucifixion. Alex wandered all around me, poking, muttering.

'Your hair.'

It was like a bird's nest – matted curls, fizz springing out in all different directions; even this pitiable woman had to comment.

'It's so alive. It's alive. So like you. Unruly, wild.'

I heard Jack giggle; it was so inappropriate, he must have been nervous. Alex Cattanach's hands pulled me towards her. Her frailness had me fooled, there was still a scrum-half in that traumatised body, and it was impossible to pull away.

'I'm sorry.'

It was a whisper into my ear that only I could hear, the softness of the voice being lost before it travelled further. Maybe things would have turned out differently if DI Bancho had heard.

But he didn't.

Bancho grabbed my arm.

I only knew I was being handcuffed by the coldness of the steel around my wrist.

'Brodie McLennan, I am arresting you for the attempted murder of Alexandra Frances Cattanach. You do not have to say anything but anything you do say will be taken down and used against you in a court of law.'

I hit the deck quickly, managing to note that the linoleum floor was green and surprisingly warm.

The first thing I saw when I came to was Cattanach's feet. The toenails were painted-red, albeit badly chipped. The only thought in my head was that I never figured that Cattanach would paint her toenails.

'I don't blame you for being mad, Alex.' My whisper was loud enough to be heard and taken down by DI Bancho. What a farce – that Cattanach and I had to be reduced to our lowest finally to understand one another.

'I promise you, Alex, I'll get the bastard who did this to you – no matter what it costs me.'

Bancho didn't bother to write that down. I knew that I must follow the instructions that I give my clients and say nothing, but, as it's said, a lawyer who represents himself has a fool for a client.

'Detective Inspector, you can hold the suspect in my room, it's just down the hallway.'

Doctor MacPherson had been watching too many bad cop shows and he was delighted to be part of the thrill of the catch. He couldn't keep the excitement out of his voice. I looked at his trousers to see if he'd pissed himself.

Detective Constable Peggy Malone had been standing outside. She came in at this point and addressed Bancho.

'Duncan, we've discussed this. I don't believe there is any need to handcuff this suspect.'

'Suspect? You should see what she bloody did to that poor woman.'

Peggy showed the whites of her eyes dramatically, indicating that he should shut up. Bancho followed her look over his shoulder to Jack, who, God bless him, had his notebook out and was writing everything down.

'Keep talking and acting that way, Duncan – there's nothing the liberal broadsheets love more than a great police brutality story,' he shouted.

'Peggy – get him out of here,' Bancho blustered.

We stopped to watch DC Peggy Malone bundle Jack out of the hospital. She looked more like a barmaid gently ejecting a customer at closing time than a hard-nosed cop warding off a potential grievance to the Police Complaints Board.

'Stand up straight and get walking, Brodie. It's bloody obvious that you were laying that on thick so that Peggy would think I was mistreating you.'

'It's true, that's all that's on my mind just now – I was trying to show you in your worst light. It doesn't take much. Your girlfriend seems ready to believe anything bad about you – doesn't bode well for your relationship.'

'Get moving – what kind of arsehole do you think I am that I would take relationship advice from you? If you ever get released from Carstairs, you'll die alone and be eaten by your cat.'

He kicked the door open to Doctor MacPherson's office. The word had obviously spread round the hospital that a dangerous fugitive had been captured. Nurses, auxiliaries, even one or two older guys who looked like consultants, had somehow found that they had a pressing appointment in the vicinity. I can confirm the government has indeed employed more nurses in recent years.

'Ah, Doctor MacPherson. I see you've come to watch.' I couldn't resist it – if he had lived during the revolution, he'd have been in the front row with his sandwiches.

'I thought you might like to know, Miss Brodie, exactly what effect your actions have had on that poor demented woman.'

168

'Brodie is my first name – Callum. You live in Scotland so you presumably know that under the Scottish system I'm innocent until proven guilty.'

'I'm her doctor. What more proof do I need? Since she was transferred here from Raigmore Hospital, further to her initial injuries, Miss Cattanach has slit her veins open to provide enough blood to write your name on the wall on a regular basis. When she can't get enough blood, like this morning, she uses her own faeces. All that is important to her is that she sees your name – your name on the wall.'

It did sound pretty damning to me, but I couldn't keep my mouth shut.

'And as her medical practitioner, you couldn't think of ways to stop her from causing such damage to herself? Haven't you heard of Crayola, Doctor MacPherson?'

Touchily, he seemed to take this as an insult to his skill as a psychiatrist. Duncan Bancho was enjoying this too much to stop him or step in; he stood with his back to the door, barring my escape, as MacPherson let rip.

'You buried my patient in a shallow grave in Ruthven Barracks. She was still alive, but that wasn't enough for you. You mutilated her face and wrapped her in a shroud. It was a lonely place – you must have been surprised when she was found breathing.'

I needed to find out what the evidence was against me so I continued to bait him.

'Okay, I know she's lost weight, but believe me, the Alex Cattanach I knew was a big girl – no jury would ever believe I could carry her up that hill.'

169

'Sodium pentathol. As you well know, you drugged her so she couldn't fight for her life. And tell me this: if you didn't do it, how did you know she was taken up a hill?'

Over my shoulder I could sense Duncan taking a more professional interest in this. I wasn't such a fool that I would admit the truth. A truth Duncan knew and would shortly remember. The alibi I'd given him when he had arrested me under Section Two could prove my downfall. Like a hyena, he circled me.

'Brodie McLennan – you have already told me that you were at Newtonmore at the MacPherson Clan gathering when Alex Cattanach disappeared.'

'So?'

I tried to sound nonchalant – but Dr Callum MacPherson stepped in; it was obviously a common name in these parts.

'Newtonmore is only three miles from where Miss Cattanach was found,' he said. 'She had been staying in a hotel in Kingussie to attend the gathering. The Cattanachs are part of the MacPherson Clan – if I was the police I'd want to know what a McLennan was doing at the MacPherson games.'

'You're in deep shit, Brodie.'

'With respect, Detective Inspector Bancho, her troubles are not as dire as those of Miss Cattanach. As a result of her trauma, she is suffering from a very rare psychological disorder – Cotard's Syndrome. The patient believes that she is immortal – that's why she cuts herself and attempts suicide daily. In her mind, the fact that she survived being buried alive means she is invincible. To her, the rest of us are ghosts. There is no cure, no drugs that will work on this condition. On Monday I am going to try a course of electric-shock treatment, which I understand may bring her some relief but to what extent I don't know. Of course, if by some miracle she did recover, there would still be the mutilation to come to terms with.'

Last night's fish supper started repeating on me – or maybe it was dismay at the hand fate had dealt Alex Cattanach. I was relieved to see Peggy Malone; she had brought the police car round to the front of the hospital.

It had to be a bad day when the highlight was being arrested and taken to a police station in Inverness.

Chapter Twenty

'Getting locked up is becoming a bad habit – do you like men in uniform that much, Brodie?'

For once, Robert Girvan was a welcome sight.

'Thanks for coming, Robert. I wasn't sure if you would make it. I know that you had agreed to work for Bridget this week.'

'Have you ever tried saying no to Lavender? Although, between you and me, I think she's a bit pissed off you didn't ask Eddie to represent you.'

That was all I needed. I knew Lavender would be hurt, and that was a lot harder to deal with than asking Robert Girvan for help. He threw a pack of chewing gum at me, which hit me on my shoulder and broke my trance. I had been staring at the putty-coloured walls of my cell, praying for a way out.

'Why did you ask for me anyway?' he continued. 'Everyone knows that you feel uncomfortable around me. I would have thought at a time like this you would want a lawyer you liked?'

'Everyone knows I feel uncomfortable around you? Am I so transparent?'

'You are when it comes to me.'

'I wanted you because you're good – you remind me of someone.' Girvan looked pleased; he thought I meant myself, but I didn't, he just struck a chord with me.

'Robert, I'm sorry if you've misunderstood my feelings in the past. What I felt for you was pity, but don't take that the wrong way. You're bright, funny, good looking,' I laid it on thick, 'and you were shafted by your senior partner. McCoy put you in a position that is damned hard to fight your way out of.'

Angus McCoy was senior partner in McCoy and Boyd SSC – Solicitors to the Supreme Court. Two years ago, Cattanach discovered that McCoy had embezzled over ten million pounds from banks and building societies by conning them into making loans of up to £500,000 a time, which he then ploughed into disastrous business ventures. McCoy got wind that he was about to be arrested. He left a taped confession and fled to South America.

Robert and his other partners were left to clear

up the mess. Robert had only been made a partner six months before. He was on a salary, he didn't get a share in the profits, which meant he was basically a slave. A junior partner works all the hours of the day and night and gets paid little more than an assistant. In fact, I'd worked out when I was in that position that I wasn't even on minimum wage for the hours I worked.

McCoy's actions meant that Girvan was liable in terms of the partnership agreement for McCoy's debts. Robert Girvan was declared bankrupt. He'd played the game and he lost big time.

McCoy had a lot in common with my senior partner, Roddie Buchanan. I toiled in that office so I wouldn't end up like Robert. The irony is, both Alex Cattanach and I would now trade places with him in a heartbeat.

'McCoy handed himself in, he's serving ten years. He did the crime and now he's doing the time. Have you ever met him?' Robert asked.

'No, I don't know that many conveyancing lawyers.'

'He's a cool guy – a player. If it had worked out he would have been a hero. After all, he didn't steal from grannies. It was all institutions, and I reckon he figured if it all went belly-up then they could afford to lose it. Even ten million is tax deductible. McCoy doesn't hold a grudge against Cattanach for taking him down. But someone does.'

'And you think that someone's me?' I asked him. 'I don't have a grudge. Believe me, no one who saw her now would.'

'It's that bad? I heard them talking outside. I

can't imagine it, Brodie. The point is, the police obviously believe you were willing to take her out rather than face being in McCoy's situation.'

'Whoever goes down for this won't be in his shoes, they'll be in Carstairs. When you're found criminally insane you never get out. Did you tell Bridget that you were representing me?'

'I thought she might object – so I left it up to Lavender. You couldn't blame her if she did take it badly – she and Alex were pretty much an item. I expected them to go through a civil partnership in a couple of months when the legislation goes through. I'm not looking forward to telling her.'

'Why should you tell her anyway, I suppose? It's only some temporary work, she can't expect to own you.'

'Sorry, Brodie, but starting next month Bridget's offered me a permanent position, with a view to giving me a partnership. My bankruptcy ends in September so I can apply for a full practising certificate.'

I couldn't tell him that he would be getting his partnership sooner than he thought. Bridget Nicholson's appointment to the College of Justice had to remain a secret until it was officially announced. The fates were certainly smiling on Robert Girvan. I didn't begrudge him, I just wondered when it would be my time.

'Back to you, though: it doesn't look good, Brodie. You have a motive, everyone in the job knows it. You were in the vicinity. Christ, even when she was catatonic she still pointed the finger at you. Why does she hate you so much? From what I can tell, she has always hated you.'

174

'I *used* to think that.'

'Don't tell me seeing Alex in a lunatic asylum is making you soft.'

'No, although I would understand if it did. I just didn't know Alex as well as I thought I did. Did you know, she painted her toenails?'

'Alex is a dyed-in-the-wool lesbian, how would I be likely to know that? What difference does it make anyway?'

'I know it's just a little thing, but it got me thinking that she was more feminine, more in touch with her feelings, than I had given her credit for. I always used to think she was an emotionless machine who had it in for me. But what if I was wrong? I do judge books by their covers. Alex didn't have a vendetta against me, she just genuinely, but erroneously, thought I was involved in something dodgy.'

'You not calling her Cattanach any more now that you've gone soft? How does all this make a difference anyway?'

'It makes it easier for me. No one wants to be hated for no reason.'

'I thought you would be used to that by now,' Robert threw back.

'That doesn't deserve an answer. No one wants to be hated. It makes it more acceptable to me that Alex was just doing her job. I made her life hell, I wouldn't answer her letters, I was petty – I thought she had it in for me because of Bridget.'

'So you've had an epiphany. That won't cut any ice if this goes to court.'

'What will?'

Chapter Twenty-One

When I walked into the dock I knew there was a God.

The courtroom was empty because I was on petition and the application for bail is heard in chambers. Which can mean the sheriff's private room or that the public is excluded from the ordinary courtroom.

Peggy Malone and Duncan Bancho had returned to Edinburgh, leaving me in Inverness. If the sheriff clerk or the police officers guarding me were surprised they didn't show it. Maybe Bancho had already been mouthing off about how guilty he believed I was and they all thought this was a done deal.

Anyway, I have never been so pleased to see a Fiscal in my life. Frank Pearson came into the dock and threw his arms around me. For the first time I cried without trying to hide it. I laid my head on his cheap shirt and my tears soaked through to his skin. He stroked my hair; he smelled of the mountains and fresh air.

'I see you forgot your comb.'

Self-consciously I raised my hand in an in-effective attempt to pat my hair down.

'Is it that bad?'

'Am I one to talk?' he joked, smoothing his receding hairline dramatically. It was good to laugh. I could almost forget what I was facing for a second. Only a second, though.

'You're in deep shit, Brodie.'

'Oh, Frank, I know.'

'Well, we've been there before, honey, and gotten out of it.'

Frank Pearson and I had been to university together, when I got back from searching for Joe in the states. He was older by a few years, but the rest of us still thought of him as a mature student. He had been the Fiscal involved in Kailash's murder trial. My stepmother had almost killed him. Joe and I broke into his flat and found him lying on the floor after being half-strangled by a noose. Pictures had been taken of him in an auto-erotic pose complete with PVC harness and mask.

Honest information didn't circulate, but what did were the photographs of Frank.

'I'm not opposing bail, Brodie – although DI Bancho was insistent that you were a threat to the public because of the nature of the crime. I had to remind him in no uncertain terms that in Scotland the Fiscal brings the prosecution, not the police.'

'Did I ever tell you you're my hero, Frank?'

'Get a grip. To get out of this, Brodie, you're going to need all the friends you have.'

'They're scarce on the ground at the moment.'

'I guessed as much. So, when I heard you'd been lifted I immediately put in for a secondment back to Edinburgh.'

My heart leaped. An ally in the Procurator Fiscal's office was just what I needed.

'Do you think you'll be able to come back?' I

had to ask him.

'Well, it'll be a bit embarrassing – again – but for you I can stand it.'

'That's not all I meant – how can you just transfer back to Edinburgh?'

'There's a shortage of Fiscals in the service because the pay is so bad. There is even more of a dearth with my experience. I could go anywhere I want, because all the regional offices are willing to cut one another's throats just to solve their staff problems.'

'You'd do all that for me, Frank?' I asked. 'The safe money's on me going down.'

Frank smiled.

'Well, let's just say I've learned never to bet against you. One way or another, you usually find what you go looking for,' he said.

Now was not the time to tell Frank I was going after Alex Cattanach's attacker.

Chapter Twenty-Two

'The police believe that Alex Cattanach was attacked by a lawyer with a grudge,' said Jack as we got back to business.

'No, Jack, the police believe that *Brodie* attacked Cattanach. They have a motive and she was in the vicinity when the attack occurred. They've stopped looking for anyone else now that they've got you, Brodie.'

I'd been released on conditions of bail, and

Frank, Jack and I were all huddled in the hack's car like a bunch of terrified hoodlums.

'Well, there must be other lawyers who hate Cattanach – Brodie wasn't the only one she was investigating. Anyway, I've done some research,' said Jack. I could have kissed him.

'Alex Cattanach was appointed Chief Accountant to the Law Society in 1998. Since that appointment she has pledged to weed out rogue or bent lawyers. She sent teams of investigators into firms on routine inspections – these routine inspections have resulted in nineteen solicitors on petition charges, which means they will serve a minimum of five years in prison if they are found guilty. With such scrutiny Alex has, naturally, made enemies. As she was fond of saying in the press, "It all depends on how well your firm is doing; if it's not doing well that seems to be an excuse for turning a blind eye to money laundering."'

'So that's why she was determined Brodie must be guilty?' asked Frank, as Jack put his notebook down. 'After the business with Kailash and Roddie, the firm is in dire financial straits. But, still – I thought lawyers were supposed to believe that you were innocent until proven guilty?'

'Alex Cattanach is a bean counter. She has an excuse. The rest of the Bar also believe I'm guilty and they don't have an excuse,' I said, peeved.

Frank looked at me with sympathy.

'I've heard Cattanach lecture on crooked solicitors – she seemed calculating but fair. I don't get why her treatment of you, Brodie, has been anything but. Could someone else have thrown a spanner in the works?'

He'd asked just the right question. 'I've always thought Bridget Nicholson was behind it,' said Jack.

'I think we've got to concentrate on the facts. It's not a story for a Sunday newspaper, Jack, it's Brodie's life we're talking about.'

'Well, you're naïve beyond belief if you think this isn't going to hit the papers.'

'I didn't say that. Look, Brodie, here's a list of the solicitors currently on remand.' His finger was agitatedly hitting the page he held.

'There are twenty names on this list, Frank. Do you really think Alex's attacker is here? Where do we start?'

Frank had a plan already worked out. 'I thought we'd better visit McCoy, Robert Girvan's old boss. I wouldn't put it past him to have paid someone to carry out the attack.'

'God, Frank, you haven't seen Alex Cattanach – this was no hired assassin. Her attacker is sadistic, when you look at her wounds you can feel the sick pleasure he got. He enjoyed this.'

My phone had been ringing throughout. 'You'd better answer that mobile,' said Jack.

I pushed my hand into my pocket, pulling out discarded sweetie papers at the same time. Even before I looked at the number I knew who it was and I didn't want to take his call in Jack's presence. I felt as if I was committing adultery. I wasn't going out with one of them and I was no longer married to the other, so I don't know why I felt in such a dilemma, but that's what was going through my mind. You could cause trouble in an empty house, Mary McLennan used to say to me. She was right. I flipped my phone open.

'Joe.'

'Why did you go to Inverness without telling me? Why did Jack Deans take you? What's he expecting – a medal?'

I think he might have gone mad if I'd told him what Jack was hoping for.

'It was Jack who found Alex Cattanach,' I started to explain.

'Yeah, and the stupid bastard didn't realise Bancho was tailing you. This isn't a time to put your trust in amateurs, Brodie.'

He was right. But I still felt guilty.

Go for the easy option, Brodie girl, I told myself.

I switched my phone off.

Chapter Twenty-Three

The doorbell rang. I tried to ignore it.

After the kind of day I'd had, I craved solitude. The journey back from Inverness had been quick, given that I'd slept all the way, but I'd had more stress in a short time than anyone should have to cope with. A continuous peal pierced my ears. The bastard wasn't going away. It sounded like they had left their finger on the bell. Stomping up the hallway I shouted at the closed door.

'I'm coming, so shut up!'

Even I was offended by my inhospitality.

Lavender was made of sterner stuff. Unusually, she was not a welcome sight.

'You'll have had your tea,' I snarled.

'Not on your nelly, Brodie. Your cooking is the only thing I came round for. It certainly wasn't your sunny disposition.'

Although it was a beautiful summer evening, Lavender wore a coat. She didn't follow me into the kitchen straight away, she stopped to take it off and hang it up. Lavender took an inordinate amount of time doing mundane tasks – I wasn't sure whether she did it to bother me or whether she used the time to work out a strategy for whatever she wanted.

'So it was okay up there, Brodie?'

We sometimes did this – carried on deep conversation with each other whilst in different rooms.

'Fine,' I lied. Being thrown into jail hadn't been fine at all.

'Was DI Bancho a bastard?'

I could tell from her voice she was hiding something. Slowly, she poked her head around the corner and it was obvious straight away; her red eyes let me see that she had been crying. She pulled a used paper handkerchief from her pocket that was much the worse for wear. It looked like she had been sobbing all day. Lavender blew her nose. It trumpeted round the kitchen.

'Your body makes the most unladylike noises – how are you managing to hide that from Eddie?'

'With difficulty,' she answered.

I turned my attention to the tomato sauce that was in danger of burning. Lavender looked at the table and saw that it was set for one. Without being invited, she set herself a place. I tore the purple basil to bits. I was too rough and it disintegrated in my hands before I threw it into the pot.

'Don't take it out on the food, Brodie – I'm going to be eating it,' Lavender chided.

The events of the day started to hit me – and Lavender's obviously emotional state didn't help. It sounded cold, but I didn't want to spend all night listening to how Eddie had been drinking again or what his latest screw-up was. It was hard to breathe, and I felt as if ice was melting in my chest. Gravity seemed to weigh me down, and it took a great deal of effort to lift the crème fraiche. Large blobs dropped into the blood-red sauce and swirled, the spirals reminding me of Cattanach. It was like a free association test – when I thought of Alex, Duncan Bancho came to mind, immediately.

Lavender's words interrupted my woozy spell.

'I got a phone call today – from the witness in the Alchemist trial.'

I lifted a large knife from my kitchen drawer. Lavender instinctively stepped back.

'What is that, Brodie?'

'It's just a knife.'

'That's not an ordinary knife. You don't get those in a box set in Debenhams.'

'It's a Scottish whinger. My grandad gave it to me – it's a MacGregor artifact. Whoever takes it into battle is supposed to be invincible.'

'It's lethal looking.'

'The blade's twelve and a half inches long. They

reckon that's the length of a man from his belly button to his spine – it's meant to be some sort of old traditional thing but it makes a fine knife for chopping.'

To test its sharpness I placed the point against the top of my thumb and ran its edge along my skin. A bright crimson bead formed along the line.

'You know I didn't believe the Alchemist,' Lavender continued. 'I nearly dropped when this man called to say he was phoning in response to the advert I had placed in the *Evening News* personal column.'

I picked up the chorizo sausage that lay alongside my marble chopping block.

Lavender picked up a notebook that was lying beside her handbag. 'Mr Wilson. Lives in a large Georgian house that looks onto Leith Links. On the fourth of May he took his poodle for a quick walk, to pee and poo before bedtime.'

'Information overload, Lav.'

She reached into my wine rack, pulled out a bottle of 1978 Rioja, and proceeded to open it before she went on.

'Mr Wilson was walking along Leith Links. He said it was a bright spring evening, he didn't meet anyone else on his walk. Trixie, that's the dog, became agitated and began snuffling around at the base of a hedge. Trixie was on one of those extending leads, so Mr Wilson couldn't see what was exciting her, he thought she was just about to do her business.

'As he got closer, he saw something sparkling in Trixie's mouth. He rushed towards her but she

184

wouldn't give it up. Apparently she's a bit of a madam. Dog obedience classes have made no difference. Her owner dived down at her, ripping a hole in his trousers but managing to grab a necklace. It didn't break as he pulled it out of the dog's mouth so he knew it wasn't fake. Whilst he was down on the ground he saw more diamonds sparkling; they were hanging deep in the privet. He scratched his hands quite badly – but once he was certain he'd got it all, he continued on his walk. Leith police station is just on the edge of the Links. Mr Wilson is certain that he handed the items in to the police station; the police officer told him that DI Bancho was dealing with the matter.'

I started to slice into the chorizo sausage. The knife made a satisfying thumping sound on the board. Lavender poured herself a large glass of wine and took a sip. I continued to chop noisily as she went on.

'DI Bancho couldn't come out to see Mr Wilson because he was interviewing a suspect in the case. Mr Wilson said there was a scantily clad young woman at the front desk, who had just been arrested. I think it made his night seeing her.'

None of this made me feel good.

If the Alchemist had been lying, then my position would have been safer. I knew now without a shadow of a doubt that Duncan Bancho would have no qualms about planting evidence on me. He had previous in that department.

Lavender placed her hand on mine, stopping me mid-chop.

'Who do you think you are? Lorena Bobbitt?'

'Before my time, Lavender.'

'Rubbish – unless your mother was hiding newspapers from you when you were a teenager. Lorena chopped off her husband's penis with a knife – then threw it out the window.'

I winced as I remembered the story, but felt a sense of deep satisfaction at the thought. I shucked Lavender's hand off mine and continued my chopping with gusto. She was happily listening to the sound of her own voice and quaffing my wine. I was still waiting for her to pour me one.

'Just tell me what's gone wrong, Lav – don't keep me waiting.'

'I got overexcited when Mr Wilson told me his story – it seemed like the first good news that we'd had in ages. I kept thanking him – he couldn't actually see me dancing round my desk, I wasn't that obvious, but he must have guessed. He asked me why it was so important.'

'Tell me you didn't tell him everything, Lavender.'

She turned away and stuck her nose deep into her glass.

'Lavender, we've spoken about your lack of discretion before.'

'I know! I know! That's why I feel so bad.' She waved her hands dramatically in the air. I took a ladle and slopped the chorizo and potato casserole onto her plate. Before she'd even started eating it, she asked for more.

'I'm feeding you, Lav, not fattening you. Tell me what Wilson said.'

Stuffing her mouth, she chewed before she started.

'He said he was delighted that he'd made my day, but he had gone to the police station to assist the police, not to let criminals off. To quote him, he said there was no smoke without fire and the thieving little bastard deserved what he got. Apparently some young thugs turned over his garage a month or two ago and the insurance company won't pay up. Even when I told him that he wasn't getting the reward unless he testified for the defence in court, he wouldn't budge.'

Lavender is the equivalent of a pit bull when it comes to looking after me.

I ladled more casserole onto her plate. Unfortunately, it didn't keep her quiet.

'Joe's been trying to get you all day – he's going off his head with worry. He's upset, and I think he suspects about you and Jack.'

'So what? Joe and I aren't an item.'

'Your problem is you always throw your hat into the ring for the wrong man. You instructed Robert Girvan. You should have asked for Eddie – you know he's a better lawyer.'

'He's an alcoholic, Lavender. My life is on the line. I can't afford to be sympathetic, not even for you.'

'Jack Deans is a dipsomaniac, Brodie, but it seems to be one rule for him and another for everyone else. Any sane person would have taken Joe to Inverness. He's the one who'll always be there for you, always protect you. There is absolutely no way that Bancho would have arrested you if Joe had been there. You can trust Eddie and Joe not to stab you in the back – can you say the same for the other two? Did you ever stop to ask yourself how Bancho knew where to find you?'

Sweat started to break out on my top lip as a wave of heat ran through my body. The kitchen was airless and I'd left the cooker on. I switched it off and opened the sash window. It made little difference.

The whiff of a neighbour's barbecue came wafting in. It was approaching seven and my neighbour and his girlfriend were having fun. She'd changed into white shorts that rode up the crack of her ample backside and made her look ridiculous to everyone except him. He was better-looking than she was, but he looked at her like a cat who'd got the cream.

A sharp pain sliced through my heart and I slammed down the window. I could live with the heat.

'I told Joe that I'd make sure you go down to see him tonight, Brodie.'

'So, that's why you hogged all the wine?'

She ignored that comment. 'I hate to cut and run, Brodie, but I've got places to go.' Lavender pushed her chair away from the table. She looked very smart in a new tailored navy business suit, in spite of the fact that it was two sizes too small. Lavender always squeezed into clothes on the basis that she would slim to fit them.

'I got this free in a packet of cornflakes.' She held a pedometer in her hand. 'It won't do much good. I've eaten far too much.' Lavender was having difficulty squeezing the clip of the pedometer onto her waistband. Eventually she managed by undoing a button.

'What's with the training shoes, Lav?'

'I'm walking everywhere – the only Americans who aren't fat are New Yorkers because they don't drive everywhere.'

'That's a bit of a generalisation, isn't it?' I asked her. 'How many minutes do you think it will take to walk off that second huge portion?'

'About five hours; so I'd better get started.' Lavender reached up and kissed me. 'I'll show myself out – you put some make-up on and go down and see Joe.'

I heard her fumbling in the hallway, putting on her coat. I was determined I was going nowhere, until the laughter from my neighbours' garden drove me out.

Chapter Twenty-Four

I was dead tired as I walked into the Rag Doll.

Unusually, there was no bump and grind music in the background. A crowd had gathered round the large-screen TV. Even the dancers were spellbound. Were Hibs playing in a European cup match I didn't know about?

'Turn the TV off, she's here,' said Moses in an unsubtle stage whisper that only served to draw my attention to the telly.

A really scabby photograph of me filled the screen. I looked as if I had a five o'clock shadow across my jaw. Those media types do it deliberately. If you're the villain of the piece they find a photograph where your eyes are half-shut and you look as shady as hell. In my case they had done their job magnificently.

'Leave it on. She has to know what she's facing.'

Joe overrode Moses. The newscaster's voice told everyone in the pub the same story that they had been listening to since the six o'clock news. I had been arrested and had appeared on petition in Inverness Sheriff Court. I had made no plea or declaration and I had been released on bail.

The piece added that the Law Society accountant Alexandra Cattanach had been found and was recovering in a hospital in Inverness. The plastic blonde reporter added that Miss Cattanach was suffering from extensive injuries and shock. Cue a photograph of the Law Society's Chief Accountant. It was not taken from their files.

'Are they allowed to do that?' a voice asked.

I could barely hear Moses above the rumbles of disgust. The photograph of Alex had been taken this morning.

'It doesn't matter if they're allowed to. They've done it. Brodie? Why didn't you plead not guilty? It looks bad, man.'

'Moses. I was on petition. I'm not allowed to enter a plea of not guilty.'

'Sit yourself down,' said Glasgow Joe as he manhandled me into a seat. 'Turn it off now,' he added, 'I think we've all seen enough. Get Brodie a drink.' He indicated to the girl behind the bar that she should execute as many of these demands as possible.

'I don't want a drink, Joe, and I don't need you to be my nursemaid, Moses.'

'Believe me, I'm not,' he answered.

Joe motioned and the music started up again whilst another lardy lass jumped up and grabbed the pole. I knew the Rag Doll wasn't at the top end of the market, but it always looked like a WeightWatchers meeting in here. This one's thighs were shaking in time and her cellulite held the tune, but I was in no mood to be superior tonight. Anyway, her clients seemed to love her, as usual. I looked across the table towards Moses. His hands were very white, and his nails were immaculate in their black polish as always; even his cuticles stood to attention. His splayed fingers were keeping control of a pile of papers. My mobile rang, and I went to answer it just before he took it out of my hand.

'We need to talk about these,' he said.

I knew what they were.

I'd handed enough of them out in my time.

They were mandates. Instructions from clients written on odd scraps of paper, all of them telling me that I was no longer wanted. They had found a bigger, brighter lawyer, or, at the very least, one who wasn't more likely to end up in jail than they were.

'Look at them, Brodie.'

'I don't want to,' I whinged.

'I know you don't, but we have to deal with it. All of the Dark Angels are going to Bridget Nicholson. I can't understand it. After I sorted out Bruce, they should all be shit-scared of me – something bigger must be happening. Is that bastard Robert Girvan enticing them away?'

'Robert? I know he's planning on working with Bridget and has done a lot for her already, but he's loyal, Moses. I'm not comfortable with him around, but I trust him. To be fair, clients wouldn't take much bribing at the moment – they're rightly terrified of you and what you might do to them.'

'True – but this just seems like an organised plan of attack on you. The Angels started handing these to me even before the news had hit the papers or the TV. I just wondered who'd told them.'

'Bad news travels fast.'

'It's not that quick – unless it's from a text. With you instructing Girvan, Brodie, you've given him credibility. I was surprised by your tactics, but thought you must know what you're doing.' He flapped the mandates as he spoke. 'Now I'm not so sure. Why didn't you instruct Eddie Gibb? He's good, he supports the right team, and I know he wouldn't have stabbed you in the back.'

'You're guessing, Moses. It's all any of us can do just now. Is there anything we can do about the mandates?'

'No. I can't ask them to go back to you. You've given Robert Girvan an endorsement I never would have. Funny thing is, the only Dark Angel you're still acting for is the Alchemist. I don't know whether he's pleased with you or frightened of me after the Bruce farce.'

'What's happening with that?' I had to ask.

'I handed myself in – but Bancho wasn't there. Now we know where he was – chasing after you.

Anyway, some radge interviewed me. As usual I said nothing, and Bancho is still otherwise occupied. But he's going to come after me. It's just a matter of time.'

'Well, I'm glad I can be of some assistance, even if it only buys you a few weeks.'

'I'm in no danger even if it went to court – no witness is going to turn up. The worrying thing is Bancho thinks he's got a shot at taking me out. He's not answering any messages left in the chat rooms for him and some Mr Big is muscling in on my patch. I think he's got Bancho in his pocket.'

Joe put down a steaming cup of espresso in front of me; he'd made it himself and it was in the nice cups he kept in his flat.

'You're drinking too much coffee, Brodie,' Moses admonished.

'Why do you say that? Are my teeth getting stained?' I rubbed my finger self-consciously over my front teeth.

'No – you're wired. You need to calm down.'

'I am knackered; I need every legal stimulant I can get my hands on. I've got to find the man who attacked Cattanach, stop my practice from going down the toilet, and, on top of that, my trousers are getting too tight because I can't find the time to do anything about it. Look...'

I pulled at a muffin top that was just beginning to creep over my trousers.

'I've got things to do, people to see, keep in touch.' Moses got up to leave. He touched me on the cheek as he left – it was somewhere between a pinch and a caress.

193

'Joe,' he said as he went out, 'I'm going. I want an update on that stuff we were talking about. Catch you later.'

Moses swaggered out of the Rag Doll. His presence parted the crowd and the last I saw of him was his full-length leather coat swinging in the wind.

'He's some boy,' said Joe as we both looked out after him.

'He thinks he's a man, Joe.'

'Well, that's where he's wrong, and it's not the first mistake he's made. Mind you, Moses doesn't have a monopoly on being an arse.'

'What do you mean?' I asked, waiting for the insult that was surely coming my way.

'Where do I start? You seem to be drawn to people who are going to stab you in the back. Jack Deans – how much did he get paid for tipping off the news?'

'It could have been anyone.'

'Grow up, Brodie. He's in the business – why do you think he's suddenly so interested in you? It doesn't matter how good Girvan is in court, because if this gets to court then we both know you're fucked. Any jury is going to take one look at Alex Cattanach and they want someone to pay – the person holding the tab will be the numpty in the dock, and Duncan Bancho is determined that it's going to be you.'

I needed to get out of this conversation. 'Frank's transferring down to Edinburgh – he'll be here before the end of next week,' I offered Joe as a diversionary tactic.

'I know. He sent me a text – it's the first good

news I've heard in a long time.'

'What about your girlfriend?' I said in what I hoped was an offhand manner.

'Who?'

'Your girlfriend.'

'Oh – you – mean Tricia?'

He coughed as he said her name and it was obvious he wanted to change the subject. I was puzzled by my feelings. It was if my heart had become warmer. Joe's girlfriend couldn't be a great shag if a text from Frank was the best thing that had happened to him recently.

'Frank told me about the list as well – have you done anything about it?'

'I haven't had time.'

'What do you mean? You haven't had time? You're sitting here doing fuck all. You've got to get your arse into gear, Brodie – there is nothing more important right now than clearing yourself.'

'I'm just out the cells, Joe – I don't intend to sit on my hands but I'm exhausted.'

'Well, it's a good job one of us isn't. I phoned Donna Diamond.'

I stared at the list in front of me. Donna Diamond's name was well down.

'I would have started at the top – alphabetically,' I told him.

'That's why I said you're not to rely on amateurs. I checked with some people I know and, looking at Donna's background, I thought she was a likely candidate.'

'Why? Because she's a lesbian?'

'Is she? He? Christ, I can't keep up. Anyway, no – it was because he was a rugby player before his sex-change operation. They both played at the same club – different teams, of course – and he, I mean she, never matched the illustrious career Alex had.'

'This list isn't taken from Cattanach's phone book, Joe – it's the contact details of supposedly bent lawyers that she was investigating.'

'I know that, you stroppy bint – but Donna Diamond was reported to the Procurator Fiscal after Cattanach went in on a routine enquiry. They discovered anomalies in the client's accounts of thirty thousand grand.'

'That's not very much, Joe.'

'I know – but it was the sum needed to fund his sex-change operation.' Joe was still messing his words up. 'He swore he was going to pay it back one way or another, but, of course, Cattanach didn't give Donna – or David, as he was known before – the chance. Donna – Christ – David has been trying to contact Alex, to the point where Cattanach's secretary has accused her of stalking. A report was made to the police about him. Her.'

'What does that say about the list? I haven't been charged, nor have I stalked Cattanach.'

'Before you start with the "why me?" crap, Alex didn't write Donna's name in blood and shit on her hospital wall. Donna, as far as we know, did not admit to the police that she was within three miles of the victim on the night of the attack. Do you want me to go on?'

Chastened, I shook my head. I didn't know how to respond to Joe's accusations because, much as it pained me to admit it, even to myself, I had made a right cock-up of this case.

'Cheer up, Brodie. I've made an appointment to see Donna in her office at nine thirty tomorrow. Lavender has arranged cover for the courts, so you don't have to worry. I thought I'd come and collect you on the trike and we can go for a run or we can catch a show. I've checked the weather; it's supposed to be fair.'

'Do we have to, Joe?' I felt too embarrassed to go anywhere.

'You're going to get your fancy gear on and we are going out to paint the town after we see David. Donna. If you hide, people will think you're guilty; you can't let the bastards grind you down.'

I looked at him, hoping he was joking, but he wasn't. He was there for me again. Just as he always was. His lips were set in a grim line but still his mouth looked generous. His hair was ruffled, lived in, and it hung thickly about his face.

'You can do it, Brodie. You've got the heart of Bruce,' he told me.

'Robert the Bruce or Blind Bruce?' I asked him.

'Doesn't matter, Brodie – just make sure you survive.'

Chapter Twenty-Five

'Feel free to stare, Brodie.'

The person in front of me urged me to give in to my curiosity, but it was said sarcastically. I wished that I could have risen above the peepshow mentality, but I was spellbound. Donna Diamond was a commanding presence, six feet tall, taller in her chunky wooden sandals.

'You're prettier than I thought was possible – I mean for an ex rugby player in a pink floral dress,' said Joe.

'Thanks, Joe, I'm flattered, but there was a lot more to sexual-reassignment surgery than simply cutting off my cock.'

Joe crossed his legs. The clock on the wall behind Donna's desk showed that it was 10 a.m. The client waiting room was empty except for her wife (ex-wife?), who doubled as her receptionist. We'd been in her offices in the New Town for fifteen minutes and the phone hadn't rung once. Business was bad.

Donna was a conveyancing solicitor, so our paths had never crossed. Obviously I'd heard of her. She was slightly more notorious than I was, an unenviable accolade.

'You said on the phone you wanted to speak to me about Alex Cattanach? It's a terrible business.'

I stared into Donna's face. Her green eyes were shiny with tears. Was she just a great actress? In an unguarded moment, my thoughts must have been transparent, for Donna answered my unasked question.

'You're here to find out if I did it. Well, I hate to disappoint you, but the answer's "no".'

Marjorie, Donna's wife, walked in carrying a tray laden with teacups. Marjorie wore a plain navy trouser suit, which looked as if it had cost no more than twenty-five pounds from a supermarket. Her grey hair was short and unflattering, she wore no make-up and the lines on her face were etched by something that was probably worry. The cup rattled in its saucer, and I took the tea from Marjorie's hand.

'What a lovely ring,' I said to her as I looked at her hand. I don't normally comment on rings worn by the wives of solicitors because they are pretty standard – three diamonds in a straight line, the success of a practice judged by the size of the diamonds. As children are added, the career can be traced by the size of the diamonds on the eternity ring.

The three diamonds in Marjorie's engagement ring, however, were sizeable and well cut. This was a ring to shout about.

'We've seen better days,' Marjorie answered, looking at the piece of jewellery.

'Unfortunately, Marge is right,' interrupted Donna. 'As David Ross, I never failed to meet expectations in the boardroom or on the rugby pitch. Let's just say Donna's never been given the same chance. Except by you, dear.'

Donna's manicured hand reached out and stroked Marjorie's. A look of genuine affection passed between them. All I could see was that it cost more per week to do Donna's nails than Marjorie paid for her suit.

'I had a very successful practice doing conveyancing, wills and executries – but after thirty years of keeping Donna a secret I couldn't go on. I told Marjorie first, of course. I would rather be hated for what I was than loved for something I wasn't.'

'How did she take it?' I asked. Joe was busy holding the door to let the long-suffering Marjorie out.

'Badly. She left me. I was warned that would happen – most transsexuals lose their families and the suicide rate for pre-op men is horrendous. I tried to survive on my own – you can't have the operation unless you live as a woman for a year. I couldn't take the loneliness. I reversed my breast-augmentation surgery and begged Marjorie to take me back.'

'It must have been hard to keep your business going,' I commented, thinking of myself, and how hard I was finding it to keep my focus on clients.

'Well, I can't deny that the shock people got when they saw me sometimes drove them away. I can't help but think if only I'd had the courage to stick it out the first time, it would have been different. I'd be further along the road.'

I didn't want to disabuse her, but the shock of seeing their sporty macho lawyer turn into a drag queen at any time other than Hallowe'en was not a good marketing ploy to launch at any client. The few enlightened souls who would have stayed surely must have been confused when Cinderella turned back into Prince Charming.

'I knew Alex before all this happened,' Donna went on. 'We were members of the same rugby club. I never attained her achievements on the rugby pitch, though. It's funny, but as David that would have irked me. Now, as Donna, I find my old personality traits have gone. I used to love restoring vintage Porsches – I have one in the garage at home, the bonnet is still up, but I haven't touched it in years.' Donna held her hand in front of her face and examined her blood-red talons.

I tried to move her on. 'So you knew Alex socially?'

'Yes, in fact she was rather kind to me when the news first came out – it was only later that things changed – although, to be fair to her, it wasn't personal.'

Joe was standing by the window looking out onto the street, checking for traffic wardens. He wasn't wearing his kilt, and leaning against the window in his black leather bike trousers, he looked like sex on legs. What was happening to me? Had Lavender being putting something in my tea? The white T-shirt Joe wore was sparkling and tight across his chest. He had obviously found the time to work out in amongst luring Tricia.

Donna was staring too.

'I hope you don't mind me asking,' she began, talking directly to Joe. 'But what conditioner do you use? Your hair looks so soft and silky.'

Joe shifted uncomfortably, his size-thirteen leather boots hopped, as if the floor had suddenly become red hot. Donna was out of her chair in a flash. In her heels she matched Joe inch for inch – in some departments.

'What a lovely shine it has.' Her hand reached out to touch it. I was sure Joe was going to back away, but he stood like a patient Labrador being stroked by a dangerous toddler. His eyes implored me to intervene, but I was enjoying myself too much.

'Don't worry, Joe – I'm not going to pounce on you. I didn't have the surgery because I was gay,

201

I had it because I knew I needed to be a woman,'
Donna assured him.

I couldn't deny it, the thought had crossed my
mind. Not only was I politically incorrect, I was
also bloody confused.

Donna was seated at her desk again and I
hoped she was ready to tell me the story of her
run-in with Alex Cattanach. Sadly, she wasn't.
Donna was in the mood to talk and talk about
anything except what I was there to hear.

'After the op,' she went on, 'I found that I was
gay. I'm sorry to disappoint you, Joe, but I'm more
likely to jump on Brodie's bones than yours.'

Now it was my turn to squirm.

'What about traffic wardens?' I hissed.

'I can afford the fine.' He smiled that slow,
infuriating smile of his.

'So, that's another thing you have in common
with Alex,' I went on.

'What's that? You've lost me, Brodie.'

'Well, you and Alex are lesbian rugby players.'

'I've told you that when I became Donna I lost
interest in masculine pursuits. I can't even bear
to watch it on television.'

'What went wrong? If Alex was one of the few
people who understood your predicament, how
come you're on petition?'

Donna took a long sip of tea. Was she deliberat-
ing on whether or not to tell me?

'Marjorie! Marjorie, darling! Come in here for
a moment.'

The thudding sound on the floor told me that
the long-suffering Marjorie was obeying the
command.

'What is it, dear?' The smile on Marjorie's face told me that she would have liked to have stuffed the pen she was holding up Donna's nose. That happens in the best of relationships.

'Our conversation last night – remember we discussed changing lawyers?'

Marjorie nodded obediently.

'Well, I've decided to use Brodie's firm.'

I squirmed and forced a smile upon my face. Anything Donna now told me was subject to client confidentiality and I couldn't use it in my defence. Knowing this, why did I agree? Perhaps because preparing a defence is like untying the Gordian knot – untangling the first knot would let me know it could be done. If Donna did tell me anything, I could find another way of using it. My gut was singing and I knew she was the key.

Marjorie left the room, consigned to her lonely spot in reception beside a phone that was unlikely to ring, unless it was her mother.

'Have you got a copy of your petition?' I asked.

Donna reached into the top drawer of her desk and handed me a rather thin file. I tried not to look disappointed.

'Is this all there is?'

Her eyes shifted from side to side and I could easily tell she was lying.

'Yes.'

I had to accept her answer for the moment.

'I see you were formerly represented by Bridget Nicholson?'

Joe groaned so loudly that Donna looked at him sharply and asked, 'Is that a problem?'

'No, it's not a problem – but you'll have to sign

a mandate.'

Thankfully there was a copy of the petition on file.

'You embezzled thirty thousand pounds from the Royal Bank of Scotland. That's a pitiable sum really, Donna – why so little? McCoy at least took ten million.'

'I don't regard myself as in the same category as Mr McCoy,' she threw back sniffily.

'At least his theft was worth it. Unless you're going to tell me Cattanach's made a mistake – and I think we both know that whatever failings Alex had, ineptitude wasn't one of them – why so little?'

'This surgery isn't cheap,' Donna informed me. 'Especially when you get it done twice.'

I was looking at her ample bosom as she spoke. I wasn't sure why I was being so cruel – but there was something about her that really annoyed me.

'When I started out down this path, money was no object. I was naïve, I didn't foresee the effect this would have on my business but I prided myself on being a good lawyer and I thought at least some of my clients would remain loyal.'

'Big mistake,' I said. 'Clients are rarely loyal.'

'Too true – even my best friends took their business away. They acted as if transsexuality was a disease they would catch. Even to admit to having known me or been my friend would be tantamount to an admission of ... well, homosexuality, really. They didn't understand any of it.'

'So, you had no money and you decided to steal it.'

'I would have paid it back – but I didn't get the chance. Alex came in on a routine inspection and noted the fraudulent loan application to the Royal Bank of Scotland.'

'Was it worth it?'

'Do you mean were the hours of electrolysis, the voice therapy, the hormone treatment worth it – or are you talking about the thirteen hours it took for a San Francisco surgeon to peel off my face, shave my brow bone, feminise my skull, shorten my chin and shave my Adam's apple?' she asked.

'When you put it like that, Donna, getting your cock chopped off sounds easy.' Joe smiled at her and broke the atmosphere.

'I meant, was it worth losing your practising certificate?' I brought the conversation back round again.

'There was no choice. I had to do it.'

'Did you attack Alex Cattanach?' Unfortunately I already knew the answer I'd be given.

'No – and if it hadn't been for the routine inspection the loan would have been repaid. No one would have been any the wiser.'

'So, Cattanach spoiled your plans?'

'Unlike you, I'm not into revenge, Brodie.'

'You think I attacked Alex Cattanach?'

'If I did I wouldn't be alone – but I'd say you probably have a lot of people on your little hate list; I don't think you'd be the forgiving type exactly. Anyway, we all know that the firm's in trouble and that you're in the thick of it.'

She had a point, but it wasn't one I wanted to listen to. Dragging Joe away from his newly found comfort zone, I left. None the wiser, and no closer to confirming my innocence.

Chapter Twenty-Six

Any little hope I might have had of finding Alex's attacker and clearing my name quickly was extinguished after our visit to Donna. To ensure that the day wasn't a complete write-off, I intended to pack a great deal in.

When you've a lot to accomplish, start with the one thing you don't want to do. Which is why I found myself outside Edinburgh Sheriff Court at 11.30 a.m., waiting to go in and look for Bridget Nicholson.

'Are you scared or something?' asked Joe as he dropped me off. I wondered how quickly I could get rid of him. I didn't need someone peering into my soul right now.

'No – I was just thinking back to when I first qualified. I hung about here dreaming of shaping a successful career.'

He didn't come back with the immediate reassurance I wanted. 'Maybe you got it all too quickly, Brodie – in the past wee while you've hardly had time to draw breath.'

'I'm a big girl now, Joe – if you ever actually thought I could take care of myself, you'd know that you can't keep every bit of wind off my face. I'm okay. This is my turf. Why don't you go? I'll phone if something comes up.'

'Well, if you're sure you're okay. The brewery's delivering today and I want to be able to explain why we don't need that much beer from them.' The Rag Doll was always busy, but Joe could buy alcohol from the cash and carry cheaper than he could from the brewery. Naturally, the brewery didn't like their profits going to someone else, so they tied publicans up in shitty contracts. A man like Joe had no qualms about breaching this; it was just sometimes he had to do some sweet-talking to get out of trouble.

'Just go.'

'I'll leave you the trike. You give me the keys to the Fat Boy and I'll fix the oil leak. How's that?' He handed me the keys with the beam of the Man Who Will Sort Things Out. I had a few men in my life who thought like that, but when push came to shove it was down to me to get my arse out of the fire. So I agreed with him, even though I hate driving the trike because it's so conspicuous. Even worse, you don't wear a helmet on one of those, and I was still trying to avoid seeing Duncan Bancho. The Sheriff Court was quiet. The hustle of the morning was over and all parties were set-tling into procedural matters. The security guards looked at me out of the corners of their eyes, probably afraid to say hello in case they had to arrest me later on. My bike boots thudded as I walked along the empty corridors. I may have been in trouble, but I didn't want to announce my presence, so I tried to walk on my tiptoes, and that's how Bridget Nicholson found me – creep-ing along the corridors like a thief in the night.

'Brodie,' she said calmly behind me.

I was caught short and had just enough time to force a smile onto my face as I turned. My cheeks hurt already.

'Bridget – I was looking for you.'

'That was nice, Brodie. I knew you'd understand that I needed to know about Alex.'

I pushed the mandate I had for her back into my pocket.

'Yeah – well, I knew that you two were close.'

She held my eye steadily.

'That woman was the love of my life for over two years. I seriously thought she was the one. We even talked about a civil partnership early next year.'

Well, that was one wedding I wouldn't have been invited to. However, it was still interesting that Bridget knew enough to make her certain that the partnership would never happen. What did she need to know from me if she already had information about the state of Alex?

'I would have phoned you, Bridget, but I wasn't sure what reception I would get – you know, with the TV coverage.'

She stared at me before adding, 'And the fact that the police have charged you with the attack.' It was a statement, not a question. 'I know we haven't always gotten along in the past, Brodie, but, actually, I don't think you are anywhere near capable of attacking Alex like that.'

Bridget started to walk along the corridor as she finished her words. I had difficulty keeping up with her. I got the feeling she was running for cover and I wasn't objecting. I didn't want anyone else witnessing our little téte-à-téte. We stopped on the top corridor outside the agents' room, staring out over the rooftops of Edinburgh. It never ceases to amaze me how many trees can grow in guttering.

'My love for Alex was almost like a sickness, Brodie. Have you ever felt like that?' Thankfully, Bridget didn't actually want an answer. She wouldn't have got one anyway. 'She was everything I wanted, and she just dropped me.'

A large blob of snot dripped from her nose. She was too upset to do anything about it but I watched it dangle up and down as she breathed. I raked in my pockets and found my usual stock of grubby paper hankies. She wasn't so upset that she didn't notice that the one I offered her was rank.

'Don't worry, it's clean,' I assured her.

'I just feel so guilty – there was such a bond between us and I can't bear to see her like that. When I saw the television clips, the newspaper – do you think she'll be upset? Can she feel upset? Did she mention me? Did she give you any message? Any sign?'

Bridget was beside herself, pulling at me for answers. If she was putting on a show, as I strongly suspected, she was doing bloody well.

'Look, I don't know what anyone has told you, Bridget, so I don't really know what to say.'

'Nothing – they've told me nothing because I'm not family. I am the only family she had! Her father's dead and her mother is in a nursing home and thinks she's seventeen. I need to know, Brodie. I need to know. I can't pick up scraps from the media. I need to know.'

Why did she need to know? Because she had loved her? Because she still loved her? Or because she needed to know what clues, what evidence, Alex Cattanach was spewing out?

I had to tell her something.

Best to keep it to a something that I couldn't be tripped up on at a later date.

'I'm not an expert, Bridget, but it's bad. It looked pretty bad to me.' There was no point sugar-coating the little I did know.

'Alex has Cotard's Syndrome. It's very rare. If you went to see her, she'd probably just think you were a ghost. The facial scarring she has? She looks as if she has been attacked by some really evil bastard. It's dire – even worse than on telly. It really is much more serious than a simple nervous breakdown – they can't give her tablets because they don't work, not with Cotard's. The doctor – Doctor MacPherson – told me they would start electric-shock treatment because sometimes that's helpful.'

Bridget looked stunned.

I didn't think she was acting this time, but I guessed, even if she was the perpetrator, the facts would still seem cold and shocking.

'Thanks for telling me, Brodie – I know it wasn't easy. I've got to pull myself together. I'm starting a trial in ten minutes.'

A silence fell between us. I felt a slight niggle of guilt over the fact that I hadn't told her the complete truth about Alex self-harming and writing my name with her bodily fluids. I was just so pleased Bridget was being nice to me, that she thought I was innocent. Pathetic, I know; but sometimes we all yearn to be liked.

'I'm sorry that we've been at loggerheads

recently,' I said rather pitifully.

'It was my fault as much as yours,' she graciously admitted. 'Maybe I was just tetchy over the Alex situation. It doesn't matter now; my star is rising.'

And yours is falling. It was unsaid, but it lay between us like a brick wall.

'I'm grateful for your help, Brodie – is there anything I can do for you?'

I shoved the mandate from Donna Diamond further back into my pocket. Why spoil a good thing? I searched around for something non-committal to say. 'I don't suppose you've the name of a good cleaner?'

I had to say something.

She paused and thought for a while.

'Actually, I do. I have a really good cleaner. Give me your number and I'll get the firm he works for to call you. I think they're called Fresh as a Daisy, or something naff like that.'

I reached into my left pocket where I kept my business cards that had my mobile number on them. The business cards in my right pocket had Lavender's number – only the inner circle got the former.

'Bridget! Bridget!'

The sound burned me even before I turned to see three Dark Angels placed at the end of the corridor. This sight was a pain in the arse for two reasons. Firstly, Dark Angels don't appear in court, at least not this frequently. It meant that Moses had lost Duncan Bancho's protection, so he couldn't act as a buffer for me. Secondly, the Dark Angels formed the basis of my practice. It was a sign, if one were needed, that I had been wounded very badly.

A brave face was needed.

'How's it going, boys?'

They were young enough to flush with embarrassment. Bringing up the rear was the Alchemist. On his arm was Blind Bruce, as he would forever after be called. His handicap hadn't improved his temper.

'You're a bastard, Brodie McLennan. You saw what happened but you're just like the rest of these wee gobshites – you'll say nothing for fear of upsetting Moses fucking Tierney.'

'Shut the fuck up, Bruce.'

The Alchemist tried to keep him in line. I was desperate to get away. I didn't want Bridget to ask me what he was talking about. I didn't think I could lie if she asked me directly what I had seen. Blind Bruce had applied for criminal injuries compensation, but no one was likely to be convicted, and, because of his criminal record, he was on a hiding to nothing.

'Where are you going, Brodie?' he went on. 'Don't you have time to see a fucking good lawyer in action?'

Bridget did not have the grace to look embarrassed. I hoped that I would be a bigger person in her situation, but I'd already forgotten that I'd felt quite friendly towards her a moment before. The mandate burned a hole in my pocket, but to give it to her now would look churlish. I still wanted to, though.

'Bruce, will you take a telling?' interrupted the Alchemist. 'If you carry on like this, Moses will have you out on your arse – and then where will you be?'

Bruce managed to hold his tongue. Heavy bandages covered his empty eye sockets. Strangely to me, he still wore the Dark Angels' uniform. His nails were painted black, and they were perfect. Someone was taking good care of him. Blind Bruce defined Moses completely: Moses as the two-faced god. He took away Bruce's old life and yet gave him another. I couldn't justify his behaviour, but Blind Bruce looked cleaner and better cared for than he would have in an NHS hospital.

The Tannoy system broke into everyone's thoughts.

'Bridget Nicholson to Court Nine.'

'I have to go, Brodie,' she said. 'Thanks for your help.'

The Dark Angels turned to follow her, creating a stir as they walked. As their long leather coats flapped in the breeze, they made Bridget look like an alternative Pied Piper.

'Brodie! I need to see you,' the Alchemist called back. He was obviously trying to ingratiate himself with Moses.

I didn't have time for him at the moment.

'Call Lavender and arrange a time.'

They all walked too fast for Blind Bruce, and he was left behind. I stayed still, watching them all, watching him, but not wanting to engage him as he traversed the corridor. He stumbled like an old man, his cane clicking on the floor. I didn't take my eyes from him, not even for a second. It was a form of self-flagellation, though I don't know why I had to do it to myself, given that there was a fucking queue waiting to kick me.

The sunshine hit me as soon as I got out of court.

A good day's work.

I'd lost a livelihood but hopefully gained a cleaner.

Chapter Twenty-Seven

'Jesus, Brodie – that's loud enough to wake the dead.'

I pulled the trike to a stop outside the coffee box at the top of Leith Walk. It was half past one and I had time to kill before getting to my next appointment. Thank God Lizzie was already brewing the espresso. It was making me feel perkier every step closer I took.

Lizzie leaned out of the small police box that had been turned into a coffee kiosk and threw her arms around me. I felt my neck snap as she pulled me forward in a bear hug.

'Ow, Lizzie – your ring is caught in my hair. God, it's not another engagement one, is it?'

She tried to extract her finger painlessly from the coils and twisting spirals that my hair had turned into. As Lizzie fought to be free, I noted that she wasn't answering the engagement comment. She probably couldn't keep track.

She squinted her eyes at me in the sunshine. 'I saw you on TV last night.'

'You always knew I'd be a star, Lizzie.'

214

Lizzie turned to finish making my coffee; she had made me a macchiato just the way I liked it.

'Your gorgeous mother stopped by this morning,' she informed me. 'She was asking if I'd seen you. Apparently she's worried about what direction your life is going in.'

'That's some bloody cheek she's got.'

'I don't know why you're like that – I think she's fab.'

I was relieved to see the next barista walking up the cobbled pedestrian area in front of St Mary's Cathedral. I turned away from the coffee box a bit and over to the large statue of the hand with the locust upon it and sat down, carefully avoiding the insect. The coffee was reconnecting my system; I felt as though I could think straight. Even a short trip on the bike usually helped; the journey to Castle Huntly would definitely do me good as long as Lizzie didn't try to come with me.

In the sunshine, the trike looked like something from the builder bike-off competition. The copious amounts of chrome gleamed. The paintwork was more expensive than that of a Porsche. The petrol tank was shaped like a coffin; it was a bugger to fill. I hoped Joe hadn't left me short.

There was something entrancing about the warm wind on my face, despite the fact that I was heading to an appointment I didn't really want to have. Even the fact that I would look like the scarecrow from *The Wizard of Oz* was of no consequence compared to the sheer, sensuous pleasure of driving through the Scottish countryside on a summer's afternoon.

The trike was not fast, so the scent of the fields reached me. It wasn't idyllic – I had to face the smell of shit, the real odour of the countryside, assaulting my nostrils. The roads to Castle Huntly were clear and I made good time in spite of the lack of speed.

It looked almost like Cinderella's castle in Disneyworld. I understood why the tabloids made such a fuss about the place – it didn't seem quite real. As I drove in, the trike attracted a great deal of attention from the drugs barons and crooked accountants alike who made up most of the inmates of this low-security prison.

'Oi! Would you mind keeping your eye on my trike?' I shouted to a trustie who was supervising gardening duties. He nodded quickly enough, but the lascivious look he gave the trike put me on my guard.

'Where are you from?' I asked him.

'Edinburgh,' he replied. I waited for a bit more information. 'Muirhouse,' he eventually said.

Bull's eye.

'That trike belongs to Glasgow Joe – do you know him? He has the Rag Doll.'

No explanation was really necessary beyond Joe's name. I could have left the keys with the trike and it still would have been there when I got out. I went on my way knowing that Joe's toy was safe.

'It's like a holiday camp in here,' I said when McCoy came out to see me a few minutes later.

'My condolences, my dear. You must have frequented many substandard establishments.'

McCoy was dressed in a blue and green Paisley-patterned silk smoking jacket; on his feet were poncey velvet slippers that he'd probably got from Harrods. An open-necked shirt and a cravat convinced me that I was about to interview Noel Coward. He carried *The Times* under his arm, and I wondered who had ironed it for him. McCoy's hair was grey, beautifully cut and slicked back.

'So what brings you here, Miss McLennan?'

'You know who I am?'

'I have the pleasure of being a friend of your mother and I watch the news.'

'Should I be calling you "Uncle"?'

'I said I was a friend of your mother's, my dear, not a client. If it will put your mind at rest, I met her through Malcolm.'

Now we both knew where we stood.

'How is he, by the way?' continued McCoy. 'I heard the silly old bugger had gotten in tow with a rapidly ageing dancer.'

'You heard right. At the moment he's recovering from a nose job.'

'Silly girl, when will he learn? By the way, I don't know if you're aware of it, my dear, but my acquaintance with your family has not always been a happy one. Your father? One of the last sentences he handed out was mine. I came back from South America because my lawyer had promised me the deal of the century – two to four years. Your father gave me ten.'

I thought I'd be on thin ice if I said that the sentence was the one thing my father had done that I approved of. Instead, I made an encouraging noise of condolence.

'I suppose you want my help clearing your

name, Miss McLennan? But, tell me this – why the hell should I?'

The bitter old queen. I was sure he knew something, even if I didn't know exactly what it was. If he wouldn't talk, would it matter? He had been banged up for years, maybe he was out of the loop. I wasn't sure but my intuition told me that he knew something.

'I don't know why you should help me – maybe because Malcolm and Kailash would like you to? Is there anything you want from me?' I was willing to trade. 'I'm not helping you escape,' I added hastily.

'My dear – even the most senior prison officers cannot put an exact number on the amount of inmates who escape from open prison, but they are prepared to admit that the number is in excess of seven hundred each year. You give me no credit if you think I could not get out of here if I so wished.'

I needed to get back on track.

'You employed Robert Girvan?'

'Yes, almost exclusively on a full-time basis, but now he's working with Bridget Nicholson. She's offered him a partnership, I believe.'

Fleetingly, a dark look crossed his eyes, then disappeared so quickly I wondered if it was my imagination.

'If I share some information with you, we're both agreed that you are in my debt?' he asked.

'You have my word,' I quickly replied.

'My dear, the word of a MacGregor may not be worth as much as you might hope. But give me your word as Kailash's daughter and I will tell you what you need to know.'

I reached out and shook his hand. I refrained from spitting on it.

'You know, of course, that Alex Cattanach is a lesbian? You may not know that she was once an alcoholic. She had great difficulty coming to terms with her sexuality. Alex is very together professionally, an absolute machine. I like to pride myself that no one else could have sent me down.'

'Everyone knows Alex is a lesbian now, so she can't have been getting blackmailed,' I pointed out.

'Correct, my dear – but what if she was the blackmailer?'

'Upright, poker-up-her-arse Alex Cattanach would never be into that sort of thing.'

'An unfortunate turn of phrase, my dear. She never utilised a poker in her private life, as far as I am aware, but she did have certain video evidence that was damaging to certain parties.'

'Video?'

'Pre-DVD. It's an old, old scandal but still hot enough to have blown the parties' lives apart.'

'I know what a video is – could this one be hot enough to kill for?'

'Most certainly,' McCoy replied.

'You know who it is, don't you?'

He nodded.

'You're not going to tell me, are you?'

He shook his head this time.

'If you are as good as you think you are, you'll find out, and if you're not, then you're safe,' he told me.'

'Safe? You know better than anyone that I face

a jail sentence and what that would be like.'

'It's better than Alex Cattanach's life.'

'True. You don't have to tell me who it is in the video – just give me a few more details.'

'You're pushy, aren't you?' McCoy mused. 'Still, you wouldn't be Kailash's daughter if you weren't. The video was filmed several years ago in a solicitor's office. It involves one of the "stars" in sexual acts with clients. The video was kept in a drawer in the solicitor's office. Alex Cattanach found it and, as far as I know, threatened to act upon her information.'

McCoy stared at me, smiled, then turned and walked out. I was left flabbergasted – and extremely pissed off. That bastard could pick up the phone and clear my name right now.

But he wouldn't, and he was clearly revelling in that.

McCoy may have claimed to be a friend of my mother, but, as he left, it was the continuing influence of my dead father that left me wondering.

Chapter Twenty-Eight

'Don't hog the whole bed, Brodie – shift over.'

I ignored what I thought was someone else's voice, the remainder of a dream that I couldn't pull from its edges. My bedroom was completely dark, thanks to the blackout blinds. I turned in my sleep, pulling more than half the duvet with me. I felt safe and cocooned. Lately, I hadn't been sleeping well I thought it might have something to do with the amount of booze I had been consuming, but I'd still rather blame the light nights or a lumpy mattress. Anyway, tonight I had resisted the temptation to drink myself a little way into slumber – and it must have worked. I had obviously fallen into a deep sleep because my dreams were certainly vivid.

I couldn't get the dream back, but reality was kicking in.

I had gone to bed alone and now it definitely felt as if there was a man there.

'I told you to shift over.'

Jack Deans prodded me none too gently, almost pushing me over the edge of the bed. I hung there precariously whilst he settled himself. He had definitely not practised abstinence, the smell of whisky ran round my heart.

'Jack. Jack?'

'Don't scream, gorgeous; let me explain.'

He put his hand over my mouth. It was hard to breathe. I tried to bite him, but he knew what I was up to. He was almost naked, and through his boxers I could tell he was definitely pleased to see me. I didn't feel like returning the compliment. He brought his mouth close to my ear and whispered. His hot breath sent shivers down my spine; for form's sake I thought I had better continue trying to kick him. Then I heard the words, and any emotion other than fear flew out the window.

'They've found another body, Brodie. Same MO as before, except they didn't find this poor sod in time. It's only a matter of time before

Duncan Bancho turns up here and arrests you. I knew you'd need an alibi, so here I am. The old lock-picking skills are still there – and you should be damn grateful that they are. In more ways than one. I'm not just useful for scaring the cops away.'

He pulled me closer; his hand was still over my mouth and he kissed me on the neck. My body wriggled towards him. It had a mind of its own. With his free hand he reached out to investigate my nakedness further. He didn't seem quite so bothered about my imminent arrest as I was.

'You are gorgeous, Brodie – and I think we should make this look as if we're for real.'

I tried to bite his hand again, but it was more of a nibble. My mouth searched hungrily for his. I was so engrossed I didn't hear the first knock.

'I'll go,' he said. 'You stay here and be quiet.'

Jack grabbed my silky dressing gown and ran to the door. I could hear the mumbled voices coming closer as he led the visitors into my darkened bedroom.

'Just what the fuck do you think we were doing, Duncan?' he said as he came in. 'Do you want details?'

The harsh centre light was now on in the room and I struggled to get my bearings. Through my squinting eyes I could see that Jack looked both obscene and ridiculous. My pink dressing gown was far too short, and impressively it was still sticking out at ninety degrees.

Duncan Bancho nodded towards me.

'Evening, Brodie.'

I sat up in bed, covering myself as much as

possible, and let Jack continue to deal with Bancho as he was doing such an impressive job. As my eyes adjusted to the light I saw things I'd rather not, like the young police constable standing on my dirty knickers that I had dropped by the side of the bed; the tights drying on the mirror along with a selection of grey pants; and, taking pride of place, my home waxing kit, which lay in full view with what looked like a year's worth of pubic hair stuck to the roller.

'Detective Inspector – if you want to speak to Brodie then that's fair enough. You can see that I have been here with her; she has not had the opportunity to commit any crime. If you want she'll hand herself in at a time to be arranged between you, but if you lift her now, then I promise you there will be a story in the papers about police harassment by Sunday. See what that will do to your promotion prospects.'

'Are you threatening me, Deans?'

'I'm just stating the facts, Inspector – so that we're both aware of the score here.'

'I thought you were the lawyer, Brodie? You must be losing your touch if you're letting this has-been fight your battles. By the way – does Joe know this one's shagging you?' Duncan Bancho turned to Jack and looked him up and down, before fingering the edge of my dressing gown. Jack didn't flinch; thankfully, his erection was long gone.

'It might not have been such a clever move to give Brodie an alibi, Deans. Glasgow Joe's a hard jealous bastard – you might have bitten off more than you can chew, smart-arse.'

Jack stared him down.

'Put the light out on your way out, Duncan, and leave us to finish what we started. Think hard on what I said. I think Brodie's cost you a promotion before, hasn't she?'

Bancho slammed the bedroom door on his way out.

From the hallway he shouted, 'I'll be back, Brodie. You've just got a stay of execution, not a full pardon.'

We listened in silence, straining to hear their car drive away.

'Sorry about that last remark, Brodie – he riled me.'

'Was it the comment about being a has-been?'

'Fuck, no; nothing I haven't heard before. No, it's just that we both know he's on his way to tell Glasgow Joe. And he'll enjoy it.'

Jack didn't look obscene any more, just daft in my dressing gown. We looked at each other with embarrassment; we both knew the moment had passed. He left to go to the other room and get dressed properly. In the time he was away, I twiddled my thumbs and wondered where the hell we would go from here.

'Do you fancy a hot chocolate?' I asked him, shouting through. 'It helps me sleep.' I knew that it would be too straightforward for him to answer 'yes' or 'no'.

'I fancied something hot and sweet when I came in here tonight, darlin', but it wasn't drinking chocolate.' He walked back through, pushing his mobile into his trouser pocket.

'Well, that's all that's on offer – and only if you

put some clothes on. You remind me of Donna Diamond. Before the op.'

'How do you know Donna?'

'She's my client. I saw her yesterday morning. I'm representing her in the High Court on the embezzlement charges.'

'Not any more you're not, Brodie,' he told me. 'Do you carry your own fan around to throw shit at?'

'What are you talking about? Has Bridget steamed in again?'

Jack looked at me with a mixture of exasperation and pity. 'Brodie – the person found murdered up Calton Hill a couple of hours ago was Donna Diamond.'

Chapter Twenty-Nine

Pain knocked me down onto a chair.

It was difficult to breathe. Even I was beginning to suspect me.

'She knew more than she told me, Jack.'

'What are you talking about?'

'When I saw her today, I knew that she was important, that she had at least part of the key to all this. Now it's obvious she was acquainted with Cattanach's attacker. Maybe she contacted him after I left and this is the result?'

'Serial killer?'

'Only one person is dead, Jack – he didn't finish Alex Cattanach off. He's learned his lesson; he

225

made sure that Donna Diamond wasn't left the same way.'

'Alex is as good as dead; we wouldn't let an animal suffer the way that she's suffering.'

The doorbell rang, interrupting Jack's words.

'Christ, that was quick. He's sharper off his heels than I would have given him credit for.'

'What do you mean – "that was quick"?'

The doorbell went again; the caller was impatient.

'It's three thirty in the morning. Who's calling at this time?'

'Joe.'

'Why is Joe here?'

'Because I texted him. I believe it's always best to mix some truth with a lie. I knew that Bancho wouldn't be able to wait to tell him about me being here. Believe it or not, I respect Joe too much to let that bastard break the news to him.'

'You're a liar, Jack Deans.'

The doorbell went again. Jack was jumpy but I wouldn't let him answer it.

'You're scared of Joe. That's the, only reason you'd forewarn him. You hate the thought that if it came from someone else, you'd be looking over your shoulder until he decked you.'

'Of course I'm scared of him, Brodie – I'm not fucking brain-dead; but that doesn't alter anything. Until you make up your mind who you want, me or Joe, then I think it's best to play it this way.'

'I didn't know you were on the menu. I didn't know I was faced with having to bloody well "choose". Who put you in charge of deciding what my options are?' The constantly ringing doorbell was playing on my nerves. Joe was only stopping himself from kicking the door in because he knew I was in here; it wasn't enough to stop him irritating the hell out of me though.

'You've always known, Brodie, you've always known that I was waiting for you to snap your fingers. Remember that night outside St Leonard's when you were going in to defend Kailash? That's when I really knew. You got off that bike looking like something wild – you were facing them all, knowing you had a fight on your hands, and you'd never looked more gorgeous.'

'You still thought that even after I hit your dodgy knee with my briefcase?'

'Maybe because of that – you're ballsy and I like that in a woman.'

'Gee, thanks. Talking of ballsy women reminds me of Donna, though, poor sod.' The ringing continued. 'Why don't you answer that door before Joe comes through it?'

I checked in the mirror that I looked decent; letting myself know what my priorities were. Joe came in the open door like a force ten gale. Sweeping me up in his arms, he held me under the light checking for bruises. I hoped Jack hadn't left a love bite on me when I was dozing.

'You're scaring me – and I don't like it,' Joe growled down at me. 'I heard that there had been a murder and that you were involved. I thought...'

'I know what you thought, Joe, and that's maybe my fault,' said Jack.

'Maybe? You sent the buggering text! At first I thought she had been hurt – then I reckoned that

227

even an ill-mannered get like you might have resorted to a call rather than a text for that sort of news,' exploded Joe.

'Sorry,' said Jack, sounding anything but. 'Well, at least she's okay.'

He moved on to busily filling the kettle for tea, obviously not wanting to make eye contact with Joe, who might still be thinking about killing him.

'So – what's the problem?' Joe demanded.

Jack sat down to wait on the kettle boiling, but also to interject some drama into the conversation on his terms.

'Duncan Bancho was coming round to arrest Brodie for the murder of Donna Diamond.'

'Oh, Jesus – did that poor woman not suffer enough?'

'If it's any consolation, Donna's out of her suffering now.'

'I'm not talking about Donna, Deans. No, it's poor Marjorie I'm thinking of. Can you imagine how heartbreaking it would be to lose your husband and gain a narcissistic bossy pal who's better-looking than you? Then there were the other women. Now she has to deal with Donna being dead – what is she supposed to feel, for Christ's sake? The tabloids will have a field day.'

Jack backtracked on what Joe had said, neatly ignoring the comment about the tabloids. 'What do you mean, "other women"?'

'Well, after the snip, Donna was always after other women. That's how she really knew Alex Cattanach, not through rugby at all.'

'Was Donna Alex's lover?' asked Jack.

'No – at least I don't think so. I went out to help

Marjorie with the tea when we were there and she poured her heart out – she was a bit upset about Donna's shenanigans.'

'What are you on about, Joe?' I asked.

'You must have noticed the way she flirted with you, Brodie.'

'No!' I shouted, ignoring how uncomfortable I had been when we were there.

'Really?' Joe went on. 'Didn't you think it odd that she didn't think you were guilty of what you were accused of?'

'I beg your pardon, Joe? There are quite a few people who don't think I'm capable of such a hideous crime.'

Jack was keeping his head down, brewing tea in the background.

'Would anyone like some toast? That's lovely bread you've got there, Brodie. Did you make that yourself?'

'Shut up, Jack!' we both shouted in unison.

'Here,' said Joe, finally putting things in their place and pointing at Jack. 'Nobody has told me yet why he's here.' He froze a smile on his face as he reached over for the mug of tea Jack was offering him. 'I don't think you're here to be the tea laddie, are you?'

Jack was quick with his explanation.

'Brodie needed an alibi so I provided one.'

'Good. Good,' Joe nodded. He waited a few seconds before adding, 'Mind you, "alibi"? That's a new word for it.'

I tried to stare him out, make him say more. I won – sort of.

'I can see with my eyes what's going on – it's

not an alibi and it's not a fucking ciabatta-making competition either.'

'So, what is going on, Joe?' I asked.

'Well, it's obvious, isn't it?'

Jack was holding his breath whilst looking for an escape route. His eyes kept skimming over to the kitchen window – it was obvious he was thinking of jumping and that broken legs were the least of his worries.

'What are you on about? Spit it out, man.' I goaded Jack more than Glasgow Joe as Jack shook his head to me behind Joe's back. For better or worse I ignored him.

Joe looked to the nodding dog behind him.

'I don't mean to insult you, Jack ... after all, a man's got to make a living. I just don't exactly approve of you fleecing Brodie.'

'Any article I write, I'll run past Brodie,' Jack quickly explained. Quickly, but not very convincingly. There was no way Jack would give up his editorial rights, unless he thought they were a fair exchange for his testicles.

The three of us stared at each other in turn like characters out of some bad Spaghetti Western. By the time a few tons of tumbleweed had blown past, it was clear that nothing more was going to be said, and that no one was really willing to give in. It reminded me of being back at school, with the main difference being that Joe had protected me in those days. I didn't think I could rely on him to do that now.

I turned my back on both of them and made my way to my bedroom. I wiggled my arse a bit for good measure and assumed that they would either start fighting or leave.

The silence that hit the flat as I cosied myself under the duvet suggested there were no more bodies to be counted that night. The very thought brought the corpse of Donna Diamond to my mind, just in time for the nightmares to begin.

Chapter Thirty

The sounds of Elvis drifted towards me, mingling with the smell of death.

The music of the King let me know that Patch was at home and probably about to start work.

Professor Patterson didn't turn around when I entered the morgue. This gave me a chance to study my mentor. He wore a shirt reminiscent of Elvis' Hawaiian period, short-sleeved with large swathes of yellow and green. Pictures of palm trees and dusky maidens in grass skirts were in abundance.

It was hardly an appropriate dress code for the Head of Forensic Pathology at the University of Edinburgh. Patch Patterson had been born with hard Scottish religion bred into him for generations, which was why he kept his harmless vice a secret. A secret that he could only give free rein to in the bowels of the hospital, where he was pretty sure no one alive would visit without warning.

'Want a cup of coffee?'

It was always his first question; unlike Moses,

Patch was addicted to caffeine. Without turning round or waiting for an answer he simply walked off into his side office and switched on the kettle. The music blared on, and I followed Patch. His office was untidy and loose papers hung out of files laid in piles on the floor. His sturdy, hand-made brown brogues were hidden under the desk; in his domain Patch did exactly as he wanted, and so, naturally, he wore blue suede brothel creepers. Remarkably, given what he worked amongst each day, they were unsoiled. On the wall there was a 1975 calendar, kept for the magnificent picture of Elvis looking sweaty in a white boiler suit studded with rhinestones, singing live in Las Vegas.

I was handed a steaming cup of instant coffee.

'Sorry. The espresso machine is on the blink, this is all I have until the damned thing is re-paired.' Patch looked apologetic. We both shared a love of good coffee and took a rather childish pride in the quality of our palates. Unconsciously, as we spoke, his hand went up and he started to stroke the port-wine-stain birthmark that covered half his face and gave him his nickname.

'I have some rather nice homemade madeleines in my tin, Brodie, if you're interested. Some say they are to die for.'

Patch's attempts at joking always came with warning signs – I accepted that a slight smirk would get me some nice biscuits in return, so I indulged him as usual. The truth was, I hated autopsies and always had. He was incredibly blasé about it all, which seemed a good idea for a pathologist really, but as soon as I came into this room, I started sweating and my hands would shake a bit too. I even felt a little sick – but hoped that the biccies would help in that department.

'I thought you were on a diet? Whatever happened to your new mantra – a moment on the lips, forever in the aorta?' I asked him.

'That was last month – so far this month I've only been dissecting skinny people, and I realise once more that no matter what vice I cut out I'm still going to die.'

His comment made me realise how few times I had seen him recently. 'I'm sorry I haven't been round, Patch. I've been otherwise engaged.'

'I know. I saw you on TV – did you get my text?'

I nodded. Patch had sent his love and offered his services. There was no need for him to do this explicitly because I always knew he was there for me no matter what. I grew up a fatherless child, an outsider, whereas Patch was a great father without a child. We were both interlopers in Edinburgh legal circles and we stuck to each other like old pieces of chewing gum on a shoe.

'I've been expecting you, Brodie.'

'I said I was sorry.'

'Don't be so stupid – I've been expecting you because of this.'

He held up a business card.

It was so filthy that I didn't initially recognise it as mine. Patch held it at some distance from his face; he was careful to use tweezers.

'It's from your left pocket – obviously you were or wanted to be close to Donna Diamond.'

'She was my client – a recently acquired one,' I told him.

'It was a short-lived relationship, my dear.'

'What's that orange stuff on it?' I asked.

'Foam. Builder's insulating foam. If you have a gap between the wall and a window you spray some of this stuff and it expands to fill the hole. Damned useful it is too. Dries hard like concrete.'

He walked, so I followed. Patch didn't explain himself to anyone. You either understood him or you didn't. The clock on the wall ticked loudly; Patch was always reminding me: time flies. Outside, the world went on as normal. I could hear the laughter of porters joking with one another. In the morgue it was a parallel universe.

'I left her out,' said Patch, pointing to the shape at the side of us. 'I knew that you would call round and I thought it would save time.'

I nodded my thanks.

'I was out at Calton Hill last night,' he continued. 'Did the autopsy first thing. DI Bancho insisted. I take it you know him?'

All the while he walked around the gurney pulling off the sheet. I will admit to a certain morbid curiosity that was only overcome by my overriding squeamishness.

I started with the feet, then, as my sensitivity decreased, I got used to the sight of the naked corpse in front of me.

The first thing that hit me was that Donna Diamond had bloody ugly feet. They were immaculately waxed and obviously she had professional pedicures, but no amount of hot-pink nail polish could hide those bunions. Her big toe was small, much smaller than the next toe, which had a pale white band where a toe-ring had been. Donna liked her accessories, as I would find out when I got brave enough to look at her nipples.

'Bancho. He seems to think you're responsible for this.' Patch swept his hands expansively over the cadaver. 'Which was why I thought it was imperative that he didn't get his hands on *this.*' Patch waved my soiled business card in the air.

'We both know you could be in trouble for that,' I pointed out.

'Well, you'd better not tell him then, had you, Brodie?'

'Where was it, Patch?'

'We'll get to that in a moment. First, let me tell you how I procured the item and managed to hide it from DI Bancho.' Patch looked very pleased with himself as he began to recount his tale.

'He was vomiting – and you know how I feel about spewers; present company excepted.'

'You made him sick, didn't you?'

'I may have given the boy a helping hand.'

'Well, go easy on me, Patch – I'm feeling like a wrung-out dishcloth. I was having tea and short-bread with Donna not so long ago.'

Patch ignored my request and went on.

'I had the Inverness hospital email me the medical records of Alex Cattanach – it's a bloody shame.'

His words gave me quite a start. Patch rarely swore at any level.

'It's a bit unfortunate for you too – I mean what's going on – I always thought your name would be up in lights, Brodie, but not this way.'

I had managed to move my eyes upwards. Donna's hair had lost its lustre and lay around her head like a pillow of straw. Patch must have read my mind. Hair extensions to cover her male pattern baldness – it must have taken Donna hours to get herself ready to face the world.

Without her make-up and her animated expressions, the time that she had spent under the surgeon's knife looked like a waste of effort and money.

'The knife marks on her face, Patch,' I asked. 'Do you think it was the same person? The pattern looks the same to me, but it's difficult to tell because Alex's scars were swollen and infected when I saw her.'

'I've only seen scanned photographs, Brodie, so until I see Alex in the flesh, so to speak, I can't be sure ... but something doesn't smell right.'

'Perhaps the attacker is just stepping up the violence? I don't think he intended Alex to survive.'

'The smile that is cut into Miss Cattanach's skin seemed to be important to her assailant and yet it's missing here. The cheeks are untouched. We need to ask ourselves why. What was there about Alex Cattanach that necessitated a smile to be carved onto her? What message are we being given that the same violence wasn't inflicted on Donna Diamond?' He poked at Donna's face with a gloved finger as he pondered aloud.

'Alex was attacked on a hill in the Highlands and buried alive,' I reminded him. 'There are similarities – are you saying the differences are more important? Is that where we'll find the vital clues?'

Patch looked at me before continuing. 'This

236

victim was killed elsewhere and deposited on Calton Hill. The grave was shallow. The assailant intended the body to be found. The location of the victim is a busy spot known for carnal trysts. They knew it would not lie undiscovered for more than a few hours.

'The spirals on the face of Alex Cattanach were cut in a clockwise direction. The marks on Donna Diamond, on the other hand, were made in an anti-clockwise movement, indicating a right-hander made one set and a left-handed person made the other.'

'Couldn't the knife marks have been made by the same person – if that person was ambi-dextrous?' I asked.

'Is that what you're hoping for, Brodie? Is that what you're wishing for? Well, if wishes came true we'd all have had ponies when we were wee. You're best to know what you're facing, lass, then you can fight it – self-delusion is no weapon to take into this scrap.'

'The marks on the body – they don't look life-threatening. What did Donna die of?'

'I can't say for sure until the toxicology reports come in – but she was poisoned. I suspect we'll find that temazepam was used.'

'Jellies?'

'Correct – large quantity, readily available on prescription as a sleeping tablet.'

I was strong enough to keep my eyes moving on the body, attentive enough to notice the small butterfly tattoo on her shoulder. I winced as I looked at her large silicone breasts, pert and standing to attention even in death. Twinkling in the areolae were silver rings with diamond chips. One thing was certain: Donna put a great deal more effort into being a woman than I did.

'I've been saving the best till last.' Patch looked like a cat who had stolen the cream.

'Don't you always? I've already told you that my stomach can't take too much today. After Duncan Bancho left you last night he came knocking on my door, so I've had approximately two minutes' sleep.' It was necessary to lay it on with a trowel when you were dealing with Patch, anything less and you got nowhere.

The business card and the tweezers had made a reappearance whilst I was trying to get sympathy.

'Have you guessed where I found this yet, Brodie?'

'No – and I don't think I want to.' I recognised his most evil smile.

'About Donna Diamond's person … the vaginal cavity to be precise; and it wasn't the only surprise I found there.'

He paused for dramatic effect.

'Your card was found inside the vagina of a dead transsexual. And it was held in place by the builder's foam you asked about. Indeed, there was sufficient foam to block the opening completely.'

I would never look at my cards in the same way again. I'd definitely have to change the design.

'Pay attention and snap out of it, Brodie. Someone is setting you up. They want you to be the fall guy. If I hadn't hidden this evidence you'd be on remand in Cornton Vale by now. What do you intend to do about it?'

'Well, Patch,' I replied. 'What options do you think I've got? One half-murdered lesbian accountant writing my name in her own shit and blood on the walls of a mental hospital. A dead transsexual with my personal business card shoved up her fanny to the high end of nowhere. A bent copper out for my head on a plate, and a psycho Goth blinding his so-called followers for daring to question him or me.'

Patch's eyes never flickered as my own heart pounded.

'I suppose entering a popularity contest isn't an option just now, my dear,' he said. 'But if I were you, I'd stop the dramatics and start planning, or the only way you'll be getting into a court is as a client, and the only way into my morgue will be as a specimen. I'm not keen on either option, so, please, for my sake – get yourself sorted and realise that you do have some friends left.'

Chapter Thirty-One

'If I don't get something to eat soon, you'll be representing me on a manslaughter charge, Brodie.'

The farmers' market was taking place in the car park opposite the office in Castle Terrace, and it was becoming increasingly difficult to keep Lavender indoors. The vendors had travelled from all over Scotland and were plying their wares like medieval shopkeepers under the shadow of

Edinburgh Castle. Competition was fierce and marketing tactics came from the sharp end. Fish merchants from Arbroath were smoking their own haddock in whisky-soaked woodchips. They were all calling to Lavender, according to her, and I didn't know how long she could resist it.

'Stop thinking of your stomach for once, Lavender,' I entreated her. 'That reminds me, though – did Eddie like your coq au vin?'

She snorted before replying. 'Those bloody books say that the way to a man's heart is through his stomach, but Eddie just doesn't have that big an appetite.'

I raised one eyebrow, a feat I had mastered at the age of ten, even though I had to spend a whole summer holiday in front of the mirror to do it.

Lavender went on – I'd touched on her favourite subject now. 'He's not that interested in food.' Her eyes went misty as she added, 'which is how he manages to maintain his lithe footballer's physique.'

'I'll take your word for it,' I said, not wanting to spend any time thinking about Drunk Eddie's body.

'Don't you want details, Brodie? Are you not interested in my life? How about a blow-for-blow account, as it were?' she teased.

'No – intriguing as I'm sure your sex life is, Lav, I'd rather save my own arse than hear about Eddie's.'

'Spoil-sport.'

The office was quiet on a Saturday morning, the atmosphere relaxed, and Lavender and I tended to get through a lot of work. For once, the phones were silent and it wasn't a sign that business was going down the tubes. There were no courts sitting on a Saturday, and criminals tended to be lying in their beds sleeping off a drink- and drug-fuelled fugue. They needed their beauty sleep before they hit Princes Street in the afternoon for a bit of shoplifting.

I wandered over to one of the two whiteboards that hung in my office. The one on the left was known as the prison visiting board. It did what it said on the label: all our clients who were in custody were on that board, along with the date that someone from the firm had last seen them.

'Laura McGuigan, Lavender? If she was at Cornton Vale, why didn't she pop in to see Tanya Hayder? Her rehab at Fearns is only down the road.'

'You know Laura, Brodie – she's a law unto herself and this hassle isn't making her any easier to manage.'

The board on the right detailed Friday's trials – we hadn't been that busy. The firm couldn't continue to leak money like this. I wiped it clean and picked up the red marker.

'Let's start from the beginning.' I motioned to Lavender to sit down so that we could get through things. 'How are you getting on with the witness in the Alchemist case?' I knew from our previous discussion that the man had phoned up to collect his reward, but when Lavender had asked him to be a witness he had refused. However, I also knew that Lavender was not the sort of girl to take 'no' for an answer – just ask

241

Eddie. She had stalked him until he had given in. Such was the cleverness of Lav, he was convinced it had been love at first sight.

'Strangely enough, he was on the phone yesterday. Apparently DI Bancho has been harassing him. Putting pressure on him not to testify.'

'How did you manage to get that out of him, you witch?'

'He's not in the witness box yet, Brodie, he's just not quite such a fan of our boys in blue as he was a week ago.'

'They're not all like Bancho.'

'No – some are like Desk Sergeant Munro.'

Much as it pained me to defend him, in all fairness I couldn't tar Munro with the same brush, even if he was constantly horrified by the notion of a 'lassie' taking a man's job.

'Munro's honest enough, I guess – so what are you going to do to turn the reluctant witness to the dark side?'

Lavender tapped the side of her nose with her finger.

'Ask no questions and you'll get no lies.'

I had nothing definite to write on the board, so I wandered over to the window. The market was getting busier. The mobile coffee box was heaving and a large queue of caffeine addicts had formed. Lizzie was too busy meeting their needs to give her usual wave. She was working overtime trying to get enough money to purchase a pair of Jimmy Choos she'd fallen in love with in Harvey Nicks.

I saw Lavender check out where I was looking and thought I could use her calorie obsession to get out of the office for a few minutes. 'I'd kill for some chocolate right now. Do you fancy a mocha? Lizzie's working and I could text our order over?'

'I'm always up for one, but ask her to deliver because you're going nowhere until we've finished.' The striped canvas awnings on the stalls flapped cheerily in the breeze and I longed to be outside, but Lavender was a hard taskmaster. I knew she was serious. She would keep my nose in the office until our desks were clear.

'What's the score on the Tymar front, have you been able to make any headway?' I asked her.

Lavender took a small compact out of her make-up bag and applied her lipgloss. I knew then she was considering her options. It was rare for her not to just blurt out the first thing that came into her head. How much was she prepared to tell me?

'I've been trying to speak to Roddie,' she admitted. 'But he's avoiding me like the plague – so it's a sure sign that the wee bastard knows something.'

After Kailash was found not guilty of the murder of my father, I was in a position to bargain. Revenge is a dish best served cold, they say, but when I gave Roddie what he deserved, everything was still sizzling. Roddie Urquart had been shown up as the lying toad he truly was, and although lawyerly etiquette would never take everything away from a man who had done so much wrong, they all knew that I was behind his fall. Sometimes, Edinburgh legal circles needed to be reminded of that fact. Perhaps I had been too rash. As my grandad had cautioned me, I should keep my enemies close.

'Where is Roddie these days?' I asked.

'He's in Geneva – close to his money. I don't know why you're so soft with him, Brodie. He's a consultant with this firm, he draws his money every month, yet as far as I can see he does nothing.'

'Would you want him here, Lav, hanging around? Personally, I don't care how much it costs me to keep him away.'

'Has anyone figured out what he does in the Geneva office?' she replied.

'You know I'm not involved in the commercial department, but I've heard them say he's very useful in setting up offshore companies. He's also a tax specialist – maybe we're too hard on him; the others seem to think he earns his crust.'

'Brodie, he earns a fortune for doing nothing – crust, my arse; that lad's on caviar.'

The phone rang to interrupt Lavender's diatribe.

'It's reception – there are two coffees at the front desk. The doorman wonders if you want him to pay for them?'

'Tell John to come on up and I'll square up with him right away,' I answered.

John the doorman was keen not to be out of pocket because he was in our office in a flash. The mocha was still hot and sweet. There wasn't as much cream on top as I liked, given that Lizzie was quite fastidious with regards to fat content in her diet, and, consequently, in everyone else's. I really preferred it when Bob, the usual barista, worked on a Saturday. He weighed in at eighteen stone and knew how to ladle on the chocolate.

'I'm in two minds about whether or not to get Moses involved,' Lavender told me when John had gone. She looked at me anxiously. I noticed that she had a blob of cream on her nose. 'I just wanted to run it past you in case it would jeopardise your career – but then I thought it was a bit too late to start thinking about that.' She winked.

Lavender didn't usually bother to consult me on such matters.

'You must be worried.'

'Aren't you? I looked at what I knew about Alex Cattanach and the one thing I had to conclude is that she's not an idiot, or at least she wasn't before the attack.'

'Tasteless, Lavender.'

'You know what I mean – she wasn't one to waste her time chasing wild geese. Alex was hunting you because she knew there was money laundering going on in this firm.'

'That's a serious accusation. If you're right, then I'm facing fourteen years under the Proceeds of Crime Act.'

'Well, if you get done for the attack on Alex Cattanach then we'd better hope that your grandad can get you concurrent sentences.'

'I can see why you're thinking of seeing what Moses can find out, Lav, but he's wrapped up in his own troubles. Can't you find out if Roddie's been up to anything and just fix it yourself?'

She stared at me, knowing what I was really asking.

'That's a tall order even for me, Brodie. I've

245

spoken to some of my friends and we're working on it, actually, but nothing's concrete yet.'

Lavender's 'friends' were a group of computer nerds that she'd met on a course called 'How to build a firewall'. This course was for would-be security experts but the first thing they were taught was how to tear a firewall down. I'm not sure Lavender, like many of her fellow students, bothered to stay for the rest of the course.

'So,' I said. 'Have you found out anything about Tymar Productions?'

'I started by looking at the way Alex worked – and she is absolutely bloody certain that we are at it. I asked myself why?' Lavender liked to do full justice to her stories. I just had to sit back and be patient.

'Cattanach was appointed Chief Accountant to the Law Society in 1999. It was a surprising appointment because she was young and female. Alex made a pledge to weed out bent solicitors. The first thing she did was to increase the frequency of the routine inspections. That meant she sent her teams of investigators into offices without warning to go through their books. Nineteen solicitors were charged with fraud as a result. We had a routine inspection – so what did she find that worried her? I think the fact that we are losing money as a result of Kailash and Roddie set her alarms off.'

'I was hoping you'd have better news – have you got any sweeties in your bag to sugar the pill?'

She threw a rumpled paper bag of aniseed balls at me.

'Will you let me finish? Cattanach's golden rule

is: if the firm is not doing well, the partners will turn a blind eye to money laundering. Who am I to say she's wrong? I then spoke to Kailash about Tymar Productions. She knows that Roddie set this group up. It's an offshore company registered in Cyprus with a Swiss bank account.'

'So, where are you at the moment?' I asked, not letting on that I knew this already.

'I'm trying to get the client details of the Credit Suisse, but it's easier to get into a nun's knickers than this lot.'

I nodded. I had faith that, given enough time, Lavender would get to the bottom of it. The question was – could I buy her that time? I didn't really want to know the answer to the question after that. I thought that the ostrich approach was eminently sensible, but knew that I had to ask.

'What's happening with the mandates?'

Lavender drew breath. A good sign, because she had a tendency to hold her breath when she was tense. I immediately relaxed.

'I spoke to Moses yesterday morning. I told him not to worry, I was just calling because I was worried about him – the word on the street is that he can't hack things just now. I said I didn't mind the fact that the Angels were going elsewhere – I was just vexed for him.'

'Devious – when did the phone calls start coming?'

'By eleven thirty most of them had phoned begging to come back ... and they'd already called Bridget.'

The phone rang before I could congratulate her.

'It's for you – David Ross' wife,' she told me.

It meant nothing. I shrugged my shoulders.

Lavender started scribbling on a piece of paper. *Donna Diamond's wife – she's outside the office.*

'Tell her I'll be right down,' I shouted as I ran down the stairs.

Maybe my luck was turning after all.

Chapter Thirty-Two

'Do you fancy a buffalo burger?'

Marjorie shook her head at my offer. 'I've gone right off food since they found him – I mean, since they found Donna.'

'You don't mind if I go ahead, do you?'

As soon as I'd got the burger in my hand, it was gone.

'Thanks very much – how did you know I'd be hungry?' Joe said as he grabbed it.

'What are you doing here? Apart from nicking my food?' I asked.

'Marjorie asked me to come,' he told me.

I threw an evil look in his direction. It bounced right back.

'She was afraid to meet you by herself – I can't think why,' he said in a lower voice.

'I asked Joe here because he makes me feel safe,' Majorie said, practically nuzzling up to him. Joe towered over her, his dark blue and red Ferguson kilt swinging gently in the breeze. He had no right to wear any kilt really, being of Irish

248

descent, but he had chosen the modern Ferguson tartan because he liked the colours and the pattern. It was all vanity to tell the truth. His antique badger-fur sporran was more effective than sticking a sock down his Y-fronts.

Bitchiness bubbled up inside me, even though Marjorie was about a hundred and dog plain. I didn't like the way she was proprietarily hanging on to his arm. I wanted to say, 'So you still like a man in a skirt?' but thankfully I managed to control myself by biting down hard on my remaining burger.

'Have you told Brodie yet what you mentioned to me on the phone, Marjorie?'

So, they'd been having chummy wee chats now? I knew that I had more to bother about than that, but it still niggled me.

'No, Joe – I told you in confidence and you suggested that I tell her. It was your idea, not mine.'

Widowhood wasn't bringing out the best in Marjorie, and I didn't feel sympathetic enough not to ask what was bothering her. 'You seem to have some problem with me – whatever I've done to cause this, I'm sorry,' I lied. I was only trying to make a stab at amends because my hunch told me that she knew something. She had some information I needed and, unless I could gain her confidence, there was no way I was getting it. Even her pensioner lust for Joe looked unlikely to overcome her caginess with me.

'My husband has just been found murdered up Calton Hill, Miss McLennan.'

Husband? It was hard to think of Donna

Diamond as anyone's husband.

'I can see what you're thinking.' Marjorie must have been a good mind-reader then. 'How could I still love that freak as a husband?'

Did she think portraying me in a bad light would give her a better chance with Joe? I was getting less and less keen on the grieving widow with every passing minute. In fact, she was downright creepy – her husband, wife, partner, pal, whatever, had just been found slaughtered, and her main concern was getting up Joe's kilt.

'I liked Donna,' I said, trying to take the wind out of her sails. 'I'd certainly never think of her as a "freak" and I'm very sorry for your loss.'

An elderly woman struggling with a box of organic vegetables barged past me, knocking me into Joe. Marjorie didn't look pleased. Under other circumstances this would be funny; I'd often joked with him that he was the pensioner's toy-boy.

'Let's stand out of the way of the crowd.' Joe took command of the situation. Taking my elbow, he led us both away towards the relative quiet of the car-park railings. He was being bloody mean. I felt sick as I looked over the edge down to the bottom level. As usual with my vertigo I felt myself being pulled over the brink. The aversion therapy with Lavender clearly hadn't worked. My eyes fluttered and I felt dizzy. Joe grabbed me and hauled me back. I looked into his eyes and I knew that he understood me completely; his arm stayed around my back to steady me.

Marjorie bridled at my side. I pushed Joe away; if I had to be his pimp to get the information, well, that was just a sacrifice we'd both have to make.

'Donna's murder has to be avenged, Brodie,' continued Marjorie, as I tried to get back to a normal colour. 'Don't get me wrong, I mourned the loss of my husband the first time he had breast implants. The pain I feel isn't about my bereavement – I've been crying inside for David for years. But Donna was a good person and she didn't deserve to be trashed like that. She'd gone through so much to live life on her terms, and it was snatched from her just as she healed and was about to live her life her way.'

'She was your friend,' I said, and Marjorie nodded. It seemed at that point as though we might at last have reached some understanding – she might have struck me as distinctly unlikable, but it was obvious that life had dealt her a pretty raw deal. Joe stared at his feet. We passed an informal moment's silence over the death of the man who, under the surgeon's knife, became Donna Diamond.

'How will you manage financially?' I asked. It's the sort of rude question solicitors habitually ask in the interests of looking after their clients. Marjorie was not, strictly speaking, my client, but her husband had been.

'David's life was well insured – I'll be quite well off.'

I thought I saw a twinkle in her eye but she didn't quite have the air of the merry widow about her. Maybe she'd get around to propositioning Joe sometime in the future. For the time being, she was happy enough to give him small orders that he happily carried out rather than getting involved in anything emotional or embarrassing.

'All this upset has made me thirsty – could you please get me a cup of tea, Joe?'

Marjorie watched him walk away, the muscles on his broad shoulders outlined against a deep blue shirt. I'd spoken to him before about wearing clothes that were too tight for him, but he liked to make people think he was just too broad for normal clothes to contain him. Vanity again. Joe's hair, as Donna had observed, was his crowning glory. Today he had it back from his face; presumably he was trying not to inflame Marjorie's senses, but he still looked damned gorgeous.

'You would be entitled to make a claim under the Criminal Injuries Compensation scheme,' I said, getting back to business but still trying to be helpful. I needn't have bothered. Dr Jekyll turned into Mrs Hyde as soon as Joe was out of view.

'Firstly,' she said, fixing me with an icy stare, 'I didn't want to see you again – Joe persuaded me. Secondly, I don't want any handouts.' Little flecks of spit gathered round her mouth. The hairs on her top lip and chin were evident. Donna had obviously spent the family budget on electrolysis and Marjorie had been left out. She had lived in the shadow of her more glamorous housemate and that must have been tough – even now that Donna was dead, I was still comparing them.

Joe appeared back on the scene before we killed each other. I kicked myself for not going with my first impressions – she was horrible.

'Lizzie let me skip the queue,' he announced,

like a wee boy who had done well. 'I said it was an emergency.'

'Oooh, it's lovely, Joe! Just the way I like it,' Marjorie simpered, as if he'd made the bloody stuff himself.

'What did you make of the diary, Brodie?' the lapdog asked.

I stared blankly at Joe.

'I told you, Joe, I only trust you – I don't want to air my dirty laundry in front of anyone else. I can tell she's like all the rest. Blame me, blame the wife. How can David Ross be queer? What kind of woman is his wife that she'd drive a man to cut his bits and bobs off?'

'I don't...'

Marjorie wouldn't let me start, let alone finish.

'Save it for the cocktail circuit, Brodie. I can read you like a book – and I can tell you one thing here and now: he's too good for you, and the sooner he realises that, the better.'

She motioned her head towards Joe.

'A promise is a promise, Madge.'

Joe put his arm around her. I wondered what he had done to extract any promise from her. And what was all this with pet names? Joe had already admitted – like every other man – he was a sucker for flattery, and 'Madge' was playing him like a jukebox. Any other time and I would have suggested that she gave Lavender some advice, but, looking at Joe, I thought I should be asking her myself.

'You give it to her then, Joe – it's in my bag.'

She handed Joe a large battered synthetic-leather handbag. I could see the fabric showing through on the corners and I knew that Donna Diamond would never be seen with such a cheap style statement. Once again, it occurred to me that David's transformation into Donna had been the least of Marjorie's worries. Keeping up with her spending habits, which reminded me of those of a lottery winner on coke, must have been frightening – especially as business slowed.

Despite my dislike, I couldn't keep the pity out of my eyes. Ever vigilant, she noticed and tried to snatch her bag back from Joe. Thankfully, he was aware that I would blow his good work and he was too quick for her. He swung the bag high above her head, scattering cut-price cosmetics as he turned around.

As Joe handed me a black five-year diary, he slipped his arm around Marjorie and pulled her close. He whispered into her ear just loud enough so that I could hear; he was binding me too.

'I promise that Brodie and I will catch whoever killed Donna. You'll get justice, Marjorie, and then you can move on; start again. I'm telling you, you'll find some man who will love you for the woman you are.'

She looked crushed, realising that Joe wasn't offering himself. He manoeuvred her away from where we were standing – he was actually really good at this type of thing. Mind you, it wouldn't be the first time he'd found himself between two warring women – even if they weren't his ex-wife and the widow of a transsexual.

Joe walked with Marjorie to her car and a fleeting thought stole across my mind – would he be safe or would Marjorie have one final go? However, all thoughts as to Joe's safety or otherwise were quickly dispelled when I looked inside the diary. Any clandestine pleasure I anticipated was gone as soon as I opened then quickly closed the pages again. I'm not a sadist – that bit of my father wasn't in my blood. The pain of David Ross's transformation to Donna looked like it would be too much to bear on a half-empty stomach. I snuffled around looking for the buffalo-burger stall but the guy was closing up for the day. I spied Lizzie at the other end of the market. A coffee and homemade bran and raisin muffin would set me up for what I was about to endure. I wandered over with the diary in my hand.

Lizzie was peering over my shoulder whilst she poured a double espresso into foaming milk and chocolate syrup. I needed all the help I could get.

'What have you got there?' she asked.

It seemed a straightforward-enough question.

I sat down on one of the bistro chairs with the diary and looked intently at some of the cartoons Donna had doodled inside. They were labelled 'The Biggest Lie'. They appeared to depict the time that David told Marjorie that he had found the source of his pain. David confessed that he was a transsexual but that he still loved the woman he shared his life with. Marjorie said she was not a lesbian, sex was important to her and she had found someone else. No wonder naughty Madge didn't want anyone to see this. Sweet-talking Joe as if she was some sixteen-year-old virgin when, all along, she had her eye on some-one else whilst Donna was still in pain.

'So, the writer of the diary didn't go ahead with

the operation,' continued Lizzie, peering over at what I was reading. It was no use trying to get rid of her – she was looking at the diary as if a new issue of *Heat* had fallen onto her lap.

'No, he did,' I assured her.

'But the last drawing there shows him promising that he won't change, that he won't be a transsexual – I hope his wife didn't believe him, Brodie.'

'She did.'

After all Marjorie's insults to me, I could gossip with Lizzie, because 'Madge' had declined to be my client. There was no confidentiality issue, but I wondered whether Marjorie herself had even bothered reading this diary – why had she given it up to me, given what we thought of each other, when it portrayed her so negatively?

'I know I'm thick compared to you – but how is this poor sod's diary going to help you, unless there's something you haven't told me?' asked Lizzie. She smiled. She was dressed in the worst possible taste. Although it was midsummer she wore a woolly Bob Marley hat in bright green, yellow and black. Her hair was piled inside it and, even for her, it was an unusual statement. The only explanation could be the skinny youth she had been seeing recently.

'What's your new beau into?' I asked, distracting both of us for a welcome moment.

'Is it that obvious?'

I nodded, and Lizzie continued. 'We're going to an open-air reggae festival in the Meadows this afternoon – do you fancy coming?'

'Playing gooseberry is bad enough at the best of

256

times. Amongst the great mass of unwashed adolescents who will be dancing on the grass today, it will be even worse. Besides, Lizzie, I'm too old for that sort of thing, so you certainly are.'

She ignored my comment. 'Who said you had to come alone? Bring Joe.'

'I don't think so. If he comes back looking for me, tell him I'll be with Moses at the diner.'

I threw away the rest of my muffin and mocha; suddenly I had lost my appetite.

Chapter Thirty-Three

The Lost Knickers Diner was Moses' idea of a joke. He had believed that the term 'money laundering' had come from the 1950s when the Mafia had bought laundries to 'clean the money' from their illegal gambling operations. It was an urban myth but one that had become yet another money-spinning scheme for Moses.

The boy wonder could do no wrong when it came to dragging cash in, even legitimately. I wasn't resentful, though – as Mary McLennan would have said, I wouldn't have had his life for all the tea in China. No one who knew him, even those who rightly condemned some of his actions, would fail to understand how such a personality was formed, given his history.

The Lost Knickers Diner was primarily a laundry. It was in a good area so its clientele was mostly made up of young professionals. Moses the businessman had read in the *Financial Times* that young professional types were having difficulty meeting partners, hence the rise of speed dating. He had already observed some romances spring up amongst his customers as they watched their whites being tumble-dried. After a lightbulb moment, he thought he would capitalise on the romance of soap suds and open a café-style diner. The coffee, burgers and chips went down well, because they could eat their tea, get a shag and still have a clean shirt for the morning. A multi-tasker's paradise.

'Did you bring your washing?' Moses shouted from the back as my entry tinkled the door chime.

'No, I just brought myself – isn't that enough?'

'I just wanted to rifle through your dirty knickers, Brodie – but I hear Jack Deans got there first.'

Now this was clearly a lie – obviously not about Jack Deans and my knickers, but the fact that Moses wanted to get into my thong. I tried to change the subject, so I switched to a topic that always diverted Moses.

'How come you always look so good?' I purred. I had learned a thing or two from Marjorie.

'You know the story, Brodie.'

'No, I don't – I want to know why you always take such time to groom yourself and stuff. To me it seems like there's never enough time in the day,' I said, casually brushing the remaining muffin crumbs from myself onto the floor.

'It's not something I like to divulge.'

He handed me a Diet Coke with a slice of lime

and crushed ice in a highball glass with a curvy lady in a swimsuit on it. Fifties' music blared out of the speakers.

Moses may not have been wearing a Fifties' swimsuit but his costume was just as outlandish. It wasn't the Goth clothes that I was interested in but the excessive neatness behind the Dark Angels. Their hair never had roots showing through the peroxide-blond. The black nail polish was always perfect, and that's not easy when you're ripping a car apart. If I found out how they motivated themselves to do it then maybe I could do it too and keep Kailash off my back.

'Most of us lived in that home.'

I knew which one he was referring to – it was out in South Queensferry and my late father and his wife used it to operate a paedophile ring. The children of the ring were the original Dark Angels and Moses was their leader.

'Every Sunday, prospective parents would come to the home to look for children,' he went on, not really talking directly to me. 'We were told to put on our best clothes and clean our teeth and then maybe we would get a new mummy and daddy. Some of us scrubbed our necks so hard they were bleeding. None of us ever got adopted – they all wanted babies, not ten-year-olds like us. We thought it was our fault and every Sunday another one of us joined the band that scrubbed so hard they bled. Old habits die hard, Brodie.'

Kailash would just have to bear my messiness. She had also been in the home and subject to my father's treatment – or I wouldn't be here to tell the tale. I suppose Moses' story gave me a greater understanding of Kailash; she was just trying to get the best for me, and that wouldn't happen in her eyes unless I looked 'neat'. I didn't think I could manage even that to cement mother–daughter relations.

'Do you want another one?'

Moses pointed to my empty glass. Fear had made my mouth dry and I'd gulped it down.

'I'm fine, thanks.'

'Why are you here, Brodie? No offence, but with a budding romance on the scene I would have thought that you had better things to do on a Saturday than hang around with me. Not that I'm not glad to see you, you understand.'

'It's not a romance, Moses. It is absolutely not a romance.'

'You're risking a lot for a quick shag, Brodie, if you don't mind me saying.'

I did mind, but I didn't tell him because I didn't want to fall out with anyone else today. I was still shaken by Marjorie. 'In case it's escaped your attention, we are both in deep shit, and when I'm in deep shit my sex drive flags.'

'Liar,' he whispered at me.

It was true. I was lying. Since this whole thing had started up I had felt like I was on heat. The old primal urge that linked sex and fear was kicking in again. I hadn't wanted to admit it even to myself but, this morning when I'd looked at Joe, I'd remembered how good we had been together. Flashes of passionate nights under the desert sky in Vegas had come into my mind. I had caught him smirking at me; he always knows what I'm thinking.

'Even if I am lying, Moses, I'm not admitting it to you. You'd trade the information for a cheap deal on soap powder.'

'Only if I thought you secretly wanted me to.'

He winked at me. He was anxious to get into Glasgow Joe's good books and any news that would give Joe an insight into me would be hot property, although he must have been a little concerned that the messenger might get shot.

'Cut the crap, Moses. How are you getting on with Duncan Bancho?'

'Well, the little misunderstanding we had over the man now known as Blind Bruce has gone away – since there were no witnesses.' He looked me in the eye. I said nothing. 'There were no witnesses,' he repeated. 'And even Bruce has admitted to the police that he was extremely unlucky to fall on his own knife and poke his eyes out.'

'It was a harsh punishment, Moses, and you know it.'

'Who made you God, Brodie? You're here because someone is setting you up. Is that fair? At least Bruce had a chance – he knew the rules. If at any point he had grovelled, said he was sorry, things would have been different, but no, he challenged me, he kept on challenging me, and that couldn't be allowed to pass. It's the law of the jungle, Brodie: eat or be eaten.'

I watched a girl doing a service wash. It was quite therapeutic, seeing her fold the snowy-white sheets and towels.

Moses watched me watching her.

'Funny you should be drawn to watching that

261

girl. She belongs to Kailash, she's given me the contract for her places. Kailash is very loyal; but I wouldn't like to cross her. She's not daft, mind, she runs a very tight ship, she really screwed me down on price, and if it's not perfect then it's handed right back for me to have another go.'

'Moses, keep to the subject – we're both being fucked by Bancho – you've been paying him a lot for protection and information and now he's taking someone else's money and you have no idea who that is or why. Am I right?'

Moses raised his eyebrows at me and I sensed that there was something going on here that he didn't want me to see. In the background the Alchemist had come in. He'd slunk round the back through the multicoloured plastic streamers. With him was a fattish merchant-banker type, maybe just the right side of thirty, three stone overweight, wearing salmon-pink cords that had probably cost a fortune, even though there was never a decade in which they were in style.

Five minutes later the man came out, pockets bulging, looking bright-eyed and bushy-tailed.

'You've missed some!' I shouted to him and he wiped his nose.

'You know how I feel about drugs, Moses. I thought I knew what you thought about them too.'

'You're fucking naïve about them, Brodie, that's what I think. Despite your job you don't seem to understand that there is a difference in drugs – I don't do heroin, I don't deal with smack-heads. That guy who just walked out – do you think he thinks he's a junkie? He could buy and sell you.

He's probably buying stuff to take to his shooting lodge in the Highlands. It's just recreational stuff I'm involved in, nothing else.'

The Lost Knickers Diner is an excellent shop-front for Moses' pharmaceutical industry, which is way too big to be called 'cottage'. I remember reading an article saying that cocaine use amongst twenty- and thirty-something Scots had doubled in a year and that it was now the drug of choice for young professionals. Moses wasn't one to pass up an opportunity.

'Anyway,' he said, getting back to my original question, 'if Bancho has his way I won't be in this business any more – and I don't mean that he wants to put me behind bars. No, that greedy wee bastard has got someone who's paying him big-time, muscling in on my supply chain. I'm losing dealers left, right and centre. Whoever's paying Bancho is paying him to supply the drugs and the information. When the Alchemist gets there they've already got their gear. No amount of doings is going to pull them into line. My best hope is the Alchemist's trial – have you found the witness?'

'I'm not telling you because I know what you'll do – and that's not good for anyone.'

'So you've found the witness and, surprise, surprise, he's not co-operating.'

'Drop it, Moses,' I warned.

'Don't worry, it's dropped – now, I'll ask you again. What did you come here for?'

I didn't believe a word he said about not going after the witness, but I would have to give this job to Glasgow Joe – he was the only one who could control Moses. I handed him Donna's five-year diary. I wanted to see what his reaction was – he had great intuition, but he also knew more than anyone else I was in touch with about the seedy side of life, which would hopefully lead him to answer some questions I had about the contents. He opened the pages as if he was trying to give the matter due attention. He was attempting to get back into my good books. I expected a few schoolboy jokes as he flicked through, but perhaps he acknowledged a fellow human being's suffering in those lewd cartoons.

'Well, fuck me sideways, Brodie!' he shouted out and started to laugh, leaving me to regret my warmer thoughts about his empathy.

'Keep your voice down,' I whispered at him, now more unsure than ever of the ethics of touting this diary around town. He ignored me and started jumping around and punching his fist in the air, shouting, 'Ya beauty! Ya beauty!' I was desperate to know what it was that excited him in the heartbreaking diary.

'Well done, Brodie, you've only gone and brought me details of my fucking supply chain! Whatever poor Donna Diamond went through to keep this diary, at least in the last six months, he's – sorry, *she's* – detailed the comings and goings of the bastard who's been muscling in on my line of dealers.'

'I've read it already, but it didn't make complete sense to me – what does it mean?' I asked him once I had pulled him off me and dried my cheeks from his kisses.

'It means that whoever killed Donna killed her

because of this.' He waved the diary in the air. 'We just have to find who's been stealing my customers and we find Donna's killer! Plus, we nail this bastard, then we get another go at nailing Bancho, and that's got to be good because we're doubling our chances of getting that bastard off our backs.' He was looking at the diary all the time he said this, and exclaimed, 'Bonus news for you, Brodie! Look…' His black fingernail pointed to an entry dated the fourth of January:

Alex Cattanach contacted me today – as a client! Who would have thought? How the mighty have fallen. Enough drivel. Obviously, she knew that whatever she told me was bound by client confidentiality (the bitch – it's such a juicy tidbit). Even so, she was pretty cagey. She came up with some story that two friends of hers were being blackmailed. Apparently there's a video of her 'friend' and a.n. other engaged in what she called 'lesbian acts' (I'd like to see it). It gets better – it's shot in a legal office and involves young female clients (better and better). Alex Cattanach is no better than she should be, yet she still had the bloody cheek to act holier than thou with me. On her way out she asked me if I intended to plead guilty to the fraud charge and save the Crown some money. Maybe if I find her blackmailer she'll get the charges dropped.

Now I was definitely walking in Donna's shoes. To prove my innocence I had to find the same people she was after and try to ignore what had happened to her when she had done so. I shuddered as I thought of my business card.

Chapter Thirty-Four

'I've never seen this place looking so clean, Brodie – well, not since...'

Patch didn't finish his sentence. We didn't speak about Fishy, my ex-flatmate. He might have been handy for washing the dishes but he had a less useful side when he got in league with my stepmother and tried to kill me. Give me a sink full of crockery with mould on it any day.

'Thanks, Patch. I've got a new cleaner – recommended to me by Bridget Nicholson no less. I've never met the lovely Agnes, but she's doing a great job. I might start asking her to fix the rest of my life up too.'

I handed Patch an exceptionally hygienic cup of tea.

'You see, Grandad, I can keep my enemies close,' I whispered as I handed him his porcelain cup with a saucer.

We were having a war-council meeting. Frank had phoned late in the afternoon to say that all the Crown production documents and evidence were in. For once, I was delighted to suggest to the crew that they came over. I even asked Kailash, just so that I could show off my sparkling pad. Fresh as a daisy indeed, just as the cheesy advertising leaflets for the company said. I usually went into the office on a Sunday as it was so quiet and I could catch up on things, but today I was taking it easy. Not too much of a problem, given that we still weren't as busy as I would like. I had cooked a feast using a Madhur Jaffrey cooking book I'd got in a charity shop for one pound fifty. Normally, I would just have ordered the food in, having had to spend all my time making the place sanitary. Today, I enjoyed baking my own naan bread and puris and hoped they would be impressed.

Frank insisted that we worked first, then ate.

He opened his briefcase and took out the ten-by-eight black and white photographs of the productions. I felt myself go a bit woozy as I remembered the last time I had sat here looking at photographs pulled from an envelope. It didn't seem that long ago that a serial killer had been sending me pictures of friends with nooses around their necks, and images of butchered schoolgirls. This time Alex Cattanach stared up at me and my appetite went out the window along with her vacant stare.

The knife marks on her face were particularly evident in the starkness of the picture. Spiral welds formed a grotesque pattern on her cheeks. It was expert knife work. Acid reflux came into my mouth as I looked at her, not helped by the smell of the lamb biryani that was burning on the stove.

It was hard not to stare; it was even harder not to want to cry with sympathy at the ruination of this once proud, intelligent woman. She wouldn't be starring in any naughty videos this side of Christmas, a horrid little voice in my head said. I was grateful that no one else could hear it. I must state in my defence that when people are faced with a dark situation the natural reflex is for them to laugh. I told myself it was natural, but not forgivable.

I didn't feel like laughing at the next picture.

'Would someone mind explaining this to me?' Grandad tapped his arthritic old finger against the grainy black and white photograph.

'I would have thought the picture explained itself, Lord MacGregor.'

Patch and Grandad had a thing going on – too small to be called a feud, too big to be dismissed. I don't know how it started, I suspect it began in some court case, God knows how many decades ago, and I didn't know when it would end. Certainly not anytime soon, I thought, by the looks of them. Like two old rams, they were locked by the horns, neither one willing to back down, Grandad smarting at the implication that he was losing his marbles.

'Okay, calm down.' My voice sounded calmer than I felt. 'It's my name, Grandad, written on Alex Cattanach's wall, by her. The material she has used is her own blood and shit.'

'Oh.'

'Is that all you have to say?'

'Well, regrettably, in this instance I am forced to agree with Professor Patterson. The photograph really does speak for itself, and I think we all have enough brain cells left to shudder at what any sane or reasonable jury might think of it.'

'I think we should serve the food now.' Kailash got up from the table and moved to the cooker. Her face was hidden from me and I feared she might have been crying.

I had set the places before they arrived and it looked lovely. My table was antique rosewood, chosen from a shop in Stockbridge. My only worry when I'd first bought it was that Moses seemed to recognise it. Even the glasses were old. Grandad had given me some of my unknown Granny's dishes and glassware and his eyes shone with pleasure as he recognised them.

Tonight we were eating in the dining room because there were so many of us. I took particular care not to seat Jack Deans next to Glasgow Joe, then I also had to keep Grandad and Patch apart. I missed Moses because, remarkably, he was a great peacemaker and in this assorted group of my friends and family he would have worked wonders. Strangely, my grandad adored him and it was not unusual for me to find Moses up in Grandad's flat in Ramsay Gardens, as they chewed the cud together. Tonight, however, we had both agreed that it was more essential for Moses to get on with tracking down the blackmailer.

Kailash carried the basmati rice to the table in a huge Victorian soup tureen. The pattern on the china was blowsy and colourful – rust marigold edged in gold with dark blue leaves – not exactly true to nature, but a fabulous centrepiece to the table. A silver candelabra, with eight beeswax candles, showered us with a glow that the content of the evening didn't merit. The pakoras were superb, and although the lamb was burnt I hoped that none but the most discerning palate would notice. Frank wolfed his down, and Grandad and Kailash toyed with theirs, claiming lack of appetite. Disappointed, I decided not to bring out the handmade mango ice cream, created from the gelateria that Joe had bought me for Christmas.

I cleared the dishes away quite quickly; the fun had gone out of the evening when the first photograph of Alex had appeared. It wasn't helped by the fact that I'd been distracted and then ruined some of the dishes, not just the lamb. I really take pride in my cooking and usually my guests are well satisfied eating in an untidy kitchen around a cramped table. Tonight, I had really wanted to pull it off – it was the first time that I'd used my granny's dishes and I wanted to show Grandad that I could do something – even if it was only to be the cook in Cornton Vale.

Now it was ruined.

Jack came into the kitchen laden down with dishes that I hadn't collected yet. He placed them on the thick wooden worktop, still overflowing with food. I was scraping it into the bin like pigswill, too annoyed to save it to be reheated – I preferred the grand gesture, as always. Jack came up behind me and pulled me close. He bent and kissed my neck; he knew my secret. Learn how to kiss my neck properly and I will hang around for life; or at least until I get bored.

I responded to him. I would have responded to anyone who kissed me there like that. But Joe didn't see it like that when he came into the kitchen – he only saw Jack and I sneaking away from everyone to steal some moments together. Too large a presence to sneak out and conceal his hurt, he stomped out of the room.

We had been caught.

In that split second, I knew what I felt.

Knew what I wanted.

I had made up my mind about Joe and Jack without even having to spend too long thinking about it, but I wasn't in a position to tell Joe that. He had already headed off to the dining room and I was left with the one I knew to be the fuckwit. No matter how he might protest that he would change, that was what Jack Deans was.

And it wasn't enough.

Maybe he was all I deserved, but I knew he wasn't all I needed.

It was hard to face Joe as I went through to the dining room. Logic told me it wasn't the case, but my heart felt as if I had betrayed him. Divorced or not. The ways that he had helped me over the years since the divorce had more than made up for any mistakes he'd made.

Joe was standing at the side of the fireplace away from everyone else, fastening his biker's jacket. He looked at me without any anger. I was desperate for an argument; that would have meant there was something I could try to fix. Being like this, so quiet, made me unsettled.

As we tried not to meet each other's eyes fully, Jack came up behind me.

'I think it's best if I go, Brodie,' he said. 'Give me a call and let me know what Frank's got.'

As soon as Jack said the words, Joe started to unzip his jacket whilst staring at him. Jack's words made me see Joe's point. I was unsure whether Jack wanted to know what the evidence was to help me, or whether he simply wanted to write good copy. He never pretended to be anything

271

other than a drunken hack, even if I, for some reason, saw something different. My hormones had blinded me to Jack's rotten qualities and let me believe he was a better person than he really was. And I had willingly gone along with it all just for a quick one. Or two...

I couldn't doubt that this was all hard for Joe, but the difference between the two men was that he stayed. He stayed in case I needed him.

I needed alcohol. Quickly. Lots of it.

'Does anyone want a drink?' I shouted.

They all started clamouring like fish on a farm at feeding time.

'Anybody would think your throats were cut!' Joe shouted. 'If this was in the Doll I'd be telling my staff to keep an eye on you lot, you greedy set of buggers. Now, one at a time. Ladies first. Kailash?'

'I'll have a Hendrick's gin, with finely sliced cucumber and fresh borage.'

Would she now? Trust her – anyone else would have a Gordon's gin with flat Schweppes and, if they were lucky, a slice of lemon that had a tiny bit of life left in it.

'I don't have that,' I snipped.

'Yes, you do, I brought my own. It's chilling in the fridge. Just bring a few leaves of borage – I brought that as well.'

It felt like a relief to escape from the dining room, but Joe followed me.

'Don't worry, Brodie,' he began. 'I'm not going to make a scene. We both know that I've no right to.'

'That's right – you divorced me.'

'I know, and maybe I've lived to regret that. But remember, I didn't sign those papers because I didn't want you. I signed them because I thought you'd have a better life without me. Mind you, looking at the cock-up you're making of it, I think I was wrong there too.'

He walked out of the kitchen with Kailash's glass. I knew that all I had to do was call him back and we could start again. He had made a decision once that he was bad news for me; if I loved him, then I would have to say that I was bad luck for him too. I was facing a prison sentence for attempted murder at the very least, with possible fraud and murder charges hanging over me. By the time I got out of prison I would need an ovarian graft to have children.

I grabbed a beer from the fridge and drank it straight from the bottle. I walked into the dining room in my leathers and tight white T-shirt. I had been so busy cooking I had forgotten to change. I knew there was a love bite on my neck and I didn't exactly look classy. They all turned to look at me as I came in.

Frank was the first to talk. 'It's not as bad as we feared, Brodie. Not as bad as it could have been. There's no DNA evidence against you. The only evidence the police have is a motive for the assault. They have you in the vicinity when the attack occurred and they have a weapon.' Frank held up a photograph of a Stanley knife.

'What good is that to me? That's available in any and every DIY store in the country!'

'I know smiled Frank. 'It's good, isn't it?'

'Well, it's time to be thankful for small mercies

I suppose,' I said, feeling that I needed to cheer Frank and everyone else up. For myself, the mercies in my life seemed so damnably small, I couldn't even find them to be grateful over.

Chapter Thirty-Five

'Darlin', you look terrific – have you lost weight?' I knew Tanya Hayder was lying but I smiled politely anyway. Moses had decided that we had to pay a visit to one of the 'premier escorts of the *Flowers of Scotland* website'. It was time to call in our markers. Tanya knew more than she had let on yet, and we needed that information now.

The Castle was a very upmarket rehab set in the Scottish Borders. The psychotherapist was from California, and had written several books – consequently, celebrities flocked from all over to pay homage at his feet. I had read one of his tomes, *What Cheerful People Know*. It had impressed me so much that I had even tried some of the strategies. Basically, he said we were hotwired by our genes to be scared all the time so we had to have courage even when we didn't feel brave at all. When I drank or Tanya chased the dragon, we were just giving in to our reptilian impulses. It cost me £7.99 to follow his advice for a fortnight; here, it was costing the state £1,000 a day. I would lay good money on the truism that you can't teach an old dog new tricks. Unfortunately, sitting in the sumptuous common room of The Castle, Tanya looked like a very old dog.

'Not like you, Tanya,' said Moses as he pulled a straight-backed dining chair out of the corner of the room, ignoring the fact that she was all skin and bones. 'You've put on some weight there – your cheeks are filling out again.' Moses didn't slump in chairs, but rode them like horses, giving you the impression that he was on the starting line in a race, ready to bolt at any moment. Watching him in the bright sunshine, I easily imagined him grabbing the chair and smacking it off Tanya's head if he didn't get the answers he wanted. I think Tanya felt it too.

'So, darlin,' Moses continued, 'I think you know that we're not here to measure each other's waistlines. I've been good to you in the past, and so has my friend Brodie.'

He didn't say 'too good to you', but that was to be understood. Tanya shifted uncomfortably in her chair, and, although I was fond of her, she reminded me of a sewer rat. By that I mean a tremendous survivor although, as I looked at her in the harsh sunlight streaming through the full-size bay windows, even her mannerisms were reminiscent of the creature. Heroin had robbed her of her humanity.

It was fascinating how she twitched. Her small beady eyes darted between our faces, summing us up, guessing which one of us was the softest touch.

'Brodie,' she began.

I guess I lost in the poker-face stakes.

'You and I go way back.'

Her head was nodding, trying to get me to agree with her. I knew as soon as I did that, then the truth was lost. I remained still. She reached out and touched me with her skinny claw-hand. I fought the urge to pull back. Using every available vein for junk destroys your circulation. Her wasted arm was mottled with purple blotches, as if she had sat by a fireside for too long.

'See, darlin', we understand each other.'

She patted my leg in a manner that was meant to soothe but just set my teeth on edge. Her arm twisted just enough to show me the pale under-side. Barely healed puncture marks were visible.

'What the fuck!'

Moses grabbed the same arm so hard that I thought he had broken it. The patient who was sitting quietly in the corner scurried out of the room, sensing the trouble before it had even fully begun.

Alone now, Moses squeezed Tanya's arm so hard it brought tears to her eyes. She was an excellent actress, but Moses wasn't falling for any of it. As soon as she knew that the victim role wouldn't work, she became angry, spitting like a cat trying to bite him. Moses jumped back and slammed her head into the wall. He wasn't dealing with some-one that he thought would understand anything but the language of violence – Tanya was just an Edinburgh junkie. 'Shut the door, Brodie. If we want anything out of this bitch we're going to have to make her talk. And I, for one, am looking forward to it.'

My feet sunk into the thick carpet. I couldn't stop to think of the rights and wrongs of this situation. Could I plead the Nuremberg Defence? Who would believe that I would take orders from a barely literate boy? Moses knew best how to handle this situation – there were too many people depending on me for squeamishness to come into it.

'We can do this the easy way, Tanya,' said Moses, 'or we can do it the hard way. I know you've got a stash. If you don't want me to grass you up to the people who run this place then you'd better start talking.'

All the fight left Tanya. She returned to her chair, deflated. There was no pretence at niceness, no camaraderie or talking of old times. Maybe it was the first time that I truly understood that when you're dealing with a junkie, they have no soul to negotiate with.

'I'm not going to ask you how you got the smack – it's not my business. It's enough for you to know that I know, and I won't hesitate to get you thrown out of here and straight into the poky.'

She flicked her matted stringy hair out of her face.

'What do you want to know, you little shit?'

Moses handed her the diary.

'You a tranny boy these days?' she said, flicking through it.

Moses didn't rise to her insults. Despite appearances, he generally abhorred gratuitous violence.

'Keep your smart comments to yourself, waster, and tell me about these ships.'

'What am I? A fucking sailor?'

'No, but you've shagged enough of them to

make a stab at it – now, tell me about those boats.'

Tanya started squirming again. I wondered if she had pissed herself; it wouldn't be the first time a client had done that. I checked under the chair but the carpet was still in pristine condition.

'You might be scared of whoever you think you're protecting, but I can't see any of them around. Me? I'm here and I'm seriously annoyed.'

'Your mouth's full of shite, Moses,' Tanya replied, cocking her head towards me. 'She's a lawyer; she'll not let you near me. They've got rules.'

I reached over and grabbed her T-shirt.

I could feel the bones of her chest against my fingertips. I stood up and picked her up with one hand – she only weighed about six and a half stone but the action still stretched me.

'My bosses in the Law Society keep telling me that there are rules to follow as well, Tanya. I don't listen to them either. I'm facing at least fifteen years for stuff I didn't do, I can take a bit extra for roughing you up. Now look at me and listen.'

With my free hand I pushed her face in front of mine so that she was forced to look into my eyes. Addicts hate to look you in the eye because their confidence has gone. I pointed to Moses without looking at him. 'I'm his witness that you struck the first blow and he thought you had a knife. Now answer his questions and be quick about it.'

The Leither was coming out in me now that my back was against the wall. After days of being at the mercy of others, it felt great, even if I was picking on the weakest in the pack.

'Tell me about these boats,' I said.

'They're fishing boats.'

'Where from?'

'Peterhead.'

'What are they bringing in?'

'What do you think? It's not fags.'

'Tell me the types of drugs they're hauling.' I resisted slapping her as I said it.

'Heroin from Pakistan.'

'Nothing else?'

Tanya shook her head emphatically. Maybe she thought that if she dramatically denied everything, we would believe her. Moses looked perplexed. He didn't supply heroin or crack cocaine on moral grounds. So whoever was muscling in on his supply chain got their recreational drugs from somewhere else.

'Who's the Mr Big, Tanya?'

Tanya laughed so hard at Moses that she fell off her chair. The drama-queen act was wearing thin.

'Oh, you crack me up, you do. What's with the lingo, Moses? Been watching too many cop shows? And are you expecting me to do your job for you now? Work everything out for poor wee Moses? I'd heard you'd gone soft. I never believed it until now.'

The overacting victim turned in a second and spat at him. A greenish glob of mucus left a snail-like trail down his face. Moses took a paper handkerchief out of his pocket and wiped it away. He didn't retaliate, which made a shiver run through me. The last time he had seemed to be calm in the face of insults, he had moved on to slicing a man's eyes out – I wondered whether this silence was more than him just losing his bottle? It would be hard either way. If Moses had lost his guts then what would I do?

Suddenly, I remembered the guru who ran this place and the £7.99 piece of advice he'd given me.

WE ARE ALL ALWAYS AFRAID.
BUT SOME HAVE THE COURAGE TO ACT

I picked Tanya up by the scruff of the neck and threw her against the wall. It didn't really hurt her but it was theatrical to watch – I've had years of being a drama queen, just ask Joe, and I wasn't prepared to give up my title yet.

'He might have lost the lead out of his pencil, Tanya, but I'm just getting mine.'

I thought about throwing in a 'bitch' to sound suitably tough, but even though my mind was working fast with all the adrenalin, I wasn't quite quick enough to get my dialogue perfect.

Tanya's face was squashed against the wall. I hissed into her ear.

'Who is the Mr Big, then, Tanya, if you don't mind the cheesy terminology?'

Obviously, she did, because she didn't reply.

I leaned my shoulder against her – we were close enough for me to smell her last cigarette.

'You'd better start talking, Tanya,' I warned her, 'or you'll be out of here so fast your arse won't have time to hit the pavement before you're back in Cornton Vale.'

I leaned against her again. The good thing about her completely ignoring me was that I couldn't be that heavy otherwise she would be capitulating and screaming in pain. Even then I was thinking of diets – how bloody pathetic was that?

'Okay, I'll tell you. Just get off me, you fat bitch.'

She'd found my weak spot. So I leaned in once more, just for good measure.

'You've got it all wrong – both of you,' she hissed, moving away from the wall and smoothing herself down. She looked no worse than if she'd had an uncomfortable night's sleep. I would make a pathetic bouncer.

We stood shamefaced on the thick-piled carpet as she circled around us, the playground bully, taunting us for our stupidity.

'"Who's the Mr Big? Who's the Mr Big?" Arseholes.'

This was her moment, and we had to let her have it. Although it had to be said that we were kind of at a loss for words.

'There is no Mr Big.'

Moses and I could forget being Butch and Sundance, we couldn't even make it to Thelma and Louise.

'Okay,' interrupted Moses. 'We get it – you're so smart and we're so dumb. Just tell me who it is before I break your irritating scraggy junkie neck.'

She stared him out.

'I've seen your sort before, Moses Tierney,' she finally said.

I doubted it, but said nothing.

'You're pathetic. You know nothing about me, about my life.'

Again, she was wrong – she couldn't imagine in her worst nightmares what Moses had been through. Neither could I, even though I knew some of the story.

'And you know nothing about what I know. So, I'll give you a free bit of help – I don't know who Mr Big is. Now, can you piss off and leave me alone?'

'If you're lying to me, Tanya, I'll come back and get you,' Moses informed her. 'You obviously don't know what happens to people who cross me, people who disrespect me. You lie – I get hacked off. I get hacked off – you hurt.'

Tanya couldn't have looked less bothered.

'Oh boo hoo, Tierney. If you two idiots have spotted I've got smack in here, I don't suppose it'll take the staff long to catch on. I know I'll get kicked out – at least in Cornton Vale I'll be safe from your pathetic threats and crap double act. Now piss off before I get you thrown out for upsetting me.'

Pathetically, we were happy to oblige.

Chapter Thirty-Six

'Slow down – you're going too fast, Brodie!'

I refused to listen to Moses. I wanted to get back to Edinburgh fast and he was a lousy passenger on a bike, whether I went fast or at a snail's pace. He just didn't get it.

I loved the twisting country roads that led from

Tanya Hayder at Castle Fearns back to Edinburgh, but, like most men in my experience, he couldn't follow me. Lavender was great as a passenger. When I leaned into a corner, she came with me. Once she even fell asleep on the back of the bike; not something even I've been able to achieve.

Moses was another story altogether. When I leaned into a corner, he went the other way trying to straighten me up. Instead, we almost came off. This didn't help his nerves.

'I swear I'm never getting on this bloody bike with you again, Brodie,' he screamed in my ear. 'My arse is numb and my coat is covered with dirt and shit from the road – I'll never get it clean.'

'Stop moaning; you own a bloody launderette and dry-cleaner's, you soft get! Have you figured out who Mr or Mrs Big is yet?'

We were approaching Biggar, a pretty market town in the Borders about twenty miles from Edinburgh. We'd left Tanya over an hour ago and we still weren't any closer to figuring out who the mystery mover was. The Fat Boy was attracting attention, as usual. I had slowed to thirty miles an hour to go through the centre of the town. It gave the pedestrians a chance to gawp at the Harley, which looked pretty magnificent

Joe – why did every thought lead back to him? – had fixed the oil leak in the engine. He'd also had all the chrome on Awesome shined to within an inch of its life, restoring my beloved bike to his glory days. I tried to persuade Moses to wave back at the children along the route who were desperate to catch our attention, but he didn't want to play.

'Sulking's no good – we're still no nearer finding out who's behind this,' I shouted at Moses, trying to be heard over the engine.

'Alex Cattanach knows who's behind it,' he shouted back.

'If you'd seen her, you'd know that she's not in a fit state to talk about anything.'

'I thought you said that she was going to be given electric-shock treatment, not drugs, because that was the only thing that worked?'

'The only thing that *might* work. Moses, I don't think she's got a snowball's chance in hell of ever making it back to the real world.'

That thought depressed me. To make matters worse, the skies opened and a heavy summer shower fell on us. I had an open-faced helmet on and the rain was splashing in my eyes making it difficult to see. Luckily, Moses was too busy moaning about his boots getting soaked to notice that I was having difficulty handling the bike.

At the moment, Alex Cattanach's recovery was my only chance. Even if she did recover, I couldn't see why she'd want to do me any favours, given how much she'd hated me before the attack in fact, in her madness, the only thing anchoring her to reality was her hatred of me.

We struggled on.

The rain was coming down so heavily it was almost like a flash flood. Just outside Edinburgh's city boundary, I pulled over to the side of the road and suggested that we take shelter under an oak tree. Moses was only too delighted to jump off the Fat Boy. The Pentland Hills behind us were lost in mist.

'Sorry about this, Moses – my boy's built for the long, dry roads of California, not the crap of Scottish weather.'

'Spare me your petrol-head nonsense, Brodie. You going to break into a Beach Boys' number next?'

'Just hurry up and get under here before you catch your death – there's nothing worse than a summer cold,' I told him, sounding like Mary McLennan.

We slumped miserably against the thick, gnarled trunk. Moses placed his foot on a raised root. In spite of the fact that he was now making a valiant effort to get on with it, he was sadly out of place. Dark Angels don't do countryside or daylight very well. It was a good job there was no mirror nearby; the rain had caused Moses' mascara to run, giving him panda eyes. I knew it wasn't a look he would appreciate so I kept quiet.

'There are things that are worse than a summer cold, Brodie,' he pondered

'Okay,' I indulged him. 'What's worse than a summer cold?'

'Him.'

Moses pointed to the police car that was parked behind Awesome in a lay-by. Duncan Bancho was out of the car, clearly having recognised the bike, and was scanning the surrounding area, looking for me.

'Trying to catch me having a piss behind a hedge, Duncan?'

Peggy Malone, who had been driving, sniggered behind her man. Moses hit me in the ribs with his elbow.

'DI Bancho. How's it going? Can we do anything to help you?'

'You're as bad as one another, Moses,' he answered. 'She's a cheeky cow, and I'm not fooled by your offer of useless assistance. Is this your bike?' he asked officiously.

'Cut the crap, Duncan, you know it is.'

He lifted his boot and kicked the brake light with such force that the Fat Boy fell on his side.

'No rear light, Miss McLennan – you've got seven days to hand in your driving licence and insurance details to the nearest police station.'

Peggy Malone wasn't smiling now. She shrugged her shoulders at me; there was nothing she could do. I hadn't expected her to. I tapped Bancho's shoulder and faced him up.

'Why don't you go after the people who are really committing crimes, Duncan? Find out who was blackmailing Alex Cattanach about a porno video she'd made. Another thing you could do that would be a bit more useful is to find out who's bringing heroin into Peterhead on fishing boats. Don't know? Maybe it's about time you did.'

He pulled away from me; I was so angry I was almost spitting.

'Don't forget,' he sneered back at me, 'hand those documents in within seven days.'

Without looking back, he jumped into the passenger seat beside Malone. We stood and watched them disappear, then Moses playfully punched me in the shoulder and jumped up and down.

'That good cop, bad cop routine of ours is really effective. But you're getting to be a real bad ass, Brodie; I've never been the good cop before.'

'Rubbish! You're always crawling to cops – scared they might get you on something if you don't at least look like you're co-operating. Anyway, it only works if we get results, which we didn't – how come he was out here?'

'He must have been following us.'

'So he knows we both went to see Tanya?'

'Ach, that's nothing. Brodie, you're her lawyer – you have to go and see her.'

He had a fair point with only one snag. Moses had no reason for his visit. The two of us together could only mean that we had gone to pump her for information.

'I'll tell you something that freaked me out.'

'If it's sexual, Moses, I don't want to know.'

He kicked me on the backside as I climbed back onto Awesome. Although my darling bike was hurt, he started first time.

'Bancho doesn't know who Mr Big is either,' continued Moses. 'And that is fucking scary, because if *he* doesn't know who his paymaster is – who does?'

'Don't let nerves make this harder than it is, Moses – everything we know points to Duncan Bancho. He's setting me up, for Christ's sake – I've been arrested twice because of him.'

'Are you sure? Because my gut's telling me he's not our ring-leader. He's no fucking Snow White – I've paid him off in the past and I've no doubt that he's bent, but he didn't know about the video.'

'Are you sure?'

'Just because you don't want to hear it, Brodie, doesn't make it a lie – I saw it in the man's eyes.'

Moses was used to making life or death decisions based on what he saw in someone's eyes.

'Well, if he's not involved, why is he pursuing me?'

'Has anyone ever told you that you are very irritating, Brodie McLennan?'

I sat in silence for the rest of the journey, pondering what he'd said. Traffic, as usual, was busy, but unusually it was flowing quite well and gave me plenty of time to think. Moses was also obviously deep in thought or he would have complained that I was taking the long route back to dropping him off at the Dark Angels' headquarters.

I drove down my favourite street in Edinburgh. When I was a little girl I used to badger Mary McLennan to take me there, after I had been to St Bernard's Well. Ann Street, named after the painter Henry Raeburn's wife, hasn't changed since it was built in 1817. The road is narrow and cobbled and it is tapered in even further by the fact that cars are allowed to park on both sides. The houses look as if they have been designed by Enid Blyton. If a child has to live in a city, then how blessed they would be to live in one like this. Each house has a long front lawn, intended for games of cricket on hot summer afternoons, so there is plenty of birdsong. I used to think that the children who lived behind these walls were the luckiest kids alive. The strange thing was I never actually ever saw a child playing in the grounds.

Awesome didn't like cobbles, and the noise from his exhaust disturbed the peace of the street. The Georgian windows reached from the floor to the ceiling, offering the casual passer-by an excellent chance to snoop.

The owner of number 189 looked out and watched, as did many of her neighbours. But, unlike them, she waved hello at me. Her guest didn't. Moses almost fell off the back of the bike and it wasn't because of my driving.

'Slow down, Brodie! Let's go back there a minute. I can't believe what I just saw!'

I ignored Moses completely and opened up the accelerator faster than a greyhound out of a trap.

Unfortunately, I could still hear him wittering behind me.

'Christ, Brodie, who would have thought it? Glasgow Joe shagging Bridget Nicholson?'

'They were hardly shagging, Moses,' I snapped. 'He was in her kitchen having a glass of wine and some supper.' I couldn't keep the snippiness out of my voice.

'No such thing as a free lunch – or supper,' he replied in his version of a posh voice. 'I thought she was supposed to be a lesbian? Do you think big Joe's enough of a man to turn any maiden's head, eh? Well, almost anyone.'

Moses was enjoying my discomfiture. I wasn't going to make him stop by telling him about the reality of the past I'd had with Joe.

'Don't worry,' he went on, 'my loyalties won't be divided. I don't want to shag either of you.'

He jumped off the bike, laughing at his own wit, and blew me a kiss whilst swaggering up the road in his own unique fashion.

I was left a bit annoyed, a bit afraid – and a lot alone.

Chapter Thirty-Seven

From: Frank Pearson
Sent: Tuesday 23 August 2005, 2.30 p.m.
To: Brodie McLennan
Subject: Are we fucked?

Can you hear my screams from here? Have just come in from court and plain brown paper envelope was on desk. Had a really bad feeling about it as soon as I saw it – please tell me am wrong. Open the attachment and email me <u>immediately</u>. I'm in Crown Office – have feeling am being watched. Don't phone me.

Frank xxx

I stared at the screen. The time had passed slowly since Bancho had harassed me and I had seen Joe cavorting with that cow. Nothing of particular interest had happened, apart from my heart breaking and my bowels going hell for leather. Now, I wanted more of nothing.

I was reluctant to open the attachment but knew that if Frank was not at his desk waiting on my email, then he was in the toilet being sick. I felt like joining him. Frank was definitely not a drama queen like myself, so whatever had spooked him was sure to send me running to the ladies.

'Lavender – do you remember the vodka that was left over from Harry's retirement do? Any of it still left in the office?' I shouted through to Lavender in the next room.

'You're out of luck – we finished that lot off when the jury decision came in on the McTavish case and you'd won.'

Unconsciously I rubbed my head. I remembered that night vaguely. A police officer, Julie McTavish, had been wrongly accused of a crime because her fingerprint was at the scene – we had taken on the ScotCrime Fingerprint Bureau and had identified several anomalies in the way they carried out fingerprinting techniques.

Julie McTavish was a fine police officer. Not only was her career saved but I got lots of good publicity over my courtroom skills. This was the only type of press I relished.

Lavender's mention of Julie reminded me that she owed me a favour, a big one. And one that I needed to call in against Duncan Bancho. Now.

'Lavender? Call Julie McTavish for me and arrange a lunch, will you?' I was still shouting to her through the open door – I wasn't sure I could trust my bowels when I got up.

'You sound as if you need this more than we do.'

Eddie Gibb came into my room with a screw-top bottle of wine, already open. The glass in his left hand didn't look too clean but I was past caring. I clicked the mouse and opened up the attachment. As I'd hoped, Eddie sat down beside me on the arm of my chair.

'You in trouble?' he asked, without adding 'again'.

'I'm just about to find out.'

We sat and watched the screen as the pixelated photograph materialized. It was like watching paint dry. The first bit came through and then it seemed to get stuck whilst Eddie and I held our breaths. A dangerous thing to do, considering how long it was taking.

'This is a crown production? I thought you had seen all the crown productions in your case?'

As we sat there, I started to feel embarrassed. I had instructed Robert Girvan, a man I didn't get on with, to represent me. It was a real slap in the face to Eddie.

'Eddie, I'm...'

'It's no big deal, Brodie. I just want you to get off – who else would employ Lavender and me if you weren't here? I hope Robert Girvan's up to the job.'

I took a deep breath; it sounded strangulated. Eddie instinctively put his arm around me. Lavender came round the back of my chair and we all stared at the screen. Lavender knew what she was looking at; she grabbed my glass and took an enormous swig.

'Holy shit!' she said through pursed lips so that it almost sounded like a whistle.

'Frank's waiting for a reply, Lav. What can I say?'

My fingers flew across the keyboard; I'm not sure whether it was wine or adrenalin that increased their speed.

From: Brodie McLennan
Sent: Tuesday, 23 August 2005, 2.38 p.m.
To: Frank Pearson
Subject: We should be having a fag by now

Good news – your instincts are spot on. Bad news – we appear to be up shit creek without a paddle.
   How did this happen?
   Brodie xxx

We sat as we were, waiting for his reply. Eddie and Lavender silently joined hands behind my back. I had the uncomfortable feeling they were praying. Unfortunately, we didn't have long to wait.

From: Frank Pearson
Sent: Tuesday, 23 August 2005, 2.40 p.m.
To: Brodie McLennan
Subject: Post-coital etiquette

Post-coital etiquette demands that you tell me the truth.
   a) Is this lethal-looking weapon – with, I might add, the MacGregor clan badge and motto on it – yours?
   b) If the answer is in the affirmative, I would like to ask why you have such a killing blade in your armoury? As a friend I would like to know – do you have any other weapons of mass destruction about your person?
   c) How has this now come to be in the Crown Office productions? When I saw you, I showed

you the photographs that the police had supplied to us. The weapon they had originally was a simple Stanley knife that could be purchased in any DIY store, as you pointed out.

I await your answers
Perplexed of Edinburgh x

From: Brodie McLennan
Sent: Tuesday, 23 August 2005, 2.48 p.m.
To: Frank Pearson
Subject: Who else is screwing us?

Hi Perplexed,
The answers are as follows:

a) The knife in the photograph is, as you guessed, mine. It is known as a whinger specifically designed to be the length of a man's gut from navel to spine. It is a MacGregor family heirloom, another wonderful legacy from my father.

b) It is in my possession because it always belongs to the heir apparent. The family legend is that whoever takes the whinger into battle is invincible. Ha bloody ha. Until recently, i.e. last week, it was in my cutlery drawer. It's marvellous for paring vegetables with. I can confirm I have no other weapons of mass destruction – if I had I would use them on the bastard who planted that evidence.

c) I don't know how the whinger is now in the Crown Office productions. There has been no break-in to my home. The only person I can think of who could have planted the evidence would be DI Bancho.

Brodie xxx

I pressed the send button and we all waited.

'I phoned Joe and told him what's happened,' said Lavender. 'He's on his way.'

'You take too much on yourself sometimes; most secretaries would say, "I hope you don't mind..?" or "Is it all right if I...?" but not you. Lavender knows best.' I couldn't help snapping at her.

Eddie jumped off the chair; he hated confront-ations. It didn't take a psychic to figure out that there was one coming this way very soon.

'You need Glasgow Joe, Brodie. I need Joe. Thank God he's on his way.'

'Joe this, Joe that – do you know he's shagging Bridget Nicholson?' I screeched at her.

Eddie's ears pricked up and he broke the habit of a lifetime – he got involved.

'I don't believe Joe is shagging that woman.'

'Is that right, Eddie? Well, sadly your love antennae aren't too sharp because I saw him in her house.'

He puffed. 'Not even if I saw him in her bed would I believe it – she's not his type.'

Eddie was stalwartly defending Joe. Why did he inspire such loyalty? I hated to admit that I was jealous.

I was relieved when Frank's email came through.

From: Frank Pearson
Sent: Tuesday, 23 August 2005, 2.55pm
To: Brodie McLennan
Subject: Shit

What about that new cleaner you were so bloody

pleased about?

Send me details now – what contractor was she from? Will do a police background check.

Frank xxx

Lavender began, 'I've got the cleaner's details in my computer next door. Maisie who cleans for me is off on holiday next week and I thought it would be handy to use your new girl rather than an agency. I'll send them straight through to Frank as he'll need to contact Fresh as a Daisy for all the personal stuff on her.'

Lavender left my office to go next door. Her mood had immediately lifted now that she had something to do. Eddie and I faced each other, wondering what to do next.

He decided on the easy option. 'I'll make a fresh cup of coffee – it sounds as if we'll all need our wits about us.'

Eddie shut the door between my office and outside. It was odd, that door was never closed. I put my hand on the brass handle to open it again, then I checked myself – obviously they wanted privacy. Maybe he was advising her to leave whilst she still had a job. It's far easier to get another job when you have one.

My paranoia was running riot.

'How's it going?' A voice said as the door opened.

Eddie hadn't wanted privacy for himself; it was for Joe. He must have seen Joe park the bike outside and he scampered. Joe was still pulling his helmet off as he walked into the office; he must have run upstairs.

Dressed all in black leather biking gear, he looked like a gorgeous Darth Vader – with more of a face, obviously. He wore a Liberty silk scarf round his neck, pale pink with delicate flowers. Far from detracting from his stinking manliness, it added to it.

I reached up to feel it.

'Why are you still wearing that old scarf? She wasn't your greatest fan, you know.'

He ran Mary McLennan's best Sunday accessory through his fingers.

'I know – I just wanted to have her near. We had our own understanding, Brodie. Your mother knew me inside out and she held me to a standard that I can't meet. When I wear a bit of her, at least I try.'

I wanted to cry at the thought of my mother. Instead, I sat down at the computer. Frank's reply was in. Joe leaned over me; a delicious concoction of peppermint chewing gum, fresh summer air, bike oil and sunshine. I sniffed long and deep – and openly. He looked down at me, puzzled.

From: Frank Pearson
Sent: Tuesday, 23 August 2005, 3.09 p.m.
To: Brodie McLennan
Subject: More shit

Brodie,
Have just checked out what Lavender sent through.

No Agnes McElhose living at Muirhouse Green, Edinburgh. There is a Robert Burns who resides there.

Robert, or Bobby, Burns is well-known in this office, and not because he has a famous name.

Have you ever seen him?

Daft question. Obviously not, I suppose, or you'd know a bit more about your new cleaner. It gives me no pleasure to say this, Brodie, but this is all shockingly sexist of you. Tut tut. Did you just assume all cleaners were women?

Bobby Burns, the one who you seem to think is Agnes, lives at 252 Muirhouse Green.

Have Googled and Agnes McElhose is the name of a girlfriend of the 'real' Rabbie Burns. The poet nicknamed her Clarinda and she named him Sylvander. She was a married lady and, unusually for Burns, the relationship was platonic.

Our Bobby Burns has a warrant out for his arrest for escaping from Saughton Prison. A female social worker went in on a visit, he attacked her and nicked her flowery coat and high heels. None of the guards gave him a second glance; mind you, he's not bonny. Stupid gets, shouldn't be letting them watch *Silence of the Lambs for* ideas, though.

The good news is – Bridget Nicholson is not his employer, she is his lawyer.

SO WHY IS SHE RISKING HER CAREER TO SHAFT YOU, BRODIE?

Leaving the office now – you can get me on my mobile.

Frank xxx

'Tell me you didn't?'

I could think of at least a hundred things that I would rather not tell Joe at the moment, so I kept silent.

298

He didn't.

'Tell me you didn't employ someone you'd never seen or met? Tell me you didn't give them a key and that you weren't always out when they were there? And tell me you didn't do all that with a notrious waster?'

My one overture of friendship to Bridget Nicholson and I hand her the keys to my house, whereby she promptly sets me up.

I looked at Joe, remembered that I had seen him in Bridget's house, and knew that although she had taken everything from me, it still wasn't enough to satisfy her hatred.

Chapter Thirty-Eight

'It's gone.'

'What's gone?' asked Joe.

My finger was raking about in my purse, pushing the mounds of copper pennies back and forth so hard I thought the nail on my index finger would be bruised.

'The white stone that Tanya Hayder gave me years ago when she was in Cornton Vale. I always thought that if I had it, she might come out okay, and so would I.'

'You don't need me to point out that you've got more to worry you than losing a bloody pebble.'

'It's not the stone itself, Joe. I know she probably bought a packet of them in a supermarket. It's the fact that it feels like an omen.' I was on

299

the back of Joe's bike, travelling down to Muir-house to see if we could get our hands on Bobby Burns.

Lothian Road was already busy; the rush hour was getting earlier all the time. The air was warm and balmy and, not for the first time, I thought that being on a motorbike was the only way to travel round the city. I had my arms around Joe's waist and he felt thinner. Had he been working out? For her? I leaned against him. His leather jacket was pliable and expensive. I could almost see how it could become a fetish. Bridget bloody Nicholson crossed my mind. Again. A pang of jealousy cut through me.

We were stopped at the traffic lights beside the Caledonian Hotel. It was the perfect opportunity to talk, but I didn't take it. If Bridget Nicholson was capable of framing me, what else was she up to? Had she turned Joe against me? Even though he was there, I still felt that the world was against me. I would have put money on that being impossible only a couple of days ago, but now I suspected she was a lot cleverer than I had given her credit for.

I saw our reflection in Fraser's shop window, scattered amongst the silver mannequins in expensive dresses and outlandish shorts. What story would people make up about us as we passed? Honeymooners on a biking tour of Scot-land? It did not look as though it would be out of the question, I kidded myself.

Joe had left his Harley behind. Today, we were on his Honda Blackbird, top speed 190 miles per hour. Whatever Joe had decided he was going to do, he intended to get us there fast to do it. We turned along Queen Street, which had almost entirely been taken over by lawyers' offices. Turning left at the traffic lights, we headed towards Stockbridge; the cobbles would be easier with the bike's thick, sticky tyres. As luck would have it, we were again stopped by a red light, which helped my voyeurism. This time I couldn't keep my eyes away from the house in Heriot Row which had been my father's home. It had not been sold after his death because his widow Bunny was still alive, albeit locked up in a secure private mental hospital.

I'd been born in that house and, after Bunny's death I would probably inherit it. Not something I relished or looked forward to, although the news of Bunny Arbuthnott's death would come as a welcome relief.

I held on even tighter to Joe as we followed the cobbled road round to the left and passed Royal Circus, a beautiful Georgian semi-circular development that would rival any architecture in Britain. Crossing Raeburn Place, I started to pray. We were uncomfortably near to Ann Street and I wasn't yet ready for a confrontation with Bridget Nicholson. I buried my face in Joe's jacket. He misunderstood my intentions and nuzzled back. When had he turned into a slut? I fumed all the way along Stockbridge, past the pram shop and the premises of expensive interior designers.

Turning right at the traffic lights we moved up past Fettes Police Headquarters and the school where Tony Blair had been a pupil in his youth. The allotments beside Inverleith Park were busy with gardeners harvesting the fruits of their labour. Maybe that's what I was doing too.

We didn't speak all the way up Ferry Road. There was no awkwardness, though; our bodies were too used to each other to feel ill at ease. What did I expect from this meeting ahead of us? I'd been around criminals for long enough to know that Bobby Burns wouldn't be struck by a pang from his conscience as soon as we walked in the door, and offer to go straight round to the police station and confess. Whoever was running this operation seemed to be able to wield more clout and fear than Glasgow Joe or Moses. But, much as I wanted to believe it, I found it difficult to see Bridget Nicholson in the role of Mrs Big. However, the reason I was on this little jaunt was because I'd underestimated her previously, so perhaps I best wise up sharpish.

The bike drew to a stop outside the entrance to a block of flats. Four in a block, covered in graffiti, it looked as downtrodden as its neighbours. Unsurprisingly, none of these council houses had been snapped up.

'Are you coming in?' Joe asked.

'If you expect me to stay outside and keep an eye on your bike, you're mistaken.'

'I didn't mean that. I meant professionally it might not look too good.'

'Thanks for thinking of my CV – but from where I'm standing, my career can't slide much further down.'

I followed him into the stairwell. It smelt sour, unpleasant, and reeked of the stench of human urine. I trod carefully over the debris of discarded chip papers. In the corner I heard a rustle, and my imagination immediately came up with images of rats nibbling on half-eaten cheeseburgers.

Joe banged on the door. 'Open up!' He looked over his shoulder but took no care to be circumspect; his reputation would buy him all the discretion he required.

The cheap plywood door swung open as if battery-operated. Bobby had scurried away to the living quarters, presumably after seeing Joe through the spyhole. The hall was dark and narrow, carpeted with dark brown nylon with golden onion swirls, the height of fashion in 1976. The house was clean. Burns lived there with his mother. Bobby – or Agnes as I knew him – was seated in the middle of the room on a dining-room chair covered with pink velour. Above the unlit gas fire there was a painting of a blue Chinese lady. I seemed to remember lots of my mum's friends having them and a story that they had been given away free if you bought a fire from British Gas.

'How's it going then?' asked Moses as he came out of the kitchen. I knew now why Bobby had let us in with ease – Moses had paved the way and told him who was about to arrive. He had made himself a cup of tea and helped himself to a Penguin biscuit. Waving the tea and biscuits at me, he spoke with his mouth full.

'There's plenty more where that came from – do you want some, Brodie?'

I shook my head; a wee snack was the last thing on my mind. Moses settled himself down and put his feet up on the tiled coffee table.

'You'd better not have made a mess in there or my ma will go mad,' said Bobby – Agnes – or whoever the hell it was. I felt as if I was back in confused Donna Diamond land again.

'I'd have thought that the state or otherwise of your ma's kitchen should be the last thing on your mind.'

The boy squirmed on his seat as Moses chastised him; God knows how long Moses had kept him there. His skinny legs were encased in tight drainpipe jeans, and now that I got a good look at him, I saw he wasn't in the first flush of youth. Sallow skin was stretched like parchment over his cheeks and mousy brown hair hung lankly to his shoulders. This Bobby Burns had been caught without his shoes on; no doubt his mother forbade the wearing of them on the front-room carpet. His well-worn socks scrunched the shag up and down as Joe stood on Bobby's toes, and then Bobby cried, 'What did you want to go and do that for?'

Joe was wearing metal-studded bike boots and I could see a tiny droplet of blood form on Bobby's cotton sock.

Joe got off his foot and paced back and forth in front of him. He reached into his boot and pulled out a knife that made the whinger look like a penknife. He ran his finger up the blade. Even I winced as droplets of blood formed a line along the imprint where the blade had been. Joe's hair was hanging free around his shoulders and he looked like a savage, a side of him that I knew he'd tried to suppress and make amends for. How many times had he told Moses that it was a mug's game? I had drawn him back into the mire. Guilt pressed my back into the wall.

He moved fast.

One tap from Joe's size-twelve boot and the chair fell over.

Two flicks from his knife and Bobby's jeans lay like cheese strings around him. Joe's movement slowed down as he went for the boy's cheap cotton boxers, but the skinny bugger held on to them and crouched down on the rug.

'You're a mad bastard, Glasgow Joe. You fucking leave my knackers alone.'

His hands were cupped over his balls. Joe ignored his words and pushed him over with his foot. He placed his boot none too gently on his neck and bent over his victim like a gamekeeper gralloching a deer. When Bobby felt the coldness of the blade move down and land on his groin, he started to cry.

Joe reached down and grabbed him by the scalp. Yelping, Bobby was dragged to his feet. Dancing on his tiptoes, a grotesque marionette, Joe sneered into his face.

'Start talking,' he snarled. 'You *KNOW* what I'm after.' Joe's knee connected with the testicles. Bobby crashed to the ground again. Rolling in the foetal position, he vomited on his mum's shag-pile carpet.

'Let's start with the easy questions – who gave you the order?' Joe asked. 'Bridget Nicholson?'

'Fuck off, Joe! I thought you knew the score but you know nothing.'

Joe's foot attached itself to his face; he wouldn't be entering a beauty pageant anytime soon.

'If you want to know so much, get your bitch to ask Tanya Hayder.'

It was a good idea.

If Tanya thought we had Bobby on the defensive, she might be a bit more forthcoming with what she had kept from us. I flipped open my mobile and called The Castle. The fact that it was more like a hotel than rehab meant I could call any time and get who I wanted.

'Can I speak to Tanya Hayder, please?'

I used my best telephone voice and informed them I was her lawyer.

I was asked to hold on whilst they went for her.

When the female voice came back on the line, it was obviously not Tanya. 'I believe you are asking for Miss Tanya Hayder?' the woman enquired.

I agreed, with my posh voice still working, giving her details of who I was.

More silence.

'Please wait one moment whilst I speak to my superior,' la-di-da told me.

God – did they know I hadn't exactly played ball on my last visit? Was Tanya a grass now amongst everything else?

The man who, came on the line was certainly succinct and none too friendly.

'I'm sorry, Miss McLennan – Miss Hayder is no longer a guest here.'

Shit.

She'd bolted.

'When did she leave?' I asked.

The man breathed heavily as he considered my question. He had probably been told all about me by Duncan Bancho, I'd imagine.

'I have checked your name out, Miss McLennan, and am aware that you and Miss Hayder were professionally connected. In a legal capacity,' he quickly added.

'Yes,' I layered it on, 'I'm sure you have. I wouldn't doubt that you'd be very professional – and I do appreciate it. One can't be too careful.' I tried not to look at Joe standing beside Bobby Burns as I said it.

'May I fax you confirmation that I represent Miss Hayder?'

I was praying he'd say 'no'.

'Not any more you don't,' he informed me.

I swore under my breath. I really couldn't blame Tanya for mandating, but I really didn't want it to be for Bridget Nicholson.

'Who's representing Miss Hayder now?' I asked, already knowing the answer.

'Unfortunately, where Miss Hayder has gone she won't be needing a lawyer,' slime-man told me. 'As her ex-lawyer you need to know, I'd imagine. Miss Hayder met with a rather nasty accident in the showers. I would ask you to be discreet about this, Miss McLennan – we haven't informed her relatives yet, and we don't want the papers to hear about it. It would cause panic, and many of our clients are paranoid enough as it is.'

'An accident?' I parroted. 'How bad is it?'

'Oh, rather bad. Rather bad. About as bad as it gets, unfortunately.'

There was nothing more to say.

I ended the call.

'Tanya Hayder's dead,' I told the threesome

watching me.

From the look on his face, I wasn't telling my cleaner anything he didn't already know.

Chapter Thirty-Nine

We had consciously chosen the time and venue for our meeting. It was imperative that no one saw us together, otherwise the career that I had fought so hard for would be over. The career in question belonged to Detective Constable Julie McTavish this time, not myself.

The one o'clock gun rocked the café and the tourists at Edinburgh Castle stopped to look around. The one o'clock gun goes off every day so that the good burghers of Edinburgh can set their watches; however, there is some merit in the argument that routinely firing a cannon is a rather imprudent act in today's atmosphere of red alerts. Inhabitants of the City, unless they are caught unawares, don't react to the gun – to do so would be childish and foolish and mark you out as a tourist – nightmares for the capital's would-be snob brigade.

Julie and I sat within the sharp glass angular windows that overlooked Princes Street Gardens. The walls were painted with soldiers in Red Coats – lobster backs. The murals seemed to be depicting the Battle of Culloden. It was so taste-less a scene that I lost my appetite. The food didn't help, mind you.

'How's the prawn sandwich?' I asked Julie as she picked up a stale piece of bread oozing a nuclear pink sauce with bits in it that had gone orange at the edges.

'As good as it looks.'

She owed me a favour but that didn't mean she was happy about it. I reminded her of the worst time in her life and she was a perfect example of being careful what you wish for. Sure, we had successfully restored her career, but her superiors and colleagues weren't happy about the ripples caused by her case. It was well nigh impossible for her to gain promotion, and any shitty detail that was required to be done had her name all over it. Any complaints and she would be told that she could leave if she wasn't happy. Having fought so hard for it, she thought she couldn't give it up. The conflict showed in her eyes, which were ringed with black and had large bags under them caused by cortisol, the antecedent of adrenalin. Her eyes showed a career of too many late and stressful nights and no good food.

'How are you doing – in the force, I mean? Is your career going forward again, Julie?' I asked unnecessarily; my spies already knew how crap her so-called career was.

No light shone in her brown eyes. The hair that had once been expensively cut and coloured looked harsh and brassy around her puffy face and her make-up was too thick. Julie was hiding something. Was it something more than the red broken veins on her cheeks, put there by the two bottles of white wine she drank daily when her shift was finished, according to my sources?

I needed to find out what I was here for, the information that was the real reason for meeting Julie today.

'Julie – do you know how Tanya Hayder died?'

She stared at me with something close to dislike, fighting with the knowledge that she needed to keep me onside.

'They're trying to keep it quiet, Brodie, but you can't hush up anything that happens in a rehab, especially one with celebs in it; they have too much time on their hands. Anything at all acts as a diversion and something like this...'

'Anything would help, Julie – all I know is that Tanya had an accident in the showers and she's dead. We all know Tanya's been on smack for years. I saw her a couple of days ago; she didn't look good. The slightest thing could have carried her off.'

A small child was having a tantrum in the corner, standing up in the high-chair and throwing her food around. Julie McTavish looked at her enviously. I coughed to bring her attention back to the table.

'Well, all I know is, it wasn't a small matter, it wasn't a *slight thing.*'

'It was described as an accident to me when I rang.'

'Well, it would be – you're her lawyer. You *were* her lawyer. Anyway, rehab is big business. Once this is leaked to the press, they'll have to pay people to stay.'

The child had quietened down now and had progressed to throwing strawberry ice cream at anyone who passed within two feet of the high-chair. Julie was still distracted by the child, and the wistful look in her eye made me think maybe hers was one case that I would have been better off losing. At least then she would have been able to get on with her life instead of being stuck in purgatory at Craigmillar.

'Compliments of Patch – I phoned him because I knew that he'd been called in.' She handed me an envelope. I knew that it contained photographs that I didn't want to see. So I did what I always do in these situations – I tried to distract myself.

'Patch? I thought he was on holiday,' I commented.

'You know Patch never goes on holiday – he goes to Elvis conventions. He had to delay his departure so that he could cover this. When he heard the details over the phone, he said he didn't want to leave it to his deputy. As we sit here his head and heart are at an Elvis convention in Porthcawl.'

I was surprised that Julie and Patch were so close. He didn't discuss his Elvis addiction with just anyone.

Now that I knew Patch had deferred his leaving, it made me even more nervous. In some way these photos must be connected to my case; nothing else would have induced him to stay.

The ten-by-eights were crammed into an envelope that was slightly too small for them; and, having been forced in, they were reluctant to leave. The corner of the envelope tore as I yanked them out, the photographs bent and curled at the corners. But not enough. Not enough to stop me seeing history repeat itself again – only Tanya had been luckier than Alex Cattanach. She was most definitely dead.

The grainy pictures showed a skinny, naked Tanya lying in the shower. Stab wounds covered her body. There were signs of strangulation and her cheeks had been slit from the corners of her lips to her ears. Grotesquely, she grinned at me.

'You might want to be a bit more discreet with those.' Julie's hand obliterated the picture of Tanya, as a horror-struck mother yanked her son away from my shoulder.

I put them back in the envelope to peruse at my leisure. Something to look forward to. I had other things to discuss with Julie.

'Something big is happening in this city. It involves Tanya Hayder, Alex Cattanach, Bridget Nicholson and me – not that I know anything about it. I'm caught up somehow and I'm buggered if I can figure it out yet. On top of that, I think that the balance of power is changing hands from Moses and the Dark Angels to someone else.'

'Bridget Nicholson?' Julie offered.

'It could be – but I know Duncan Bancho is tied up in all of this, he's completely bent. I need to know if you've heard any scandals, Julie, any whisperings.'

'Personally, I think that Duncan Bancho's clean. I know he's impetuous and he doesn't follow the rules, but I think he's an okay guy. He's been decent to me since the case, he even said he was sorry for all the trouble I'd gone through. Believe it or not, he even said I wouldn't have been cleared unless you had been my lawyer because you're not afraid to stand up for what's right. You take on the establishment and no one else would.'

I drank the dregs of my cold coffee to stop myself spluttering.

'He couldn't buy me with a few drops of honey from his tongue. And, to be honest, Julie, I'm getting a bit suspicious about how many people are going out of their way to tell me how smashing he is.' The tone of my voice had raised several octaves and I sounded harsh and shrewish.

I made my excuses and left. I wasn't getting anything I needed from her and we had never been friends. Julie promised to keep in touch in that awkward way people do when they have to end a conversation they weren't enjoying anyway. I had the feeling I wouldn't want to hear anything she had to tell me, because it contradicted my own views. I was too like Moses in that respect – why keep 'no' men around?

I made my way to George Street and collected Awesome. Heading to my destination, I wondered about the friendship between Julie and Patch. I couldn't explain it and it bothered me. I also couldn't explain why I was so bothered about something so irrelevant, compared to everything else in my life at the minute.

When I arrived, I followed the sound of Elvis and the stench of death straight to Patch's morgue. I knew he'd be expecting me; in light of recent developments his trip would be delayed indefinitely. I pushed open the door. A body was already lying on the slab, a sheet discreetly pulled over it. I felt sick immediately. Through the thin white cotton, I could make out the skinny form of Tanya Hayder.

'This won't take long. No need for me to scrub up,' he shouted towards me as I came in.

I immediately followed him to the gurney. With the swiftness of a magician he pulled the sheet from Tanya. Death had not restored her beauty, but it had given her a kind of peace.

'She'd lived a hard life; she's younger than you, Brodie, yet her internal organs are in worse shape than mine. She's in a better place now.'

'Patch, Elvis is addling your mind. You belong to the Wee Free Kirk and they believe that right now Tanya is being roasted in hell's fire, damned forever.'

'Well, they can be a tad harsh at times – this lassie has been more sinned against than sinner.'

'You must have known a different Tanya Hayder.'

I was sad. I didn't want Patch to tell me what I already knew. I regretted my last meeting with her but I'd have to learn to live with that.

'Anyway, she left something for you, Brodie – it's only a copy, mind, they have the original at St Leonard's. Unfortunately, DI Bancho is on the case, it being another one of the Slasher cases.'

'Slasher?'

'It's the name the police are using. Duncan Bancho is trying to put a stop to it, he's wary of the case being sensationalised, but he can't stop officers talking. He's trying to stop the press printing that there's a serial killer on the loose.'

'Is there?' I asked.

'No – there is a psychotic knife-man out and about the closes of Edinburgh but not a serial killer. The person who murdered Tanya was the same person who attacked Alex Cattanach, but – and this is something that your average Plod won't accept – the murderer of Donna Diamond was a copycat. DI Bancho, however, has accepted my findings.'

'What is this? Has Duncan Bancho been made a saint and no one's told me? How come everyone's singing the praises of a bent copper all of a sudden? Have you not heard what Moses has to say about him?'

'You let your personal likes and dislikes cloud the issue sometimes, Brodie.'

'No way – that guy is on the take. I've seen it myself, I've seen what he does.'

'Brodie, think about it – what have you seen? A young man who you have irritated beyond the bounds of sanity – of that I have no doubt as he's not the first to be put in that position – is somewhat annoyed by you. But if he's so crooked, how come you have no proof?'

'I have proof.'

As I said it I could feel my heels digging in. I knew I was right.

'It's not seemly to argue over the bodies of the deceased. It's not seemly.' Patch thought differently about the dead to anyone else. In some ways they were just empty containers to him, and yet in a more subtle way they were like old friends – albeit naked, hacked-up, dead friends – who he shared most of his working days with. To me, they just looked like a reason to empty my stomach.

'The Slasher is stepping up the tempo – look at the ferocity of the stab wounds. This time they were determined the victim would not survive. Twenty-five wounds to the abdomen and legs. She was knifed in the abdomen first and must have cowered down on the floor. There are wounds on her head and her shoulders from where she must have curled up trying to protect herself. The legs were injured when she pulled them up to try to protect them – all of the marks are predominantly around the outer thigh of the left leg and further down that side. She had curled up in a foetal ball...' Patch's voice got quieter as he said this; both of us saw the irony of a traditionally safe position being Tanya's final one. 'The shower room looked like a slaughter house,' he finished.

'The killer must have been covered in blood – someone would have seen them leave,' I said.

'I have a theory on that.' Patch always had a theory on everything. He leaned over Tanya Hayder. I didn't go and meet him halfway, rather I leaned back towards the wall.

'I believe the killer stripped naked and got into the shower with Tanya – I think it was someone she knew. The major injuries occurred before she started to defend herself.'

'How do you know that?' I asked.

'It's a hunch – nothing I can point to specifically yet.'

'The cuts on the eyes – that's not something that Alex Cattanach has. The markings on Alex's cheeks look like Celtic spirals, and these...' I wavered, not really knowing what I was looking at.

'They're runic symbols – in the past it wasn't unusual to see this sort of thing. This almost looks like primitive, ritual cuttings, but in this case the marks are not designed to promote good health or courage. The murderer continued brutalising Tanya after she was dead, the stabbing continued, and then these slits on the eyes were made post mortem.'

'This and the attack on Alex Cattanach? They're not about pagan enchantment, Patch. They're barbarism.'

'Well, I think Duncan Bancho wants to speak to you about that. He knows that you went to see Tanya and that you had an argument; one of the other residents complained to the warden.'

'I intend to avoid Saint Duncan until I've got this figured out,' I replied.

'Are you any closer to doing so?'

I shook my head. I couldn't bear to hear myself speak the truth.

'Here's a copy of the letter Tanya Hayder wrote to you.'

Patch passed me the document. I wasn't surprised. Prisoners write letters. They have it down to an art form. Some of my clients earn by making scrolls for other inmates to send to their loved ones. But this was no 'scroll'. The only decoration it had on it was Tanya's tears.

Hiya Brodie,
I'm sory we fought. I should of told you what u want to know. specialy with u being in such bother and al that.
I know about the vid cos I was in it.

317

Me and wee Moira Campbell from Pilrig Street. I dont think u met her, nice lassie, her da was a minster and then she got hooked on smack from some dodgy boyfriend. Anyway, she's ded now so u wont get any info from her. Sometimes I think I see her hanging about the foot of The Walk, seeing if she can pick up a punter, but its just some other poor lassie. i think we must all look the same, even to me.

Moira comited suicide cos of the video. She wasn't a lesbian and I think wud was terified that her da wud see it and that would end him. She had her principles, altho I used to tel her not to let it bother her. I suppose her old man wouldn't have been too happy at the sight of her seling herself. Don't get me started on ministers, though. Two-faced bastards, the lot of them.

The vid was a rite bad porno movie. It was filmed in some solicitors office. I was going to blackmale them. If I can only get myself some money toguther then I can go straight. I KNOW I CAN.

I cant name names – it's too dodgy. But I've got a copy of the tape – find it and youll know rite away whose involved.

I gave it to Moira's da – and I made him swear to me that he would never look. He's the minster of St Jude's Episcopal church in Leith.

See you soon, hunnnee. Did I say that I was sory?
Tanya xxx

I looked at Patch, who had been reading over my shoulder, and then I ran like the wind.

Chapter Forty

St Jude's Church in Leith has its own graveyard.

As I walked through the large wrought-iron gates, Joe was already there – unsurprisingly, given that I had phoned him and asked him to collect Tanya Hayder's package as I left the morgue. I may also have had a few words to say about the importance of getting it before Duncan Bancho did. The Rag Doll is less than five minutes from the church and – yet again – I knew Joe was my best chance of success. Patch would have enough questions to answer without making this a waste of time, so I couldn't allow my personal feelings for Joe to mess this up. Quite apart from the small matter of my liberty, there was a serial killer at large – for, as far as I was concerned, Alex Cattanach was dead. Maybe worse than.

Nothing with Joe was ever simple, though. He was standing in the graveyard under a leafy tree. The birds were singing and beside him stood what can only be described as a broken man. The broken man was wearing a dog collar. Joe had clearly found the Reverend Campbell, Moira's father.

I saw Joe placed his arm around Campbell and pulled him close, patting his back like a child as they stood in front of her simple gravestone, and, as I got closer, I could hear what he was saying to the man too.

'You weren't a bad father – you were an unlucky one. The streets of Leith are running with drugs – Moira was just in the wrong place at the wrong time. What could you have done?'

'I've asked myself that every hour on the hour since I heard the news, Joe. I've lost my faith and I just don't have the courage to resign from the only life I know. Moira grew up here playing in the trees. This is her final resting place – at least I know where she is at nights now. I come out and speak to her; sometimes, I think she even answers me.'

'You're doing good work here, Mike,' Joe comforted him. 'I know some of the kids you've rescued. You couldn't save Moira but you've managed to do exactly that with many others.'

'I couldn't do it without your help, Joe.'

I wasn't intending to eavesdrop – I was simply waiting for an opportune time to introduce myself – but now that Campbell had dropped that bombshell into the conversation, I hid behind the tree and planned to listen more intently. Unfortunately, Joe waved his hand at the Reverend and silenced him on the subject.

I walked out of the shadows and Joe introduced us to each other.

'We'd better get going, Mike,' he said as soon as the formalities were out of the way. 'If anyone shows up, I don't want it to be awkward for you. Just tell them that you gave it to us and let me worry about them.'

Reverend Campbell handed a white padded envelope over to Joe, who placed it under his arm. I noticed that it was unopened; the Reverend had kept his word to Tanya. Lucky for him, I thought, as we went out the back gate to the graveyard. Glancing over my shoulder, I saw Duncan Bancho and Peggy Malone walking up the path towards the minister. Unseen, Joe and I ran as if the devil himself were after us. We knew that the Rag Doll was too obvious; there was only one person to go to.

Moses.

Hillside Crescent is a much underrated part of Edinburgh. Formerly, it was classed to be at the top of Leith Walk or Easter Road. In reality the architecture is much more akin to Carlton Crescent across the road. The houses there cost well over a million and have done for much longer than the current property boom. Moses bought his for a song when he was sixteen. I never did know where the finance came from, but now I suspect my grandad had a hand in it somewhere.

The flat – or lair – of the Dark Angels was unique. It resembled a film set. In a large drawing room to the front of the flat, the walls were lined with bunk-beds like the catacombs in Rome. The place was spotless. Moses was a neat freak and I'm sure that many teenage runaways who sought refuge with the Dark Angels found it easier to live on the streets than with Moses' commandments.

The original Georgian door had been painted glossy black, and had a shiny brass door-knocker. For once I didn't feel ashamed of my housewifery skills in comparison; whatever else Bobby, or Agnes, was, he was a damned good cleaner.

After our meeting yesterday, Moses had brought him back to the lair so that we could decide what to do with him. Whoever the much-insulted Mr Big actually was, we knew that he was capable of a level of violence that few could match. I couldn't even gut a dead fish, so that was me out of the picture. But I like to think smart. The attack on Alex Cattanach had given me an idea. I had asked Moses to get some sodium pent-athol, which I intended to use in conjunction with hypnosis. I figured that Bobby would tell me all I needed to know without him suffering so much as a bleeding nose, as long as Kailash came good on her claim to be adept at putting people under. That was my hope anyway. However, that had to be put on the backburner for the time being, so that I could watch Tanya's final present for me.

The Alchemist opened the door to me and Joe.

'My trial's up on Friday,' he said without plea-santries 'I hope you've not been too busy trying to save your own arse to look after mine. The gear you asked Moses to get is in the fridge. Tell me if you're taking it today. Moses makes me keep tabs on all the drugs I have on account of the Angels – sometimes the temptation is too much.'

We followed him into the large hallway. The black and white tiles were newly polished; not only did they shine but they were extremely slippery I followed Joe to the shoe cupboard; we knew by now that Moses would expect us to take off our shoes. There were some plastic slipper-ettes available for guests but I refused to use them, even though Moses said the acid from my feet would stink his rugs. It was a point of principle. The slipperettes didn't fit Joe's feet, but I doubt that Moses would have the audacity to suggest he wore them, even if they did.

Bobby Burns sat in the corner and waved a hello as we walked in. That seemed very friendly, given our last meeting.

'Valium,' explained Kailash, who sat in the best seat in the house, a red velvet chaise longue.

'He was being a right pain in the arse, shouting about kidnapping and everything. I've got enough problems with the neighbours without him adding to them,' said Moses.

I nodded as if his behaviour was the most natural thing in the world. Moses abhorred chaos and violence in his home. Mozart played softly in the background, as he had read somewhere that listening to the composer increased your intelligence. 'Easier than reading books,' he said when I questioned him about his choice of music. Although he was trying – and succeeding – to educate himself, it was because he had been so badly let down by the state system that he was lacking in the first place. He hated having any obvious chink in his armour. My grandad was teaching him philosophy and he had taken to Nietzsche in particular. 'That which does not kill us makes us stronger' was written in gold italic script in his bedroom, the first thing he saw every morning when he awoke.

'I had a helluva job getting my hands on a video, Brodie, everyone has DVD players now.'

The battered VCR looked out of place underneath the sixty-inch high-definition LCD screen that Moses had imported from the States. Three seats were arranged around it, as if for film magnates at a private screening.

'What about him?' I asked, nodding towards Bobby.

'He'll have to stay – he's freaking out Angelina and she won't have him anywhere near her,' Moses answered.

Angelina ruled the roost. A plump girl of eighteen, she mothered them all. She had won her place by virtue of her cooking skills; we often swapped recipes and she had taught me techniques such as how to make a perfect soufflé. Moses had, at her request, sent her on a cookery course. I wondered what Nick Nairn and his middle-class cooks had made of her – if they had seen past the lip ring, black lipstick and spider tattoo, I'm sure that she would have bowled them over as much as she did us. I hoped Moses had the sense to shack up with her one day; although, somehow, I suspected it wouldn't happen as the light of unrequited love burned in Angelina's eyes every time she looked at him. All she had to do was drop three stones and he'd be eating out of her hand.

Angelina walked in carrying a large tray laden with freshly baked goods. Her shortbread was to die for. My hand shot out to grab some before she had even put the tray down. Angelina smiled; Moses and Joe looked askance.

'It's organic, fresh out of the oven, Brodie,' she told me with pride as I took my first bite.

'You have got to teach me how you get it so crisp.'

'Don't you dare, Angelina,' interrupted Moses as we chatted without concern for what was really going on around us. 'She'll be like the side of a house before you know it. Unable to get into her leathers and then always late for court.'

Moses spoke for me. If Angelina was bothered by his remarks I couldn't say, for she turned and left the room as silently as she had come in. Kailash surveyed her as she departed.

'I'd keep that girl happy if I were you, Moses. She could be very useful – curves like that are always in demand, and I'd be happy to give her employment if you don't watch your step.'

Through the closed door Angelina shouted: 'Make sure that creepy bastard stays with you, Moses.'

Bobby smiled formlessly, unaware of what was going on. He had been hastily dressed before he left his flat in what looked like his mother's trousers – navy blue polyester with a seam sewn in and an elasticated waist. Moses followed my eyes and answered my unspoken question.

'I wasn't wasting my time squeezing him into those skinny jeans.'

Joe, who had been fixing the video, nodded that it was ready. Moses stood up and pressed a remote control. The heavy gold-edged black curtains swung shut and the room became dark. Every cough and snuffle was amplified. I shifted uncomfortably in my seat as the pit of my stomach heaved and rolled as though I was on a trawler in a force ten gale. Moses interrupted the mood.

'Before we start, I want to get this clear in my

head. Angus McCoy said that Alex Cattanach was blackmailing the people in this video. Donna Diamond thought that Alex Cattanach was in the video and being blackmailed because of it. Then we have Tanya Hayder who has a copy of the video, she starred in it and admits she was going to blackmail people but hadn't gotten around to it. What the fuck is going on?'

'That's what we want to find out, Moses,' I answered, 'So if you sit down and shut up Joe can switch it on.'

Joe pressed the button and ran back to his seat.

'Is it on?' a woman's voice shouted from the screen. I recognised it. The knowledge of the name evaded me. It was on the tip of my tongue, irritating like a small piece of grit in my eye. I knew it was there but I could not put my finger on it. Which one of them was it?

The camera panned out around the room. A large desk occupied the centre of it. I could see the certificates on the wall but couldn't read the names. Law books filled the shelves, but there was nothing so far that I could identify. A photo-graph on the desk; all we could see was the back of it. The cameraman was teasing us.

Tanya came into view, even prettier than when I had first known her. Pain stopped my heart. What a waste. She was dressed like the schoolgirl she was. The uniform certainly wasn't that of her alma mater.

'Get in beside Tanya,' spoke a harsh voice, a voice that expected to be obeyed. Moira Camp-bell came creeping onto the screen, looking skinny and undernourished. Head bowed, her hair was cut in a plain schoolgirl bob. Every inch a minister's daughter. The uniform she wore probably belonged to her.

Problems had already toughened Tanya. Her defences seemed so much stronger than Moira's.

'Wipe your nose – there's snot dripping from it.'

I wondered why the voice didn't tell Moira to wipe her tears? Were those part of the enjoyment? Tanya was stripping, as if for games. Moira stood still, head bent, shoulders stooped, holding her own hand. We could hear her crying. I knew without looking at him that Moses wouldn't be able to watch this, it was too real to him, too much like the life he had known.

'Get in there and help,' the voice behind the camera shouted.

Bridget Nicholson, naked except for a schoolteacher's gown, walked on set. My head reeled back as if I had been punched. Moses sat up and took interest. Bridget Nicholson proceeded to strip the crying girl, ignoring her tears. Tanya, now almost naked, eager to be the teacher's pet, desperate to please, asked: 'Do you want me to keep my socks on, or shall I take them off?'

'Keep your socks on,' the woman's voice replied. I still didn't know her. Was it Alex Cattanach? Donna Diamond said it was.

Had she been killed for that belief?

Chapter Forty-One

'I know what you're up to, Brodie McLennan!' Joe shouted after me. 'You don't even know if she's in,' he continued.

'Well, then, I'll find her wherever she is.'

I was almost at the front door now. It was a very large impressive entrance. Stone urns stood to attention at either side, filled to overflowing with flowers in bloom.

'Are you here to protect your girlfriend?' I snarled as I rang the doorbell.

'What the hell are you on about?' He was a good liar; he actually sounded surprised.

'It's not the first time you've been here – I saw you. Moses and I saw you in her kitchen window. At least Bridget had the decency to wave.'

He grabbed me by the shoulders, forcing me to face him. I looked up at the windows to see if any neighbours were watching but the only sound was that damned birdsong. How had I ever found it enchanting? I rang the doorbell again, this time keeping my finger on it. I knew how irritating it was from my encounter with Duncan Bancho. I heard a rustling on the upper landing – someone was in and it sounded as if they were going to answer the door. Bridget obviously hadn't seen it was me, or maybe the thought of Glasgow Joe was exciting enough to overcome the obvious drawback of my presence.

'Where's the bloody fire – I'm coming.'

Bridget was out of breath. I wondered what she had been up to. The question was answered soon enough. She opened the door wearing nothing but a towel, and I sniffed some middle-aged woman's perfume – Shalimar or something equally unimaginative.

'Haven't you heard of making an appointment?' she asked me.

She left the door open and walked back into her hallway. I took this as an invitation to enter. The wide oak floorboards were smooth and golden. She didn't demand that I remove my shoes, unlike Moses. Joe followed closely behind me.

In spite of myself, I was excited that I was entering a house on Ann Street. Another childish goal achieved. However, I didn't like the fact that Joe was with me, given that he was the only other living soul who knew of my obsession with this street. He watched me closely. I suspect he had more than one reason to.

Bridget walked up the curving staircase. It was elegant, reminiscent of *Gone with the Wind* only smaller and more tasteful. A runner of red carpet went up the centre of each stair. On either side of the carpet was pristine white paint.

'Agnes does a good job of your place,' I shouted up to her. She ignored me but Joe shot me a warning look. My voice seemed to echo around the high hallway as a glass cupola showered light in. The atmosphere was peaceful elegance; no wonder Joe liked it.

Bridget walked into the kitchen. Opening the well-stocked stainless-steel American fridge, she pulled out a chilled bottle of champagne and filled three glasses. Additionally, she placed fat strawberries in a cut-glass bowl and offered me one alongside my champagne.

'It adds to the flavour,' she added helpfully, as if I'd never had champagne before.

Bridget's blonde hair hung about her shoulders. Newly washed, it shone, and I could not in all honesty say that it looked like a skanky mane, even though I wanted to as usual. The thick white towel showed off her light golden tan, no doubt obtained from a tanning salon in Stockbridge. Her toenails were also professionally pedicured. What was this with me and women's feet, was I becoming a foot fetishist? I was pleased to note the gnarly blue varicose veins that marred her otherwise attractive legs. At least I didn't have those, and, if Kailash was anything to go by, I wouldn't.

I sniffed the strawberry; it was deliciously ripe. Bridget hadn't made the mistake of sticking them in the fridge and spoiling their flavour.

'I came here for answers, Bridget. This isn't a social call and a glass of inferior champagne will not make it one.'

'Prosecco Valdo is all the rage this summer,' she haughtily informed me, but her use of 'Prosecco' instead of champagne did make me wonder: if she was the blackmailer and raking in so much money, why was she buying cheap wine?

'Bring your wine through to the drawing room,' she ordered. I was somewhat surprised that she hadn't excused herself to get dressed, but it showed me just how intimate she and Joe were –

and I didn't like it.

A Waterford crystal chandelier hung from the ceiling, and I could see our little trio in the ornate gilt mirror that was hung over the fireplace. Joe towered above us, his masculinity dominating the room. We sat down on the overstuffed sofas and Bridget and I faced each other like gunslingers. Joe took the easy way out and opted for a wooden chair on the outskirts of the action, ready to jump in if things got too rough, or jump out if they got too embarrassing.

'I've seen the video, Bridget,' I told her.

'Did you enjoy it?' she asked.

'You are one sadistic bitch. Moira Campbell didn't want to be there.'

She stared at me coldly. 'What makes you so sure that I wanted to be there, Brodie?'

'I've already told you that I've seen it.'

'And that makes you the expert?' she asked, putting down her glass and getting up from her seat.

'Would you like one?'

Picking up an antique silver cigarette case, she offered it first to Joe. He declined and, as an afterthought, she passed it in my direction. She didn't know him as well as I thought. I picked one up. Joe glared at me. I put it back.

A smile formed on Bridget's lips as if to say I was a stooge and that was how she had played me – he who laughs last laughs loudest. Let Bridget think I was a naïve idiot – more than one successful person in history had used that strategy.

'What happened between you and Alex Cattanach?' I resumed. 'You were pretty much an item. I even heard talk that you had arranged a civil partnership. After I had been to see her in the asylum, you seemed pretty upset when you asked me how she was.'

'You flatter me with your attentions. You seem to take more than a passing interest in my affairs. I didn't know you cared, Brodie.'

'Our lives seemed to overlap, much to my distaste. I was dismayed by your girlfriend's overt interest in me and I had the sneaking suspicion that you had something to do with Alex Cattanach's curiosity.'

'I can't take the credit for that – you managed to piss her off all on your own. You seem to have a talent for it. Is that her only talent, Joe?' she purred at him; she was far too old to be playing the ingénue and it was nauseating.

'Brodie has rare and unique abilities in many fields, Bridget, all of them to my taste.' Joe's voice was deep and censorious but Bridget refused to be insulted.

'What happened between you and Alex Cattanach?' I asked, ignoring how I'd felt when Joe had supported me.

'It's very simple. She found someone else and dumped me. I was hurt.'

'Hurt enough to attack her?'

'Don't be so stupid, Brodie. I got over her; thanks to you, actually.'

I shifted my weight in the chair. She misunderstood and hissed: 'Don't flatter yourself; you're not my type. Joe, on the other hand, is a different story – I have always been partial to going over to the enemy now and again.'

'I can imagine,' I said, not wanting to imagine any such thing at all. 'Who was Alex's new girl-friend?' I pressed, steering us back on course. 'And how come no one else has spoken about her?'

'I don't owe you or Alex Cattanach any favours. If you want to find out who her girlfriend was then you'll have to do it yourself.'

'I think you might want to help me slightly more than you realise, Bridget,' I countered. 'There is the small matter of the tape – what age were the girls?'

'They were over sixteen, and even if they weren't you can't prove when that video was made. I'm not talking and the other two girls are dead.'

'What about the mystery lady? The woman behind the camera? Was it Alex Cattanach?'

Bridget walked over to her music system and selected a compilation of love songs. It was dire – she whipped through the first few bars of some dirges sung by an overblown American woman before settling on Whitney Houston. It seemed horrendous to me, but there was something pitiful in the way that Bridget stood. The slump of her shoulders and the way her thin mouth turned down at the corners made me think that perhaps Alex *had* been the love of her life – everything else was just bravado.

I didn't have time for sympathy, though.

'I asked you if Alex Cattanach was the camerawoman.'

'No, she was not – she abhorred the video; it was against her so-called bloody principles. God ... you know even better than I do what Alex is like – was like – when it came to right and wrong.'

Bridget walked up and down on the red hand-made Turkish carpet, smoking furiously, drawing deep with every breath. Lost in her own thoughts I saw that this was a routine she carried out often, probably every time she was under stress.

'She couldn't take the pressure of being a lesbian, you know – she felt as if she was sinning against God. It drove her to drink, and she was a pretty mean drunk.'

'Personally, I didn't find her too sweet sober.'

'I had nothing to do with that crusade of hers against you, Brodie. I'm not saying that I didn't enjoy it, because that would be a lie. There are few things that I would have enjoyed more than seeing her nail you for fraud. But I didn't start it up, I didn't ask her to go after you.'

Her red-taloned hands picked up her glass. Draining it, she left to get a refill.

'Why aren't you saying anything?' I hissed at Joe.

'I thought you were doing well on your own,' he whispered back.

The fridge door slammed shut – so did our mouths.

'You were kindly saying how delighted you would have been if Cattanach had nailed me,' I said as Bridget reappeared.

'Of course. There's no pretence between us, Brodie. I hate you and you despise me.'

I ignored the dig and went on, 'Donna Diamond thought that Alex was being blackmailed.'

'Why?'

'Because Alex instructed Donna...'

I had barely got a few words out before Bridget interrupted me. 'Shit. Complete horse shit. There is absolutely no way that Alex would ever have gone to Donna Diamond if she had been in trouble. Think about it – it doesn't make sense. Even before her operation she wasn't a great lawyer. Donna and David before her were both too preoccupied with what was or wasn't between their legs to think about the law.'

The silver tray on the Georgian mahogany sideboard contained glasses and a decanter of whisky. I put my wine glass down and walked over. I poured myself a generous measure and offered one to Joe, who declined. Full of manners, as my mother would have said. Bridget didn't comment on my drinking habits, and I knew that Joe wanted to. I didn't care what anyone thought – the decanter contained a single malt Islay, one of my favourites. I needed *uisge beath* right now.

'Alex consulted Donna. I know this,' I told her. 'I have Donna's diary and the entries aren't faked.'

'Alex Cattanach was a blackmailer, Brodie.'

'Who was she blackmailing?' I asked.

'I'm not doing your work for you – you seem to think you're a cop these days; work it out for yourself. But let me tell you one thing – Alex Cattanach wouldn't have been up for a medal for services to law, and she certainly wouldn't be getting the sympathy she's having thrown at her these days if people knew what she was really like.'

I guessed Bridget Nicholson had been one victim of Alex's, irrespective of the fact that they had been lovers too. It didn't take a genius to figure out that the video would end Bridget's judicial career. I would see to that. Not for myself, but for Moira Campbell and Tanya Hayder, who got more than they deserved when they sought out her services.

Bridget wasn't finished yet.

'Someone is using you, Brodie. I may not like you, but I wouldn't deliberately see you sent down for a murder you didn't commit. You think you know everything about Alex because of something in Donna Diamond's diary? Alex brought about Donna's prosecution, Brodie! I don't believe she would have gone to her for help, and I don't believe Donna would have given it.

'If Alex had ever really been in trouble then she would have instructed you – she told me so. She liked to taunt me with it when she was drunk. Alex admired you, Brodie. She admired you.'

Suddenly we all saw a different reason for Alex Cattanach writing my name in excrement on her hospital walls.

She wanted my help.

Chapter Forty-Two

Opportunities make a thief.

This had been one of Alex Cattanach's favourite sayings, and she used it in every interview she gave. Maybe it had also applied to her – after all, blackmail was just theft under a different guise.

336

A text message had come in from McCoy the next day. He wanted to see me immediately – no doubt to call in his favour. I didn't mind; who would have thought he'd be right with pinning down Cattanach as a common blackmailer?

I waited in the common room at Castle Huntly for the guard to find him. The open prison was reminiscent of a run-down student hall of residence, especially with the pool table in the corner.

'Good, you came right away,' McCoy shouted as he entered the room. He was used to attracting attention and it was a hard habit to break. Sadly for him, I was the only one there. McCoy was dressed for the outdoors today. Expensive garish cords and a green wool jumper with oblong suede patches on the shoulders and elbows made him every inch the country squire, from his brown handmade brogues to his twill checked shirt. It was a costume, but it didn't do anything to hide the fact that he looked awful.

'You're not looking so good,' I blurted out.

'That's why you're here,' he said snappily.

Maybe he wanted me to make a will.

'Did you bring a car? I'm damned if I'm getting on the back of a bloody bike. I've seen the day, mind. Is Malcolm with you?'

'He's driving,' I nodded.

'Good – at least I'll have some tolerable company.'

The old queen was looking to be slapped, and he must have seen me bristle at his insult.

'Please forgive me if I sound a trifle harsh, my dear. It's just at my age it's nice to share some time with someone who can see more than liver spots and blue lips. Malcolm remembers me when I was in my prime, and I need that right now.' I did understand and I even tried to help him into the car. His heart was bothering him and there was talk of him being released early. Malcolm, however, had other ideas. He leaped round to meet his old friend, anxious to show off his new nose, which had fully healed. Arnica, he assured me, had worked wonders.

'You're looking gorgeous, old girl,' purred Mc-Coy.

'You're not looking so bad yourself, old thing,' replied Malcolm, but we all knew he was lying.

'How is the romance going?' McCoy asked as we pulled out of the prison car park. I was relegated, to the back seat. I felt like a spare prick at an orgy, an analogy that had come readily to mind as I knew they were about to start discussing Malcolm's love life. I didn't want to hear. The two old codgers in the front were already acting as if I wasn't there. I didn't want to draw attention to myself, because, like it or not, I needed McCoy.

When McCoy had contacted me he was very specific. Bring Malcolm. I owed him big-time. He knew far more than he was telling me so I had primed Malcolm to help me winkle it out of him, not that I needed to. I had quickly realised that, behind Kailash, I was his favoured one. It was a nice feeling – I had liked Malcolm since meeting him last year. He had cared so much for me, without me even realising it to begin with.

McCoy had also advised me that he wished to

go out for lunch. Just any pub or roadside café would not do – he wanted to go to Boath House, a hundred and twenty mile round trip from the prison. Malcolm was excited since it had such a fine reputation. I knew that I'd be picking up the tab; not that I minded. I had never adequately thanked Malcolm for healing me when my step-mother had injured me last year.

I tried to catch up on some sleep whilst we drove there. I was going to speak to Malcolm about giving me something to settle the sleeplessness on the way home. As I fell into an uneasy doze in the car, I heard the woman on the video. I felt that I knew her but I couldn't put a face to the voice – the harder I tried, the more she seemed to slip away.

I must have been moaning and talking in my sleep as Malcolm was unduly solicitous when he woke me up. I think even McCoy felt sorry for me; maybe the nap had done me some good after all.

I was pleased that Malcolm had awakened me just before we entered the drive to Boath House. The pink shale driveway curved graciously to the house; along the roadside, round sandstone balls acted as bollards marking the way. Boath House had been built around 1825, and the present owners had spent years painstakingly restoring it.

We were greeted by the owner, who explained that the window cleaner had just finished his work. The original windows had been in a terrible state due to the summer storms the north-east had recently experienced. The two old queens added that they too were delighted at the sparkling windows, to the extent that I wondered how McCoy had found the time to embezzle such a large amount of money when he filled his mind with frippery.

The owner showed us into a lovely drawing room. The overstuffed chairs were reminiscent of Bridget Nicholson's and they brought my mind sharply back into focus. We ordered our drinks. I stuck to a Diet Coke in case I was becoming like Eddie, plus Malcolm had indicated that I would be driving home, which, when I looked at the extensive wine list that I would be paying for, annoyed me.

McCoy put in his request. 'I'll have a Hendrick's gin with thinly sliced cucumber and some borage please.' I was surprised because the only other person I knew who drank this was Kailash; it must have shown on my face.

'My dear, I told you that your mother was a friend of mine, in fact it was she who introduced me to this tipple – we had many a fine night in Amsterdam. Of course, we were all a lot younger and more energetic in those days.'

I cleared my throat as a timely warning to Malcolm that I was present.

The owner came back with our drinks. Malcolm launched himself back into the chair and sighed whilst greedily sipping on his delicious-looking margarita. The Diet Coke I had, whilst furnished with a slice of lime, didn't exactly meet the mood of the fine old house.

'Oh, my dear, those look simply delicious! What are they? Sadly, I have to be so careful of my digestion these days.'

The owner told McCoy that they were appetisers, choux buns made with olives. They were still warm, having just been taken from the oven. I bit into the light pastry and from the initial mouthful I prayed that they would disagree with McCoy's delicate digestion. No such luck. The greedy old bugger had downed his share and mine before I had chewed my first bite.

'Steady on, old chap, a girl's got to watch her figure,' Malcolm admonished kindly.

'It's all right for you – I don't have a virile young lover to keep in shape for.'

'Not even in prison?' Malcolm asked, astonished.

I quickly turned my head and stared out of the sparkling windows, grateful that our diligent hostess soon arrived and showed us to our lunch table. The dining room had French windows that overlooked the pond and the swimming swans. Naturally, McCoy had taken the best seat, and consequently, if I wanted to see the swans, I had to crane my neck.

I had ordered the rough country pâté for a starter, whilst Malcolm and McCoy had asked for soup. When the dishes arrived, McCoy decided my starter looked more delicious and promptly took it. Yet again, I blurted out exactly what was on my mind.

'I hear from Robert Girvan that you two got on famously; even now he doesn't have a bad word to say about you.'

The thin blue lips stopped chewing. His rheumy eyes stared at me across the table. In an unguarded moment I saw a flash of pure dislike.

'It was Robert Girvan I wanted to speak to you about.'

His voice was hushed and he leaned across the table in an intimate manner. I could see the broken veins in his nose, and the quarter-inch of grey roots showing through in his obviously darkened hair.

'The favour I owe you? You want me to do something for Robert Girvan? I'm not sure he needs it – he's on the up and I'm certainly not.' Or I won't be after this meal, I thought. McCoy had already ordered another bottle of French wine, which our hostess was decanting. We were alone in the dining room apart from her. McCoy gave me a look and I knew that he wanted me to be silent. All graciousness and smiles, he dismissed our hostess from the room. He checked over his shoulder once more before he spoke.

'I don't want you to do that little fucker any favours whatsoever. It's completely his fault I'm in prison to begin with.'

This was news to me. 'Robert spoke very highly of you, and, since your little foray into fraud resulted in him losing his practising certificate and being made bankrupt, I thought it was rather big of him.'

Malcolm's kick to my leg came too late.

McCoy's face turned puce as Malcolm rummaged in his pocket and produced a vial of tablets.

'I knew, I just knew, that I'd be needing these. You silly old fool; you promised me that you wouldn't get yourself excited going over these matters. Slip this under your tongue – it's haw-

342

thorn and it'll lower your blood pressure. I mean it, you're not getting to talk again until you've followed my orders.'

McCoy meekly obeyed.

'That's better,' approved Malcolm. 'Now just wait a minute for it to take effect.' His voice was low and caressing. I knew that tone well, healing and soothing; it wasn't the one he used on me now.

'You, missy, you know better. Or you should do.'

'But I don't know anything about this matter,' I said, leaning over and whispering in Malcolm's ear for fear of causing the stroke that seemed to be hanging over McCoy.

'We have reason to suspect that Robert Girvan...' began McCoy in a slow and measured voice, 'reason to suspect... Oh, we bloody well know that Robert Girvan told Bridget Nicholson about my ... dealings. Shall we say their plan was for me to end up in here and for Robert to become senior partner of the firm I spent the best part of forty years building up. They were too thick to work out the actual consequences of their actions. It wasn't part of their plan that Robert would be made bankrupt, but he had no idea of the true scale of my...' he coughed to clear his throat, before concluding, 'transactions.'

'Okay, I get what you're saying about Robert, but what was in it for Bridget?' I asked.

'Their intention was to amalgamate the two firms: Bridget intended to be the managing partner of the new one.'

'And Alex Cattanach was the spanner in the

works, because she was so thorough that, once alerted, she found every scam you had run over the last forty years?'

'Exactly.'

There was a strange kind of pride in his voice, almost as if he admired himself and Alex for their attention to detail. He bore her no ill will – that was obvious – so I could cross his name off the list of likely attackers, plus the fact that he was in prison at the time. Indeed, he didn't even seem that hostile towards me.

'I've already exacted my revenge on Bridget Nicholson,' he told me calmly.

I thought about it for a moment. God, it was all so obvious now.

'You were the one who brought the video back in to play?' I said.

McCoy nodded smugly. His face may still have been puce but it was shining now with male-volent pride as he picked up the story.

'Tanya Hayder. I met her when she first started on the streets – a bonny, intelligent girl, excellent for "entertaining" my business clients. Until, of course, she fell too far down the slippery pole. I looked out for her – handed her a bob or two now and again, that sort of thing. I always knew about the video, but it was none of my business until that bitch overstepped the mark and made it so.'

'How did you get a copy?' I asked him. 'Even if Tanya had one to start with, I can't imagine that her erratic lifestyle would have allowed her to keep it.'

'Tanya found out that Bridget had kept a copy in her desk drawer. A punter who she serviced through that bloody awful website told her that he'd seen a porno movie of her younger sister and asked if he could get her next time.

'She was furious. She blamed her ruin on Bridget Nicholson. I don't honestly think even she believed that, but she did say that Bridget caused the death of the young lassie who was in the video with her. Apparently she was new to the game, and only fifteen.'

'But a video like that,' I queried, 'surely Bridget had it under lock and key? In fact, I'm surprised she even kept it.'

'I've found that people always carry the seeds of their own destruction with them,' Malcolm pronounced.

'That's certainly too true in my case, old chap,' agreed McCoy. 'In March, I got two lads from the prison to break in and steal it.'

'I never heard that her office had been broken into,' I said, puzzled. News of a theft from a solicitor's office would have spread like wildfire round the agents' room at the Sheriff Court.

'I gave strict instructions that nothing was to be taken or disturbed other than the video. I made two copies – I gave one to Tanya and told her to keep it safe. The other I sent to Alex Cattanach, and I have the original.'

'A sound plan,' I agreed. 'But something went wrong. If the video was taken in March then her career should have been over. Instead, she's been offered a seat in the College of Justice.'

'I know. Alex Cattanach was supposed to use the video to expose her. You can't have a judge sitting on the bench with explosive material like this lying around.' I wondered about McCoy's naïveté – there had certainly been enough going around about my father over the years, but it hadn't stopped people turning a blind eye and deaf ear to it. Or prevented him from getting to the top of the judicial tree.

'At the very least I thought Alex would have a quiet word and Bridget would withdraw,' said McCoy. 'Alex did blackmail someone, which is why I think she was attacked – but I have no idea who it is and I want you to find out.'

'Is that all?' I didn't try to keep the sarcasm out of my voice.

'No – Robert Girvan is involved with someone else in something very shady. I've been hearing rumours – I don't like him in the slightest but even I'm surprised how far he has sunk. Have you heard of a company called Tymar Productions?' I leaned across and kissed him.

'Maybe we can work together after all. What do you know about Tymar?'

'Your boss, Roddie Buchanan, set it up. He's placed your name on all the company registration documents and bank accounts. Tymar Productions is the reason Alex Cattanach was after you. Roddie has set you up nicely to be the fall guy whilst he, Robert Girvan and whoever else is involved in this reap the benefits. I've spoken to your secretary, Lavender, a lovely girl, and I've given her instructions on how to entice Roddie back to your office for a meeting. In fact, he should be leaving Geneva in a couple of hours.'

McCoy and Malcolm barely had time for a bite out of their handmade petit fours and a swig of coffee before I had bundled them back into the car and we were headed home.

I'd got more than I had dared to hope for. Suddenly, the bill didn't seem too extravagant after all.

Chapter Forty-Three

'Did you get it?' I asked Joe when I met him in the lobby of Lothian and St Clair first thing the next day.

'Of course I got it. Anybody can get into your house without a key. We've warned you about that before.'

I opened the door to Lavender's office. I had stayed at hers the night before after I had brought Malcolm back from Castle Huntly. We'd had a lot of plotting to do, and I also managed to sleep a lot better at her flat than at my own place.

'Where is he?'

'He's in the loo,' Lav answered. 'He can't contain his excitement.' She was sitting at her desk pretending to type. I wasn't sure about Roddie but I knew for certain Lavender was having difficulty controlling herself. She was wired – a nervous smile kept flicking across her face.

'You're supposed to be sad,' I hissed.

'Oh, don't be an idiot. Roddie can't imagine anyone being sad at your downfall. In any event, you know Roddie; he's so up his own arse that he doesn't know what time of day it is unless it concerns him.'

Glasgow Joe was keeping shootie at the door. I think we would have been better with a smaller lookout. The smell of fresh coffee permeated the air. Everything was ready for Roddie's showdown with me when I supposedly returned to the office from a consultation with an advocate in Parliament House.

On McCoy's instructions, Lavender had contacted Roddie to come back to Scotland because I was about to be charged with the murders of Tanya Hayder and Donna Diamond. Lavender had stated the firm was about to go tits over arse when the press heard about it, and she was sure that the only person who could lead us out of this was him.

This appealed to his vanity, and the anticipated pleasure of seeing me carried off in handcuffs was one that he could not resist. He'd caught the first available flight out of Geneva; he even soiled himself by travelling economy, so eager was he to see my downfall.

Jack Deans was coming to the office in five minutes as an appointment had been arranged with Roddie. Jack was acting as if he had a scoop, a breaking news story about my arrest. He wanted Roddie's comments on what it was like to be the business partner of a serial killer. Roddie was only too delighted to oblige. I could only assume that someone had told him that Jack and I had a broken relationship and that Jack too was out to get me – the past that Roddie and the journalist shared didn't exactly make for a blooming friendship, but, as far as I knew, men could always bond over a wrong woman and what she had done to them.

The corridors of Lothian and St Clair bustled, with everyone unaware of what was being planned. Anna, the junior, immaculately and expensively coiffed as usual, flirted with Martin, the young trainee, at the water cooler. She had switched her attentions from my junior partner, Willie, when his wife found out. Lothian and St Clair was a den of iniquity in more ways than one.

Lavender's phone rang.

'That's Andy the doorman. I ordered a basket of muffins for Roddie's meeting with Jack. Can you sneak down and get them, Brodie?'

I was only too pleased to get moving; the adrenalin was pumping round my body and, because I wasn't fleeing or fighting, I felt jittery. I took the stairs and ran down them, taking some two at a time and jumping from the third step down onto the landings. It was childish but I felt gleeful about my encounter with Roddie. Of course, he had no intentions of telling me about Tymar Productions, but I was certain I could find a way round the road block he presented. After all, I had Joe.

Roddie was completely unaware that we knew about Tymar. Lavender and her hacker friends had worked out one password, and she wanted to confront him with it; but my way was much sweeter. Bridget Nicholson had no idea that we knew she was linked to Tymar; she was only concerned with appearances – how it would look when the video was leaked over the Internet. She might even have thought that it would increase her business – I wouldn't have been surprised if it did.

'Have one,' I said, offering the basket of muffins to Andy the doorman. He was practically drooling at the mouth and I didn't blame him, even if I had other things to occupy me. If there had been no evidence and Bridget hadn't been daft enough to record that video, then she would be sitting pretty right now, telling me to sod off.

Lucky me.

I took a muffin and started up the stairs. It looked nicer than it tasted. I took my time and, as I chewed, considered my meeting with Bridget. She had stated that she hadn't wanted to appear in the video either and, despite me wanting to deny it, there was something in the timbre of her voice that made me believe her. But if her appearance was against her wishes then who had forced her into it? There appeared to be only one answer: the camerawoman, the one who was smart enough not to leave clues and still have an identity that evaded me.

I saw Jack sitting out at reception, waiting for Roddie, and I hid in the stairwell, watching through the narrow pane of safety glass. He looked great, still suntanned. Was it fake? Jack had never seemed the type to be overly concerned with his looks; he was too interested in fags and booze. I hated the fact that I was still attracted to him. It had nothing to do with my feelings for Joe. Jack loved the bad girl in me and I responded in kind. Today, he looked every inch a Pulitzer Prize winner. Was he off the booze? More likely, since his clothes looked quite fresh – maybe there was another woman on the scene?

Jack turned around, his senses aware that he was being watched. His deep blue eyes quickly scanned the room. He found me quickly and I was impressed that he didn't betray my whereabouts.

Unusually, Roddie came out to greet Jack personally.

Normally, a meeting with Mr Buchanan was like an audience with the king; you were taken into his presence by a minion. Even Abby, the front desk receptionist, stopped her phone conversation with her friend and put down her nail file long enough to look surprised. Her eyebrows rose even higher when Jack followed Roddie into his room – he stuck his butt out and wiggled it in my direction, only Abby couldn't see me.

Lavender was, as usual, well prepared.

The door between Lavender's office and my room (that Roddie had taken back now that he thought I was in trouble) was ajar. Roddie would never allow this to happen in his own world. However, since he could not conceive of a secretary who would be so audacious as to insist on an open-door policy with her boss, he didn't bother to check. We crowded into the room: me, Lavender, Joe and Eddie. Why Eddie was there was beyond me, except Lavender said she didn't want him to miss out on the fun, and that since we were his sole employers he had every right to know what was happening. Eddie looked uncomfortable and I guessed that it was not his idea. For a man who hates confrontation this would be his notion of hell.

'Do you have it?'

I repeated the question I had already asked Joe. To silence me he brought out a small brown glass bottle with a thick black cap on it. There was no label and no instructions but I had already been told all that I needed to know about sodium pentathol from the Alchemist. A few drops in the extra-strong coffee that Lavender had brewed specially, and Roddie would be primed to answer Jack's questions. It wouldn't make him pour everything out, but it would loosen his inhibitions more effectively than any booze, making him particularly susceptible to our line of questioning.

Lavender brought the coffee in on a tray and fawned over Roddie. She was a master at it. Maybe she had learned something from all those self-help books after all.

'That's a lovely tie you're wearing, Mr Buchanan,' she oozed. 'Did you buy it in Switzerland? The Continentals have such a fine sense of style.'

She completely ignored Jack and continued simpering up to Roddie. I thought he was bound to notice her insincerity but he lapped it up like a thirsty man. Having said that, I've met his wife. One thing I can say for certain is that Mrs Roddie Buchanan is not a woman to sweet-talk anyone.

'Have I said how lovely it is to have a gentleman such as yourself around the office again?' was Lavender's parting remark. She really was excelling herself, and it worked. He gobbled down her coffee as eagerly as he had swallowed her compliments. Jack had been primed not to drink it, although I would love to try some on him later.

We didn't have long to wait.

Roddie appeared to get hot. He took his jacket off and then loosened the tie that Lavender had admired so much.

'Shall we get started, sir?' Jack asked.

Roddie liked that, the notion that the addled hack who had caused him so much grief in the past was at his mercy now. He preened himself, running his right hand through his sparse and fiercely regimented hair, disturbing his elaborate comb-over.

'I'd like to ask you about Tymar Productions,' Jack began.

I felt nervous. I hadn't expected him to go straight in.

We were piled on top of each other like a human pyramid. Lavender, who was at the bottom, stuck her nose further into the room.

'I thought you wanted to ask me about Brodie MacGregor's impending murder charges?'

Damn it. Jack had blown it. He was too cocky, too sure of himself. He should have waited, tested the waters. We could have added more sodium pentathol if that was necessary. However, it was interesting that Buchanan called me by my father's name, even if he had known my true parentage long before I had.

'I want to know about Tymar Productions,' Jack insisted.

We all held our breath.

Then it happened. Roddie began to talk. 'Well, I suppose that's alright because Tymar Productions is all about Brodie,' he laughed.

'What exactly is Tymar Productions?' queried

daft Jack, playing his part.

'It's a company, of course, formed offshore in Cyprus with a Swiss bank account.'

'Does Brodie know about it, Roddie? May I call you Roddie?'

'Of course she doesn't or I would be dead. She's too like her mother that one. I spotted her number right away. I wasn't happy about employing her and, as you know, events have proved me right. Poor breeding. Not from the MacGregors, of course – but have you met her mother? That woman almost ruined me. All because I wanted to inform a childless man, a judge, no less, that he had a daughter. Don't you think every man has a right to know he has a child? Men have lost their place in the world, thanks to women. Look at the way fathers are forced to act like terrorists, just to see their children.'

'Have some more coffee, Roddie.' Jack refilled his cup and helped it to his mouth, encouraging him to swallow.

'Let's talk some more about Tymar,' Jack persisted.

A thought floated across my mind, one that I tried to dismiss but it lingered. Jack had used this technique before.

'What do you want to know?'

'Roddie, I want to know everything.' I couldn't see the smile on his face but I could hear it in his voice. 'Let's get started, Roddie. Who first asked you to start Tymar?'

Jack's pen was busy scratching. He knew he was on his way back to the big-time and he wouldn't rely on a tape recorder to get all of this down.

Roddie thought for a moment, then went on.

'Robert Girvan – yes, it was Robert who asked me. The request was rather surprising because he was a partner in another firm; he was McCoy's partner before he was busted. I asked him why he didn't do it in-house, and he said he wanted to keep his business life separate from the law firm. He was paying me well, so I wasn't going to object.'

Lavender flashed me a look that said, 'I told you so.' If it had been possible, she would have danced in front of me singing it. Eddie squeezed my arm.

'We all make mistakes,' he mouthed. I think I loved Eddie at that moment.

Roddie helped himself to more coffee.

'So, what did Robert Girvan want Tymar for?'

'Well, at first, Jack, I had no idea. I thought it might be a property company or something, then he made an unusual request. One that I was quite happy to comply with since it involved me getting paid a lot of money.'

He wiped his brow with a pristine mono-grammed handkerchief.

'I was under pressure, Jack; you have no idea what it's like working with that woman. She is quite simply infuriating. Brodie MacGregor is irritatingly good at what she does, earns a lot of fees, but that puts the rest of us under pressure. Then when I had my little contretemps with Kailash and the firm started haemorrhaging money as a result of the scandal, Brodie made no secret of the fact that it was my fault.'

'Wasn't it?'

Jack asked all the questions I wanted to put to Roddie.

'No,' Roddie whined. 'I've told you. I just wanted to reunite father and child – what could be wrong with that?'

'The father was a paedophile – some people may say that was wrong.'

'Jack, Jack ... her father was a very important man; such men are always the subject of rumour and conjecture. In any event, she was long past the age when her father would have been interested in her if he did indeed have those proclivities.'

'So you didn't like Brodie?'

'Haven't I just said that? She came in here a nobody. I gave her a start and how did she repay me? She made me look a fool in front of my partners by bringing in double the amount of fee income that I did. I was forced to work harder just to maintain my position, at a time when I should have been winding down. That's when I thought I could go to Kailash – if she had paid me enough money I could have retired and everything would have been all right. But that's not her way; she has to destroy a man. Did you see what she did to me? It was a set-up but it looked bad. Do you know what the worst of it was?'

Jack shook his head; but we all did, nodding like those dogs in the back of a car.

'The worst of it was that I had to ask Brodie for help.'

Jack poured himself some water.

'Let's get back to happier things then. Tymar is your revenge on Brodie, isn't it?'

Roddie replied, 'Robert Girvan's special request was that he needed to buy a woman's identity as a cover for the bank account and company. I sold him Brodie's; he didn't object. In fact, when he had to work under the little bitch, I think it kept him going when she was giving him patronising handouts.'

'So, Brodie's financial details are on all the registration documents of the company?'

'That's right! All her details except the important ones. Like a scan of her iris or her palm print, so that means she can't actually access any money.'

'What does Robert Girvan use Tymar Productions for?' asked Jack.

'I don't know, but it's highly illegal, because lots of cash flows through the accounts. Tymar Productions is supposedly a film production company. Not a bad idea if you want to launder money. I was always rather amused by the name myself,' he said, starting to giggle like a school-child.

'Tymar Productions?' Jack repeated, and shook his head.

'Oh, and here was me thinking you were meant to be clever! Don't you see it? TYMAR? Take your money and run.' Roddie Buchanan continued to giggle at the hilarity of it all.

Jack gave him enough coffee to send him to sleep and I was left with the prospect of seeing Robert Girvan as myself.

He had taken my identity.

He had stolen me from me.

He was a man pretending to be a woman when

357

it suited him, in this mess of confused men and women.

Suddenly, a thought swam into my head as if my dreams had come back in one piece.

The voice behind the camera.

How sure was I that it truly was a woman? Was that why I hadn't been able to place it?

Was Robert Girvan behind everything?

Chapter Forty-Four

'It worked then?' the Alchemist asked.

'Like a charm,' I replied, meeting him at court straight after Roddie's performance. He nodded as if he had known that it would.

He had changed.

Not metaphorically, but literally. His hair had been dyed back to his natural colour and he wore a suit. Not a cheap suit like the ones my punters normally borrowed – it looked expensive and, from the way it hung on his scrawny frame, I would say that it was handmade. His white shirt was not new, that would have been too nouveau riche, but it was spotless and freshly ironed. Of course, he wore his school tie. It was not the same school tie that Tanya and Moira had worn in the video – it was even posher. I was surprised; Moses had not done Bernard's background justice.

Bernard's public-school acolytes were not at his side. They had been replaced by his mother. It was obvious that Bernard had been a late baby. Mrs Carpenter came from the same generation as Mary McLennan and, from the look of her, I would say she was just as strict.

On stout flat brown shoes she marched towards me. Thankfully, I was in my suit and the court gown hid any lingering stains that might have remained from breakfast.

'Miss McLennan – I have to tell you that I was not happy that Bernard instructed someone other than our family solicitor.' She told me his name. I didn't recognise it but assured her that he was a fine fellow. She beamed, her choice of lawyers having been vindicated. Because I had agreed with her, she softened.

'Bernard tells me that you have a fine pedigree in the law and that your father was the Lord President; I'm so sorry for your loss, dear.'

'My grandad – who is still alive – was the Lord Justice Clerk,' I told her. Bernard smiled at me, relieved that I knew how to placate the likes of Jemima Carpenter. I didn't come across such posh, concerned mothers often in my line of work, but I like to think that if Mary McLennan were still alive, then I would know how to walk my own path but still keep her happy. I wouldn't betray my working-class background, but I'd be able to blend into any environment.

'Bernard assures me that he is completely innocent,' said Ma Alchemist, 'and that the police planted evidence on him. Whilst I find it almost impossible to believe that the police would stoop to such matters, I cannot believe that my Bernard was guilty of entering someone's home and stealing their jewels.'

The Alchemist blushed.

'Bernard has been wayward lately; you see, he has been trying to find himself ever since he left university.'

Mrs Carpenter was old enough to think that hippy-speak was still in vogue. I didn't want to say that Bernard had been wayward for so long he'd had enough time to find himself ten times over. She patted her hair, which had clearly been washed and set yesterday. She was nervous. The diamonds on her left hand almost blinded me and I understood where Bernard had developed his taste in jewellery. He coughed in embarrassment.

'Don't worry, Mrs Carpenter. There must have been a stray police officer behind the matter. I have found a witness who has confirmed to my secretary that he found the jewels in a hedge, or rather his dog did.'

'Did you say dog? Oh, now I have every faith that things will turn out all right. I have found that dogs are generally more reliable than people.'

She pulled a picture out of her wallet and showed me her Pekinese, Bernie. After making suitable gushing noises, Mrs Carpenter put Bernie's picture away. I had a flash of understanding as to why Bernard had gone wrong. He was named after a dog. I was told that the Bernie in the picture was Bernie IX; I just knew that the boy Bernard did not warrant Roman numerals after his name.

'I need to speak to Bernard alone, Mrs Carpenter.'

She uttered the immortal cry of deluded mothers everywhere. 'We have no secrets!'

I hoped for her sake that they did, and ushered him along the corridor out of earshot.

'The witness's name is Mr Wilson,' I told him. 'I don't know if he's here. I cited him as a defence witness so if he doesn't show up I can ask for an adjournment – but that may just be postponing the inevitable. Although he has confirmed your story about DI Bancho, he's not keen to speak.'

'Sorry if I've misled you, Brodie,' he answered sheepishly.

My heart sank. If I had a pound for every time I've had those words uttered to me on the morning of a trial I'd be a millionaire.

'Please explain exactly what you mean by misleading me.'

My voice was icy; I could have frozen milk at fifty paces. I thought I saw Bernard quake; at the very least his outsized Adam's apple bobbed about nervously.

'I don't think I specifically said it was DI Bancho – sure, he was interviewing me, but there were other coppers around. You just seemed so keen to blame him that I sort of went along with you, just to please you, like.' He smiled apologetically.

'Run that past me again, Bernard.'

I never stopped smiling as I looked into his nervous eyes.

'It's like I said. Sorry.'

I wanted to smack his face and call him a liar. Joe had warned me that this one would sell me for a bag of smack; come to think of it, he'd also told me that Bancho wasn't bent. I wouldn't

361

listen then – but I was listening now.

'Continue.'

My icy tone dropped several degrees.

'I was lifted by a woman officer – she knew the score. I never saw her again. I think by the time I saw Bancho, the gear had been put in my property.'

He shrugged his shoulders before adding, 'By the woman, I suppose.'

'And you tell me this now because...?'

'Because I don't want to get into any more trouble than I'm in. Brodie, I'm out of my depth here. You've met my mother; you can see that I'm not cut out for this life. When Moses cut out Bruce's eyes in front of me...' His voice quavered with unshed tears.

'If I just plead guilty, then this can all be forgotten. They won't send me to jail, I'll get probation. I promise I will never do anything wrong again.'

This vow is made to me each time I start a trial. This time I believed the pledge. Strangely, I also thought he was making a mistake. I was all for him walking the straight and narrow, but he would be attaching himself to Mrs Carpenter's apron strings to play second fiddle to the current Bernie, the resident Pekinese.

'At first, I thought you were throwing me a line, Bernard.'

'Well, why did you take my case to trial?'

'That's too long a story to go into here, but you don't deserve to have this on your record – the evidence was planted on you irrespective of who did it.'

'I stole the stuff – I was just unlucky they found it.'

'Bernard – the law is a system of checks and balances. My job is to make sure that everything evens out. If you plead guilty then some crooked bastard will go on to do it again to someone else.'

'I don't care about anyone else.'

Rarely has a truer word been spoken.

'Bernard shut your mouth and do as I say.'

I walked away from Bernard, leaving him to the devices of Mrs Carpenter. She would never allow her second most beloved Bernie to plead guilty.

Chapter Forty-Five

Duncan Bancho and Peggy Malone stood outside the court enjoying a last cigarette.

Bancho looked like a condemned man. The mere presence of police had cleared the usually crowded court entrance and I walked right up to them. We needed to discuss Bridget Nicholson and Robert Girvan.

Now.

I could see that Duncan had not been sleeping, which was hardly any wonder. If I was right, he would be facing five years in Saughton Prison. If Bernard was telling the truth, he'd still be belted for allowing such things to go on whilst it was his watch. But I couldn't afford to feel sorry for him now. Generously, Peggy Malone offered me a cigarette.

'No thanks, Peggy. Could I have a word with Duncan on our own? We have a bit of a history and there's some private stuff I need to say.'

DC Malone walked up the stairs to the witness room.

'You've got a bloody cheek,' snapped Bancho. 'History? That you sold Fishy down the river and want to do the same to me?'

'Firstly, I'd like to say I'm sorry.'

'Sorry? Do you think that's enough for ruining a fifteen-year career? I joined the police as a cadet straight from school; I don't think "sorry" quite cuts it.'

'You're not making it easy for me, Duncan.'

'Not making it easy? For you? You have got a bloody nerve, Brodie.'

'I want to ask for an adjournment today – tell the Fiscal you don't oppose.'

'Why should I?'

'Because someone planted those jewels on Bernard Carpenter, and I've just remembered you're the kind of cop who wouldn't approve of it.'

'You've pushed me too far this time, Brodie, I swear. I still intend to do you for Alex Cattanach's attack.'

'Just speak to the Fiscal. I'm going to say I'm ill.'

I ran back in and the case was called first on the roll in Court Nine before Sheriff Harrison.

'Bernard Carpenter?'

I spoke up. 'I appear on behalf of Bernard Carpenter. I seek to adjourn this case on the grounds that the defence agent is too ill to proceed to trial – I understand that the Fiscal has no objections.'

The baby-faced boy representing the Crown was only too delighted to get rid of this hot potato and quickly nodded his assent. Bernard looked nonplussed. He wasn't important – I didn't have to explain myself to him at the moment.

'Before you rush off, Miss MacGregor, I'd like a word with you,' said Harrison. 'If you are well enough?' he added with a smirk.

'Court!'

The sheriff clerk shouted as Sheriff Harrison left the bench. We all stood up and I made moves to follow him to his chambers. Was he going to ask me what was wrong with me? I needed to get moving fast; maybe I should tell him I had anal leakage – a friend of mine always threatened to write notes to her son's teachers saying that was what he had if he ever tried to wing a day off school. At least I'd embarrass him; I'd bet my feet wouldn't touch the ground.

I closed the door behind me. The room was well sound-proofed and my feet moved silently across the thick red carpet. Harrison's wig lay in the corner of the desk and he looked oddly human, younger than I had remembered. I was also uncomfortably aware that I owed him a favour after the Tanya Hayder case.

'I heard poor Miss Hayder died in that rehab you fought so hard to get her into.'

I nodded at him.

'Sometimes we should be careful what we wish for – if the poor wretch had ended up in Cornton Vale it's likely she would be alive today, ready to shoplift on her release. Don't misunderstand me; I am not laying Miss Hayder's death at your door, it was her wishes I was referring to. Still, let's move on to other matters, no less difficult.'

He looked down at his desk and shuffled his papers. I got the impression that no matter how much he needed to say what was on his mind, he didn't want to say it.

'Mmmm ... yes, well, the thing is ... I have a daughter. A rather brilliant, rather wayward daughter. She has just finished at Edinburgh University. Much to my surprise she managed to qualify in law, *summa cum laude*.'

'You must be very proud,' I told him, pretty sure I was on safe ground with that response.

He looked at me over his half-moon glasses. For some reason I felt sorry for him.

'You'd think that – until you meet her. Anyway, I'm sure you know from your own experience that after graduation the first thing to deal with is, erm, the future. By now she is desirous of obtaining a traineeship.'

'With her degree, the top Edinburgh and London firms will be queuing up to take her,' I said.

He shook his head.

'No. No, they will not. In any event, Louisa has decided that she wants you – she has developed a rather close relationship with her Professor of Pathology.'

'Patch?' I interrupted. I would have to have a word with him. I bet he put her up to it. Still, I was intrigued to meet the girl. She must be quite something if Patch was recommending her to me.

'If you don't mind I will call her in now,' said Sheriff Harrison, deciding that the discussion was behind us.

It didn't really matter what the snotty posh girl was like, I was stuck with her for two years because I owed her daddy a favour. Why she wanted to be my trainee was beyond me. Patch must have waxed lyrical about my abilities, and her father must have kept quiet about what he thought about me.

'Louisa! Come in now, darling, I know that you're listening at the door.'

There are very few people who make you forget what you were doing the instant that you met them. But I will never forget my first impression of Louisa Harrison. It could have been her bright pink, extremely unattractive hair, wispy to the point of thinness and hanging in a rat's tail down her back. It could have been the fact that she had her leather jacket on, which she must have thought was de rigueur office-wear at Lothian and St Clair. Or possibly it was the fact that she was one of the smallest, most misshapen people I had ever seen. I wasn't aware that I was staring until she spoke. Her voice was high and squeaky.

'Osteogenesis imperfecta,' she informed me. 'Brittle bones. And imperfectly formed ones at that. That's why I look like Quasimodo's sister.'

Her tone was chirpy and matter of fact.

Sheriff Harrison shrugged his shoulders. It seemed that she was my problem now.

'Oh, right. Your father says that you're keen to do your traineeship with me?'

She didn't answer; she wasn't going to give me any help.

'So, when do you want to start?'

'How about right now?' She was keen enough

to answer that one. 'That's why I'm wearing my leathers.'

'I don't have a helmet for you,' I said, trying to get rid of her, whilst being pretty damn impressed that she had brought her own leathers and knew so much about my devotion to the bike. I couldn't use the excuse of not feeling well to someone who had obviously gone through so much pain in her life.

'Don't worry. I've got my own.'

I gained the distinct impression that Louisa Harrison was used to dealing with people who tried to fob her off.

'You two girls have fun,' shouted Sheriff Harrison as he ran back in to court.

'It's not been easy for him,' Louisa said wisely.

I already had the feeling it wasn't going to be easy for me.

'How did you get friendly with Patch?' I asked as we made our way to the bike.

'At an Elvis convention,' she told me.

It was one of the last answers I wanted to hear.

'The thing is, Louisa, I've got something very difficult to deal with this afternoon.'

Her eyes sparkled. 'Is something "going down"?' she asked, obviously hoping that was exactly the case. 'You won't even notice me.'

'What? With that hair?' I replied.

'You'd be surprised how invisible a crippled girl is. By the way, I found this in my dad's chambers.'

She stretched out her rather beautiful hands towards me. In her palm lay a single white stone.

'You must have dropped it.'

I knew we were going to be all right.

Chapter Forty-Six

'I think he's about to make his move,' Joe said.

Moses shouted in the background, 'I know he is!'

They had both been following Robert Girvan and I'd received a phone call from them just as I'd left the court with Louisa. Joe had given me instructions and I'd made my way towards the Rag Doll as fast as I could. At the pub, I turned left and headed up to the high-rise council flats, the same estate where Joe and I had been brought up.

I joined them in their hiding place beside the seven-foot metal bins that lay at the bottom of the rubbish chutes. It was stinking. Some of the bags had burst open – potato peelings and some less acceptable things lay on the ground. In the corner I could see a mouse nibbling on a rotting apple core.

'This is Louisa,' I said pointedly to Joe and Moses as I introduced them. To my shame neither of them stared at her, just nodded matter-of-factly.

'I'm Brodie's new trainee.' The pride in her voice was unmistakable.

'What did you do wrong that you ended up with Brodie?' Joe asked.

'I met Patch at an Elvis convention and he said she was great.' Moses groaned, and I knew he was cursing the addition of another of the King's chosen ones. 'Christ, you're stuck with Brodie, but we're stuck with another bloody Elvis freak.'

I winced at the use of the word 'freak', but that was my problem, not theirs. Louisa settled herself down amongst the stinky nappies as if she had been born to it.

'Couldn't you have found a nicer place to hide?' I asked them.

'You don't hear Louisa complaining, and she's closer to the stink than the rest of us; no offence, Louisa,' Moses added.

'None taken, Moses.'

Louisa had obviously had all our biographies from Patch and was acting as if she had landed amongst the X-Men. It was rather sweet and I only prayed I could keep myself out of jail long enough for her to finish her traineeship.

Robert Girvan finally turned up. After carefully checking that no one was watching he lifted up the metal door of a garage.

'Here we go,' said Glasgow Joe. 'Here's our man – or woman, I should say. Tell you what, Brodie, once I've finished with him he won't have to put on a woman's voice; he'll be fuckin' squeaking his bollocks off for the rest of his natural...'

I had told Joe and Moses about my initial suspicions regarding the porn video. They had jumped on it as a good enough reason to beat Girvan up, given half the chance. I had asked them to call me as soon as they had arrived at the location – I wasn't looking forward to telling them that they only knew half the story, though.

Girvan was dressed in his suit; no doubt he had just left Bridget's office to make this appointment. He carried a large sports hold-all, so he must have been intending to go to the gym after he left here.

'I thought you said that Duncan Bancho was keeping a low profile on this one?' Joe pointed to the garage, where an unmarked police car had just pulled up. He could spot them as easily as if they had flashing lights and a siren going.

'Brodie?' he carried on. 'Why's Bancho here?'

'He's not,' I answered as Peggy Malone got out of the car. I wasn't surprised. Although she was in civvies she stuck to a uniform, her skirt hugging her round hips and, as usual, her blouse looking as if it had shrunk in the wash. She couldn't help wiggling and jiggling as she threw her arms around Robert Girvan.

'That's a lie for a start,' whispered Louisa.

'What do you mean?' I asked.

'Everything about her is wrong – look at her body language. She pulled out of that embrace as if he burned her. She's using him; in fact, I'd say she manipulates a lot of people. Before you ask how I know, I'm not ashamed to admit I manipulate to get my own way. If I waited like a good girl for what I wanted, I'd still be in the queue long after the shop had shut. I admire a fellow artist, though I wouldn't like to tangle with her.'

My phone vibrated.

'It's Duncan – the cat has left the house and I'm hoping she's at the trap. We're just round the corner. Can I come over?' said a voice.

'Only if you stop using that silly code stuff. Hurry up.'

No sooner had I closed my phone than two cop

cars sped up from either direction, effectively blocking off the garage entrance. We ran out to join Duncan and his boys in blue.

Duncan shouted at Robert Girvan and Peggy Malone to stand still. She looked around, saw the rest of us, and made a split-second decision. She obviously thought she could still walk out of this. She ran out and threw her arms around Duncan.

'I'm sorry for working this one on my own,' she said breathlessly as she clung on to his hand. She was too concerned about saving her own skin to even bother about all of the potential witnesses around her.

'I would have cut you in on this, Duncan, I just wasn't sure where it was going.'

Bancho stared at Peggy as if he had never seen her in his life.

'Margaret Malone – I'm arresting you for the murder of Tanya Hayder and the attempted murder of Alex Cattanach. You do not have to say anything, but anything you do say will be taken down and may be used against you in a court of law.' He coughed. It was always hard arresting a fellow cop, but one you had been shagging was bound to be particularly difficult.

'Take her in and book her.'

'No comments!' Bancho shouted at Jack Deans, who strolled up behind us. As usual, Jack paid him no attention.

'Do you have any comments, Detective Constable Malone?' he bawled at the police car as it sped off.

Robert Girvan was still pinned against the wall by an officer whilst his colleague opened the hold-all. Instead of dirty jock straps it was over-flowing with used bank notes.

'Book him and get him out of here quick,' said Bancho. Jack's arrival had hastened the departure of the police.

'I owe you one, Brodie,' Bancho said.

'No hard feelings?' I asked.

He waited before replying. 'No, none – maybe now I'll get the promotion you keep stopping.' I waved to him as he disappeared, but couldn't help wondering where my apology was.

'Okay, I admit I was wrong about him,' I said, whilst Joe tried not to look smug. He put his arm around me possessively as Jack Deans walked towards us.

'I'm off to do my usual hanging around police stations hoping to get a scoop; and praying the defence lawyer won't attack me,' he said. A secret smile passed between us; we both knew the moment he was referring to. One night, outside St Leonard's police station, he had been waiting in the rain for me. I was pissed off at having to represent Kailash and I'd clipped his dodgy knee with my briefcase. I still maintained it had been an accident, but neither of us believed it.

'Before you go, Jack – how did you know to come here?'

'Joe tipped me off.'

'That was big of him.' I looked quizzically at Joe, who was pretending not to listen.

'Not really. The Big Man suggested that this was my ticket back to the big-time. I think he wants rid of me.'

'And are you going?'

My heart already knew the answer.

'I'd stay if I thought you would make it worth my while – but as long as Joe's on the scene no one else has a chance, Brodie. It's time you faced up to that too. Don't throw it away. If he messes up again, call me. I'll come running. That's a promise.'

He took me in his arms and kissed me, before saying: 'She's all yours now, Joe. Mess up, and I'll be back.'

Jack Deans walked slowly down the road towards Leith Links and out of my life.

For the moment.

Chapter Forty-Seven

Louisa had chosen the music and she was up dancing.

There was generally only a selection of pole-dancing classics and some ancient-sounding 1970s stuff here, so I couldn't quite identify what it was – but she seemed to be having a good time. The Rag Doll was heaving but the regulars had made a very small space that served as a dance floor. Everyone was there: Grandad, Kailash, Joe, Lavender, Eddie and Malcolm. Even McCoy had come down for the night when he'd heard the news.

A lot of drink had been swallowed since DI Bancho had gone back to the police station. We were waiting on him and Patch to arrive so that we could complete the whole picture. In the meantime, Joe placed a laden tray on the table.

'I'm sorry, Kailash,' he said, 'the Rag Doll doesn't stretch to Hendrick's and cucumber. You'll have to put up with old lemon and tonic like everybody else.'

Kailash stared at him.

'When will you learn that I am not like everyone else and neither is my daughter. You might not like it, but she's mine. It really is a perfect case of nature over nurture – and if you can't accept that, then you'd better give Jack Deans a call.'

I grabbed my whisky and pretended I hadn't heard.

'I'm proud of you, Brodie,' my grandad said. 'It was a hard one to get out of, but you're as slippery as an eel and you managed it without my help. Explain to me again about Tymar Productions?'

'It started before Tymar,' I began. 'It really began with the video. The camerawoman was Peggy Malone. I think I'd become so used to slippery genders that I didn't even believe I'd heard a woman's voice when I had. When Roddie told us that Robert Girvan had stolen my identity for Tymar, I started to wonder if it was him behind the video too.

'Peggy knew Bridget Nicholson from way back; they'd been involved in a lesbian club for professional women in the late Nineties. Peggy always had that over Bridget. Peggy wasn't bothered about promotion, she was independently wealthy, so she never cared that anyone could blackmail her. Especially since she'd always had more on them. She was the one who forced Bridget to take part in the video.'

I sipped on the golden water and let it warm my throat. It had been, as Grandad had said, a close call for me. Even speaking about it made my throat constrict – whisky was my answer to the globus hystericus.

'Bridget introduced Peggy to Cattanach when they started seeing each other, and Alex fell head-over-heels for the cop. Peggy was the reason that they split up. She was insatiable, which is why she was never really bothered about whether she went with a man or a woman. As long as she was in control, she was happy. Staid Alex Cattanach was never going to be enough for her. It must have seemed like a godsend when McCoy contacted her about the video; only the video was meant to be used against Bridget.'

'But Alex Cattanach had no interest in Bridget Nicholson by that time?'

I raised my glass in salute to my grandad. He caught on fast.

'Correct. Alex Cattanach wanted to settle down with Peggy Malone, and she thought the video would bind them. She hadn't even noticed that Peggy had a certain side to her, she was so blinded by lust. Cattanach eventually worked out what was going on with Tymar and her principles would not allow me to take the blame. That's when Peggy attacked her.'

'So when we were up at the MacPherson gathering, Alex Cattanach had gone up to Ruthven barracks to be betrothed – but in fact her lover almost murdered her?'

'She's a weird bitch, but she hides it well,' I said in my own defence.

'She couldn't hide it from me,' Louisa shouted above the din of the pub. Did her disability come with superhuman hearing?

'Alex wasn't pointing the finger at me by writing my name on the walls,' I went on. 'She was trying to exonerate me. I suppose I'll have to forgive her rubbish tactics in view of her mental state.'

The door swung open and Moses entered. Patch walked in behind him. Louisa rushed up and hugged Patch; not even I did that. It was the first time that Patch had ever been inside the Rag Doll and, in deference to Patch's strict religious views, Joe pulled the nearly naked dancer from the stage.

Moses had gone to the lab to wait on the results of the toxicology tests and he was clearly excited.

Patch waved a piece of paper. 'It's conclusive. There are traces of heroin on the notes in the hold-all and on the bag itself. Peggy and Robert had muscled in on Moses' network of dealers.'

'I only do recreational stuff, nothing hard,' interrupted Moses as Grandad raised a disapproving eyebrow. I guess it did seem a little odd that a bunch of people involved in the law were all feeling sorry for Moses because his drug ring had been taken over.

'I figure that Peggy saw that she could make money from Moses by pretending to be Duncan Bancho,' I said.

'The Angels spoke to the guy over the net – how were we supposed to know it was his fancy piece?' Moses tried to defend himself for giving me plainly wrong information.

I took over again. 'The closer Peggy got, the more she saw an opportunity. She had a ready supply of dealers given all the scum she dealt with at work; all she needed was the drug, which she brought in from Pakistan. Her mistake was busting Tanya Hayder. Tanya told me that a cop was buying prostitutes for drug runners. I assumed it was a man. Her client paid her in smack, but she knew he wasn't kosher because she's serviced a lot of trawler men. The hands and the smell weren't right.'

'How do you fit in?' asked Patch.

'The money needed to be laundered. Bridget introduced Robert Girvan to Peggy when she thought they were going to be partners. Peggy spotted Robert's weaknesses and exploited them both. It was Roddie's hatred of me that brought me into the equation.'

'What are you going to do about him?' Kailash asked.

'He'd get a slap on the wrist and struck off for selling my identity; it would do the firm more harm than good,' I had to admit.

'So he walks?' Joe asked.

I nodded.

'Bridget Nicholson – what's going to happen to her?'

'She'll never be a judge, but I don't see any good coming out of persecuting her further; besides, I'm not sure exactly which crime she has committed.'

'Girvan? I take it he's going away for a long

time?' Eddie asked.

I nodded again.

'Good,' Eddie continued. 'You'll be needing an assistant – with a view to partnership, mind. I need to get a bit more organised, a bit more settled.' Oddly, Eddie was the only one who hadn't touched alcohol all night. It would take more than one night to impress me, however, although he wasn't usually so assertive.

'I'd like you all to raise your glasses!' I thought it was a bit premature of him – I hadn't given him a job yet. Eddie stood up, beaming. He seemed incredibly excited about the prospect of being my new assistant, even if it was only happening in his mind.

He hushed the pub.

'Ladies and gentlemen, I would like you all to drink a toast to the future.'

I smiled. He wasn't a bad guy and I did like a bit of attention.

Eddie smiled at Lavender who was nursing a drink – maybe she was joining him on the wagon.

'To the future Mrs Gibb!' Eddie announced, as Lavender looked on, happy enough to burst.

The deal was sealed.

I don't think anything that had happened in the last few weeks surprised me quite as much as what was going on here. As I kissed Lavender I felt her bubbling over with joy. She pulled Eddie over beside her and whispered something to him.

'Ladies and gentlemen – again!' he shouted. 'Just one more toast, then I'll leave you all to enjoy the night...' Bless him, he hadn't forgotten me after all.

'Raise your glasses, please, not only to myself and my beautiful wife-to-be, but to the forthcoming baby Gibb. Here's hoping he or she gets their mother's looks *and* brains.' Lavender patted her belly proudly as Eddie put his hand over hers.

Bloody hell.

This was turning into some night.

As Joe put his arms around me, high on it all, I answered my mobile.

'Is that Brodie McLennan? It's Desk Sergeant Munro from St Leonard's police station here.'

Sighing, I told him that I knew where he was stationed – just as he knew I had picked up my own phone. Some things never change, and this man was one of them.

'I'm calling to advise you, Miss McLennan, that we are about to arrest Marjorie Diamond for the murder of her husband, Donna Diamond.' He broke off for a second to curse with his fellow reception officers about the intricacy of it all.

'Anyway,' he went on, 'whoever she is – was – the wife – woman – has asked for you. And DI Bancho has said that you should be kept informed of everything anyway. Get here as soon as possible because we want to process her quickly.'

'Of course you do. You always do. There's probably some game on telly tonight. Haven't you heard? I've had quite a busy day myself, Sergeant Munro.'

'No rest for the wicked, miss, as my old mother used to say. Best get on your bike and get up here pronto. She's a screamer...'

The party was in full swing as I got on Awesome.

I looked back at Joe standing in the light of the pub and knew that all the people who mattered to me were behind him.

It felt odd.

It felt nice.

I hoped it would last.

The publishers hope that this book has given you enjoyable reading. Large Print Books are especially designed to be as easy to see and hold as possible. If you wish a complete list of our books please ask at your local library or write directly to:

Magna Large Print Books
Magna House, Long Preston,
Skipton, North Yorkshire.
BD23 4ND

This Large Print Book for the partially sighted, who cannot read normal print, is published under the auspices of

THE ULVERSCROFT FOUNDATION